*Sarah's known monsters…and John isn't one.*

Sarah's life isn't going well. She's divorced from an abusive jerk, been drugged, stuffed in her trunk and nearly kidnapped. Between that and a harsh winter, it's almost more than a girl can take. She's rightly distrusting of any man's affection, so an ice-skating date with John—who doesn't seem to feel the cold—isn't exactly on her bucket list. Yet something about him captures her attention.

John is determined to live as an ordinary mortal. He's moved into the city, bought a sports bar, and works there as the bartender. As a new vampire, he's never considered dating, until he meets Sarah. Prudence dictates he stay away from her, but everything about her calls to him…right down to her cute animal socks.

Sure, finding out John is a vampire is scary, but Sarah's learned not all monsters have fangs. Besides, someone else isn't too happy about their budding relationship. Sarah will have to survive before getting her chance at love.

I0600904

## Other books by Stacy McKitrick

**Bitten by Love Series:**
My Sunny Vampire
Bite Me, I'm Yours
Blind Temptation
A Vampire Wedding

**Ghostly Encounter Series:**
Ghostly Liaison
Ghostly Interlude

**Short Stories in the Following Anthologies:**
Home for the Holidays
Love's a Beach

# Bite Me, I'm Yours
## (Bitten by Love #2)

## Stacy McKitrick

Dayton, Ohio

Mythicalpress.com

Copyright © 2014, Stacy McKitrick
Edited by Paige Christian
Formatted by Enterprise Book Services
(www.EnterpriseBookServices.com)
Cover designed by Maria Zannini (BookcoverDiva.blogspot.com)

Published in the United States of America
2nd electronic edition: October 19, 2017
2nd print edition: October 19, 2017
ISBN (print version): 978-0-9967976-7-2

To Jim
(my husband, my sweetie, my best friend)

# Chapter 1

If Sarah Daugherty were smart, she'd live somewhere it never got cold. If she were smart, she'd have never let her mother get the best of her. If she were smart, she'd have never married Steven.

Yeah, if she were smart.

She stared at her reflection in the mirrored elevator doors. Somewhere beneath the white down-filled coat and pink scarf, a pathetic, twenty-four-year-old divorcee waited for doors to open and blast her with air that belonged in a freezer. They didn't disappoint.

Her friend, Lori, laughed. "What a wimp. We're not even outside and you act like it's below zero."

"It's below zero in Celsius." Ever since the events that unfolded prior to her divorce, Sarah had been cold. No matter what she did, she couldn't get warm enough. Winter wasn't helping any, either.

"Yeah, but last I saw, Dayton still measured temps in Fahrenheit." Lori stepped out and looked up. "Gee, what happened to the lights? It looks like a freakin' tomb in here. You're the workaholic. Do they normally go off after seven?"

"They never did before." Sarah examined the ceiling while the elevator still provided some light. Bulbs nearby were broken, meaning the ones leading to her car were probably the same way. The doors shut behind her. If it weren't for the oil and gasoline odors, she could be in a dungeon.

Lori unlocked her car. "Told my sister I would babysit tonight and I'm already late. Do you want to come?"

Babysit? Lori's niece was only six months old. Sarah's heart hadn't mended enough for that kind of torture. "Thanks, but I think I'll pass."

Lori frowned as she opened the driver's door. "Shit. Wasn't thinking. Sorry."

Sarah smiled her no-worries smile. She'd gotten pretty good at it the past few months. "It's okay. Now get out of here."

After a brief hug, Lori slid behind the wheel. "I'll see you tomorrow, kiddo."

Sarah headed for her little Civic, looking for her landmark. If the owner of the bright yellow Nissan Xterra ever quit his or her job, or decided to drive it to lunch, she'd be heartbroken. Ever since she started using this garage, she'd parked beside The Bumblebee—the name she'd come to call it—where it remained by quitting time. Seeing the tall vehicle brought a smile to her face. What did it mean when a yellow SUV was a bright spot in her life? Maybe that she needed a better life.

The roar of an engine echoed. Lights from behind cast long shadows ahead. Sarah waved as her friend drove by. Darkness surrounded her Civic and the SUV, and as she walked between them she stepped in something crunchy. Bits of white glass dotted the floor, glinting faintly from what little light remained. Another broken bulb.

*Crunch, crunch.*

She jerked upright. Was someone else here? She walked to the rear of the vehicles, making more crunchy sounds of her own. No one approached from the elevators or stairs, not that she could see much. Her heart crept up her throat and she swallowed.

The only sounds came from the pounding in her chest.

"You're hearing things, you idiot," she mumbled. Still, pinpricks of fear raced over her skin and she itched to go home. On legs that were no longer steady, she turned back to her car. She opened her purse with shaky hands.

*Crunch, crunch.*

She hadn't imagined that. Something scratchy and wet with a sweet smell cupped her nose and mouth.

*What the*— Holding her breath, she grabbed at the mask. Her purse fell and landed with a thud. The assailant wrapped his free arm around her waist and yanked her against his hard body.

"Time to sleep," he whispered, his breath warm against her ear.

2

*Nooo!* She hadn't escaped Steven's abuse only to have some stranger take his place. She clawed at his hand, but her gloves prevented her from scratching him. Taking hold of his fingers, she pulled. Bones cracked, but he held on. She yanked harder. His shriek pierced her ear, and he pulled away, scratching her face with the stiff material. Mouth free, she took a clean breath and screamed. Someone had to hear. The place echoed like a canyon. He clamped his hand across her mouth, cutting off her cry for help. Damn it. What would it take to stop him? She kicked him in the legs.

"God damn it," he muttered.

The attacker lost his balance and loosened his hold. Freedom seemed in reach. She leaned forward, using whatever leverage she could. He righted himself and pulled her back with arms that doubled for a vise. No amount of twisting and turning got her free. She reached behind, hoping to gouge his eyes, but he bent her head back against his shoulder. The mask scraped her face and her neck screamed in pain.

"Keep it up and I'll snap your neck," he growled.

Her heart raced. He might not kill her now, but there was no way this would end well. Wasn't there anyone around to help? Tears welled in her eyes and her chest burned for oxygen. With no choice left, she breathed in the sweet scent. Her world went dark.

\* \* \* \*

John Pennington emerged from the stairwell into the parking garage with a playful bounce. Sporadic lighting made him glance up. A few steps later, he stepped in something crunchy. Broken glass glittered in the remaining light. He shook his head. Who would do such a thing? He made a mental note to report the incident. Good thing he didn't need the light.

He headed for his SUV. A lady's loafer lay on its side in the aisle. Was some poor woman limping around with one shoe, or had it been used to break the bulbs? He picked it up. A familiar scent hit him, one that always lingered around his vehicle. Strawberries.

A man softly grunted as if straining. Always willing to lend a helping hand, John walked toward the sound and came to a sedan backed in against the wall. The trunk was open and the grunter, a man in his late twenties, struggled with loading his cargo. Cargo he had no right to load. A woman's shoeless foot stuck out to the side.

John stopped cold. "Hey! What the hell are you doing?"

3

The culprit jumped, dropping the woman. Her head hit the trunk floor with a thud. John winced. That had to hurt. While he stood there gaping at the woman, the man dashed off.

"Oh no you don't." John transmitted instructions to the man telepathically, *"Come back here."*

Like a robot, the man stopped and shuffled back to John, jerking with each step. John grimaced. One of these days he'd get better at manipulating mortals. When others took control, the human looked...well...human. For John, they looked like zombies, right down to the glazed-over eyes.

*"What's your name?"*

"Ray Brian Fowler."

*"Ray, go over to the wall and sit down."*

The would-be kidnapper followed the instructions.

John crouched before the low-life. *"Tell me your plans for this woman."*

"I'm going to take her home and play with her like I did all the others."

The others? Ray sounded like a boy talking about his favorite toy.

John grabbed Ray's hand, getting the skin contact needed to link. *"Show me the others."*

The grisly scene emerged in his mind. John gasped. Four dead and disfigured women, cut beyond recognition. Their features were not clear, but they all possessed long brown hair, and were all similar in size. Just like the woman in the trunk.

A smile spread across Ray's face as the memories played out in John's head. Cutting them had given Ray the thrill he'd needed to rape them. Death had been an unfortunate by-product. All four were buried side-by-side at an old farmhouse up north.

"Oh God!" John dropped Ray's arm, stopping the horrifying vision. How could one person be so evil?

*"Go to sleep, Ray."*

Ray's eyes closed and his head fell forward.

That would keep him out for a good hour or so. John broke the link, stood and moved toward the woman. "You might not think this now, but today's your lucky day."

She didn't respond. She was out cold.

A mask, the type popular during flu season, covered her face. He tossed the shoe in the trunk and leaned forward to unhook the elastic from around her ears. The car reeked of chloroform, explaining why the young woman was out to the world.

John lifted the mask and stared. He couldn't remember the last time he'd seen anyone so lovely. Her long lashes were real, not those fake add-ons, and her full lips... Well, he didn't need to be thinking about those. Best to see if she was seriously injured first.

Three small scratches marred her cheek. He sniffed for any major blood loss. The scent of strawberries hit him again. Lovely. Just like the shoe. Just like around his... Wait a minute. A purse lay beside her and he searched through it, finding her keys. He aimed the fob toward his SUV and hit the unlock button. The vehicle beside his honked and lit up. "Well I'll be damned."

He picked up the shoe. "Okay, Miss Strawberry. Let's get you back to your car." He slid it on her foot, chuckling at the penguin-decorated sock. "Cute."

He grabbed her purse and jogged over to her car. Opening the driver's door gave him another whiff of her perfume. Damn, he could really get used to that. Reminded him of the garden his mother had planted every year.

After tossing her bag inside, he zipped back to Ray's car and lifted her with ease. Her fragrance more noticeable now that he held her, he stared at her lovely face. What was he doing? Damn. Blinking didn't clear his head, so he held his breath. That did the trick. He situated her behind the steering wheel then licked his thumb and applied his saliva over the scratches. As the wound healed, a small heating sensation formed on his thumb and then a rush of warmth filled his palm. He snapped his hand away. What the—

He knelt beside her and slowly ran the back of his hand across her soft cheek, now unmarred. This time the warmth traveled up his arm. Oh sweet Jesus, what was she?

Wonder filled his heart. He removed her glove and took her delicate hand into his own. Luxurious warmth spread. He closed his eyes and sighed as it traveled through his system. He hadn't felt anything this good in years. No, make that decades.

Soft, whispery breaths and the intense strawberry scent caused him to open his eyes. Lips begging to be kissed were mere inches away. When had he leaned forward? His heart raced. The last time he had kissed anyone had been the night of his turning. He hadn't missed it until now.

She moved her head and mumbled. Panic gripped his chest. He jerked backward and stood, establishing a distance and clearing his head. Damn. He'd almost kissed her. What was he thinking? She was helpless. How could he take advantage?

He leaned against his Xterra and slid to the ground, landing in broken glass. Great. He leaned sideways and brushed the debris away.

Now what? In order to ensure Ray reported himself to the police, John would have to leave her alone. But she was vulnerable. John hugged his knees to his chest. He could send Ray on his way alone, and the thought tempted him, but anything could happen between the garage and the police station. He needed more assurance than that. Maybe if he locked her inside her car? No one had entered the garage since his arrival. He stood and went over to the door.

Would she get cold? Her down-filled coat appeared warm enough and she wore a scarf. Plus, she was out of the elements. It couldn't be that cold in the garage, but then, what did he know? He had to trust she would wake up before she froze.

He needed to send her a command in case she left before he returned, but her unconsciousness made transmitting the command more difficult, if not impossible. Cupping her head would be the best way to insure a connection. It would also cause him to lose control. But man, to feel that heat once more… Shit.

Maybe he couldn't avoid the heat, but he could avoid her scent. Holding his breath, he placed his hands on her. Warmth cascaded up his arms and spread throughout his body. The intensity caught him off guard, and he blinked several times before coming to his senses. *"When you wake up, you will feel refreshed. You will remember getting in your car and that you were sleepy. Go straight home and stay in for the night."*

He released her and stepped back, his breathing ragged, her heat dissipating. It was the best he could do without confusing her any more. "I'll be back to check on you, I promise."

He activated the locks and shut the door, cutting off her scent. The loss was immediate. He sighed and trudged back to Ray, kicking him awake.

*"Ray, get in the back seat of your car."*

The miscreant followed orders while John shut the trunk and got behind the wheel. He drove to the police station and parked on a side street.

Ray didn't deserve to live. He deserved to be treated as he had treated those women. However, killing him, or even maiming him, would only implicate someone else and John wanted Ray to pay for his crimes.

*"Go to the police station and tell all officers you encounter every crime you've ever committed. Tell them your conscience finally got the best of you. However, you will not remember me or the lady you abducted tonight. Now, go."*

Ray climbed out and stalked, in that jerky, zombie way, toward the station. Once he reached the entrance, John broke the link. Ray looked up at the building and shook his head as if he had just awakened. After a few moments, he walked through the doors.

Okay, one down, one to go.

John walked back to the garage, aiming to look normal, but the closer he got, the faster his pace. He barged through the stairwell door, practically flew down the stairs, and zipped to his car.

Miss Strawberry was gone.

Disappointment squeezed his chest. Sure, he was glad she'd been well enough to drive off, but he should have gotten her name. He snorted at his idea. Right. Like it would have made a difference. He'd probably never see her again. But as he climbed inside his SUV, all he could think about was her and that lovely scent.

# Chapter 2

Sarah stared at the red traffic light and willed the throbbing in her head to go away. She should have called in sick. It wasn't like she had gotten eight hours of uninterrupted sleep. More like one.

Her sleepless night had caused a headache so severe she thought her head would explode. Then again... She felt the back of her head, finding the small bump. Could that be the cause? Whatever. The four aspirin she had taken since crawling out of bed were taking their sweet time to kick in, and surviving the day pain-free was beginning to look hopeless.

Had she made the right decision to go home instead of to the police station? But what would she say? She had no proof she'd been grabbed. It was as if the man had knocked her out and stuck her back inside her car. Why would he do that?

Someone must have come to her rescue because she had the distinct impression her abductor had wanted her for some unthinkable things. If she ever found out who had intervened, she'd hug them first, ask questions later.

A horn honked briefly from behind, getting her attention. The light had turned green. After waving an apology, she shifted into first gear.

The parking garage loomed ahead and her heart raced. Fear snatched her breath away. She gripped the steering wheel and slammed on the brake. The car lurched and stalled.

"Goddammit!" What was the matter with her? She should know better. Another horn, this one not so friendly, wailed in the air. She glanced in the rear view mirror.

Oh crap! Cars lined up behind her in a zigzag fashion. She needed to get herself together. It was just the garage for goodness sake.

She took a deep breath and turned the ignition, but nothing happened. She tried again and then remembered the clutch. Idiot! She succeeded on the third try, but the car slowly jerked forward and sputtered. She slammed on the clutch and brake. Now what? After two more failed attempts, she slammed her fist against the steering wheel.

"Damn it! Why are you doing this to me?"

More horns honked.

"Shut up!" She hit the gearshift and found it still in third. She shoved the stick into first, squealing the tires as she entered the garage. The Bumblebee greeted her and she steered toward it. No, no, no. She couldn't park there. What if that was how the assailant found her? She swerved away and found another spot. Her hands shook violently as she removed the key from the ignition.

A cold sweat formed on her brow. She couldn't show up to work in this condition. How could she explain herself? If she couldn't report what had happened to the police, she certainly wasn't telling anyone at work.

A rap on her window gave Sarah's heart a jolt.

Crap. Of all the people to discover her, why Lori? No way could she convince her friend she was fine, too much history with Steven. But she had to try. Putting on her best face, she opened the car door to get out. "Hey."

"What are you doing sitting in your car?" Lori scrutinized Sarah's face. "You okay? You don't look so good."

"I'm fine." Sarah closed the door and locked it. Twice. The second time didn't make her feel any safer, but if she kept locking it—and her thumb itched to punch it a third time—Lori might grow suspicious. "I thought you weren't coming in until later."

"I changed my mind. I was hoping to run into Brian, but I haven't seen anyone matching your description." Lori scouted the garage. "Do you see him anywhere?"

"Who?" Sarah's mind was fried. Nothing her friend said made any sense.

Lori stared at her and raised an eyebrow. "Brian. You know. The guy who hit on you yesterday morning? For someone who complained about it all day, you sure have a short memory. You sure you're okay?"

Oh God. Brian. Sarah had forgotten all about him. Yes, he had asked her out, but he'd also stared at her like she was his next meal. Had he been responsible for her near-abduction? She took a quick glance around. No sign of the man, thank goodness. "Why would you want to see that creep?"

"You said he was cute. Besides, just because he hit on you doesn't make him a creep. One of these days you're going to have to stop dismissing every man who shows an interest. You don't have to answer to anyone anymore. Not all men are like Steven, you know."

"No, some of them are worse."

She beat Lori to the elevator and jabbed the button several times. The car couldn't arrive fast enough.

"You know that won't make the elevator come any quicker, don't you?" Lori said. "So what's the matter? Did something happen last night, cause you sure look like shit."

"Wow, thanks. I love you, too." A partial truth was better than a complete lie. "I didn't get much sleep last night. Neighbors kept me up."

"Well, that sucks. You want to go out for drinks after work? Linda says the bartender at Wings is some great eye candy. Then maybe you won't care how noisy your neighbors are tonight. You'll be too busy picturing him."

The elevator dinged, announcing its arrival. Finally. When the doors opened, Sarah rushed inside, comforted by the small box. The doors moved to close, but Lori was still scanning the garage. Sarah put her hand out and the doors retreated. "You coming? Or are you going to wait some more?"

"I'm coming." Lori took one last look and sighed before entering the elevator. The doors closed and the car started the slow ascent to their floor. "So tonight? Drinks? Eye candy?"

Sarah wasn't sure she would survive the day. The night looked less promising. But what did she have to lose? Another night of sleep? "Sounds great, Lori. I'm in."

\* \* \* \*

"Hey John, I need two Coronas," Ashley said.

10

John stood behind the bar of Wright Wings Sports Bar and Grill and retrieved the last two from the fridge underneath. He'd always suspected the previous owner had an aviation fixation. With Wings located in downtown Dayton—the home of the Wright Brothers—he could understand the fascination, but the references didn't stop with the name. The theme continued inside with airplane paraphernalia displayed on the walls. Since it had worked for the previous owner, John left it alone.

Every employee except Ashley had come with the place, and John had made a good choice in hiring her. She was his hardest worker and customers tipped her heavily. Her golden brown eyes complemented her curly brunette hair, which she normally pulled into a ponytail. Tonight she wore it down, softly framing her face. That meant only one thing.

"So, who's the guy?" he asked.

She smiled and leaned over the bar. "He's in the far booth."

"Ahh, so he doesn't know you like him?" he asked just as quietly.

She shrugged. "He might know. I've only checked on him five times already."

After opening the beers, he stuck a lime slice in each. "Well, good luck."

He envied her. If she wanted something, she went for it. Maybe one day, once living among mortals became routine, he could get close to someone.

Since he had taken the last Corona, he went to the kitchen and retrieved another case. When he returned, the familiar scent of strawberries lingered in the air. He placed the case on the counter and scanned the room. There, in the booth section, Miss Strawberry sat facing a blonde woman. Sure, she worked in the area—they shared the same garage—but she'd never been in the bar before. Why now?

No, no, no. This wasn't good. It couldn't be good. It had taken the better part of the day to stop thinking about her. He had nearly kissed her when she was unconscious. What might he do with her conscious? He placed the case on the floor and crouched behind the bar to put the Coronas away. Maybe if he didn't see her, he could ignore her.

"Order up," Ashley said.

Her voice came out of nowhere and he jumped, bumping his head on the counter. How embarrassing. No mortal had ever startled him before, not a good sign. He rubbed his head as he stood.

"Didn't mean to scare you." She leaned over the bar and examined John's head. "You okay?"

"I'm fine and you didn't scare me." His voice came out sterner than he'd intended, but at the moment he didn't care. The strawberry scent intensified and invaded his senses.

"Ohh-kay," she said, eyes wide. "I need a Jack and Coke and a margarita. I'll be back to pick 'em up."

He fixed the drinks and placed them on the tray. Ashley, being the efficient waitress that she was, quickly picked up the order and walked it over to Miss Strawberry's table.

No wonder the scent was so strong. Ashley had brought it with her. After she left their booth, she gathered the trash on the table near theirs, and in the process knocked over some plates. Miss Strawberry stood, picked up the plates, and placed them on the tray. In order to look busy, John wiped the bar down as he zeroed in on their conversation.

"Oh, you don't have to do that," Ashley said.

"I don't mind. It's not like you did it on purpose."

Her angelic voice cut through the din, as if made for his ears alone. He longed to hear more.

Ashley grabbed some napkins and handed them to the lady. "Thanks."

Miss Strawberry smiled and nodded as she wiped her hands and tossed the napkins on the tray before heading back to her seat.

In the three months he'd owned the bar, he'd never seen anyone do that before. Not even another waitress.

She smelled like home. She cared about other people. And her touch—he would never forget the warmth. If he wasn't such a wimp, he'd ask her out. Maybe someday he would, in like, say, six months. Or a year. Just not now.

He could watch her, though. What was the harm?

Nothing, until the blonde said with a lilt, "I think he's got a crush on you."

\* \* \* \*

"What are you talking about? Who's got a crush on me?" Sarah panicked and glanced around the room, but couldn't spot anyone she knew. "Is it Brian? Is he here?"

"Brian? How the hell would I know?" Lori grabbed Sarah's hand, getting her attention. "Will you calm down? God, you've been jumpy all day. I'm talking about the bartender. Man, Linda wasn't wrong about him. And he's been staring at you, you lucky dog."

The bartender? Sarah shot a glance in his direction, trying not to look obvious, but worried needlessly. He was talking to a customer and not looking her way. She relaxed a little. Not Brian, thank God. But damn, how had she managed to miss him when she'd come into the bar?

Lori placed her elbow on the table and rested her head in her hand while she stared in his direction. She sighed. "Boy, I wish he'd look at me. What a hottie. I can only imagine the kind of fun I could have with him."

Sarah couldn't argue with her friend. He was hot. His light brown hair, which looked wind-blown, blended with his fair skin. It also didn't hurt that the white, long-sleeved, T-shirt he wore showed every muscle in his chest and arms. Every movement he made caused something to ripple.

She swallowed back her own drool. "Why do you suppose he was staring at me? I don't know him."

"And this is why I want to strangle Steven. He's just a guy looking at a pretty woman. Why don't you go on up and talk to him? I'm sure he won't bite."

Talk to him? Was Lori nuts? Just because *she* could go up to complete strangers and share her life history didn't mean Sarah could. Granted, she needed to change her ways if she wanted to change her life. How else would she ever find companionship? Maybe she *should* make the first move, because she certainly hadn't given any man who'd asked her out a chance.

Then again, the men who'd shown an interest always seemed to have some sort of agenda. Steven wanted a trophy wife and when she hadn't fit his mold, she'd paid for it. Brian had seemed more interested in conquering her. She didn't want to be anyone's trophy or conquest, only to be treated as an equal. Was there someone out there like that? Like, maybe the bartender? She'd never know unless she talked to him.

Of course, that meant actually getting up and talking. But her abduction was still too fresh and it nailed her to the seat. One margarita wasn't enough to pry her free.

Lori waved down their waitress. "Hey, Ashley," she said discreetly. "Who's the bartender?"

"That's John. Is there a problem?" Ashley asked.

Lori shook her head. "Oh, no problem. Just admiring the view. Do you know if he's single?"

Embarrassment heated Sarah's face. If she could dig a hole and crawl in it, she would.

"He's not married and I don't think he's dating anyone." Ashley leaned in closer. "But then he keeps to himself. He's a real nice guy, though, and very popular with the women. I've never seen him interested in any of them, not that they haven't tried."

Sarah bet he was popular with the women. What woman wouldn't want him? She briefly pouted at the news, but hoped it would at least get Lori to stop.

"He's not gay, is he?" Lori asked.

Crap. Sarah hadn't even considered that.

Ashley laughed. "If he is, he hasn't shown any interest in men, either."

"See, he doesn't date customers. Just drop it, okay?" Sneaking another glance his way, Sarah finally caught him staring. The man's eyes glimmered.

\* \* \* \*

Damn. John had hoped he'd hear Miss Strawberry's name by now, but the blonde never used it. When Ashley had commented he didn't date, her expression boosted his ego, until her friend thought he was gay. Miss Strawberry didn't think that, did she? If he were to date anyone, he'd date her. Maybe he was crazy, but he didn't see the harm in watching, even if she caught him doing it.

Shortly after Ashley left their table, the blonde raised her hand to her face. He glanced in the direction she hid from, where several lawyer-type gentlemen clustered around a table. One of them, a man with sharp features and hair the color of coal, approached the ladies. The blonde scowled and shook her head when he reached their table.

"What are you doing here, Sarah?" he asked Miss Strawberry, not the blonde.

Her name was Sarah? Sarah, Sarah, Sarah. John would have been content repeating her name several more times, if it weren't for the man's possessive tone.

Sarah acknowledged his presence briefly before turning her attention to the table. "I could ask the same thing, Steven. Don't you work across town?"

"I was meeting clients and they work around here." He placed his hand on her shoulder. "Since when do you go out to a bar?"

She looked at his hand before glaring at his face. "Since I no longer have to report to you," she snapped at him, and then promptly removed his hand.

John silently chuckled at her remark—it was given with such venom—until Steven grabbed her upper arm. Sarah winced. John fisted his hands. Whoever the creep was, he had no right to touch her.

John tapped into the man's mind and quickly retreated. Damn it! What was he thinking? If he took control, he'd have a zombie walking around his bar. Yeah, that wouldn't look suspicious. He should be able to handle this situation like any mortal.

Sarah wrenched her arm from Steven's grip. The momentum caused her to tilt sideways, knocking her purse to the floor.

"You don't have any right to touch me," she said, rubbing her arm.

"Yeah. Go bully someone your own size," the blonde said.

"Stay out of this, bitch," Steven said to the blonde. "I didn't ask for your fuckin' opinion." He glared at Sarah. "And I'll touch you if I want."

John nearly jumped over the bar—another bad idea. What was wrong with him? Had his brain gone on vacation? He slapped his forehead as he headed around the bar.

Sarah stood and confronted Steven. "You do and all agreements are off. Do you understand? Now leave. Why do you insist on being where you're not wanted?"

John strolled over to the party, trying to look normal, holding in an urge to throw the bastard through the wall. God, he must be insane. If he couldn't risk controlling Steven, how would it look if he showed his super-human strength?

He took a deep breath. Diplomacy, not violence. Something Sarah might appreciate. He came up behind Steven—who seemed oblivious to anyone except Sarah—and tapped him on the shoulder. Steven twirled around, scowling.

"Sir, it seems you are not welcome here," John said as discreetly as he could over the din of the crowd. "Do I need to ask you to leave?"

Steven gave John a look of pure evil: lips snarling, eyes narrowing. All show. Standing slightly taller and carrying more muscle, John didn't need the advantage to toss the bastard through the wall. And the urge to do just that wouldn't go away. Damn. He needed to keep his cool. He not only had a reputation to uphold, he didn't want to scare Sarah. Hell, he was scaring himself. So he stood there flexing his muscles and giving back the evil eye, hoping it would be enough for Steven. It was. He took a step back.

"I was just leaving," Steven said between clenched teeth and then glared at Sarah before leaving to join his companions.

The blonde let out a huge sigh. "Thank you. I was afraid I was going to have to drag his ass out of here."

He nearly laughed at the vision she inspired. "I'm glad I could help."

Being engrossed with Steven, John hadn't noticed Sarah's scent, but it grabbed him now. The biggest surprise was Sarah, herself. Up close and conscious, she sent the remainder of his working brain cells straight to his groin. She was beautiful. Her large and expressive eyes seemed to look deep within his soul. Green with gold flecks, they were more mesmerizing than he imagined. He couldn't stop gazing at her, but then she was doing the same with him.

The blonde cleared her throat, loudly. Sarah's eyes widened and she blushed, intensifying her scent in a way that intoxicated him. Drunk on strawberries. Was it even possible? He was sure his stance waivered. When she returned to her seat, he almost stopped her. He could stare at her forever.

She bent over to retrieve her purse, flashing a bit of skin and a whole lot of derriere. Damn. No skin and bones for her, that ass was made for grabbing. He yearned to feel the softness of her skin as well as the warmth her touch brought.

His fangs emerged.

He clamped his mouth shut. Oh God, what was he doing? He had to think of something else. Anything else.

She straightened and he moved his attention from her ass to her face and her lips. Those kissable lips. He had wanted to kiss her ever since he first saw her. Kiss her until she begged him to stop. Now not only were his fangs exposed, so was his erection. What an idiot. He desperately needed to change the subject, but speaking with his lips pressed together wasn't so easy. "Can I get you two ladies anything? It's on the house."

The blonde glanced at his crotch and smirked. Better than looking at his mouth, at least his erection was normal. Lucky for him, her staring caused his fangs to retract.

"No, I think we're okay. By the way, I'm Lori and this is Sarah."

At the mention of her name, Sarah smiled. Her face lit up and captivated him all over again.

What was wrong with him? He shouldn't be here. He shouldn't be interested. It would only get him in trouble. He should leave and forget her.

Yeah, like that was possible anymore.

"Nice to meet you Lori, Sarah." Did his voice get softer when he said her name? "I'm John. You sure I couldn't change your mind and get you anything?"

Lori glanced at Sarah before turning her attention back to him. "No, I think we're done for the night."

"I don't have to go home yet," Sarah said.

John smiled. She wanted to stay. Then the realization hit him. Shit. She *wanted* to stay. Not good. Not good at all.

"I am kind of hungry," she continued. "Why don't we get something to eat?"

Lori looked at Sarah quizzically, then smiled at her. "Okay, yeah. I could eat something, too."

John outwardly smiled while inwardly he cringed. What had he gotten himself into? He had to leave. Would his feet obey?

"Great. I'll go get Ashley to bring you menus. Please let me know if you need anything else." Walking away from Sarah was like trudging through molasses, but staying was unthinkable. Still, he couldn't resist one more look at her. Was she checking out his ass? Her gaze drifted up and met his. That wonderful blush covered her face and her scent drifted toward him. He smiled.

No one had ever said he was subtle and his attempts at acting nonchalant were for naught. He caught her looking as often as she caught him. Hope and happiness bubbled at the surface, emotions he'd thought had died many years ago. He couldn't let them take hold now and propel him toward something stupid like asking her out, because nothing good could come from being with her. He'd only screw it up or worse, hurt her. When did life get so complicated? Why did she have to come into his bar?

And why did she have to leave?

They waved to him as they departed and his heart sank. Would she be okay? Would she be safe from Steven? Some strange draw compelled him to follow her, but he resisted the urge and concentrated on his work—something he hadn't been able to do since she'd walked through the door.

Fifteen minutes later, Ashley approached him, wiping down a cellphone, and placed it on the bar. "I found this under the booth those women were at."

John picked up the phone. Lori's or Sarah's? The rag Ashley had used contained a cleaning agent, wiping out any lingering scent of the owner. He kind of hoped it was Lori's, because seeing Sarah again would be a bad idea.

Ashley drummed her fingers on the bar. "So, did you ask her out?"

He looked up from the phone. "Did I ask who out?"

"Umm, the one you were obviously hot for all night." Ashley stood there grinning, enjoying herself way too much.

Oh great, now the whole staff would know. He put the phone down and quickly changed the subject. "So, how'd it go with the guy tonight?"

Her face fell. "It didn't. His girlfriend showed up. Why does it seem like all the good ones are taken?"

He didn't know what to say and wasn't sure she expected a response, so he shrugged and smiled. She shook her head and went back to work.

He picked up the phone. If he went through the address book, he could probably figure out who owned the cell. He pushed the required buttons and it listed only two names: Grandma and Lori. Well, it was definitely Sarah's phone. But no Mom or Dad? Didn't she have any other friends? No boyfriend?

The phone rang in his hands. Even though the display didn't specify the caller, it had to be Sarah. Who else would it be? He took a deep breath and answered the phone on the second ring.

"Oh thank God you found my phone. My name is Sarah. Where did you find it?"

She even sounded angelic over the phone. "This is John from Wings. Ashley found your phone under the table."

"What a relief. I'll have to thank her when I see her. Can you hold it for me until tomorrow night?"

Tomorrow night? His heart lifted just thinking about seeing her again.

"Uh, sure. I'll put it under the bar with your name on it. What's your last name, just in case I'm not here to identify you?" Or in case he chickened out and disappeared. He searched for a pen and paper.

She hesitated for a moment. What was that about?

"It's Daugherty." She spelled it for him.

"Okay, Sarah Daugherty." He liked the way it sounded off his tongue. "It'll be waiting for you."

"Thanks so much, John. Maybe I'll see you tomorrow."

He could hear the want in her voice and he shook his head. Seeing her again would be wrong, wrong, wrong. "Maybe you will. Goodnight, Sarah."

John disconnected the call, found a rubber band, and wrapped the note around the cell. He ran his fingers over her name. Oh, who was he kidding? He couldn't stay away if he tried. He held her phone as if he were holding his future.

# Chapter 3

Sarah opened her desk drawer to retrieve her purse. Five o'clock had finally arrived. Took its sweet time, too. The day had moved at a turtle's pace and all because she'd been itching to see John again. Well, she wouldn't have to wait much longer.

Her boss, Mark Thomason, peeked inside her office. "Oh great, you're still here."

"What's the matter?" Please let it be something quick.

"Jeff has a client due any minute, but something came up and he has to leave. Do you mind taking it? We've already had to reschedule twice. I'd hate to do it again."

He stood there with an eager look on his face. Shoot. Wasn't this the kind of incident she'd hoped for? A sign maybe they would keep her? John could wait. It wasn't like they had a date.

"You don't need to have him reschedule. I can do it." She closed the drawer. What was another hour or so?

"Great. I won't forget this. I'll send him your way when he gets here."

She looked at the clock. Was the second hand moving slower?

\* \* \* \*

John glanced at his watch. Six o'clock.

All day he had deliberated whether or not he should be in the bar when Sarah arrived. Then five o'clock had come. The need to see her again consumed him. Besides, it wasn't like they had a date. She'd come in and get her phone and that would be that.

He glanced at his watch again. Where was she? He'd expected her arrival by now. Didn't most people get off work at five?

A couple had just left and John grabbed a tray to police up their mess, anything to pass the time. As he lifted the dirty glasses, Perry strolled through the front door. Shit. Of all the nights to visit. John cursed his bad luck.

Perry spotted him and smiled. "Hey, Johnny. You short a busboy?"

John put the glasses down, grabbed Perry by the collar, and dragged him over to the pool tables, which were currently deserted. "I thought I told you not to troll for food here."

"You want to twist that knife? I think you missed my heart." Perry readjusted his Hawaiian shirt, one that had seen better days. The front pocket had been ripped off years ago and the seams contained several small holes.

John stepped back. Maybe he had over reacted a little. "I'm sorry, I just wasn't expecting you."

Perry eyed him suspiciously. "You never are. What gives now?"

Shit. Trying to keep anything from Perry was like keeping a secret in a hospital—impossible. Of course, with him here, maybe John could get some answers. The questions were liable to get him in trouble, though. "If I ask you something personal, can you be honest?"

"Since when am I not honest?" Perry swung his arms out, acting innocent, but like everything else he did, he over played it.

John raised an eyebrow. "Seriously? What about the time you said I couldn't get drunk?"

"Minor technicality. I said you couldn't get drunk from alcohol, not from a donor who was drunk." Perry chuckled. "You sure were funny." When John didn't laugh with him, he became serious. "Okay, what do you want to know?"

John shoved his hands into his pockets. He was so going to regret asking Perry, but there wasn't anyone else. "Not that I'm looking to do it, but if I were, if I wanted to date someone, and I'm careful, is it possible?"

Perry's face lit up and he slapped John on the shoulder. "Johnny's found a girl? Well, well, well. It's about damn time. But date?" He frowned and shook his head.

"What does that mean?"

"It means there isn't a law against dating, but I'm not sure you can handle it. However, there's nothing wrong with having some fun with one night stands. Hell, I do it all the time."

"So, you are trolling?"

Perry placed his hand over his heart and threw his head back. "Oh, the pain. Is that what you really think of me?"

John refused to react. One slip and he'd never get rid of his friend.

Perry peeked open one eye, sighed, and then opened the other. "Actually, I came to visit you, but see you're busy with a girl. Is she here?" He searched the dining room as if he could spot her on his own.

"No."

"But you're expecting her?"

Why did Perry have to keep digging? John kept a straight face, hoping not to give anything away. Oh, who was he fooling?

Perry smiled and nodded. "You *are* expecting her. Hmm. Maybe I should stick around."

John drew in a deep breath. He must remain calm. Perry was only trying to get to him. "There's nothing to see. I don't even know if I want to date her."

Perry leaned in and studied John's face for all of two seconds and then stepped back. "Yes, you do." He rubbed his hands together and grinned. "Oh man, this should be fun."

Damn it. John lowered his head. He *did* want to date Sarah. Whether or not he went through with it was another matter and he certainly didn't want Perry anywhere around if he decided to go for it. And if she rejected him? Oh, God! "Please don't do this. Just leave. You can come back later."

"You're no fun, Johnny. You know that?"

John looked up. A rare feeling of hope came over him.

"But good luck. You'll need it." Perry laughed his way out the back door.

\* \* \* \*

Sarah shot a glance at the clock. Six-fifteen. Her client gathered up his papers and shoved them inside a briefcase while yakking about some trip he planned to take in the summer. Why couldn't he leave already?

He stood. Finally. Hoping it would get him moving faster, she rose with him.

"Thanks so much for seeing me, Miss Daugherty. I sure hope I didn't keep you from anything."

Oh great, now she felt like a chump. It wasn't his fault; any other day she would have willingly helped him. "No problem, Mr. Reynolds. Glad I could help."

He'd barely cleared the door when she grabbed her purse from the drawer and headed for the closet.

Coat—check. Scarf—check. The elevator car arrived and she stepped inside. As soon as she pushed the button for the garage, fear tingled down her spine. What the hell was she doing? Why hadn't she asked someone to accompany her? She took a deep breath and willed the fear away. Well, if she couldn't face the demons of the garage, what hope did she have of changing her life?

The elevator opened to a lighted garage. Someone had replaced the broken bulbs yesterday and the place didn't look as ominous as before. Still, her heart thumped wildly. Maybe she wasn't quite ready to face those demons, but what choice did she have? Her car was here. She spotted the Bumblebee—she'd parked beside it again, some habits were just hard to break—and nearly trotted to it while she scanned the area. No matter how nutty she appeared, no one would surprise her again. Not if she could help it.

Quickly, she slipped inside her car and drove off. Less than two minutes later she arrived at Wings, but the closest parking spot was almost as far as the garage. She placed her head on the steering wheel. What an idiot. Thank goodness she was alone. Lori would have never let her live it down.

Sarah exited the car and locked it. Street lights illuminated her way, so at least she'd see anyone coming. When she arrived at the door to Wings, she stopped. Her body tingled as if she were near an electric current. What if John wasn't there? What if he was?

"God, Sarah. You weren't this bad in high school," she muttered. One cleansing breath helped gather the courage to open the door.

The warmth of the room welcomed her and she savored it. Well, maybe it was a little too warm. Sweat formed on her upper lip. She lowered the zipper, but it stopped halfway, stuck in the fabric. Crap. She tugged to free it.

"You need some help?" John asked.

She jumped. Where the heck had he come from? She should have heard him, the place wasn't that noisy. She looked up at the most amazing blue eyes she'd ever seen. And like the night before, they appeared to glimmer. She was lost in his gaze.

"I uhh." What the hell was wrong with her voice?

"Here, let me."

She pulled her hands away and he freed the zipper before she'd finished thinking *God, he's gorgeous.*

"Thanks," she murmured.

He gave a two-finger salute. "John Pennington at your service. Come, sit at the bar." As he passed a stool, he patted it and she dutifully sat. "See, safe and sound." He held out her phone.

"Thank you." In taking the phone, her hand brushed against his. An electrical charge shot up her arm, causing her heart to skip a few beats. She gasped in surprise. A shock, but not a shock—it was more enjoyable than that. As the contact broke, the wonderful tingling sensation remained.

He stood back. "Are you okay?"

She tore her gaze away from her hand and looked up. Oh great, he'd noticed. She took a deep breath, hoping it would calm her heart. It didn't work.

"I'm fine. Can I have a Diet Coke?" If she was having a heart attack, might she have one every day.

John filled a glass and put the drink on the bar. She hoped for another touch, but he pulled away too fast. When he leaned against the bar, he kept his hands to himself. Had he felt it, too?

"What do I owe you?"

"It's on the house. So who was the man who bothered you last night?"

He would have to mention the one person she'd rather forget. After taking a few sips, she said off-handedly, "Oh, that was Steven, my ex-husband. He's having problems with our divorce." Yeah, like he hadn't wanted one to begin with.

"I take it the divorce was your idea?"

"It was. You're sort of my hero, you know?"

He jerked back as if she'd accused him of a crime. "I didn't do anything."

"You managed to make Steven leave. I couldn't. You might want to watch out for him, though. He has a pretty bad temper."

John relaxed and smiled. "I'm not afraid of Steven. I can take care of myself."

In that she had no doubt. She still couldn't get over how he filled out a T-shirt. His body screamed power.

A petite waitress she didn't recognize approached the bar and handed John an order. Sarah had never seen purple hair up close before. The waitress caught her staring and smiled. Sarah reciprocated then turned her attention to John. He prepared the drinks with such speed. If she tried any of those moves, she'd end up with broken glass at her feet, if not a wet floor. He never made a mistake. His fingers were long and slender; she imagined him running them through her hair and maybe over other parts of her body.

"Are you okay? Did he hurt you?"

She blinked out of her dream. Had he asked about her marriage? How did he know? Oh wait, he'd probably seen Steven grab her.

"I'm fine." Her blouse covered the bruise Steven had left behind. And here she'd thought her abused days were over. "He tries to rattle me, but I try not to let him get to me anymore."

John nodded. "Good. I don't think he deserves your time."

He seemed sincere, and it caught her by surprise. Besides Lori, she couldn't remember the last time anyone really cared about her. Guess if she wanted to know him better, she should ask him out. She swallowed her nervousness.

"I know this is out of the blue, and I hardly know you, but I'd like to, and I wondered if you wanted to go out. On a date. With me." Oh God, she sounded like an idiot. She'd be lucky if he didn't laugh her out of the place.

His expression changed from one of shock to one of delight. Dare she hope? Before he had a chance to answer, the purple-haired waitress returned.

"Sorry to interrupt, Boss, but can I talk to you?"

"Sure, Heather. I'm sorry, Sarah. Would you excuse me? I'll be right back."

Well, he hadn't laughed at her. That had to be a good sign. "I'm not going anywhere," she said with a smile.

\* \* \* \*

What timing. John had been ready to ask Sarah out when she beat him to it. He hoped whatever Heather wanted wouldn't take long. Sarah might change her mind about the date, or worse, leave.

He followed Heather toward the back door. "What's the matter?"

"It's about that step. I thought you said you'd fix it. I nearly broke my neck tonight."

"What? Are you okay?" Heather didn't appear to have any scratches on her legs and he wasn't smelling any blood.

"I'm fine, but you should really do something about that step. I'd hate to see you get sued."

He entered his office and retrieved his hammer and some nails. "I fixed it the same night you told me about it. You sure it's the same board?"

She opened the door and hugged herself when the wind came through. "Yeah. Maybe you should screw it in, instead, 'cause the nail's not holding. And while you're at it, you might want to look at the handrail. It's barely holding on."

John puffed out a breath as he examined the loose boards. What the hell? He might have only been an obstetrician in his previous life, but he could nail down a board. At least, he thought he could.

* * * *

John and Heather went out the door in the back, leaving Sarah at the bar with nothing to do but suck on her soda. They hadn't been gone long when a man sat on her right. The bar was practically empty, couldn't he sit at the other end?

"Wow, you smell like jasmine. You by yourself?"

"Excuse me?" Had he just sniffed her? She turned toward a rather handsome man with eyes the color of emeralds. They had to be contacts—people's eyes weren't that green. And what was with this place? His eyes glimmered like John's. Did hers sparkle, too?

"Are you sitting here by yourself?" He spun on the stool to face her and put his arm on the bar, leaning toward her. He ogled her as if she were his next meal.

He invaded her personal space and she trembled. But he wasn't Brian and he didn't sound like her attacker. Just some guy hitting on her. And a raggedy one at that. He looked like a beach bum with his sun-bleached hair pulled into a ponytail and wearing a Hawaiian shirt Goodwill would probably pitch in the trash.

She inhaled slowly, getting a whiff of vanilla, and her bearings. "How is that any business of yours?"

"I make it my business whenever I see someone as pretty as you. Pretty women shouldn't sit alone."

His statement set fire to her gut and she welcomed it. The guy had some nerve. What a boor. "Oh, so if I were ugly, it would be okay if I were alone, then?"

He leaned back and raised his eyebrows. "Well, when you put it that way, probably not, but I wouldn't care."

He came back toward her, even closer than before. His eyes practically glowed. If he tried to kiss her, she'd have to smack him. She might be able to do it, too.

"You really are quite intoxicating. Did you know that?"

"Perry? What are you doing?" John asked.

John was scowling, but Sarah breathed easier.

Perry sat back, looking like a kid caught with his dad's *Playboy.* "I wasn't doing anything. I happened to spot this gorgeous thing sitting here all by herself and thought I would visit. Is there a law against that?"

"I thought you left," John said through clenched teeth.

"I changed my mind. I was curious." Perry looked back and forth between John and Sarah; he raised his eyebrows and then asked, "Oh! Is this her? Shouldn't you introduce us?"

Her face heated up. John had talked about her? With Perry? The guy was a creep.

John took a deep breath as if resigning himself to some horrible fate. "Sarah, this is Perry Davenport; Perry, Sarah Daugherty."

Perry extended his hand. She lifted hers, expecting to shake, when he took it and kissed the back of it, his lips lingering. A faint electrical-type current ran up her arm and his eyes widened.

"How do you do, Sarah? What a pleasure to meet you." His voice flowed like honey, and her heart fluttered. First the glimmering eyes, now the electricity. Was it the bar or just these two? She snatched her hand back.

"Now that I've introduced you, can I talk to you in private?" John said.

Perry's lower lip stuck out a bit. "Sure, Johnny, I suppose so." When he stood, he bent and placed his mouth near her ear. His breath wasn't exactly cold, but it wasn't as warm as she expected. He slowly inhaled.

"Mmm, just like home." His sultry voice gave her goose bumps. "So lovely to meet you, Sarah. Maybe we'll get a chance to talk some other time?" He straightened and motioned for John to lead the way.

John leaned over the bar and whispered to Sarah, "Sorry to do this to you again. I won't be long. You'll wait?"

She smiled and nodded. Oh yeah. For him, she'd wait.

\* \* \* \*

At this rate, John would never get that date with Sarah. She'd get tired of waiting for him. Or wonder what kind of friends he had. Leave it to Perry to spoil things.

John walked through the back door and headed for his office. He waited for Perry to enter before closing the door and lashing out. "What the hell were you doing?"

Perry rubbed his mouth. "Oh my God, Johnny. Where did you find her?"

John stretched his neck first to the right then to the left. He couldn't afford to lose it, not at the bar. "Why did you come back? You said you'd leave."

"No, I didn't say any such thing. It just looked like I left. You really think I would leave knowing you were meeting a girl?" Perry cackled. "I thought you knew me better than that."

John shook his head. No one else to blame but himself, if he'd only kept his mouth shut.

"But don't worry, Johnny. Now that I've seen her, I'll leave. She is quite a find, though. I can only imagine what she must taste like. If it's anything like she smells—"

He shoved Perry in the shoulder. "You wouldn't dare...."

Perry raised his arms in defense. "Relax, Johnny. I know what you must think of me, but I won't do it. I'll be good. But aren't you even curious?"

John was curious about a lot of things regarding Sarah, but her blood wasn't one of those things. "She's not food to me."

"We're vampires. They're all food to us. When are you going to get that through your head?"

John folded his arms across his chest. He wasn't having this discussion again. Feeding from people he knew was weird, plain and simple.

"Hey, I didn't come here to argue. I really only wanted to see who captured your attention. You have good taste. Maybe in more ways than one," Perry said with a chuckle.

Sure, he had his faults, but he'd been there when John needed someone. John eased the tension in his shoulders. Maybe he had overreacted a bit.

"Better get on back out there before someone steals her away. I'll let myself out. See ya later, Johnny!"

John made sure his friend left for good this time. He rubbed his face. He needed to get it together. Sarah was waiting.

She sat hunched over her drink, sipping on the straw. When she had entered earlier, he hadn't paid attention to her outfit because he was too busy unzipping her coat and avoiding her scent. Now with the coat off, her black slacks and long-sleeved, maroon blouse were in full view. As were her socks—gray with pink pigs. So, the penguins weren't an anomaly. With the exception of her socks, she looked very businesslike. And very feminine. He was getting hard just looking at her. For over fifty years, his penis never twitched. Now it wouldn't shut up and it was all because of her.

He walked behind the bar, using it to hide his erection. He needed to get his libido under control, especially if they ended up dating. Not that she would discover his secret, but he'd like for her to think he was a gentleman and not some horny bastard.

She still hadn't noticed his return, but walking on light feet was part of the perks of being a damn vampire. He leaned onto the bar and whispered, "So, what did you have in mind?"

\* \* \* \*

The question and nearness of John's voice startled Sarah and she looked up at his handsome, smiling face. God, he was beautiful. Quiet, too. Lost in his eyes, she suddenly realized he'd said yes.

All thoughts left her head. How did he make her forget everything? She had asked him out, the hard part was over. Right?

"I-I-I don't know. I guess I didn't think that far in advance," she said with a nervous laugh. "Do you like movies? We could see a movie."

"Yeah, I like movies. Was there one in particular you wanted to see?"

His smile melted her insides, along with her brain. How on Earth could she remember what movies were playing when she could barely remember her name?

He seemed to notice her problem and pulled a paper from underneath the bar. "Will this help?"

She smiled and nodded. Good thing his brain worked, hers had certainly disintegrated.

"What night works best for you?" she asked.

"I'm available any night. How about tomorrow?"

"What do you mean you're available any night? Don't you have to work?"

"Not really. Well, I do. You see, I own this place, which means I can come and go as I please, as long as I make arrangements. I trust my employees to take care of things here."

"I've been here before. How come I've never seen you?" She never would have forgotten meeting someone like him.

"That's probably because I've only owned it a few months. So, is tomorrow okay with you?"

Was this really happening? Was she actually planning a date? Her heart pounded with pleasure at the thought. She nodded, afraid her voice would crack and give her away.

She hovered over the paper, her head nearly touching John's, and tried concentrating on the movie times, but his closeness nearly did her in. Whatever musky, woodsy cologne he wore, he smelled better than any man had a right to smell.

"How about the eight-thirty showing?" He moved back and her head cleared.

She nodded. Sure, it was a work night, but suddenly work didn't matter.

"What time should I pick you up?" he asked.

"I asked you out, I should pick you up."

"Maybe. Where do you live?"

Irrational fear glued her lips shut. She didn't know this guy, but if she couldn't trust him, why ask him out? She swept her paranoia aside. "At Patterson and Far Hills."

"Then you're on the way. I'll pick you up." He found a pen and piece of paper and slid them across the bar. "Write your address down, along with your phone number. In case I run late."

Maybe he was right. She was on the way. Certainly not worth an argument, why get him mad before they even went out?

He stuffed the paper in his back pocket. "I'll be there at eight. That'll give us plenty of time to get there. Do you have someplace to be tonight, or can you stay awhile?"

A frozen dinner waited at home. An empty home. John's company alone beat that easily. Only one problem: it was getting late. Who knew what waited for her outside? Her enemy—fear—reared its ugly head.

"I need to get home," she said, her heart hurting a little. Baby steps, that's what she needed. She'd taken one big step tonight. That had to be enough.

He frowned, but nodded as if he understood. "Hold on and I'll walk you to your car."

The night was turning out better than she ever imagined. If she had known he would offer to walk her, she might have stayed. Now it would look strange if she changed her mind. She donned her coat and scarf while he left to inform someone he'd be gone. When he returned, he held the door open for her.

She glanced at his hand. Would he object if she held it? Probably not, but she couldn't bring herself to do it. Still… Now that they were outside, would she feel the electricity?

With a push on her fob, she unlocked her door and he opened it for her. She glanced at his eyes. Even outside they glimmered, so it wasn't the bar lights. How strange, yet wonderful. The most beautiful eyes she'd ever seen.

Sarah slid behind the wheel and John wouldn't close the door until she buckled her seat belt. He wished her a goodnight.

Excitement built up inside her as she drove through each intersection on her way home. She actually had a date. Lori would be so proud of her!

# Chapter 4

The night seemed clearer, the stars brighter and John's spirits soared. He couldn't remember the last time he'd felt such joy. Real joy. Not that crap Danielle had sprung on him prior to his turning.

He banished all thoughts of the bitch who had ruined his life and concentrated on Sarah instead. Sweet, beautiful, Sarah. Sure, her scent intoxicated him and her touch gave him back what he'd lost long ago, but there was more to her than that. Around her, he felt human. Normal.

The drive to her apartment complex only took a few minutes. He parked the Xterra and slowly got out. Butterflies flitted in a stomach perpetually empty and if he could sweat, he'd probably be soaked. The bar had introduced him back to the mortal world and Sarah opened the door to the possibility of companionship, however brief. But he must be careful. If she even suspected he was different, he'd wipe her memory and leave her. He prayed it wouldn't come to that.

He found her building and took the stairs two at a time, stopping on the second floor. First door on the right. He knocked, anticipating the beginning of something wonderful.

Sarah opened the door and smiled, lighting up her whole face. It took a tremendous amount of control not to pull her into his arms and kiss her.

"Hi," she said and stepped aside. "Come on in." She wore jeans and a pink sweater. Thank goodness she didn't feel the need to dress up for a movie.

"Good evening. You look lovely tonight." As he walked past her, he snuck a look at her feet, but her socks were hidden. Maybe he'd get a peek in the car.

"Thank you," she said, shutting the door. "Let me get my coat so we can go."

Her living room was small, but orderly. A loveseat stood against the right wall with a coffee table between it and an overstuffed chair. To the side of the seating arrangement, a bookcase displayed an assortment of paperbacks. He pulled out one. Then another, and another. Since when did people write romances about vampires?

She returned with a scarf around her neck and carrying her coat. "Uh oh. Looks like you found my guilty pleasure."

"You like vampires?"

"Well... Who doesn't love a good fantasy?"

Fantasy. Right. Because the real thing was just too scary. He returned the books, then took her coat and held it up. She stared at it a moment before slipping her arms inside.

"You live here long?" he asked.

She zipped the coat to the top, as if she was afraid something would get inside. "A few months, why?"

"Most people have knick knacks and pictures." Of course, he wouldn't tell her his place looked pretty much the same. Pictures weren't a good thing for him to have around.

"I don't like to dust."

His expression must have looked funny because Sarah laughed. It was light, airy, musical.

"Am I supposed to know what that means?" he asked.

"Sorry." she said, putting on a more serious expression. Oh no, he didn't want her to do that. He would have to watch what he said. "When I was married, it seemed all I did was dust the artwork Steven insisted on displaying. I decided this place wasn't going to be like a museum. You ready to go?"

More than ready. He opened the door and sweeping his hand out, bowed. "After you."

He waited while she locked her door. Should he take her hand? Better if he waited until they were in the darkened theater. Then she wouldn't notice if he looked dreamy-eyed.

He led the way. After he opened the passenger door for her, she paused and stared at his SUV with her mouth agape.

"What's the matter?" He glanced inside. He'd made sure the seat was clean before he left.

"You own The Bumblebee?" she asked, shivering.

"The bumblebee?"

Her eyes widened. "I'm sorry. That's what I call it. Do you live at your bar?"

"Well, technically, yes. I live in the apartment above it. You work near Wings?" He knew the answer, but she didn't know he knew.

"Yeah. In the building above the garage. Small world, huh?" She climbed into the SUV and he closed the door.

It was a small world all right. If she only knew.

He pulled out of the parking lot and cranked up the heat. It amused him how much she hated the cold. She couldn't shove her hands any deeper into her pockets if she tried.

"Are those cows?" he blurted as he pointed toward her feet.

She looked down and turned her foot. "You noticed my socks? I don't think anyone ever noticed my socks before."

John shrugged. What could he say? He had eyes like a vampire?

"Are you from around here?" she asked. "I mean, did you grow up here?"

Her scent intensified inside the vehicle and he had to know, because if this date didn't work out, he would buy a gallon of the stuff. "What kind of perfume are you wearing?"

"What? I... I'm not wearing any perfume." She lowered her head and discreetly sniffed herself.

"Oh. Well, don't worry, you smell nice." Okay, he'd screwed that up. What else would he do wrong? "To answer your question, I grew up about forty miles northeast of here, in Urbana. I left after I graduated high school and it's only recently I returned to the area. In fact, I moved to Dayton when I bought the bar, since the drive was too far to make daily."

"You have family in Urbana?"

"No, not anymore. How about you, you have family around here?"

She shook her head. "Not in the Dayton area. I'm originally from Cambridge. While at college, I met Steven and Lori. They're from Dayton, and of course, I came here with Steven. After the divorce, I didn't want to go back to Cambridge and since Lori was still here, I stayed. Is Perry your friend?"

Sarah didn't appear to like Perry, which was strange. No woman had ever resisted his charm, but maybe there was a first for everything. John smiled. "Yes, I hope you don't hold that against me."

"No, I wouldn't do that." Her laughter filled the interior of the SUV with music. He needed to make sure she laughed often. It was the loveliest sound.

John pulled into the theater's parking lot and found a slot. He exited the Xterra and walked around to open Sarah's door for her, but she was already out by the time he arrived. Sure, times were different, but it still bothered him. She was a lady and he would treat her like one.

"I heard it was a really good movie," she said as they stood in line to purchase the tickets.

Frankly, he didn't care what movie they saw. He just liked being near her.

He accompanied Sarah to the next open window and she placed their order. He pulled out his wallet, but she shook her head.

"Put that away. I invited you, I pay." She slid her money to the cashier.

His mother had always told him a gentleman paid. He picked up the two tens and gave them back to her. "I insist."

"But—"

"No buts." He paid the cashier and took the tickets. When he handed one over to Sarah, she frowned. What had he done wrong?

"Can I at least get you something from the concession stand?" she asked.

Food. Now that would be a problem. "No, thank you. I ate a large meal."

And had he ever. He made sure he'd fed well before the date. Sure, he could wipe her memory if he went and lost his mind and actually sampled her—regardless of what he'd told Perry, he was tempted—but he'd rather not resort to those tricks. A gentleman behaved accordingly and he would, too, no matter how great she smelled.

"Oh," she said.

Another frown. He certainly wasn't off to a very good start.

While the previews were playing, Sarah took his hand and interlaced her fingers with his. A rush of warmth traveled up his arm through his body and ended at his groin. He nearly gasped in pleasure. Shit, if he wasn't careful, he'd end up coming in his pants. Yeah, it'd been over fifty years since his last orgasm, but that was no excuse for losing it like a virgin.

He concentrated on her as her warm hand became lost inside his. Her pulse raced. Maybe she felt something, too?

So what was she thinking? He could read her and find out. Nothing deep into her consciousness—that would be rude—just enough to understand her frown earlier so he wouldn't make the same mistake. That would be okay. Right?

He concentrated, but came up blank. That was strange. He concentrated harder. Still nothing. He'd never had any problem reading another person.

Until now.

Maybe prompting would help. *"Tell me how you feel."*

No reaction. Had she heard him at all?

He tried another route. *"Release my hand."*

Her hand remained inside his.

Oh, shit. If he couldn't read or control her and she found out…no, no, no. Not good. What was she? Why did she have to be different? He had to break it off and quickly. He untangled his hand from hers. The hurt look on her face nearly broke him in two and disappointment weighed heavily upon his heart. So much for a promising future. He might have cried if he still had the ability.

The movie went by in a blur. He was unable to concentrate on anything but Sarah. Sitting next to her, enjoying her scent, wanting to touch her and knowing he could never have her, tortured him beyond belief.

After two hours and ten minutes of enclosed anguish, he took a step outside and breathed deep. The clean air cleared his head. While guiding her back to the Xterra, she asked him if he enjoyed the movie. He didn't want to hurt her feelings and admit he hadn't watched it, which was silly since he was about to hurt her even more.

"I've never seen anything quite like it," he answered truthfully.

Sarah covered her mouth and laughed. "Yeah, I thought it was awful, too. Sorry to put you through that."

"Hey, I picked the movie. You don't have anything to be sorry about."

She placed her hand on his arm. "Are you okay? You seem lost in thought."

Maybe he should wait until he got her home. It would make the drive back less awkward. "I'm fine."

He pulled out his key and pointed the fob to his SUV. A man stood between two cars, staring at them. No, not just a man—Steven. His clothes were disheveled and he reeked of liquor. Shit. John placed a guiding hand on her back. Maybe he could get her in the vehicle before—

"Hello, Sarah."

Okay, maybe not. But she kept on walking so he stayed right with her, positioning his body between her and Steven.

"Is that how it's going to be from now on?" Steven yelled. "You can't even say hello?"

Sarah stopped and turned. The tangy scent of fear emanated from her trembling body, but she held her head high. "What do you want?"

Steven glanced at John before speaking to Sarah. "I want you back," he pleaded. "Don't you know that?"

That did it. Was the man blind? Couldn't he see how much she despised him?

John stepped in front of her. "She doesn't want to see you. Why do you keep bothering her?"

Sarah tugged at his arm. "John, no. I can take care of him."

Her eyes glistened with unshed tears. He wanted to protect her, but what right did he have? None, if he planned on breaking it off.

She stood straight and brave. "You know our deal. It's over and I've moved on. It's best you did, too. Now if you don't mind, we have someplace to be."

Sarah took John's arm and headed for the SUV.

"So you're out whoring yourself now?"

She froze. John fisted his free hand. He could rip Steven a new one—the man was clearly itching for a fight—but John had no right to interfere. Besides, how would he explain himself? With anger burning throughout his body, he might not be able to rein in his strength. Then what? He couldn't very well wipe her memory. Better to walk away.

Shielding Sarah from Steven, John whispered, "Don't let him get to you. He's not worth it."

She nodded and continued walking. John opened the door for her, went around to the driver's side, and had just clicked the seat belt together when Steven appeared at Sarah's window. He banged his fist against it, causing Sarah to jump and cry out.

"You're a cunt, you know that? It won't take long for him to realize that, too!"

John took this as his cue to drive away and he fought the temptation to run over the bastard.

"I'm so sorry." She was shaking, and not from the cold.

"Why should you be sorry? You didn't do anything wrong."

"I know, but as hard as I try otherwise, he still gets to me. Even ignoring him doesn't seem to work because he just won't go away." She rubbed her temples. "This has been some week."

"Because of Steven?"

"That's part of it." Her forehead wrinkled as if she debated on whether to tell him something else. He was about to drop it, when she continued. "Earlier this week I was attacked in the parking garage."

"What?" Shit, he'd forgotten all about that. If he couldn't get into her mind this evening, he certainly couldn't have had success on Monday.

"Crazy, huh? The whole incident is kind of fuzzy. I remember someone grabbing me and then the next thing I know I'm in my car. So if I wasn't attacked, then I'm losing my mind."

He would have given anything to ease her mind.

"Did the police catch him?" He hadn't bothered checking the paper, if an article even existed yet.

She stared at him, dumbfounded. "What? No. I mean, I didn't call the police. What would I say? I didn't have any proof. They would probably think I was crazy or drunk or something. I wasn't hurt or robbed. It was really strange."

Okay, so she didn't know about Ray. If she hadn't reported it to the police, how would she? "But you're okay now," he said, more as a statement than a question.

"Yeah, I'm okay as long as I don't think about it when I have to park in that garage," she said with a nervous laugh.

Oh man. All the more reason to break it off. He could only imagine how she would react if he ever told her his secret. Vampires were worse than abductors, right?

After he parked the Xterra, he rushed to reach her door, but she managed to beat him to it again. He walked her to her apartment and struggled with the words he needed to say when she spoke first.

"I had a nice time before Steven showed up," she said, smiling. "Do you want to come in?"

If he were human, he'd say yes in a second, but he wasn't human any longer and he was stupid to think he could be. "No, I don't think that would be a good idea."

That wonderful smile morphed into a frown and confusion flashed in her eyes. "What do you mean? Did I do something wrong? Is it because of Steven?"

God, he was such a prick. It was for the best, he just had to remember that. He shook his head. "No, it's not anything you did. I'm sorry."

"I don't understand."

He couldn't bear looking at her face and lowered his head. "It was a mistake for me to go out at all. I'm not ready for this." He took one more look before he turned to leave.

She grabbed his arm. "John, you're not making any sense. If I moved too fast, I'm sorry."

It wasn't fair. If he wasn't a damn vampire, he'd be in her apartment right now. He would have been happy with her. But he couldn't stay. "This was a mistake, Sarah. Let me go."

She lowered her arm. He ran down the stairs, needing to get as far away from her as he could. If he didn't, he'd never leave.

He stood beside his SUV and took one last glance at her apartment windows. Whatever feelings she had for him couldn't have been strong and she'd eventually forget him. He, however, would never get over her. She'd be in his heart forever.

# Chapter 5

Misery set up camp inside John's empty heart.

Passing the time without Sarah infiltrating his thoughts became impossible. He'd tried playing video games, but saw her in every character. She even appeared in the movies he watched. By late morning, he'd immersed himself in work, but there were only so many ways to restock the shelves and his mind kept wandering back to her. When the first customers arrived in the afternoon, he used them for conversation. Good thing they only needed a listener with their beer.

By five o'clock, he could almost function as a normal person. The place became noisy with the Friday night crowd.

He left the dining area to grab more napkins and upon his return Sarah was sitting at the bar. He ducked back into the hallway before she noticed him. What was she doing here? Had he not made himself clear? He should turn around and go back to his office. If he was smart, he'd do just that. But curiosity grabbed hold. So instead of turning around, he dropped the napkins off and headed in her direction.

She spotted him walking behind the bar and her eyes widened. He stopped in front of her, keeping a safe distance away, except no distance was safe from her tantalizing scent.

Her cheeks and nose were red as if she had been out in the cold. The whites of her eyes were red, too, but he didn't think the outdoors caused that. She looked as miserable as he felt. And he felt pretty miserable knowing he was the cause.

"Hi, John. Can we talk?"

He indicated an empty booth across the room. Gathering her coat and purse, she slid off the stool and headed in that direction. He followed and sat across from her.

She squirmed in her seat, adjusting her slacks. Once she finished, she placed her hands on the table, fingers intertwined. "I came to apologize."

Apologize? "I don't understand."

"I'm sorry I wanted to pay for the movie. I'm sorry for being too forward. I can do better. You acted like you liked me. I just want to make it better again."

What the hell had Steven done to her? John had made the mistakes last night, not her, yet she was the one apologizing. "You didn't do anything wrong. I did."

"What did you do wrong?"

More than she could comprehend. "It's complicated."

She touched his hand. Caught off guard, he gasped at the sudden warmth. Her eyes widened in surprise. Shit. He pulled his hand away.

"You feel something, too, when we touch, don't you?" she asked with a hopeful expression.

He didn't want to hurt her again, but she gave him no other choice. Too chicken to look her in the eyes and see the pain he would cause, he stared down at the table, but she spoke before he had a chance to lie.

"Oh," she sighed. "You must have loved her very much."

She wasn't making any sense. He looked up. Now she was the one staring at the table. "Loved who?"

"The person who hurt you. I understand. I'm afraid, too." She looked up. "But I'm tired of my mind talking me out of everything. I want to listen to my body for a change. I get a thrill when I touch you, John. If you feel the same thing, don't you want to try and see if it could be something better?"

He shook his head back and forth ever so slightly. She'd just given him the out he needed. It would be a lie—a big fat lie—but maybe this one wouldn't hurt as much.

\* \* \* \*

Sarah held her breath. Had she gotten through? Was John giving in?

41

He sat back and crossed his arms. "I still need time to get over...her. I'm sorry. It wouldn't be fair to you."

Oh God. How could she compete with another woman?

"Well, I tried," she said, shrugging. "I hope you're able to heal your heart. I think you have a lot of love to give." She scooted out of the booth, grabbed her coat and purse, and headed for the door.

Her nose stung and eyes burned. She had to get out, and fast. She stopped long enough to don her coat. If he was watching, she didn't know because she refused to turn around. She would leave with her head held high and no tears. After zipping up, she walked outside and took a deep breath, letting the cold air slap her. She'd made it, and without a scene. The breakdown could come once she got home.

In her haste to see John, she had left her car in the garage and now she was forced to walk back. Alone. The fear would eat her alive if she let it. Well, if she could confront John, she should be able to confront the garage. After another deep breath, she headed for her car.

She wasn't but a few steps from Wings when someone grabbed her shoulder and spun her around.

"So, I find you here again, huh?" Steven's breath reeked of beer and she grimaced.

Could the day get any worse? She wrenched her shoulder free. "It's none of your business where I go. How many times do I have to tell you?"

He grabbed her throat and slammed her against the building. Pain blossomed on contact and she winced. His grip cut off her air supply. Crap. Why couldn't she learn to keep her mouth shut? She grabbed his fingers and pulled—it had worked with her other assailant—but it only caused him to dig deeper into her neck.

"It's my business if I say it's my business, Sarah. Why do you have to torment me?"

White dots floated across her vision and her chest burned. If he didn't let go soon, she would pass out. "I'm sorry, Steven. I didn't mean it," she croaked. "Please let me go. You're hurting me. I can't breathe."

"I should strangle you, then maybe you wouldn't make my life miserable."

He slammed his mouth against hers. This was always his way. Scare her and then apologize by seducing her. It had worked in the past because she thought he loved her. But he didn't love her. He only loved her looks and the status that had brought him—the only reason he'd never hit her face. Well, she wasn't his damned status symbol any longer.

She rammed her knee into his groin. A squeaky moan escaped between his lips and his eyes bulged in pain. Or was that shock? Whatever, the best result came when he released her.

If only she'd hit him square, he might have fallen to the ground. Instead, he doubled over, the same as Sarah did to catch her breath. But she didn't have the luxury of time on her side. Quickly gathering her wits, she ran toward the garage. With luck, he'd be down long enough for her to reach the safety of her car.

The garage door was in sight; the handle beckoned. He slammed into her and she cried out as she crashed into the building. Grabbing her shoulder, he spun her around. He backhanded her before she had a chance to block his punch or catch her breath. Pain exploded in her right cheek. She went flying and bounced off the wall.

# Chapter 6

John's heart broke as Sarah walked out. How could he let her go so easily? Wasn't it his goal to feel normal? To feel human? He had felt alive being with her. Now his heart had truly died.

"What did you do to her?" Heather stood at the booth, hands on her hips.

Oh shit. Not now. He rose, but she shoved him back down. Sure, he could have resisted easily enough, but what was the point? He'd already lost the only thing worth fighting for.

"You aren't going anywhere until you tell me what happened."

"Nothing happened. Just leave it alone."

She sat across from him and leaned on the table. "Like hell. You were happy yesterday. I thought there was hope for you, yet. Then today you're moping around. I thought maybe she did something to hurt you. Until I saw her," she said as she tilted her head toward the door. "Now I'm thinking you did something to hurt her. So, are you a jerk, John Pennington? 'Cause if you are, I quit. I have enough jerks in my life. I don't want to work for one, too."

His insides were twisted into knots. He placed his elbows on the table and held his head in his hands. "I thought I was doing the right thing. She's better off without me."

"Why would you think that? Up until now, I thought you were the sweetest guy I knew. Don't you like her anymore?"

It certainly would have been easier if he didn't. He lowered his arms and shook his head. "That's not it."

44

"Well, then, why don't you let her decide if you're good enough for her. I bet it's not too late to tell her you're sorry."

Could he let Sarah decide? Could it be as easy as that? Just the thought of seeing her again sparked his poor, dead heart. Wasn't part of being mortal taking risks? He looked up at Heather. "You think she'd forgive me?"

Heather sat back and smiled. "Oh yeah, I think she would."

\* \* \* \*

The pavement was cold and hard...and dirty. Cigarette butts lay not six inches away from her face. Sarah slowly rose to her hands and knees. Her body hurt in more ways than she could count.

At least Steven had run off after hitting her. He could have stayed and done more damage. It wouldn't have been the first time.

She placed her hand on the wall while she got her bearings.

"Sarah?"

Oh God. What was John doing out here?

In a flash, he was there, wrapping an arm around her waist, supporting her as she stood. "What happened?"

"Nothing. Let me go." Her throat burned and her voice sounded strained. She wanted to go home and forget the whole thing. She wriggled away, but her legs weren't exactly ready for work and she wavered in her stance. He held on.

He grasped her chin. The contact caused her heart to flutter, but the pain in her neck won out. She winced.

He scowled and looked around the area. "Did Steven do this?"

This was only getting worse. As badly as she wanted to be in his arms—and man, did he smell good—she couldn't have him. He'd made it clear. She brushed his hand away. "Just let me go. I'm okay."

"You're in no shape to drive. Come on inside. I'll get an ice pack."

The tears she had fought to control came flooding back. Why was he being nice? Why couldn't he be a creep? It would be easier to hate him, then.

John hugged her and she let him. He felt good. He felt safe. "Ah, Sarah, I'm so sorry. If I wasn't such a fool... Can you ever forgive me?"

Had she hit her head? Nothing he said made any sense. "Forgive what?"

Gently, he gripped her shoulders and moved her back. Agony etched across his face. "For being an idiot. For letting you walk out that door. If I hadn't let you go, none of this would have happened."

No way. He had to have heard the commotion, that's why he came outside. "I don't want your pity, John. I understood what you told me. Let me go so you don't have to see me anymore."

It hurt too much to see his magnificent blue eyes. He appeared in front of her and blocked her way. She kept her sights on his shirt and tried not to notice his muscular chest.

"Sarah, please look at me."

No way, one look and she'd be putty. He crouched down to her level. No matter where she averted her gaze, he moved to meet it.

"Stop it!" God, he was driving her crazy. "Why are you doing this?"

With tenderness, he gripped her chin and her heart danced in her chest. "Sarah, please give me another chance. I swear I came out here to ask for one. I had no idea you were hurt."

He seemed sincere. Could she dare hope? "Really?"

John smiled at her. "Really. Come on. Let me get you an ice pack for that."

Oh hell, the smile did it. She nodded and slowly followed him. He unlocked and opened the door next to the bar's entrance. She couldn't make out a thing beyond the opening.

"Sorry about the light. I don't use this entrance very often. There are handrails on both sides."

Once he closed the door behind them, complete darkness enveloped her and she tensed. After feeling along the wall, her hand hit the railing and she grabbed on tight. He placed his hand against the small of her back and helped guide her up the stairs.

Halfway up, a dim light appeared. At the top, a hallway continued forward and he urged her on. She passed a door and then the source of the light—stairs heading down to another hallway. Sounds of muted conversations and music indicated it led to the bar. John stopped at the next door on the right and inserted his key.

"It's not much, but I call it home." He opened the door and flipped a switch. A lamp turned on, but barely lit the room. "Make yourself comfortable. I'll go down and get the ice pack."

This tiny apartment was his home? He must not entertain much. Any more than two people and they'd be bumping hips. She shrugged out of her winter gear and sat on the couch—which took up one whole wall—sinking into the comfortable cushions. It wouldn't take much to fall asleep here. Across the small room, the largest TV she'd ever seen sat on top of a huge entertainment center, crammed with numerous gaming systems and a DVD player. She would have put her feet up on the coffee table, except she'd disrupt the game cartridges and controls which littered the surface.

Her throat still burned from talking and swallowing. Maybe some water would help. She rose and shuffled to the kitchenette, but when she flipped the light switch, nothing happened. Okay, so she would have to search in the dark.

She opened the first cabinet and found it empty. Each one turned up the same, not a cup or plate in sight. When she investigated the refrigerator, she found it warm and smelling of mildew.

The front door opened as she shut the fridge. John glanced at the empty couch then turned and saw her in the kitchen. The startled look on his face almost made her feel guilty, like she'd been snooping. But how can you snoop when there wasn't anything to find?

"I got the ice pack," he said, holding it up.

She smiled and returned to the couch. Knowing the pack would be cold, she donned her glove before taking the item. The icy pack almost felt good against her burning cheek.

After moving the controllers aside, he sat on the coffee table and placed his hands on his knees. "Did Steven do this?"

She looked down. She *so* didn't want to have this conversation.

"Damn it," he cursed through clenched teeth and then muttered something she couldn't make out. "Why are you protecting him?"

"It's not that," she whispered.

"You should report him to the police."

Lori had told her the same thing before the divorce. "How would that make things better? Even if he went to jail, it wouldn't be forever. He'd get out and then come for me, angrier than ever. I just want him to go away." She met his gaze. "Please don't call the police."

He frowned. Would he call anyway? "Okay, I won't. I don't agree with your theory, but I'll go along with you. For now."

Really? No argument? No talking her into it? There had to be a catch, but she wasn't willing to look for it. It would find her eventually, it usually did.

"Did you mean what you said outside?" she asked. "You want to try dating?"

His frown transformed into a smile, lighting up his face. When he took her free hand, her heart raced. Would she ever get used to his touch? Did she want to?

"I do. I just hope you don't come to hate me."

She didn't think she could ever hate him, especially with the way his thumb rubbed across her knuckles. Every little touch excited her. What would it feel like to kiss him, to have his arms wrapped around her and be lost in his embrace? It would be heaven, that's what. The lower half of her body throbbed in anticipation. Hell, it would probably give her a real heart attack. Maybe she better change the subject before she did something she regretted, like scare him off again.

"You know, you commented on my lack of pictures, but I don't notice any in your place, either."

He shrugged. "Guilty as charged."

"Your bedroom must be tiny." Why'd she bring that up? She certainly didn't want him thinking she had sex on her mind, but why else mention the bedroom? Geez, she needed to get a new brain.

He smiled. "It's big enough. I do have a larger home up north, but this place is convenient for now."

"What do you mean a larger home?" Why would anyone want to live in this cramped place by choice?

"I have a house, with a yard, and garage," he said slowly, as if explaining it to a child, but his smile told her he was teasing. "It's in Urbana. I inherited it from my parents."

Inherited? John looked like he was around thirty, awfully young to have lost both parents. "I'm sorry for your loss. When did they pass?"

"Awhile ago," he said. "How's your throat? Is there anything I can get you?"

She couldn't swallow without wincing, but it wasn't worth a complaint. "No, I think maybe I should go home. A nice soaking bath sounds good about now." That and a bottle of aspirin. "Would you walk me to my car?"

He stood and helped her up. "Are you sure you can drive? I can take you if you want."

The world around her didn't spin—a good sign. "I'll be okay, I promise."

She wrapped the scarf around her neck and slipped her hands inside the coat John held for her. He really was a gentleman. No one had ever treated her so special before. Not even Steven during their courtship.

# Chapter 7

Sarah drove into the city toward John. What a difference twenty-four hours made. She'd gone from despondent to joyous. Even her cheek and head couldn't spoil her mood.

Traffic on a Saturday was practically nonexistent, making it easy to spot a dark blue BMW in her rear view mirror. Damn. Was Steven following her now? After the stunt he had pulled the night before, she couldn't be sure. The man was seriously crazy.

She yanked the steering wheel left at the next street, unintentionally cutting off another driver. The long blare of a horn made her jump. Her heart nearly stopped and she pulled over. Every cell in her body shook. She looked out the back window. The BMW drove on without turning. God, what a fool. She could have been in an accident and for what? All because she *thought* she saw Steven?

After taking several deep breaths, she continued on her way. By the time she arrived at Wings, she was back to being her plain old paranoid self. She parked in front and took one last glance up and down the street for the BMW.

Yeah, she was an idiot. Not a car in sight.

She approached the door John had said to use. Remembering the cave-like environment, she hesitated for a moment. She really needed to get her shit together. It was daylight. She'd be able to spot anyone lurking inside before she closed the door. She slowly turned the knob and pulled. Instead of darkness greeting her, the stairwell was brightly lit. She placed her hand over her heart and smiled.

She'd climbed partway when John appeared at the top. His grin brought on one of her own.

"Everything okay? You look a little rattled."

Boy, he was observant. "I thought I saw Steven and overreacted. Turned out to be a false alarm."

He frowned at her statement. Maybe she better not mention Steven again. John had invited her over for a movie, not to talk about unpleasant things. When she reached the top, he took her hand. She gasped. Would she ever get used to the sensations he sparked with a simple touch?

He glanced down at their hands. "Did I hurt you?" He opened his hand to let go, but she held on.

"No. Must have been static."

As always, John held the door for her. Unwilling to release his hand, she entered and pulled him behind her. The longer she held on, the more accustomed her body became. Her heart rate slowed and her breathing was almost normal.

"Why don't you sit and tell me what movie you'd like to see. Of course, I'm going to need my hand back to get it." She smiled at his tease and reluctantly let go. As soon as she did, her body missed him.

She placed her belongings on the kitchen counter before she sat on the couch. "What do you have?"

John went to the entertainment center and opened a cabinet stuffed full of DVDs. He started calling out titles and she picked one she'd never seen before.

Once he inserted the DVD into the player, he sat beside her and took her hand again. Her heart jumped in her throat and she breathed unevenly. If she didn't watch it, he might think she was having a heart attack. Then again, maybe she affected him the same. She hoped so.

He smiled briefly, then furrowed his brow as he gently probed the bruise on her cheek. "It doesn't look so bad today."

Crap. Why did he have to notice at all?

"That's because I'm wearing make-up." She only winced a little, but enough to cause him to stop.

"Sorry. Well, the swelling's down anyway. Do you mind if I look at your neck?"

She rolled the turtleneck down, feeling like a patient at a doctor's office.

He gently probed the area. "Does it still hurt?"

"Just a little. At least it doesn't hurt to swallow anymore. You know, you'd make a good doctor. You have a very nice bedside manner."

"You think so?"

She smiled and nodded. "Yeah, I do."

While she sat beside him watching the movie, he never released her hand. He would occasionally rub his thumb across her knuckles and it took a lot of effort on her part to pay attention to the film. They were sitting close together, her leg next to his, her shoulder against his arm. This was so much better than the theater. No armrest got in the way. Would he kiss her? Would he try?

The movie ended and John kissed the back of her hand before releasing it and standing. Well, he'd kissed her. Just not where she'd hoped. But while kissing him would most definitely be better than great—his touch titillated and then some—she should take it slow. Why scare him off again? Besides, she had rushed into things with Steven and that turned out disastrous.

"What are your plans for this evening?" Sarah asked. "I know you said you wanted to surprise me, but can I at least get a hint?"

John put the DVD away and then sat back beside her. "It's not so much that I wanted to surprise you, I just wanted to tell you in person. Anyway, there's an ice skating rink down by the river and I'd like to take you."

"Ice skating? Outside? Isn't it kind of cold out there?" Then there was the possibility of falling and making a fool of herself.

"That's why I told you to wear layers. Once you move around, you'll warm up okay. It's really quite fun, but if you don't want to do it, I'll understand."

Well that was a surprise. He wasn't coercing her. Yet. "It's my choice?"

"If you don't want to go, we can find something else to do. But I think you'll have fun if you try."

Falling on ice didn't sound like fun, it sounded downright painful. "I don't know how to ice skate." There, she'd said it. Let the embarrassment commence.

"Hey, don't worry about that. I can show you how and I promise, I won't let you fall. So, did you want to grab something to eat downstairs before we go? We still have a couple of hours before sunset."

Sunset? "Why can't we go now? While the sun's out?"

Frowning, he stood and started pacing. What the hell had she said to get him all riled up and could she take it back?

"Uh, yeah, about that." He ran his hand through his hair. "You see, Sarah, I can't, I mean, the sun, uhh."

"Oh heavens, just spit it out, John. What's the problem?"

He stopped. "I can't go out into the sun. I-I'm allergic."

"You're what?"

He sat back beside her. "I know, I should have told you sooner. I just didn't think it would come up this soon. I mean, you work during the day. I hope this doesn't change anything…"

It all made sense. She put her fingers to his lips and little sparks of electricity raced through her hand. His eyes widened and he gasped. Damn, that wasn't her intention. She put her hand down. "Is that really why you tried to break it off? Because you can't go out during the day?"

He nodded and grabbed her hand as if he wanted more of the same. Whether or not he felt anything, she certainly did. He was like a drug. If she didn't watch out, she'd be addicted. That's if she wasn't already.

"I guess we'll wait until sundown, then."

He smiled like a kid at Christmas and it was infectious. "Thank you. You'll have fun tonight, I promise."

Ice skating still scared the crap out of her, but how bad could it be if he held her? And he'd certainly keep her warm. Okay, maybe ice skating wasn't such a bad idea after all.

"Did you mention something about food?"

As John led them to the bar, Sarah got a whiff of grilled hamburgers and her stomach growled. Oh God, she hoped he hadn't heard it, but his staring at her with one eyebrow raised told her otherwise. She shrugged. "I ate a light lunch."

"Well, then let's get Pete to fix you up something."

Except for the music playing, the place was practically a library compared to the last time. Only two people sat at the bar and four at a table.

"Are Saturday afternoons usually this slow?"

"Not always, but there aren't any games on today. Next Sunday it'll probably be busy with the Super Bowl. Sometimes I enjoy it when it's quiet. It can get hectic in here when a game is on." He snatched a menu and showed her to a table in the back, near the pool table, where it was more private. "Is this okay?"

She nodded. He held the seat for her. Who did that anymore? He made her feel like royalty. She took the seat and he sat in the one next to her. He handed her the menu.

"I'm afraid my selection is limited, but if there's something you'd like that isn't on the menu, Pete can probably whip it up, provided I have the ingredients."

She looked over the menu. "What are you going to have?"

"Nothing."

"What, don't you eat?"

"Oh, I eat. I'm just on a special liquid diet. But don't let me stop you. I don't want you to feel uncomfortable eating in front of me. I'm okay with it, really."

Special liquid diet? Well, whatever kind of diet he was on certainly did wonders for him. He looked healthy. And strong. And beautiful. Hell, maybe she should try his diet, but right now her stomach craved real food and Pete's hamburger won out.

* * * *

John nearly pinched himself. No day could be so perfect, could it? Sarah filled a part of him that had been empty too long, and now he couldn't imagine his life without her. To think he'd almost let her go.

Heather winked at him and gave him a nudge as she placed Sarah's meal on the table. What? No sly remark? She went on her way instead.

Sarah took a bite of her sandwich and her eyes lit up. "Wow, this is probably the best burger I ever ate. Pete is a good cook."

"That's what I heard."

She looked at him with widened eyes. "You sound like you've never tried his food. Do you want a bite?"

It smelled tasty and if he hadn't come up with that stupid liquid diet excuse, might have taken a bite. Too late now. "Thank you, but I'm not hungry."

She hit her forehead with the heel of her hand and laughed. "Oh, that's right. Liquid diet, duh! I'm really not as dense as I seem."

John laughed with her. He liked how she could be silly with herself and didn't seem to take things personally.

Might she be able to handle the truth? Yeah, if he lived in Fantasy Land. He quickly squashed that thought.

At a quarter to six, John suggested they leave. It was funny how she agreed to go, but still looked scared. He hoped she felt differently once he got her out there.

Back upstairs, he helped her with her coat and smiled when she zipped it up high. Her pink scarf peeked out through the neck opening and she placed the earmuffs over her ears. The ensemble was complete with her pink knit hat and pink gloves. She certainly looked cozy and he hoped she stayed warm enough. He didn't need this to backfire because of the weather.

Without thinking, John nearly grabbed his light jacket, but quickly came to his senses and donned his winter gear. He followed her down, but snuck in front to open the door. After he locked up, he offered his arm. Her gaze darted down the street before landing on him.

"What's the matter?"

"We're walking?"

"I thought so. It's not that far."

"Oh, okay." She took his arm and snuggled close.

If this was what he got for walking in the cold with her, he'd take it.

Two blocks later, they arrived at the rink. He obtained her shoe size and left her huddled on the bench while he went to the rental booth. He passed a temperature sign. Thirty-two degrees. Hopefully it wouldn't get too much colder; he wanted her to have fun. When he returned, he handed her the skates. She eyed them diffidently before taking them.

"You know how to put them on, right?"

"I think so."

"The trick is to lace them up tight. That way your ankles are supported better."

She nodded and he quickly put his skates on. Once he finished, he checked on her. She had tangled the long laces and was tugging on a knot. He knelt in front of her and took over, noticing the pink socks.

"Kittens today, huh?" How many types did the woman own?

She shrugged. "Guess I was in a kitten mood."

"Let me know if it's too tight, I don't need to cut off your circulation."

"Okay."

Sarah was rather quiet, but John supposed it had more to do with the weather or her fear of another attack than anything else. But if that was the case, wouldn't she have asked to drive?

He finished lacing her boots, rose, and offered his hands. She grabbed on tightly and stood, wobbling on her skates. He slid his arm around her waist and steadily walked her over to the rink.

She stopped at the ice's edge.

"Come on, Sarah. I promise, I won't let you go."

Her whole body shook and the scent of fear emanated from her. Maybe it wasn't just the cold. Maybe it was the skates. She wrapped her arm around his waist and her other hand held onto the arm he had wrapped around her. She must have thought he would let her go. No way would he do that. He had promised. Plus, he enjoyed holding her.

She placed one foot onto the ice, then the other, as if she were testing its solidity. Her legs were a bit wobbly at first, and her feet scissored a few times, but she managed to attain her balance. Soon she was gliding, and with each glide, her grip became less tight.

At the mid-way point she said, "I think I've got it now. Just hold my hand, okay?"

As much as he hated letting her go, her confidence was more important. He slowly released her waist and held her hand. Her feet scissored briefly, but she brought them under control. Each unaided glide across the ice made her smile grow. A couple of times she lost her balance and squeezed his hand, but for the most part she was doing well on her own. He was proud of her.

As they came full circle, she raised her free hand and cheered, "I made it!"

The movement caused her to lose her balance and her feet slipped out from under her. Her free hand clawed at thin air and he quickly grabbed her around the waist, steadying her.

"You kept your promise," she said, holding tightly onto his arms.

"I always do."

Her feet were still slipping and she laughed. "Maybe I should have waited to celebrate after I sat down."

"You want to celebrate?" He lifted her enough to clear her feet off the ground and twirled her around. In the process, she put her arms around his neck and giggled like a little girl. She was so soft and her fragrance so enchanting, he didn't want to let her go. When he stopped twirling, their faces were inches apart and he gazed into her eyes. She glanced briefly at his lips before meeting his eyes once more. Did she want him to kiss her? Was she daring him to do it? If only he could read her mind.

# Chapter 8

It would have been awkward to ask, "Would you kiss me?" So Sarah did the next best thing. She kissed him.

When their lips touched, her heart raced, but he felt cold at first. Like ice. Well, they were outside on a skating rink, what did she expect? Hers were probably frozen, too. She pulled back and stared into his eyes. Instead of sparkling from the lights, an iridescence radiated from them as if they were glowing from inside.

John slid his hand behind her head and claimed her mouth with his. What started out cold quickly became oh-my-God hot. She welcomed his tongue as he aggressively explored her mouth. He tasted good, like cinnamon candy, and she suckled. She couldn't get close enough and silently cursed their coats. Parts of her body tightened and throbbed.

Kids nearby snickered.

Crap. They were outside. In public.

She broke away, but before she could say anything, someone collided into John and as he fell forward, he quickly twisted his body. He landed with a thwack, but kept his arms around her, protecting her from the ice.

He wasn't moving. She'd landed with her face buried in his chest, and she squirmed and looked up. "John? Are you alright?"

He wore a silly grin and raised his eyebrows. "Couldn't be better."

What did he mean by that? He couldn't be comfortable with her on top of him. She moved to get off when her leg rubbed against something hard. He uttered a moan that sounded more like pleasure than pain.

Hard. Pleasure.

*Oh my God, oh my God.* As she struggled to stand, she kept rubbing against him. How big was he? Each touch sent shivers through her body. Damn, just touching him got her excited. She'd climb off him, but his arms were like a vise holding her.

He brought his lips to her ear and whispered, "As much as I'm enjoying this, if you keep it up, I'll surely embarrass you. Just lay still for a minute."

Unfortunately, they'd already drawn a crowd. "I think it's too late. At least try to sit up."

A skater approached, waving his arms as if trying to regain his balance. And he was headed for them. As Sarah prepared for the impending crash, John stood and whooshed her safely out of the line of fire.

"That was close. You okay?" he asked.

Damn, that was some fast moving. If only she could be so coordinated. "Yeah, I'm fine."

"You want to try and make it around the ice again?"

Skate. Ugh. What she really wanted was another scorching kiss from him, but if that wasn't going to happen, she'd settle for his touch.

After two more trips, her feet and ankles protested the abuse and her face was numb from the cold.

"You ready to quit?" he asked.

Thankful she didn't have to bring it up, she nodded.

She sat on the bench and worked at untying her laces while John left to fetch their shoes. She had one boot unlaced by the time he returned.

She yanked the skate off and the cold air attacked her socked foot. "Thanks, John. I had fun tonight."

He straightened from untying his boots and stared at her. "Did you really? Or are you just saying that?"

The question caught her off guard. She might never request to skate again, but she'd do anything that included him holding her. "I had fun with you. But maybe next time we can find something to do indoors?"

He went back to his boots and laughed. "I think I can manage that. I'm sorry you didn't like skating, but thanks for trying."

She opened her mouth to protest, but he raised an eyebrow as if taunting her to deny it. Damn, she couldn't do that, not without lying anyway. "You're welcome." She bent over and worked on the other skate while John chuckled.

What a relief to get those heavy things off. When she stood and started walking, she almost glided across the ground. It amazed her how she'd adjusted in such a short time.

Sort of like how her body adjusted to John. The longer she touched him, the calmer her heart beat. Of course, being covered in coats and gloves, they hadn't had much skin contact. Except for that kiss, that wonderful, electric kiss. Maybe she would have to get used to him all over again, but she could live with that. What's a heart attack—or two or three—when it felt so good?

During the walk back to Wings, she relived kissing him. His lips were everything she dreamed of and better. It certainly kept her mind off turning into a Popsicle.

He unlocked the door to the staircase. "Can you stay a little longer? It's not too late for you is it?"

She should go home, it would be the sensible thing to do. But she'd been doing sensible all her life. Besides, there wasn't any place she'd rather be. "I can stay."

He grinned. "Great."

Once inside his warm apartment, Sarah took off her winter gear while John shed his own. She shook with excitement, and a bit of nerves, but when he faced her and stared at her with those beautiful blue eyes, desire raced through her and shooed any nervousness away.

In one step, he captured her face and bent down for a kiss. A tingling sensation rode through every nerve. Why had she thought her body was used to him? Like before, he explored her mouth with his tongue, searing her. She grabbed those massive shoulders of his and melted against him. Oh God, she loved the way he kissed.

Slowly, he backed her to the couch, where he lowered her to the cushions. She felt nothing but his lips and hard body.

John left a fiery trail of kisses to her neck, where he stopped to nuzzle. He licked her, which got her juices flowing. Damn. Who knew that was a sensitive spot? When he fondled her breast, she arched into his hand. Even with all the layers she wore, her nipples hardened at his touch and the lower half of her body tightened. The man practically burned a hole through her clothes.

He grabbed her hip, rubbing his erection against her thigh. God, she wanted him. Her heart nearly exploded from the excitement of it all. He could take her now and she'd let him. But was she moving too fast? No, she was thinking too much. Let him do whatever. But she'd let Steven do whatever and look where that had landed her.

Damn! It took a tremendous amount of willpower to push gently on his chest, when she really wanted to hold him closer.

John pulled back. He looked stricken and he was panting as hard as she was. He shot up off the couch. "I'm so sorry, Sarah. It won't happen again."

She didn't want it to never happen again, just not now. "What? Don't be sorry. I'm sorry." She sat up and lowered her head. "I feel like I led you on."

He sat beside her, tugged on her chin, and kissed her forehead, nearly igniting her all over again. "No, you just wanted to kiss. I got carried away, and I'm sorry."

John put his arm around her shoulder. Sarah smiled up at him, relieved. Whenever she had tried to stop Steven, he'd never listened. Instead, he'd always managed to talk her into whatever it was he wanted. Looking back, she could see Steven had never cared about her feelings at all.

"Maybe we both got carried away. I do like you, John. I'm sorry I'm not more like Lori."

He laid two fingers over her mouth, hushing her. "If you were more like Lori, you wouldn't be here. I like *you* Sarah. Don't ever apologize for being you."

Why couldn't she have met John first? He really was the sweetest man; there wasn't anything phony about him. But instead, her history with men overtook common sense and that little voice in her head said, "He's going to hurt you like Steven did."

So, she couldn't trust her body. Not yet.

"I should go home. It's been a long day."

"I understand." He stood and offered his hand.

Reluctantly, she took it. She didn't want to leave. She wished she didn't have to leave. But taking it slow was better. Smarter.

\* \* \* \*

After agreeing to another date on Sunday—which Sarah would plan—John waited until she drove away before he discreetly followed, wanting to make sure Steven wasn't lurking around her apartment building. Maybe she hadn't seen the bastard earlier, but why chance it?

Once she made it inside her apartment, John thoroughly inspected the area. No sign of the creep, and a good thing, too, who knew what John would do to the guy? That man didn't deserve his freedom.

John took his time walking back to Wings. Damn, he was still hard for her. Her scent refused to leave.

Thank goodness she'd had the presence of mind to stop him. Bad enough his fangs had emerged while he nuzzled her, he'd nearly made love to her right there on the couch. With her around, his other head did all the thinking.

Keeping his secret was harder than he imagined, but oh, so worth it. He just needed to take it slow. Steven had certainly scarred her and he would do his best not to do the same. That included getting her involved in the relationship. He got the impression she'd never made any kind of decisions before, and had seemed surprised when he asked her to choose what they would do on their next date. He couldn't wait to see what she came up with. Hell, he couldn't wait to see her again.

# Chapter 9

Sarah whipped the scarf around her neck and was out the door before securing her coat. She'd been waiting all day to visit John and finally she could leave. As she approached her car, there, standing beside it, was Steven. She froze. Crap.

How the hell had he found out where she lived? Was he here to hurt her again? Part of her wanted to go to him and punch him silly, tell him he had no right to stalk her. The other, sensible part told her to turn on her heels and head back to her apartment. She listened to sensible. She'd tell John something came up, just not what that something was.

"Sarah, wait. Don't go."

She stopped. If she didn't confront him now, he'd only come back. Shoving her hands inside the coat pockets, she faced him. "What do you want?"

When he advanced, she stepped back, putting her hands out in a stop motion. It worked. He halted.

"I'm not here to hurt you, I came to apologize. I was drinking too much, I know that now. I overreacted. Please forgive me. It won't happen again, I promise."

She'd heard it all before, but not quite as robotic, as if he'd been reciting a speech. Either he'd lost his touch or she'd finally woken up. "Forgive me if I don't believe you. And if you try anything like it again, then I'm contacting the police. Do you understand?"

"Please, Sarah, I mean it this time. I still love you. I only want you back. We'll have all the babies you want. Please come back to me."

How dare he bring that up? She'd had enough. "It's over, Steven. Go away and leave me alone."

He took a step forward and she retreated, cringing. If he took another step, she would scream. No way would he hit her again.

He put his hands up, surrendering. "Okay, Sarah, I'll leave for now. But I'm not giving up on us. You'll see, you need me." He got into his car and drove away.

She trembled all over. After spending several moments taking long, deep breaths, she got the shaking under control and hightailed it out of there. Steven might return sooner rather than later.

She parked in the alley behind Wings as John had suggested, her hands still shaking as she pulled the key from the ignition. If she went inside like this… Damn. John picked up on her moods quicker than anyone she knew. No way would she tell him about Steven. He'd gone away without incident, which was fine with her, but John might not be so forgiving. Why test him?

After a few deep breaths, she got out of the car. The nippy breeze slapped her face, but also helped clear her head. She opened the trunk and pulled out a shopping bag. She almost felt normal, if there was such a thing anymore. Rushing to get out of the cold, she hurried up the wooden steps to the back door. As she stepped on the middle board, it crackled a split second before giving away. She grabbed the rickety handrail. If she'd been falling, it would have surely fallen apart. John might want to think about fixing this thing before someone got hurt.

She patted her racing heart and entered the building. Toasty air greeted her. She shrugged the coat off as she passed John's office.

What kind of work did he do in there? Feeling for the light switch, she flipped it up, but nothing happened. Didn't any of his lights work? Afraid she might bump into something and disturb it—not to mention hurt herself—she settled for leaning against the door jam and letting the hall light illuminate the room. She could make out the desk, and there appeared to be a lamp on it. Picturing John at work inside the small office made her smile.

"You okay?" John asked.

Sarah twirled at the sound of his voice. He always surprised her. But okay? Far from it. She needed an excuse that didn't include Steven. "Your...your step is loose outside and your handrail's about ready to come off. It startled me is all."

He sprinted to her and grabbed her shoulders. "What? I thought I fixed those. Did you hurt yourself?"

"No, no. I'm fine. Really." She looked up at his beautiful face. How did she get so lucky to find someone like him?

"I'm so sorry. I'll make sure to fix them later." He caressed her cheek and her heart went wild. Zeroing in on his lips, she rose on her toes, but before she could reach her destination, he cupped her face and kissed her forehead before gently pushing her away. "What's in the bag?"

What kind of kiss was that? Putting the bag behind her back, she said, "Don't I get a kiss hello? My lips work."

John frowned. "It's not that I don't want to kiss you."

She palmed his face. "Sometimes willpower is knowing when to stop, not avoiding it completely. I don't want to be avoided."

"I don't want to avoid you, either."

Bending down ever so slowly, he pressed his lips to hers. What started out light and sweet, grew hungry and urgent and she welcomed it. He could kiss her forever and she wouldn't care.

His eyes shone from within as he gazed into hers. "How was that?"

Too short. A sigh escaped. "Much better. See, I knew you could do it."

He peered over her shoulder. "Now are you going to show me what you brought?"

* * * *

Sarah's warmth lingered on John's lips. Damn, he wished he could kiss her forever, but that wasn't very likely, or wise. He peeked inside the bag and raised his eyebrows. "Board games?"

She grinned. "Yes. You said to pick something safe and we can play them indoors."

"How did you think playing board games alone in my apartment would be safe?" When he thought safe, he pictured being out in public. Some place he would be forced to keep his hands to himself. Which was unrealistic since he couldn't go out until the sun set. Shit.

The grin on her face vanished, replaced with a furrowed brow. She lowered her head. "Should of known I'd come up with something stupid."

He was an idiot. She'd made such an effort and he'd just shot it all to hell. He had to fix this, and fast.

"You know, on second thought, you're right. I was just thinking about it all wrong. We'll play in the bar. It'll be fun."

And there would be a table between them, so no hanky-panky. It could work.

She raised her head. A flicker of hope flashed across her face. "Are you sure?"

God, he never wanted her to doubt herself again. He placed his arm around her shoulder and squeezed. "It's a great idea. Honest."

When her smile returned, he relaxed.

They had played Monopoly and were finishing with Scrabble when John glanced at his watch again. It was nearly eight o'clock and Sarah still hadn't asked for anything to eat. He'd asked her at five and then six, but she had refused each time.

"What can I get you from the kitchen?"

She picked up the remaining tiles and tossed them in the box. "Nothing. I'm good."

He knew the sound of a hungry stomach and hers was growling up a storm. Why would she lie? "You haven't eaten anything all night. Are you feeling well?"

"I'm not hungry, John," she said with a stern voice.

He wished he'd never mentioned the damn liquid diet. He could have eaten, as long as he was near a restroom. But if he started eating now, and he assumed that's what it would take for her to eat, she'd probably feel guilty he was off his diet.

She rubbed her temple. "I had a lot of fun today, but do you mind horribly if I call it a night? I'm kind of tired."

Her question brought him back. "No, I don't mind, well, I *do* mind, well, you know what I mean." He laughed, trying to make light of the situation, but only got a small smile in return.

Her stomach rumbled once again, but he didn't let on. Maybe it was better she went home. Maybe she planned to eat there.

He took the board games and went upstairs to grab her things. The evening had turned out better than he imagined. Not once had he made a move to seduce her or bite her, even when he had kissed her. Dating was getting easier. Maybe that's all he needed—practice.

After she donned her winter gear, he held the back door open for her. The way she braced herself for the cold air by hunching her shoulders and shoving her hands inside her pockets made him grin. She was so predictable.

Seeing her leave made his chest constrict, almost as if she were taking a part of him, but he'd make sure to see her tomorrow. After turning her around, he leaned in for a goodbye kiss when movement outside caught his eye. It might have been a bird, but her car caused him to stop and stare.

What the hell had that bastard done now?

\* \* \* \*

John's horrified expression startled Sarah and when she turned in the direction of his gaze, all the blood rushed out of her head. Her car! All four tires were flat, almost mutilated. And scratched deeply into the hood was the word WHORE.

She stumbled for a closer look, fingered the scratches in the cold metal, making sure they were real. "Who would do this?" Oh wait. Who else?

"I'm calling the police this time," John said. Her world wavered and he was by her side in an instant, holding her up. "Come on. Let's go back inside where it's warm."

Okay, so not eating wasn't her smartest idea, but eating in front of John was worse than eating alone. She suspected he missed real food by the way he had stared at her hamburger last night. If she didn't have to eat in front of him, she wouldn't. Next time she'd eat more than soup for lunch. Light-headed and dizzy, she prayed she wouldn't pass out. She didn't realize they'd walked all the way to his apartment until he sat her on the couch.

John slipped his phone inside his pocket. "The police will be here soon. Can I get you anything?"

"What am I going to do? I can't afford to fix that." She was already living paycheck to paycheck. And credit? Ha! Steven had made sure everything was in his name alone. How the heck would she get to work without a car? Her nose started tingling and her vision blurred. "The tires alone…"

He put his finger to her lips. "Shhh, don't worry about it. You have insurance, right?"

"Yes, but will it cover this?"

"If not, I'll help. Now, I can give you a ride home tonight, but do you think Lori can take you to work tomorrow?"

"Ah, damn it!" How would she ever be on her own if she was constantly asking for help? Buying that car had been her first step toward independence and now it was gone, or at least out of commission for a while.

"Sarah, it'll be alright. I'm sure Lori will give you a ride."

"That's not it. I'm sure she will, too. It just seems lately like it's been one thing after another and it's making me mad."

He pulled her in close and his scent comforted her in a way nothing else would. "You don't have to handle it all by yourself. Let me help you."

Did it make her a weak person if she always needed help or a strong one to admit it? Or just lucky to have people who cared? She'd been leaning on Lori for too long, now, but did John deserve to be next? He didn't seem to mind, but feelings could change. She'd seen that firsthand.

\* \* \* \*

After screwing the loose step in place and reattaching the handrail again—a job he had also accomplished four nights ago—John stood beside Sarah's car and assessed the damage. The police had taken their statements, but it appeared nothing could be done. Steven's alibi was airtight and he couldn't possibly have caused the damage to her car. Didn't mean he wasn't still involved. He could have hired someone else to do the deed. Or it was just some random act of vandalism, like the police suspected.

John examined the back of the building. He should install a camera in the alley, just in case something like this happened again.

The sound of a rock hitting a dumpster echoed. All the businesses were closed for the night and there weren't too many residents in the area. Heck, since he'd moved into the area, crime had decreased, thanks to his interventions. He headed toward the sound as a figure appeared.

Perry. Shaking his head, John headed back. Ignoring Perry was impossible, but why wait to be harassed?

Perry caught up easily. "Hey, Johnny. How's the little woman? I bet she's hot in bed. Does she taste as good as she smells? Or don't you want to bite and tell?" he asked, flashing his eyebrows.

John lowered his head. He should have known better than to ever tell Perry about Sarah.

"No! You didn't have sex with her?" Perry laughed. "I suppose that means you didn't dabble, either."

"No, I didn't... What is with you? Is that all you do with women? Have sex and feed?"

Perry shrugged. "What else is there? Besides, they don't seem to mind. Whoa! What happened here?" He stopped at the damaged car.

"I wish I knew."

"Seems like you need better security. Do you have time to play some video games or are you too busy being a bar owner?"

Perry could switch gears faster than anyone John knew. However, playing video games sounded like a good idea. Thinking about Sarah and who might have vandalized her car wouldn't benefit him or her. He hoped she could sleep. Even though she'd looked absolutely beat, she'd still been rattled and worried.

Inside the apartment, Perry draped himself on the couch and slowly inhaled. "Ah, I see Sarah's been up here. How do you do it, Johnny? How can you touch her and not make love to her? How can you be next to that wonderful scent and not take a sample?"

John opened the game cabinet as an inner alarm went off in his head and the back of his neck tingled. He didn't like the way Perry acted while he talked about her. He looked downright dreamy. "Does she affect you, too?"

"She's very intoxicating, and when I touched her..."

The game cartridge John had pulled from the cabinet slipped through his fingers. "What happened when you touched her?"

Perry stood and peered into the cabinet. "Buy any new games lately?"

John grabbed Perry's shoulder. "Don't avoid the question. What happened when you touched her?"

"I think maybe you already know. But when *I* touched her, I felt this incredible rush of warmth and it traveled up my arm to the rest of my body. It was quite exhilarating."

John lowered his arm. How could that be? "Did you excite her?"

Perry paused for a moment. "You know, now that you mention it, she was kind of put off by me. Why do you suppose that is? I mean, what woman doesn't love this?"

John had noticed it, too. Sarah pretty much hated Perry. Was the fact she couldn't be controlled making her immune to the vampire charm? Did that mean her feelings for him were real? He certainly had real feelings for her. Or did he? Shit. Did she affect all male vampires?

"Don't worry, Johnny, I won't go after her. Not until she dumps you first."

But Perry was the least of his worries.

# Chapter 10

No one at work noticed Sarah's bruise like Lori had when she picked up Sarah. And Lori would never blab about something so personal, but couldn't resist spreading the news about Sarah's car. Maybe she was only warning their co-workers about parking on the street, but whatever her motive, Sarah was inundated with people offering their own vandalism horror stories. By late morning, she needed a breather from the evil well-wishers.

She hid out in the break room and was pouring coffee when her cellphone vibrated against her hip. John. Her heart lightened and she smiled.

"Did you get any sleep last night?" he asked.

Sleep? What was that? Was three hours enough? "I got enough. You hear anything about my car?"

"I had it towed last night, but I haven't heard anything yet. I called to see if you liked ice hockey."

After the tiring morning, she was in the mood for some fun. "Gee, John, you saw how badly I skated. You really think I could play?"

The brief silence on the line made her grin. "Uh, Sarah, I didn't mean for you to play. I meant to watch."

She couldn't hold the laughter any longer.

He laughed with her. "Okay, you got me. Does that mean you're interested? The game's this Friday."

"Yeah, I'll go. I like sports. I might not always know what's going on, but it's fun to watch." Sitting next to John would make it fun.

"Great, I'll get tickets. Give me a call when you're ready to leave tonight, and I'll meet you in the garage. Can you make sure it's after sunset?"

It was the least she could do. They said their goodbyes and she put her phone away. She picked up her coffee cup and walked toward the door when she nearly ran into Lori. "How long have you been there?"

Lori folded her arms. "Oh, long enough. You're seeing John again tonight?"

"He's taking me home. Is there a problem with that?"

"I could have taken you home."

Yeah, but then she wouldn't see John. "You're already bringing me to work. Besides, he wants to. What's wrong with that?"

"I'm only looking out for you, Sarah. I don't want to see you get hurt again."

"Hey, weren't you the one who wanted me to go out?"

"Yeah, but to get laid. I didn't think you were ready for anything serious."

Too late. As for getting laid...

"John must be really good in bed, huh? I mean, you've seen him every night."

Sarah looked down at her mug. There were some things she couldn't talk about.

"Oh my God. You haven't done it yet. Is there something wrong with him?"

Sarah shook her head. "No."

Lori put her arm around Sarah's shoulders. "Okay, I take it back. Maybe you do know what you're doing. It's only that I see the same signs and I worry."

"John's nothing like Steven. And I am trying to take it slow." Agonizingly slow. Why was she waiting? He seemed interested. She was interested. Damn.

Lori pulled away. "You've got more willpower than me. I'd have nailed him the first night. But then, I only wanted him for his body."

With the workday over, Sarah rode the elevator to the garage and John. She found him leaning against a pole—arms across his massive chest. Once he saw her, his face lit up and he straightened. His smile brought a lump to her throat. No one had ever looked so good. Bouncing like a giddy schoolgirl, she approached him, smiling back.

After taking her hand, he bent down and kissed her lightly on the lips, causing her heart to flip-flop. At least she didn't have to beg this time.

"Did you have a nice day?" he asked softly, his breath tickling her lips. He seemed to take in her scent, but she didn't care since she was doing the same thing.

"I am now." When he got close, she lost track of everything. His scent made her want to snuggle against his body. And the way he smiled at her with those glimmering blue eyes made her all gooey inside. He was kind and beautiful, and he could be hers. All she had to do was say the word. "Do you have any plans tonight?"

He rubbed his thumb across her knuckles. "I made arrangements for you to get a rental car. I thought we could walk over and get it."

While her head swirled with the sensations their touch caused, his comment brought her back down to reality, if not disappointing her altogether. "I can't afford a rental car. If you can't take me home or it's too much trouble, I'll get Lori or ride the bus."

"I didn't say you were paying for it." He started for the exit and tugged at her hand. "Come on, it's not far."

She kept her feet planted and bravely said, "No."

John closed his eyes and shook his head. This was the point when Steven would lash out at her. Oh why couldn't she just keep her mouth shut?

"If that's the way you feel, I'd be honored to take you home. I just didn't want you to have to wait each day until sunset."

What? No argument? No yelling? No hitting some sense into her? Was he for real? God, she certainly hoped so.

"I don't have a problem waiting, thank you." The words seemed inadequate. She stood on her toes and kissed him on the cheek. "Now, do you have any plans tonight?"

"I thought I would feed you dinner and then maybe we could play another board game. But if you'd rather go home…"

"I'd rather be with you. I don't care where."

John did try to feed her, but this time she had purposely eaten a large lunch and truly wasn't hungry.

They were playing their third game of Scrabble when Sarah noticed a theme to John's words. When he first formed *coitus*, she didn't question it. It was after he placed *erotic*, *genital*, and *semen* that she started contemplating him. Someone had sex on the brain and it was coming out in words. She would have laughed if she didn't feel the same way.

She'd laid out her word and was picking out replacement tiles when Perry appeared out of nowhere and slid beside her. Oh God, now what? She scooted as far away as possible, but he slipped his arm around her shoulder and brushed against her neck. Her heart fluttered from the contact and his musky, vanilla-like scent came alive. She gasped.

"So what are you two love birds doing?" Perry stared at the board game and laughed. "Can I guess which words Johnny formed, or are you the naughty one, sweet Sarah?"

"What do you want?" John asked.

Why hadn't she noticed how good Perry smelled before? She'd assumed he would stink because he just didn't look clean. He still wore that nasty Hawaiian shirt and a pocket on his cargo pants looked as if it had been torn off.

"To say hi." Perry flashed a smile toward her. "Hi."

His scent fogged her mind and she swallowed hard. Her body's reactions confused her. As hard as she tried to keep her distance, the end of the booth kept her from going any further. She could shove him off the bench, but she didn't want to make a scene. Besides, Perry was probably only doing it to annoy John and sure enough, he glared at Perry with a furrowed brow and eyes that almost glowed. Afraid John might do something he would regret later, she placed her hand over his.

They had last touched over an hour ago and her heart went into overdrive. Now this she loved. How could she even think Perry's touch was similar to John's? There was no comparison.

Her action drew his attention from Perry to their hands and then to her. His face softened and he gave her a small smile. She smiled back, but Perry sucked the joy out of it.

John scooted over and moved the game so it was in front of her. With a voice calm and neutral, he said, "Perry, please take your arm off of Sarah."

Perry's green eyes sparkled more than she remembered and his gaze seemed to penetrate her soul. And he did that sniffing thing again. The fog in her mind grew thicker and breathing became difficult.

Taking his free hand, he grabbed her chin and examined her face. The smile disappeared. "What happened to you?"

"Perry, leave her alone."

Blinking the fog away, she wrenched his hand off and found her voice. She leaned toward John. "It's getting late and I didn't get much sleep last night. Would you take me home, please?"

His dejected look pained her, but Perry's closeness was intoxicating and way too pleasant. Why was her body being a traitor? She needed as much distance from Perry as she could, even if that meant leaving John.

John nodded. "I'll go get your coat."

He stood and they both looked at Perry.

Perry stared at John and then turned toward Sarah. He flashed his pearly whites and stood, offering his hand. She ignored it and got up on her own. John jogged to the stairs.

"You know I was only yanking his chain, right? So what did happen to your face?" Perry asked.

"None of your business."

"Are you leaving because of me?"

She almost said yes, but caught herself. He was so full of himself, he'd probably take it as a compliment. "I'm tired. I was ready to go before you showed up."

Nodding, he leaned into her, inhaling. She put her hand on a solid chest and pushed him back. "I wish you'd stop doing that."

"Doing what?" He gave her a wide-eyed, innocent look, but she wasn't buying it.

"Sniffing me. You're acting like a dog and I'm the bitch in heat. I don't like it."

John returned with her things before Perry had a chance to defend himself. John held the coat for Sarah and then spoke to Perry while she finished zipping. "I want to talk to you when I get back. I'll see you in my apartment, okay?"

"Sure, Johnny. Goodnight, Sarah. Hope to see you again soon." As Perry headed for the stairs, he glanced over his shoulder before disappearing behind the door.

The moment he left, she relaxed. How could someone she despised get a rise out of her body like that? What the hell was happening?

# Chapter 11

Sarah stood in the break room gazing out the window. Gray clouds slowly encroached on the city, eating up the blue sky in front.

"It looks like it's going to snow," she said to Lori. "Do you know if it was forecasted?" What she wouldn't give to have a fireplace. Something to keep her warm on a cold winter night, and it was looking to be one of those if the clouds were any sign. Of course, John could probably warm her just fine if she let him. His kisses certainly did. Damn, there went her mind again. She really had it bad when she couldn't go two minutes without thinking about the guy.

"I didn't have time to watch TV this morning." Lori said, her head buried in the newspaper. "Have you read this?"

Sarah glanced at the paper. "Read what?"

"This article. It says they found the graves of four missing women. They were sexually assaulted, then killed. It says it's the work of a serial killer."

"What?" Sarah pulled the paper over. Color photos lined up side by side under the headline. All four women possessed long, brown hair. All four women were young, in their twenties. All four women resembled her.

The moisture in her mouth disappeared. Pressure squeezed her chest. Holy shit. Would she have been number five if not for... Would he come for her again? Oh God. Where did the air go? Why was it hard to breathe?

But wait. An article meant they'd caught the guy. She was safe. Easy breathing returned.

"We need to take precautions," Lori said.

"What do you mean? He's been caught. Right?"

"Not according to the article. If we make sure we're not alone, I'm sure we'll be okay."

Back to thin air and difficult breathing. Lori probably thought she'd offered comfort. Then again, Lori didn't know about Sarah's near-abduction. She certainly wouldn't say anything now. She could freak out enough for both of them.

"So now I not only have to worry about Steven, I have to worry about this serial killer?" A serial killer who probably knew who she was and where she worked. Shit. With shaky hands, she crumpled up the paper and threw it toward the trash can. Of course, it missed.

Lori picked up the paper and tossed it in can. "I'm sorry, but when I read that article, it scared the bejesus out of me. I don't want to walk outside alone."

What did Lori have to fear? She didn't have brown hair. So why wasn't the guy in jail? Wouldn't her rescuer have made sure of that? She'd give anything for one worry-free day.

By seven, Sarah's last client had gone and she called John about her imminent departure. She saw no sense in bringing up the article. His presence alone calmed her and that's what she counted on.

After shutting down the computer, she flipped off the office lights. Lori had departed earlier with some other co-workers, because she knew Sarah had made plans to meet John. Sarah donned her winter gear, grabbed her purse and gloves, and then headed for the elevator.

While she waited, a man at the end of the hallway paced with his head down. He seemed to be talking to himself. Crazy or a stalker? Her stomach tightened into knots. Anyone could be the serial killer. Even him. Then she saw the phone in his ear and relaxed. She really needed to stop being so paranoid.

The elevator doors opened. She entered the car and pushed the button for the garage. A hand came in between the doors before they fully closed, forcing them to retract. The man from down the hall stepped inside.

She backed up and he smiled.

Okay, maybe not so paranoid. Was that how the guy worked? Lurking around hallways waiting for his prey? Luring them in with his dimples and snappy dressing? How hard would it be for him to push the button for a floor on the way, grab her, and do whatever?

Her heart crept up her throat. The elevator car shrunk before her eyes, the walls caving in around her. She was drowning in fear and couldn't catch her breath. The elevator jerked to a stop, but the doors opened as if they weren't in any hurry to empty the occupants.

* * * *

John leaned against the pillar. Tonight was the night. He wasn't putting it off any longer; Sarah deserved to know the truth. But how did you tell someone you were a vampire? All day long he'd been rehashing how he would tell her and he still didn't know what to say. Hoping inspiration would strike when he needed it, he stopped thinking and waited for Sarah.

The elevator doors opened and he smiled, until she emerged wearing a frantic, wide-eyed look on her face. He straightened as she bolted toward him.

"What's the matter?" he asked as a man exited the elevator after her. "Did he bother you?"

She was quivering, and reeked of fear. "No," she said, shaking her head.

John pulled her into his arms and held her tight. She relaxed a little, but that didn't stop her tremors. If he could take away the fear, he would.

He rubbed her back, hoping that would calm her. "What happened?"

"Nothing. I'm okay." She buried her face into his chest and her words came out muffled.

"You're shaking all over. You're definitely not okay. What's got you so scared?"

"It's silly, really. Lori showed me an article she read in the paper about some recent murders."

Well, it was about time. Thinking the police might not believe Ray—because who confessed for no reason?—John had called in an anonymous tip about the graves. But why would this scare her? "What about the article?"

She pulled back and bit her lip, but kept her head down. "There were pictures of the victims." He lifted her chin and nodded for her to continue. "They all look like me," she whispered.

"But they caught the guy, right?"

She shook her head. "Not according to the article."

What? John furrowed his eyebrows and looked away. Shit. Ray had turned himself in days ago. Hadn't he? What the hell had happened?

"Do you think my attacker was the serial killer?" Her words came out faster and faster; she almost sounded hysterical. "Or was it just a coincidence? If not, why am I still alive? If he was interrupted, does that mean he'll come back to get me? Every strange man I see I wonder if it's him. I think I'm losing it, John. I'm jumping at everything. I even thought that man in the elevator was him. I can't go on this way." Sobbing, she put her head in her hands.

John pulled her close once again and stroked the back of her head. How was he going to fix this? She was a wreck. "It's okay. You're safe now. Come on, I'll take you home."

"No. We have a date, don't we? And what if he's watching? I don't want him to know where I live."

"We'll go to Wings, then. Okay?"

She took a deep breath and nodded while wiping her eyes. He drove them the short distance because he didn't think she could handle the walk. With no vacant spot in the front, he pulled into the alley. He came around the SUV expecting to meet her, but instead of standing outside waiting as she usually did, she sat inside with her head down.

This was his fault. He should have made sure Ray had been apprehended first. How had his suggestion failed? They never had before. Well, except with Sarah. But no, he had controlled Ray. They weren't the same.

John opened the door and she lifted her head. Her eyes were brimming with tears and her bottom lip quivered. All he wanted to do was ease her mind, but the only easing he could do would most likely cause her to run. He was so screwed.

He offered his hand and she clutched it.

When he guided her up the steps, the middle board gave out. He caught her before her foot went through.

"Damn. Are you okay? I swear, I fixed this last night."

79

She went on inside without a word. At least she wasn't limping.

John found an open booth in the back and told Ashley not to disturb them. Sarah scooted on the bench, put her arms on the table, and rested her head on top of them. She looked wiped out.

He sat beside her and rubbed her back. Bending forward, he spoke softly, "Sarah, sweetie, do you want me to get you something to eat?"

"I'm not really hungry."

Her standard answer, but he wouldn't accept it. "That may be the case, but you should eat something. Please try. For me?" He didn't want her to faint on him and she seemed to be on the verge of passing out.

"Okay, but nothing heavy. Do you have soup?"

Seemed he did. One bowl later, she relaxed and smiled, her natural scent coming to life.

"You feeling better?"

She nodded. "So what did you plan for tonight?"

"Nothing important. It can wait until tomorrow."

"Not even a hint?" she asked with a silly pout.

She looked so darn cute, he couldn't help but smile. He pressed his forehead against hers. "No, not even a hint." She stifled a yawn and struggled to keep her eyes open. "I think maybe I should take you home so you can rest."

"I feel bad. That's two nights in a row I've cut short."

"I'm not counting, so don't worry about it." John stood, fetched Sarah's coat and held it out. He didn't want to stop touching her, so once the coat was settled, he turned her around, put the scarf carefully around her neck, then zipped the coat. All the way to the top. Must keep the cold out. He grinned.

"You know, I'm perfectly capable of dressing myself."

"I know, but humor me. I'm having fun." He handed over the gloves, but wasn't sure how she wore the hat. Every time he put it on her head, it looked like it was backward. She laughed and took the hat, placing it on the correct way.

He walked her to the hallway and grabbed his coat before they went outside. When John opened the door, he smiled at the view.

"Snow!"

They said it in unison. However, she said it in disgust and he said it in glee. Two inches blanketed the ground while it continued falling steadily.

John laughed. "You really hate the snow, don't you?"

She scrunched her face. "What's to like? It's wet and cold."

"Yeah, but it's also beautiful, don't you think? I look around and see how it's cleaned up everything. It's peaceful, like it muffles the sounds. How can you not love this?" When she raised her eyebrows in a yeah-right look, he smiled. "Come on, you can sit in the car while I clean it off."

"No way, I'm not that frail. I can help."

He retrieved the snow scraper and brush and held them out for her to choose.

She took the scraper. "I'll let you get the front half and I'll get the back."

John started the engine to help warm the interior while they worked on cleaning the exterior. He was brushing the snow off the front windshield when something wet hit him on the side of the head. He spun around to find Sarah grinning at him.

"You're right, John, snow can be beautiful." She lobbed another snowball as laughter bubbled from her.

"Oh, so you want a fight, do you?" He grabbed some snow off the Xterra and threw it at her.

Squealing, she turned in time for the snowball to smack her in the back. Armed with another, she hit him square in the chest. Using the snow from the SUV, they continued throwing, their laughter filling the alley. They stopped once the car was clear of snow.

"That's one way to clean it off," he said.

Sarah puffed out several breaths. "Look at me, I'm soaked. Oh well, I guess that's what I get for starting it." She looked at John and beamed.

God, she was beautiful. On legs with a mind of their own, he walked up to her and kissed her, getting a taste of snow. Holding her head, he slipped his tongue into a moist heat, savoring the essence that was all Sarah. She put her arms around him and molded her body into his.

When she rubbed up against his erection, he nearly exploded. Did she know how she affected him? Did she know how much he wanted her? If not for his secret, he'd carry her upstairs and make love to her, taste her whole body.

Tomorrow. He would tell her then. But now, he needed to get control of himself. Kissing a trail to her ear he whispered, "We better get going or we're going to have to clean it off again."

"If you say so." Her sigh just about did him in.

John escorted her to the passenger side and helped her up. He put the brush and scraper away and settled in behind the steering wheel.

"Thank you," she murmured.

"For what?"

"For helping me feel better. For being there for me. You don't know how much I appreciate that."

He ran his thumb across her cheek. "I care for you, please know that." Her face was so soft and he was tempted to kiss her again. But that would only start up what he had fought so hard to stop earlier. He slowly pulled his hand away.

"I know." She closed her eyes and leaned back on the seat.

The windshield was already covering over with snow. "I hope you don't have any trouble getting to work tomorrow."

"Lori's driving. I'm at her mercy."

Their trip took a little longer than usual and finding a slot at the complex was impossible. People had parked haphazardly, leaving large gaps between cars, but not enough for a vehicle to squeeze in. He pulled up to the stairway. When they arrived at her apartment, she pulled her keys out. He took them and unlocked her door. "In you go."

She placed her hands on his chest and stood on her toes, puckering for a kiss. Her lips were soft and yielding, and his plans of giving her a quick kiss goodnight ended when her tongue invaded his mouth. His erection popped up instantaneously, straining inside his jeans. It took everything in him to keep his fangs from extending. She drove him wild with need.

If he didn't watch out, she would find out what he was by accident. Her heart pounded against his chest and he almost scooped her up and took her inside. The voice of reason spoke up and it took all his willpower to break away from her again.

"Don't get me wrong. I want you. Badly. But now's not a good time." He couldn't recall having such a hard time catching his breath since his turning. She was creating new experiences for him on a regular basis. He could only imagine what it would be like to make love to her and hoped he'd get the chance.

"I suppose you're right," She pulled away with a pout. "I guess I should just tell you goodnight."

Each time he found it harder to leave. Once he told her the truth, there was a good possibility he'd lose her forever. Could he live without her? The sharp pain in his chest told him no.

# Chapter 12

Sarah stared out the window at work. Four inches of snow had fallen overnight and the sight made her smile. The stuff wasn't so bad, not if she could have fun in it like she had with John. Despite the rotten day, the night had ended on a high and would have been perfect if John had stayed, but she'd been out of it and he was such a gentleman. Maybe he thought he'd be taking advantage of her weakened state. But damn, she was always in a weakened state around him. The rip-his-clothes-off-and-throw-him-to-the-floor kind of state.

Tonight she would talk to him and then rip his clothes off. Going slow? History. Her body wanted John. Her heart wanted John. She might as well have John.

Many clients had cancelled their appointments, leaving Sarah with little work. Just as she filed the last folder, her boss called her into his office.

Oh crap. He'd never called her in before. Was her temp-to-hire time up? Were they going to let her go? She wrung her hands. If she lost this job, then what? Worry ate at her gut as she walked toward anticipated doom.

Mark Thomason stood when she entered his office. "Thanks for getting here quickly, Sarah. Take a seat."

She sat across from his desk and discreetly rubbed her sweaty hands on her slacks. "Good morning Mr. Thomason."

"Now, how many times do I have to tell you to call me Mark?"

He was older than her, practically her father's age. Calling him by his first name didn't seem right. But why would he go to all that trouble if he was going to fire her? Hope sprung and she smiled. "Okay, Mark."

"We have a client in Lima who needs our help. You've been doing such a great job I thought you'd be the perfect one to send. Their previous accountant up and left them with a mess. Hopefully, it'll only take a couple of days to clear up. I know this is last minute. Do you have anything preventing you from leaving immediately?"

She was perfect? If she didn't watch out, she'd end up with tears and then he wouldn't think she was so perfect. "No, no. I'm free. Thank you so much for thinking of me. I won't let you down."

"You might not thank me after you've seen the mess." He picked up a packet and handed it over. "Here's the information you'll need. Give me a call once you see what you're up against and we'll determine what to do then, okay?"

He stood, an indication he was finished.

Sarah scrambled out of her seat and shook Mark's hand. "Thanks again. I'll need to go home and pack."

"No problem. They don't expect you until one."

Four hours. Plenty of time. She turned to leave, and then remembered. "Oh, I don't have a car. Mine's in the shop."

"Get with Linda. She'll get a rental for you."

Perfect. She still couldn't get over it. Things were definitely picking up. First John, now her job. She felt valuable for the first time in her life and liked it.

* * * *

John pocketed his cell and frowned. Sarah had sounded excited and apologized for not calling him sooner. She wouldn't be gone long—only until Friday—and he was truly happy for her, but he craved her company something fierce and already missed her.

He couldn't believe he was postponing his plans once again. Was karma trying to tell him something? Or torturing him for not sharing his secret earlier? Whatever, now he'd have to wait until Friday, so he might as! well do it after the hockey game. At least that would give him one last night with her in case it went badly.

Standing behind the bar, deep in thought, he wasn't paying much attention when a woman sat. On autopilot, he placed a napkin in front of her. "What can I get you, Miss?" He glanced up and smiled. He'd only met her the one time and even then he'd never gotten a chance to remember her scent. Sarah's had overridden everyone else's. "Hello, Lori."

"You remembered."

"Now how can I forget Sarah's best friend?"

Lori smiled at him. "Aren't you sweet? I'll have a Jack and Coke."

He scanned the area for a companion and found none. "What brings you in?"

"You do." She rested her arms on the bar and smiled.

While he prepared the drink, he eyed her cautiously. She was probably after some answers; he just couldn't figure out what the questions would be. He placed the drink down and she dropped a ten on the bar.

"Your money's no good here." He slid it back, then folded his arms on the bar and leaned forward. "So why did you want to see me?"

"I... I came here to talk to you about Sarah." She swallowed hard and put her hand up to her chest. Glazed eyes. Racing heart. Shit. He'd forgotten the effect he had on women unless he consciously stopped it.

He straightened. Best to give her some room. "I kind of figured that much. Do you want to talk somewhere more private? We could sit in one of the booths."

"Okay."

She slid off the stool and strolled toward an empty booth.

"Is Sarah okay?" He sat opposite her and mentally hit himself. He was starting to sound like Perry, jumping to conclusions. Hadn't he just gotten off the phone with Sarah? If something was wrong, she would have said.

"As far as I know, yes. But I am worried about her."

"About what?"

"You need to know something. She'd kill me if she knew I was here talking to you, but I love her like a sister and I don't want to see her get hurt again." Lori played with the straw.

"Go on, say what ails you."

She stared straight into his eyes. "Did Sarah tell you Steven beat her?"

Steven's abuse toward Sarah still riled him. "Not in so many words, but I've seen his handiwork."

"That's right. She said you knew. But let me tell you a little more about Steven. Sarah was his trophy wife. If she didn't behave like it, he punished her. It started out with bruises on her arms. She didn't think I noticed, but I did. When it became a regular occurrence, I said something to her. She didn't want to admit it and would make up some excuse. I think she was embarrassed. But then she became pregnant."

"Sarah had a baby?" he blurted out. Now he was being ridiculous. Wouldn't he have noticed a baby by now?

Lori picked up her drink and sipped at it, as if she was trying to get the courage to continue.

The wait made him crazy and he nudged her along. "So what happened?"

Finally, she put the near empty glass down. "Steven...he..." Tears streamed down her cheeks and after searching in her purse, she pulled out a tissue. She dabbed at her eyes. "Sorry, I thought I could do this without crying. It's like it's happening all over again."

What the hell had that bastard done? John patted Lori's hand to offer comfort, but her thoughts ran close to the surface and he received his answer. Sarah's face cut and bruised. Her arm and leg in a cast. He quickly pulled his hand away and when Lori looked up, he masked the horror that swam in his stomach. "What did Steven do?"

"He killed her baby." She wiped the tears away. "Oh, she'll tell you she fell down the stairs. I say he pushed her. She's lucky she only miscarried. I tried to get her to press charges, but she refused. She just wanted a divorce. But I know what he did and I could kill him for doing it, too."

Not if he got to the bastard first. Anger at the injustice of it burned him. How could Steven not be in jail? "Why are you telling me this?"

"In case you hadn't noticed, Sarah's fallen for you. And when she falls, she falls hard. Now, I'm not saying you're like Steven, but I don't want to see her hurt again. He has caused her so much pain and suffering. She deserves to be happy. She deserves a normal life."

A normal life. That was the thing. Could he give her a normal life? He could love and cherish her until her dying day, but would that be enough?

John nodded. "Sarah is important to me. Her happiness is important to me."

"Good, because you seem like a good guy." Lori finished her drink and gathered her things. "I thank you for hearing me out. I'd ask you to not tell her about our conversation, but I don't want you to lie to her, either. So if you let something slip, don't worry. We've been friends for years. She already thinks I'm a mother hen. If she found out I talked to you, she'd forgive me. Eventually."

Lori scooted off the seat and John followed. "Let me walk you to your car."

"Thanks. I can see why Sarah likes you so much."

He helped her with her coat. "Do you think Steven is still dangerous? Do I need to be worried?"

"Before that stunt he pulled on Friday, I would have said no. Now I'm not so sure. I don't know if he's mad she's dating you or if he's mad she's on her own. But yeah, be worried. I know I am."

"Please let me know if you see him around, okay? Sometimes I think she runs into him and doesn't tell me about it."

"Yeah, I think that, too. But that's Sarah. She doesn't like anyone to worry about her. I'll let you know if I see him, though."

When they reached her car, he held the door open for her. "She's lucky to have a friend like you. I don't want to stand in the way of that friendship. If I ever do, you make sure to come and tell me, okay?"

Lori met his eyes, looking stern. "Don't worry, I will." Then she smiled at him. "Thank you for the drink, and the walk. Goodnight, John."

By eight o'clock, the patrons had dwindled to a few. John was conversing with a regular when Perry walked in and sat on a stool.

John excused himself and stood in front of Perry. "Where'd you go off to on Monday? I wanted to talk."

Or punch his lights out. Leave it to Perry to disappear whenever someone had a bone to pick with him.

Perry spun around on the stool. "Where's Sarah? I figured the two of you'd be joined at the hip by now."

John slammed his fist on the bar, tempted to put a hole through it. "Damn it, Perry. What are you up to?"

Perry put his arms up. "Easy, Johnny. I'm not up to anything. I was only yanking you around. I told Sarah that. Did you two have a fight?"

John ran his fingers through his hair. He was losing it, clear and simple. When did he become so paranoid? "No we didn't have a fight. She's in Lima on business."

"Lima? I always thought it was pronounced 'leema.'"

"In Peru, it is. In Ohio, it's pronounced like the bean."

"Oh. Where is that? How long is she gone for?"

"Up north and probably only a day or two." Might as well be a month. Damn, he missed her. "What's with the questions?"

"You look like shit. If she's not far, why don't you go there or don't you know where she's staying?"

"I know where she's staying. But how needy would I look if I just showed up? I don't want her thinking I can't trust her. She got enough of that from her ex."

"You still haven't had sex with her, have you?" Perry shook his head. "What did Danielle do to you?"

The mention of that bitch's name put him on edge. He grabbed his cleaning rag and squeezed. "You know what she did to me," he said through gritted teeth.

"I'm not talking about your turning. But did she turn you into a virgin, too?"

"Very funny."

"Then what are you waiting for?"

John concentrated on cleaning the countertop and refused to meet Perry's eyes. He really didn't want to have this conversation. If Perry discovered Sarah's mind was closed and that John was one step from exposing all vampires, what might he do?

Perry patted John's arm. "Johnny, Johnny, Johnny. I knew this would happen."

John froze. What the hell? Had he just zoned out? He yanked his arm free. "Knew what would happen?"

"That you'd get in over your head. I figure eventually I'll have to pick up the pieces when she breaks your heart."

Okay, so maybe that made sense. He was in love with her and nothing would change that. For a minute there he'd thought maybe Perry had read his mind. "I'm fine. You don't need to worry about me."

"Uh huh. But I'll worry anyway. Don't be surprised when you see me around." He abruptly got up and then strolled out the door.

John shook his head. His friend sounded sincere, but he'd fallen for the act before. Had Perry changed or was he up to something?

* * * *

Sarah trudged into the hotel lobby and waited by the front desk. What a day. What a mess. And to think she'd get to start all over again in the morning.

The clerk, a young college-aged woman, smiled. "How may I help you?"

"I'd like to leave a wake-up call for seven. The name's Sarah Daugherty, room 212." If she got lucky and fell asleep right away, she'd get almost eight hours of rest.

"Well, fancy meeting you here."

Sarah jerked around at the familiar voice. "Perry? What are you doing here?"

"I have business here. What about you?" He drew that last word out and raised an eyebrow.

Business? What kind of business did a bum have, because he was still dressed the part. Hadn't he been wearing the same outfit the night before? And what was with the look? Did he think she was up here cheating on John? Maybe that's what he thought, but she wasn't in the mood—nor did she have the energy—to placate him.

"Me, too. It's been a long day and I have to get up early, so if you'll excuse me." She headed toward the elevators.

"Wait, Sarah. Can we talk?" When she didn't answer him right away, he pleaded. "Please? It won't take long."

God, if she didn't he'd probably only follow her to her room. She gave in and headed to a chair in the lobby. She made sure it only fit one person. After the effect he had on her the other night, she would never sit beside him again.

She plopped down, ready to turn in, not sit and talk. Hopefully, this would go quickly. He lifted another chair and placed it in front of her. His body was leaner than John's, but he'd moved the chair as if it weighed nothing. Heck, maybe it did.

He sat and their knees almost touched. "You like John a lot, don't you?"

"Yes, I care for him very much. What's this about?" And why was he invading her personal space? She would have scooted back, but the wall was in the way. His scent was too enticing. Would he notice if she breathed out of her mouth?

"John has a large heart. For some reason, I think you'll break it."

"Why would you think that? You don't know me." She was starting to see him in a different light. Who knew he cared? It was something she expected of Lori. Ah, crap. Had Lori already given John the third degree?

Perry placed his hands on her armrests and leaned forward. She shrank back into the cushion. Avoiding his scent became impossible. Damn man smelled better than he looked, she'd give him that. His gaze smoldered. If he kissed her, she'd smack him. And she'd have no problem doing it, either.

"If John weren't in the picture, do you think I would have a chance with you?"

She blinked for several seconds until his question sank in. "Oh my God. You're hitting on me? Again? Really? I thought you were his friend."

He sat back and then took her hand, causing her heart to flutter. His vanilla scent twirled around her head and focusing almost became impossible. When he stared at her with those sparkly green eyes, she forced herself to look down at her hands.

"Do I do anything for you?" he asked. "Do I affect you at all?"

More than she was willing to admit. His mere presence caused her body all sorts of commotion. It scared her. How did he do this? What did it all mean? She liked John, so why was her body betraying that fact? Tears dripped onto her blouse leaving small wet dots. "I can't believe you're doing this. John should know what kind of friend he has."

He released her hand and gently wiped the tears away with his thumb. She flinched at the touch. Why couldn't he just leave?

"I'm sorry. I didn't mean to upset you. Please don't tell John. Next time you see me I'll behave, I promise."

He returned the chair and walked away. Sarah took a deep breath, clear of his scent, and shook her head. Was he checking on her or testing her? Did she care? No. She hadn't done anything wrong. And if Perry lied, John would so get an earful.

# Chapter 13

Sarah tugged her suitcase along as she walked from the car rental agency to the garage. The sun shone brightly, warming the air to a balmy forty degrees. What little snow remained had become a muddy, slushy mess. It might start out making the world look cleaner, but eventually it dirtied up like everything else, if not worse.

Even as she maneuvered around the puddles and dodged the occasional splash, her mood grew lighter with each step. Perry's visit had messed with her mind. It had taken her longer than normal to fall asleep only to wake and find she'd left the door unbolted. And the cheery disposition upon arriving at her assignment morphed into grunts and groans on her last day, all thanks to Perry. Whether or not he behaved, he'd be smart to stay away from her forever. She was liable to belt him one.

John had told her he parked her Civic next to The Bumblebee. Not that he called it by that name—said the Bumblebee was a yellow Camaro Transformer—but she couldn't call it anything else. She found his SUV without a problem, but where was her car? Had someone stolen it? Then she spotted the license plate. Dang. Her little car gleamed. Not only was the hood flawless, but all the older scratches were gone. Tires looked pretty spiffy, too. For a ten-year-old car, it looked remarkable.

She opened the trunk and a lone piece of paper lay inside. She picked up the note and stared at it. Written in red were the shape of a heart and the letter J. Her own heart ached and her nose tingled. God, she missed him. Was it wrong to care for him so quickly? Or were some people just meant to be? She hoped for the latter and if she didn't have work, she'd head on over and thank him properly. Instead, she kissed the note, placed it in her purse, and stuck her suitcase in the trunk.

After the busy job up north, her normal day seemed much slower, but eventually six o'clock arrived. She wasted no time changing into her jeans and pink sweater—hopefully suitable for a hockey game—and then rode the elevator to the garage.

The doors wouldn't work fast enough as she squeezed through the opening. Just as he promised, John stood there, waiting. And like the last time, she rushed to him, but for a different, better, reason. It took everything in her not to run into his arms.

She ached to touch every inch of him, and if they weren't going to the game, she might have done just that.

"Hi stranger," he said as he took her hand.

Her heart flip-flopped and it made her day, causing her to smile. Yes, it had been too long, but his touch felt wonderful. She was in heaven.

His smile hinted that he knew the reaction he caused and he lightly brushed his lips against hers. "I missed you."

Tempted to hold his head and get a better kiss, she resisted. The garage was no place to make a move and she certainly didn't want to deal with a rejection. She'd wait until after the hockey game, once she got him alone in his apartment. "I missed you, too."

Sarah held her keys out. "Do you mind? I'm kind of tired of driving."

"Then we'll take my car."

"Drive mine. Please?" She placed the keys inside his hand. "This way we don't have to come back here." And if she played it right, her car would be parked at his place all night.

He closed his eyes and shook his head, but kept the keys.

"Where do you want to go for dinner?" He opened the passenger door and helped her inside.

Ah, dinner. Should have known he'd bring that up. Stupid her, lunch had consisted of a salad when she should have ordered the pasta or something filling. If her stomach growled, she'd have no one but herself to blame. But a restaurant? No way. "I'll get something at the game."

"You promise?"

Why did he feel responsible for her eating habits? He ate when he wanted, what he wanted—whatever that was—and she didn't harp on him. But it didn't warrant an argument. "Yes, I promise."

They arrived well before the game started. After getting their tickets scanned, they headed toward their seats. Her mouth watered at the scent of cinnamon almonds and funnel cakes. Would he constitute snacking as eating? She'd find out later.

The size of the arena didn't hit Sarah until she glimpsed the seating area. She'd never seen anything so large and eagerly examined everything in sight.

John led them down to their seats. "Not bad. Practically center ice."

"Is that good?"

He held her coat as she shrugged it free. "If you like hockey, yeah."

She placed the coat on her seat and sat back as John did the same.

"How did you get such good seats at the last minute?" Of course, as soon as the question left her mouth, she noticed the vast amount of empty seats.

"The team isn't really all that good, but I enjoy the game." He stared at their surroundings as if he'd never been, either.

"Have you ever been to a game?" she asked.

"First hockey game. Actually, the only sports game I ever attended was when my dad took me and my brothers to a Reds baseball game."

"You have brothers? How many? Where do they live?" She clamped her mouth. Could she sound any more idiotic?

John smiled and took her hand. "I had two brothers, but they died awhile back."

"Oh, I'm sorry. Do you have any family left?" Again with being idiotic. What kind of person talked about their dead loved ones on a date?

"No, it's just me," he murmured.

If she kept up this conversation, she could have them both in tears by the end of the night. Didn't make her plans of hot, monkey sex afterward sound very appealing, if at all possible.

"I thought I'd go up and check out the place," he said. "What can I bring you back?"

Disappointment stung at not being invited to tag along, but how clingy would she seem if she asked? Maybe he just needed a break from the depressing talk. Couldn't blame him there. Now to see if he minded what she ate. "Those cinnamon almonds smelled heavenly. I wouldn't mind those and maybe a pretzel and a Diet Coke."

He frowned. "That's all? It doesn't seem very nutritious."

"John, we're at a hockey rink. Nothing they sell is nutritious."

"If you say so." He kissed her lightly on the cheek, then headed on up, taking two stairs at a time. She couldn't help but admire his nice tight ass. God, she was horny. Yeah, tonight was the night. She'd make sure to lighten the mood when he returned.

Once his fine derriere left her sight, she sat back in her seat. The players skated around in warm-up, making shots on the goal. She had a vague idea about the sport and had only come because she wanted to spend time with John. Didn't mean she couldn't learn, though. If he enjoyed hockey, she would try, too. What was the point in being a couple if you couldn't enjoy the same things?

The seat beside her filled sooner than she expected and without the scent of those nuts. "What'd you forget?" But John hadn't returned. Instead, Steven sat beside her. Fear prickled her skin for a brief moment when something boiled inside of her. The nerve of him. "What are you doing here?"

"Wow, is that any way to say hi? I saw you come in and thought I'd visit."

"How many times do I have to tell you I don't want to see you anymore?"

He nodded toward the top. "Who's the boyfriend? He looks familiar."

She would not take his bait and turned her attention back to the men on the ice. "None of your business. Now leave me alone and quit following me around. It's bad enough you vandalized my car."

"I didn't vandalize your car and I'm not following you. I told you I saw you come in. God, lighten up, Sarah. I'm only trying to be sociable."

Yeah, right. He might have an alibi, didn't mean he wasn't behind it all. "Fine. You said your hello, now you can say your goodbye. So goodbye," she said, waving him off.

He slid an arm across the back of her seat, getting much too comfortable. "Come on, Sarah, why won't you talk to me? I told you I was sorry. I do want you back. You can have all the kids you want, I promise. Just come back, okay?"

Why did he have to keep bringing up that subject? She'd been devastated when she lost the baby, and it was all his doing. "I think it's a little late for that," she said, her voice cracking. "It's over. I don't love you anymore. Please get that through your head. Now will you please leave?"

"No. I don't believe you. I think you still feel something for me and I can prove it."

Prove it? What would it take for him to get the message? Belting him one? Before she could question him, he grabbed her head and kissed her. She pushed at his chest, but it was useless. He wouldn't budge. His tongue swiped against her lips. She clenched her jaw and struggled to get free. Her cheek and head were still tender from her last encounter with him and his grip hurt. Damn him. She clocked him on the back of his head and he finally let go. Her face burned.

"You are *mine*," he said into her ear. "Don't ever forget it." Someone or something caught his attention and he stood. "We'll talk later. See you around."

What the hell just happened? She wanted to lay into him, but he left before she could utter a word. He walked back to his seat and sat beside a blonde woman. Why had he come over—and freakin' kissed her—if he was on a date with someone else? Too bad she didn't carry wet naps in her purse. Her face felt downright filthy.

When John finally returned she nearly jumped out of her seat. Damn man was much too quiet. Then again, music blared over the speaker making it hard to hear, period. She needed to get her wits together or else John would suspect something was wrong. No way would she mention Steven's visit.

"What's the matter? Are you okay?" He placed a bag at his feet.

"You just startled me." Which wasn't technically a lie.

He raised an eyebrow as if he didn't believe her. Had Steven left marks on her face? She should have gone to the bathroom to check it out. Too late now.

He handed over her food order. She placed the drink and nuts on the floor, and when she sat up, John was scanning the crowd. No, no, no. Couldn't have him spot her ex.

"What did you buy?" She kept her attention on the pretzel. He didn't answer, but after a while his movements stopped. She held her breath and prayed.

"Did Steven come here and bother you?" His voice held a hint of irritation and he sounded like he talked through his teeth.

Crap. She couldn't look him in the face. He'd never been mad at her before and she certainly didn't want to see it now. She picked at her pretzel.

"Forget about Steven. I'm trying to." See, she could be strong. In the past, she would be bawling at this point, begging for forgiveness.

He tugged her chin toward him. Zings of desire shot through her, but she was pretty sure he wasn't feeling the same. She closed her eyes. What a chicken.

"Shit..."

The anger laced through that one word gave her chills. She opened her eyes to find his glowing. Uh oh. "Please don't be mad at me," she pleaded. "I swear I didn't know he would be here."

His jaw dropped for a moment and then his face softened. "Oh God, Sarah. I'm not mad at you. I'm mad at him. I'm going to have a talk with him."

Relieved his anger was directed elsewhere, she still didn't want him talking to Steven. She grabbed his arm, keeping him in his seat. "Please don't. I just want to have a good time."

He caressed her cheek, soothing the burn. "I'm concerned about you. That man is dangerous and you have to tell me when he bothers you. You should get a restraining order against him."

He was right. She had let it go on too long. "I'll call Monday, okay?"

He cupped her face in his hands. Where Steven had been rough, John was gentle.

"That's my girl," he said, smiling. He then planted a light kiss on her lips.

His girl. She liked that. She also liked how his kiss tingled all the way to her toes. He really knew how to make her relaxed and lustful at the same time.

She took a bite of her pretzel. "What else did you bring? Or is it a secret?"

He chuckled. "No secret." He reached inside the bag and pulled out two jerseys. "I bought us a present. You looked like you were getting cold and I thought we could be twins."

"How sweet." Already Steven's visit was fading from her memory.

John put his jersey on over his shirt, so she did the same. Another layer never hurt. It hung loosely on her, but then most people who were wearing jerseys wore them big.

"So, how do I look?" she asked, facing him.

"Irresistible," he said, then gave her another light kiss on the lips.

With the way his kisses affected her, she wouldn't need any extra layers. She could kiss him all night and stay warm. John turned his attention to the rink, so she followed suit. Within a few minutes, he took her hand again. After the initial flip-flop of her heart, his presence calmed her nerves and relaxed her muscles better than any massage.

During the first intermission, the entertainment crew set up big red and white targets on the ice. As she watched with interest, a black puck appeared in front of her.

"I saw these when I was upstairs earlier and thought you might enjoy playing," he said. The closest to the target wins a prize."

Sarah took the rubber puck and he held another. When they announced it was time to throw the pucks, she stood and threw hers. It sailed through the air, hit a kid on his head, and then landed on the ice, well short of a target. The kid rubbed his head as he looked around. Crap. Good thing it was rubber. "I hope he's okay."

John laughed. "I'm sure he's fine. That's the risk you take for sitting up front."

Taking aim, he lobbed the puck. It flew high into the air and, when it came back down, landed smack dab in the middle of the target. It didn't even bounce or roll.

"How did you do that?"

He puffed his chest out. "Maybe it's from my years of playing football in high school."

"You played football?" She sat, chuckling.

"What's so funny about playing football?"

"Nothing. I was a cheerleader in high school." One of the few extracurricular activities her mother had approved, as long as it didn't include dating any of the football players. And now look, she was dating one. Wouldn't her mother just love that.

He sat and leaned into her. "I bet you were a cute cheerleader."

And he was probably one hot football player, but something he said didn't make sense. "How did you play football with your allergy?"

His eyes widened for a moment. "My allergies didn't occur until later. I had a bad reaction to…a bite."

"What bit you?"

He shifted in his seat. "Some animal. I don't remember a whole lot. It's kind of fuzzy."

What animal bite caused an allergy to the sun? "I didn't know that could happen."

He shrugged. "Neither did I, but it did. Oh lookee there. I think I won."

The buzzer sounded and sure enough, he had. He seemed rather proud, especially when they plastered his picture on the big screen. When he returned with his prizes, he put the hat on Sarah's head.

"Don't you look cute?" he said. "Would you like to come back, or should I give these away?" He held up two tickets and fanned her face while he wore a silly grin.

She'd go anywhere with him. "I'd come back. This was fun."

Their team won—a rare event according to John—and she cheered right along with the crowd. She still didn't know all the rules, but loved the energy. If he hadn't won tickets for another game, she might drag him back. She was hooked on the sport, as well as the company.

The night was unseasonably warm for January—hovering around forty degrees—but still cold to her. She huddled inside her coat while John took off his jersey and placed it in the back seat along with his jacket. Of course, there was one way to warm up fast and she couldn't wait to get back to his place.

He slid behind the steering wheel, teasing her with that snug-fitting, long-sleeved T-shirt. Did he have a hairy chest or was he smooth? She longed to rip the shirt off and find out. Anticipation was killing her. She grabbed the ends of her scarf and squeezed. Didn't help. If anything, it caused other body parts to clench. Fighting to keep all erotic thoughts at bay, she rambled about the game while he drove, happy she could talk intelligently. Next thing she knew, he turned down the alley. Thank goodness.

He shut off the engine and stared out the window. He'd been quiet during the drive, or maybe just polite. Not like she'd given him a chance to speak. But why hadn't he gotten out? Had she done something wrong?

She took his hand. It was cool at first, but warmed up quickly. "What's the matter?"

His expression became serious and he squeezed her hand. "Do you think we can go upstairs and talk?"

Talk? She wanted to go upstairs, but not to talk. Talking meant bad news. Disappointment wrapped around her heart. She'd been so sure he would finally take this relationship to the next level, not end it. How had she misinterpreted everything? Unable to look him in the face, she stared at her shoes. "John, if you're going to break up with me, just do it here and get it over with."

"What? I don't want to break up with you."

She breathed in relief. "You don't?"

"No. What makes you think that?"

"Because that's what people say when they want to break up, isn't it?"

He closed his eyes briefly and turned in the small seat to face her. "I'm sorry, I guess I wasn't thinking like that, because it's the last thing I want to do. It's just that I do have something to say and I thought it would be warmer for you inside."

Her face burned in embarrassment. What an idiot. Teach her to jump to conclusions. The man was nothing but a gentleman, always looking out for her comfort. When would she realize that? She smiled weakly. "Oh. Well, then let's get out of the cold and go where it's warm."

When she opened her door, John was there to meet her, his hand extended. Was he getting quicker or she slower? Whatever. She graciously took it, using any excuse to touch him. Hopefully, whatever it was he wanted to say would be over quickly and then she could rip his clothes off and that hot, monkey sex could commence.

\* \* \* \*

With her heat traveling to his heart, John stared into Sarah's eyes, falling a little deeper in love. That's why he was doing this. That's why he was ready to risk exposing the whole vampire race.

100

He loved her.

And he could do it. He could. Somehow he'd get her to understand and not come to think of him as a nut case. Because, hey, that's what he'd thought when Danielle told him. Of course, the act of being turned had pretty much proved her case. He wouldn't—couldn't—do that to Sarah.

He closed the passenger door. Sounds of feet shuffling came from a distance and he froze. A breeze from that direction might help determine if Steven was in the area, but the air was still and with Sarah's proximity, her scent overpowered everything.

She gripped his arm. "What is it?"

Should he go down the alley and investigate? Delay the inevitable a little longer? Sarah was nervous enough he couldn't leave her alone, but he could leave her inside Wings. She'd be safe there. "Probably nothing. Why don't you go on inside while I check it out?"

Her grip tightened. "Don't go, please. I see you put a camera back here. Let it do its job."

He smiled. She was worried for him, when he was probably the most dangerous thing in the alley. But she was right. The camera would catch anyone approaching her car. Damn it. That's what he got for being efficient. Better to get it over with and pray for the best. Besides, maybe her worry was a good sign. A sign she wouldn't bolt out the door once he told her his secret.

"You're right. Go on up. I'm right behind you. And don't worry about the stairs. I fixed them." He'd even made sure to use extra-long screws this time.

She smiled. "As I knew you would."

Sarah took the first step. The whoop-whoop of a police siren echoed in the alley, most likely warning someone to pull over. But Sarah jumped and landed hard on the middle step.

Wood cracked and splintered. Her foot went down as the other side of the step went up. She grabbed onto the handrail and it practically disintegrated. What the hell? That shouldn't have happened. He'd even jumped on the stupid thing after his last fix. Pulled the handrail, even. While he stood staring at the ruined steps, her movement brought him out of his trance.

Sarah was falling! Shit.

John zipped toward her, hooked an arm around her waist, and pulled her close just as she brought her hand up, the splintered wood still in her grasp. She probably didn't realize she still held it—hell, he hadn't even realized that—and with his speed, the wooden weapon skewered him but good.

As he toppled onto Sarah, a woman's laughter floated on the air. Someone in the bar was having a good time, too bad it wasn't him.

# Chapter 14

Sarah couldn't scream. John had knocked the air out of her when he'd fallen on her. But it wasn't his weight she wanted to scream at. It was the blood covering her hand. She was still holding the handrail that was sticking out of him. She jerked her hand away. What had she done? What had she done?

His eyes widened in shock. He clutched his right side. Blood poured through his fingers and dripped onto her coat. He rolled to his side, giving back her breath.

"Oh, John! I'm so sorry." She looked left and right. "Where's my purse? I need to call 9-1-1." It had fallen behind her and she pulled it into her lap.

"No!" He grabbed the purse, causing the phone to slip through her fingers.

"What do you mean, no? You need a doctor." Sarah reached for his shirt. Maybe it seemed worse than it was. But how could that be? Part of the handrail was sticking out of his side. And there was all this blood. But before she could get a look, he wrapped his free hand around her wrists.

"Sarah, you can't call 9-1-1," he said, panting. "I'll be fine." He then proceeded to pull out the railing while spitting out curse words. The blood stain grew larger.

"What are you doing? What are you doing? You'll bleed to death!" She yanked to free her hands, but his grip was too strong. Why was he doing this? "Please, John. Give me my phone. Let me call for help."

He released her hands. His breathing was labored and he winced, sitting up. "Despite what this looks like, I'm not going to die and I can't go to the hospital."

"What are you talking about?"

"This isn't the way I wanted to tell you, but I guess I have no choice now." He lifted his shirt and removed a few splinters that stuck to his skin. Where was the hole? There should have been blood gushing from the wound. Instead, the wound looked hours old. "See? I'm almost good as new."

He'd healed already? How was that even possible? "I don't understand. What's happening?"

"There's a reason I heal fast. There's a reason I can't go out into the sun and eat real food."

"What does your allergy have to do with—"

"I'm a vampire."

She felt for bumps on the back of her head. "Did I hit my head? I could have sworn you said—"

"You heard me correctly."

She leaned over and whispered, as if anyone was actually overhearing their conversation, because he was talking crazy. Maybe he had hit his head. "But John, vampires don't exist."

"We do. We just hide our existence."

All this time she'd thought that maybe he'd been the one. He was either crazy or…what? She was? For wanting to believe him? No way was any of this real. Tears formed in her eyes. "You're just making fun of me because of the books I own. Aren't you? If you wanted to end things, you didn't have to resort to these lies."

"End things? Sarah, I don't want to end things. I love you."

The cold air finally seeped into her bones and she shivered. She lifted her hands to cover her face, but blood covered one hand so she hugged herself instead. This was all a bad dream. It had to be.

"Can we go inside and talk?" he asked.

Talk? What could they possibly talk about? Would he try and bite her next?

\* \* \* \*

"Oh my God, you're nuts! I have to get out of here." Sarah grabbed her neck as she scrambled upright.

She couldn't go, not yet. John didn't want her to leave upset and confused and he stood when she did. With his blood reserves low, the sudden movement caused a cramp so severe, he doubled over. She flinched away from him, tearing a hole in his heart.

His fangs lowered and he talked, hoping she wouldn't notice. "Please don't leave. Let me explain."

She stood there shivering, but she didn't move toward the car.

"Can we talk inside, where's it's a little more private?"

"No. I don't want to go inside."

"How about the car?"

"No." She sat on the ground, shoved her hands in the pockets, and huddled inside her coat.

John sat with her, giving her enough space. "Sarah, I'm not nuts. Please believe me."

"Okay, say I believe you. Has this been a game all along? How many times have you bitten me?"

"I've never bitten you and you'd know it if I had. This wasn't a game for me. I love you, Sarah. That's the truth." Not exactly the way he'd planned to tell her, but there it was. He prayed she believed him.

"You love me? Can vampires love? Aren't they something like soulless creatures?"

"Your idea of what a vampire is and what a vampire actually is are two completely different things. I want to explain them, but you can't tell anyone. It's important no one finds out what you know."

"What, like someone would believe me if I started saying I know some vampires? Hell, I'm not even sure I believe." She sounded bitter, not that he could blame her.

"Then how do you explain this?" He peeled the wet shirt from his skin. The puckering would eventually fade, but for now it was puffy and red.

Her eyes widened. "Are those fangs in your mouth?"

"Yes, but I would never bite you. I swear."

"Why haven't I seen them before? I mean, we kissed..."

"They come out when I need...food." No use telling her they popped out when she aroused him. Let her figure that out later. If there was a later.

"You mean blood." She grabbed her neck again and what little color she had in her face fled. "Oh God."

"Does that mean you believe me?"

"I don't know. Maybe."

Close enough for him. "This wasn't the way I wanted to tell you and I understand your confusion, but you can't tell anyone. Not because humans won't believe you. It's because other vampires will and they'll want to shut you up. Our number one priority is to keep the secret."

"Didn't you kind of blow that one when you started dating me?" Her gaze bored into him, accusing. "What were you thinking anyway?"

Hadn't he been asking himself the same thing? The phrase *love is blind* had never made sense to him, but it did now. He'd been blind to reason. "You're right. I wasn't thinking. But if you recall, I did try to break it off."

"Yes, and you succeeded, too. I left you, John. You came back to me."

Shit. What was he doing? He couldn't blame this on her. "I'm sorry, you're right. What can I say—I was weak? After the first time in the garage, I was sure I'd never see you again, but then you walked into Wings and I was curious. I felt something with you I'd never experienced before."

Her eyes rounded. What had he just said?

"Wait a minute," she said. "You saw me before I came to the bar? When was that? Why don't I remember?"

Oh, crap. Think before speaking, stupid. An encounter he'd never wanted her to discover and he'd blurted it out as if it were common knowledge. Great. Now what? Well, he wouldn't lie to make himself look good. Not if he ever hoped to have a relationship. Ha! As if that were even possible now.

He scrubbed his face. "You don't remember because you were out cold. That was the night you were attacked."

Her jaw dropped. "You were the one who attacked me?"

Damn it. Nothing he said came out right. "I didn't attack you. I stopped the man who had. I just happened to be in the garage when I saw him putting you into his trunk."

"What?" She looked down at her lap and murmured, "So, you're the one who put me in my car?"

"Yes. After I took care of your attacker, I came back to check on you, but you'd already left. Figured it was better that way. I just never dreamed…"

"That I'd ask you out?"

"Yeah." He sighed. "I should have said no, but I didn't want to. There's something about you, Sarah. I need you." She looked up at that and raised an eyebrow in accusation. Everything he said to her she read the wrong way. That, or his blood loss had destroyed his thought process. "Not that way. I don't know how to explain it. I just know I feel whole whenever you're near."

Tears rolled down her cheeks and seared his heart. He hated hurting her, wanted to hold and comfort her instead. Yeah, like she'd let him do that. She hadn't run off yet, so why tempt her?

"Ah, Sarah. I'm sorry. I'm sorry for hurting you. I'm sorry I wasn't upfront earlier. But I'm not sorry for loving you. You're the best thing to happen in my life. Can you ever forgive me?"

She sat there, wiping her face and quietly shivering. He'd wait forever for an answer, but not at the expense of her comfort.

"You sure you don't want to go inside?"

"I want to go home." Her eyes glistened as she met his gaze. "Are you going to let me go?"

"Of course." Did she think so little of him? Hadn't he shown her what kind of person he was? Then again, she'd been hit with a major shock. Maybe once she processed the information, she'd come around. "Are you sure you're up to driving? I could take you." It would be difficult, but he'd find a way.

"No!" The fear on her face hurt him more than the stake had. "I can drive myself."

Her words cut deep. Forgiveness seemed far off, almost impossible. "Okay. Please promise me you'll keep the secret. I don't care what happens to me. I don't want them coming after you."

"You don't have to worry about me." She stood and wiped her backside.

John rose with care, using what was left of the handrail for support, keeping the cramps at bay. "I'm sorry about your coat. I'll replace it for you."

"No. I don't want you to do anything." Her voice was cold, uncaring.

He couldn't let her leave without knowing how he felt. "I hope you can come to forgive me, but I'll understand if you can't. You mean the world to me, Sarah. Please don't doubt that. If you have any questions, call me. Any time."

One lone tear ran down her cheek. Would she cry if she didn't care about him? It gave him hope. Maybe she only needed time. He could give it to her. He had plenty of it.

She walked to the driver's side and opened the door. "Goodbye, John."

She drove off with his heart.

# Chapter 15

*A full moon lit up the park as a warm breeze caressed her skin. John strolled toward her and she smiled. When he reached her, he cupped her face and slowly backed her into a tree. Her heart flip-flopped as it did every time they touched. Glimmering blue eyes gazed into her very soul. She wrapped her arms around his neck waiting for his kiss, wanting his lips next to hers. As he bent toward her, he flashed his fangs, turned her head, and bit her neck.*

Screaming, Sarah bolted upright. Where the hell was she? Was she bleeding? She ran her hand across her neck. Dry. Sun filtered through the curtains. The familiar surroundings of her bedroom brought her back to reality.

"Just a dream." She fell back on the bed. But the dream lingered and she trembled. Sleep had eluded her most of the night. So why did she have to dream of John when it finally claimed her?

Vampires. They didn't really exist, did they? He was nuts. But how did that explain his super-fast healing? Or his fangs? Wait. Maybe the whole thing had been a dream.

She sat up and smiled. Yes. That was it. She had dreamt it. They went to the hockey game and then…what? Her coat, draped over her dresser, displayed bloody smears. No dream did that. Crap. She pulled her knees up as an ache spread in her chest. What was she going to do?

She needed a place to escape, a safe haven. A shower. She could always think more clearly while the water poured over her. She crawled out of bed and headed for the bathroom.

The water steamed all around her, but she stood and shivered under the stream. John had warmed her. He had made her world better, more enjoyable. Had he only used her? Her chest tightened. He had become a big part of her life in the short time she'd known him. How had she let it get out of hand? Because she'd thought he was different. Yeah, he was different all right.

The shower a bust, she dried herself off and broke down in tears. How would she ever get through the weekend? It wasn't like she had her job to distract her.

She searched for projects in the apartment: cleaning, mending, anything to keep her mind off John. She brought up Lori's number, because her friend could talk up a storm, but couldn't push the send button. Lori would want to know what happened. What would Sarah tell her, *My boyfriend's a vampire and we broke up?*

Sarah put the phone back in her purse. There wasn't anyone she could call. She was alone. Again.

Searching through her cookbooks, she decided to fix an elaborate and time-consuming dinner, requiring a trip to the store. She opened the closet for her coat when she remembered it was soaking. Great. She wore several sweaters under a lighter jacket and felt like a Sumo wrestler. She could barely bend her arms, but damn it, she'd be warm.

The grocery store was neutral territory, since John had never accompanied her there. Walking up and down the aisles became therapeutic and she took her time perusing. Of course, maybe she shouldn't have come on an empty stomach or a sad heart. Besides the ingredients she needed, she also filled the cart with comfort food—cookies and ice cream. She could eat herself to oblivion. Then she wouldn't only feel like a Sumo wrestler, she'd look like one, too.

After the order was rung up, she searched for her wallet and found the note that John had left in the trunk. Pain slashed her heart open. Tears gushed out. She'd never been so embarrassed. *Get a grip, Sarah.* Wiping her eyes, she apologized to the cashier, paid for the order and scrambled out of there as fast as she could.

With the groceries stashed in the trunk, she settled behind the wheel. Was it safe for her to drive? How many more times would she break out sobbing? She leaned her head back and closed her eyes.

Ah heck, if she kept that up, she'd end up falling asleep. She started the car, put the stick in reverse, and twisted in her seat. John's jacket and jersey were on the back seat. She immediately stopped and shut off the engine, probably disappointing the person waiting for her spot.

She retrieved the items and stared at them. What should she do? Throw them away or mail them back? She buried her face in his jacket, taking in his scent. God, she missed him. It hadn't even been a day and she missed him so much it hurt. She cried into the jacket until no tears remained.

If this was how her life would be from now on, she might as well hide inside a closet. No one would want to be around her for fear of another breakdown. Heck, she wouldn't want to witness that, either. Finding the strength somewhere, she managed to drive home.

She placed John's things inside the trunk. Her fingers lingered on the jacket sleeve before she closed the lid. Returning his items wasn't an option at the moment, but she couldn't throw them out.

Cooking helped keep her mind busy, mainly because she wasn't very good at it. It took all her concentration to follow the directions. Her mother never taught her to cook and Steven had always made her nervous. A botched-up dinner led to a blow up and bruises. She was under no such scrutiny now. If it turned out bad, at least she wouldn't get slapped for it.

But when it came time to eat, her appetite had disappeared. She couldn't even bring herself to taste it. Instead, she packed it up and stored it in the refrigerator.

She headed for bed with a book and a heart that weighed more than it did when she woke. Would it ever lighten? Would she ever feel like living again? Maybe if she gave herself some time, she would. Saturday was a start. She had survived the day, even if it was miserable. She could only hope Sunday would turn out better.

\* \* \* \*

John stood outside the apartment complex and looked up at Sarah's bedroom window. He'd tried staying away. Wings had kept him busy for most of the night, but as the last few customers left, his mind had returned to Sarah. Was she okay? Not knowing was nearly killing him and the last twenty-eight hours had been the worst of his life. He'd thought he could park by her building and that would be enough. He'd thought wrong.

A dim light illuminated her curtains. What the heck was she still doing up? It was three in the morning. Maybe she had fallen asleep with the lamp on. God, he hoped so. He was about to commit the worst offense ever and if she were awake... Oh hell.

He climbed the brick wall, using the small spaces for his fingers and toes, and stopped at her window. The curtains were closed, but she'd left a gap in the middle. She lay on the bed, a book on her stomach and her eyes closed in sleep. Thank God. He pushed up on the window and smiled when it opened.

Quietly he entered her room, being careful not to knock anything off her dresser. This was so wrong—damn, they put guys in jail for this crap—but he couldn't stop. He needed to see her. Just one minute and he'd leave.

John knelt beside her bed and took in her scent. Oh, how he missed it. How he missed her. Her breathing was slow and steady and one foot stuck out from under the blanket. He smiled at the socks. Puppies.

Would she ever forgive him? What would he do if she couldn't? Check on her every night? Oh, God. He probably would. Just crouching beside her brought him peace.

He reached out, wanting to feel her warmth one more time, and then stopped with his hand hovering over her cheek. It certainly wouldn't be points in his favor if she caught him in her room. Reluctantly, he pulled away.

For an hour he knelt by her side. If he stayed much longer, he risked being discovered. Maybe next time he would come earlier, but he didn't want there to be a next time. That would mean she hadn't forgiven him. He whispered in her ear, "I love you, Sarah. I hope you can forgive me."

She stirred and mumbled. The book fell to the floor. He held his breath for a moment and then slowly rose. Leaving her was torturous, but if he wanted any chance of getting her back, he couldn't blow it. He lifted one leg over the sill.

"John?" Sarah was sitting up and staring straight at him.

Shit. He jerked backward. With no support to stop him, he lost his balance and fell through the window. He flailed his arms and grabbed for the sill, but it was just out of reach. Great. So much for leaving unnoticed.

\* \* \* \*

A thud sounded from outside. Sarah blinked her eyes. Was she dreaming again or had she really seen John fall through the window? If a dream, what was it doing open? Crap! She rushed to the opening. Cold air slapped her awake and the security light illuminated a body lying face-up on the ground below. Her heart stopped. It was John. Oh God!

She grabbed her robe and ran outside, passing the Bumblebee. By the time she reached him, he was on his hands and knees. She stopped within a few feet, afraid to get any closer. How was he able to move?

"Are you okay?" A stiff breeze kicked up and she hugged the robe closed.

"I will be." As he straightened, his bones made small cracking noises and his breathing seemed labored.

She winced at the sound. It had to hurt. If she had fallen through the window, she would have broken something. Could he heal that fast? "Are you in pain?"

He met her gaze and cocked his head. "Not much."

Maybe he thought she would run screaming from him. A good question: why wasn't she? She should be furious he'd been in her apartment uninvited, but couldn't bring herself to be mad. She'd been too damned happy to see him. "What are you doing here?"

He lowered his head. "I needed to see you were all right. I shouldn't have intruded the way I did. I'm sorry. It won't happen again. Now go on inside before you freeze."

He headed toward his SUV, but his gimpy gait gave him away.

"You're hurt. Are you sure you're okay?" she asked.

He stopped and let out a small chuckle, but did not meet her gaze. "No, but it doesn't have anything to do with the fall." Burying his face in his hands, he moaned. "I love you, Sarah, but if you want me out of your life, you need to go inside."

Out of her life? As in forever? "I don't know if I want that."

He lowered his arms. A flicker of hope splashed across his face. "I never used you. Never. If you don't believe anything else, please believe that."

The sincerity in his voice seemed real. She wanted to believe him. A gust of wind slapped her face and she shivered. The robe only reached her knees and her pajama pants were thin, but she couldn't leave him. What if she never saw him again?

113

John took two steps toward her and then stopped. "Sarah...you're not even wearing shoes. Go inside before you get sick."

She looked down at her feet. In her hurry, she hadn't even put on slippers. Now that he mentioned it, her feet became wet and cold. "Will you stay until I see you from my window?"

His face softened and he smiled. "Sure."

She rushed inside. Not because she was cold, but because if she stayed outside another second, she would have run into his arms, regardless of what he was. She clearly couldn't think in his presence.

With the window wide open, her bedroom had become a walk-in freezer, giving her another chill. She looked outside and found John. He waved before getting inside his vehicle and driving away.

How had he gotten in her room? She'd found him on the sill, was he coming or going? Did he climb the wall? He must have, there weren't any trees near the building. Wow. Was there anything he couldn't do? She glanced at the ground.

Well, apparently he couldn't fly.

A blast of frigid air forced her to shut the window. The room remained cold and she hugged her robe tight as she cranked up the heat. No way could she go back to sleep. Besides being uncomfortable, she couldn't stop thinking about him. She had questions. Lots of them. He said to call any time. Why not now?

First, she changed her socks and put on slippers. Then she grabbed her cell along with two blankets and settled in on the loveseat. He answered before her phone even acknowledged the ring.

"I am so sorry, Sarah. I swear, it'll never happen again."

Somehow, she believed him. He'd never hurt her before, so why start now? "Did you mean what you said? You'll answer my questions?"

"I'll do anything you ask, but wouldn't you rather finish sleeping first?"

"I can't sleep. After witnessing what I did, I realized I know nothing about you. I just don't know where to start."

"I can tell you my story. If you still have questions when I'm done, I'll answer them the best I can."

She found herself eager to know all about John.

# Chapter 16

"I was born in 1925," John began.

"1925! I think my grandma was born that year." Oh geez, that sounded bad. "I didn't mean to imply..." Crap. Sarah pounded her forehead. Could she be any ruder?

He laughed. "That's okay. It's old. I know."

"You don't look old, though."

"And I never will. In 1957, at the age of thirty-two, I was cursed. Frozen in time."

"You didn't want to be a vampire?"

"No, but Danielle didn't care. The crazy vampire thought she was in love and without me even knowing they existed, took it upon herself to turn me. When she explained what she had done, I was confused, just like you are. I didn't believe in vampires, who would? She wasn't prepared for my questions. She wasn't prepared for my hunger. That's when she realized she needed help and contacted the Committee."

"What is that?"

"Our form of government. They monitor all vampires and enforce the rules."

"But wouldn't you have broken a rule when you told me?"

"While the Committee prefers to be informed before I reveal myself, legally, I'm allowed to tell a prospective...well, mate, but I don't like that term. Sounds animalistic. How about love interest?"

"Oh." She swallowed. He thought of her as his mate? Why did that sound sexy and why did she like it so much? She pulled the blanket closer. "So what happened with this committee?"

"Danielle definitely wasn't thinking straight, because she pretty much confessed to breaking their newest rule: no turning a mortal without getting permission. Then again, she thought she'd gotten it from me except I was under her control, so it didn't count. She'd completely forgotten about getting the Committee's permission.

"After they arrived and cared for me, she thought everything would be okay after that. She didn't count on the Committee making her an example and she was sentenced to death."

"Death? Is that how they enforce all their rules?" God, she didn't want him to die. She'd rather go back and discuss being his mate.

"No. Telling a mortal about vampires is not punishable by death. Mainly because the mortal's memory can be erased. Problem is, I can't erase your memory, and I'm pretty sure no other vampire can, either."

"You tried to erase my memory?" What else had he attempted? While she was relieved he wouldn't be sentenced to death, what gave him the right to go digging into her mind?

"God, no! I only tried to get into your head. Remember that movie fiasco? You scared the crap out of me."

"Why did you even try? Did you want to control me?"

"No. Never. You frowned at everything I did, I just wanted to know what I did wrong."

"I was trying to be assertive and you kept taking charge."

"Yeah, I got that. Later. But at the time I was doing what my mother always taught me: to be a gentleman."

And he was, too. More than Steven ever could be. What did it say when a so-called monster was a better person? "You never manipulated my thoughts? What I feel is real?"

"I don't know what you feel, but I swear, I've never controlled you and I never wanted to. I was only curious. You've gotta believe that. But do you understand our predicament? If you start spreading the word that vampires exist, I'm pretty sure it won't be good for either of us."

"Yeah, I understand." She could never tell anyone. She wasn't sure she wanted to. It wasn't like anyone would believe her. "How did they kill Danielle? After seeing you survive a stabbing and a fall, I assume it can't be an easy task."

"We are a hardy bunch, that's for sure, but not indestructible. The only way a vampire truly dies is from burning, whether from fire or sunlight."

"No staking, huh?"

"No. A stake to the heart will only immobilize a vampire."

Wow. No pile of dust? No messy goo? Not that burning wouldn't leave a mess. "So how was Danielle burned? Did they put her out into the sun?"

"I was told they set her on fire."

"You didn't witness it?"

"No. Too busy learning about my new life. I didn't find out until months later. But when I was told, I was...glad." His voice broke at the end.

"John, there's nothing wrong with wanting justice."

"I know, but still...to take another life. It's hard for me. I never believed in the death penalty, still don't, but what she did was unforgiveable."

As she'd always thought, he was a good man. It wasn't an act. If she was sitting beside him, she'd probably give him a comforting hug. And then jump his bones. Another reason they were talking via the phone. "What characteristics do vampires have that I might have heard in the myth?"

"There are many different myths, but I am strong and my hearing and eyesight are superior. I feed from humans, but I don't kill them. Thank God I don't need much."

"You sound like you don't like...feeding."

He chuffed. "It's not my favorite activity."

"Have you ever tried blood banks or animals?"

"Animal blood doesn't work. Basically, I'd starve. And bagged blood loses something when it gets old. I don't get the energy like I do from a live donor and then I require more of it. Besides, I'd rather not take blood that is allocated for humans."

"But how can you...feed and not leave evidence behind? I would think you would leave bite marks and be discovered."

"We have the ability to hide our presence. Our saliva can heal small wounds, so basically we leave no sign behind, no bite marks. Being able to control minds, we make sure the donor feels no pain. And of course we erase their memory. Feeding only takes a minute or so and we are discreet. If we weren't, you're right, we'd have been discovered by now."

The things he could do boggled her mind. "What about some other vampire myths? Do you sleep in coffins, turn into bats, only enter houses that you've been previously invited into?"

John chuckled and she could hear relief behind it. "Do you think I would have fallen if I could turn into a bat?"

He had a point.

"But yeah, those are myths," he said. "We use them to our advantage. We don't sleep in coffins because we don't sleep. So if I don't have a coffin, I'm not a vampire, right? If you can see me in the mirror or take my picture, I'm not a vampire. If you see me awake during the day, I'm not a vampire. If I can enter your home without an invite, I'm not a vampire. And if I can't turn into a bat, then I'm not a vampire."

It made sense, except the sleep part. "You don't sleep? At all?"

"Nope."

"I don't know whether that would be a good thing or a bad thing."

"It was a little strange at first. Like living one long day that never ends. But I eventually got used to it. So, have I answered your questions? Do you understand why I did what I did? And can you forgive me? Or am I expecting too much right now?"

He needed reassurance, but how much could she give him? As badly as she wanted to be with him, could she be with someone who never aged? Someone who could hurt her with little effort? Sure, he had never lifted a finger against her, but there was always a first time, wasn't there? Steven hadn't hurt her until after the wedding.

"I wish you could have been truthful from the beginning, but I understand why you weren't. We all keep secrets, don't we? It's part of what we are. Granted, your secrets were doozies, but I don't hold that against you."

"Thank you. I know it's probably too soon, but where do we stand?"

"I honestly don't know."

"The last thing I want to do is rush you. I love you and I'll wait for however long it takes. If you decide it's over, and that you never want to see me again, I'll abide by your wishes."

"I'll call you soon. I promise I won't make you wait too long."
The thought of never seeing him again hurt too much—she wanted
to see him right then and there—but could she trust herself? He
said he wasn't manipulating her mind, but what if he was sending
out vampire vibes he couldn't control? If that was the case, then
wouldn't separation cause it to fade? Nothing had faded so far. If
anything, she wanted him more. So what did that mean?

Was she really considering dating a vampire?

# Chapter 17

"I think I hate the Super Bowl," Ashley said as she placed the beers on the tray.

Standing behind the bar, John smiled and decided to tease her. "Are they treating you bad? Do I need to bounce someone out of here?"

"That's not it." She glanced at the crowd.

And it was a good crowd, one that John was grateful for. It helped get his mind off Sarah.

Ashley turned back to John. "With the same customers all night, I don't anticipate a lot of tips."

"They might surprise you." Sure, he could send a suggestion so the customers all left hefty tips, but he knew he wouldn't have to. Everyone loved Ashley.

"We'll see." She picked up the tray and left to deliver the order.

His phone vibrated and he pulled it out. Sarah. His heart skipped a beat. It'd been nearly fifteen hours since they last talked. That couldn't have been enough time to make a decision, unless she'd decided to end it. His mood nose-dived as he answered the phone.

"Hi, John." Her voice sounded upbeat. "How's your back?"

He still couldn't believe he'd fallen out the window. Talk about graceful. "Good as new. Do you have more questions?"

"Are you busy?"

She acted as if nothing had happened. Dare he hope? "I can't leave, but I can talk. What's up?"

"I want to give us a try. I was going to invite you over, but since you're busy, is it okay if I come there?"

His smile couldn't get any bigger. "You mean it, Sarah?"

"Yeah, I mean it. I miss you."

No more than he missed her. His heart swelled. "You're always welcome here. It's kind of busy, so you might want to park in the back."

She laughed. It sounded sweet to his ears. "I think I'll avoid the alley for a while if it's all the same to you. I'll just park on the street and come in the front if that's okay."

He could kick himself for mentioning the alley. What was he thinking? "Anything you want. It'll be great. Call me when you park and I'll walk you over."

"I'll be there as soon as I can."

He wished her a speedy but careful trip and hung up. Never in his wildest dreams had he thought she would come to a decision so fast. He'd make sure she wouldn't regret it, either.

The crowd cheered and John glanced up at the TV. Someone had scored a touchdown. With the noise level on par with a jackhammer, the bar wasn't the best place to talk, but he had promised Mike the night off. Well, the game wouldn't last forever. Then he could take her upstairs. To an apartment that was currently a mess. Shit. He needed to clean it before she arrived. He headed for the stairs and made it to the door when he stopped. The bar, he couldn't abandon it. Double-shit.

Ashley approached the kitchen window. Before she collected her order, John pulled her aside. "Can you watch the bar for a few minutes? I know I'm asking a lot, but something's come up."

Nodding, she said, "Sure, John. Don't worry about it."

He kissed her on the cheek. "Thanks, Ashley. I won't forget this."

Practically flying, he burst through the door and raced up the steps to his apartment. Sarah was coming!

\* \* \* \*

Sarah turned down the street and found an open spot a block from Wings. Her heart beat double time in anticipation. If she hadn't slept the day away, this trip would have happened sooner.

After her conversation with John that morning, she still couldn't sleep so she had watched a movie to relax. She'd relaxed, all right. Ten hours later, she had awakened on the loveseat, stiff and sore. It had taken a good soaking in the tub to loosen up. At least she had put the time to good use. She'd finally realized that it didn't matter what John was, it only mattered who John was. And he was the sweetest and kindest person she'd ever known. She cared a great deal for him. It didn't hurt that he could do all those cool things, too.

With the car parked, she got out, and took one last look at her reflection in the window. She hadn't planned on going out and looked bulky with her sweater and jacket. With any luck, she wouldn't have them on for long. She hit the lock button on her fob a few times.

Oh crap. John had wanted her to call. What the hell was she thinking? She wasn't, that's what. She rummaged inside her purse for her cellphone when an arm came around her neck. Memories of her attack flashed and she tensed.

"Hold still and be quiet and you won't get hurt," the man said, the scent of apple strong on his breath.

No, no, not again. Was she jinxed or something? She squirmed to get free, but he tightened his grip, nearly cutting off her airway.

"Listen, I have a knife and I'm not afraid to use it."

A knife? She stopped struggling. Her skin tingled with fear and her heart tried to climb up her throat. "Take my purse. Take my car. Please, just let me go."

"I want you to get in your car. If you try to run, you better make damn sure you can get away, because you won't like it if I catch you. Do you understand?"

She looked down the street. Many cars were parked along the road, but there wasn't one person in sight. Even Wings seemed a mile away. She'd never make it. "Yes."

"Good. Now give me your keys and get in."

"If you want my car, just take it."

His lips brushed against her ear. Goosebumps broke out all over her skin.

"I don't want your stupid car, I want you. Now give me the damn keys."

His voice. He sounded familiar, but from where? With shaky hands, she found the keys inside her purse and held them out. He reached for them and she opened her hand. They landed on the ground with a jingle.

"Very funny." He unhooked his arm from around her neck, but grabbed onto her hair, pulling her head back. "Now pick them up and give them to me."

She hadn't meant to be funny, she just didn't want to touch him. As she bent over, he let up on her hair so she could pick up the keys. He plucked them from her fingers and pushed her into the car. Sarah headed for the passenger door, but he seized her by the shoulder. "You're driving."

He pushed her fob and unlocked the doors. The street was still deserted. Where was everybody? She opened the door and slid behind the steering wheel. Locking him out quickly crossed her mind, but since he held the keys, she squashed that thought. The horn looked hopeful, but she wasn't willing to risk her life on a chance someone would hear in time. What could she do?

He slid onto the backseat and pulled out his knife, shiny and long: over six inches. She stared at it as the moisture left her mouth. Thank goodness she hadn't honked the horn.

The man threw the keys in her lap. "Drive off."

She examined him in the rearview mirror and he looked nothing like she'd expected. No unruly hair and unkempt appearance, instead, he was cute and neatly groomed, with dark hair and brown puppy dog eyes. In fact, he looked familiar. "Do I know you?"

"Why aren't you driving?" He glared at her in the mirror.

Brian. That's who he was. The same creep who had hit on her the day she'd been attacked. Coincidence? Not looking likely.

John said he'd taken care of her attacker, but what were the odds someone else would be grabbing her now? She picked up the keys. Her nerves were shot and her hands shook as she put them in the ignition. "Where am I driving?"

Using the knife, he pointed ahead. "Go. I'll let you know when to turn. Now keep quiet and drive off!"

The streetlights glinted off the blade, inches from her face. Keeping quiet? Not a problem with him waving that thing around. But leaving with him would be a death sentence. No one would ever find her in time. How could they? She wasn't giving up her life that easily.

\* \* \* \*

John glanced at his watch. Should Sarah have arrived by now, or was time moving slower than usual? Granted, he hadn't spent much time in his apartment, but certainly enough for her to drive over. He needed to keep busy before he drove himself nuts. Polishing the glasses seemed like a good time killer and it could be done close to the door.

The crowd was into the game, cheering and cursing, and normally so would John, but his mind was on Sarah. Even the goofy commercials couldn't distract him. So he stood there and polished, taking a break to fill a drink when required.

A tremendous crash sounded outside and he jerked, nearly dropping the glass. He rushed to the door and looked in the direction of the noise. Down the street, up against a building, smoke was trailing around a mangled car with the same shape and coloring as Sarah's. Where was the stinkin' license plate? His heart lurched. Oh dear God. He yelled at the first person he spotted, "Ashley, Call 9-1-1. It's Sarah."

He rushed to the Civic, ignoring any possible audience. The air reeked of oil and transmission fluid, but not gasoline, and what he perceived as smoke was actually steam hissing from the radiator. He peered through the cracked driver's window. The airbag had discharged leaving Sarah leaning against the steering wheel. She wasn't moving. Thoughts of her demise stabbed him in the heart and he went wild with terror. "Please don't die, please don't die."

He pulled on the mangled door, but it wouldn't budge. The passenger door was just as crumpled. Damn it! Desperate to get inside, he nearly yanked the door off its hinges when common sense told him to look around. Several people in the bar had come out to investigate. Too many witnesses. He could punch a hole in the window. It wouldn't take much effort. However, that would only get glass all over Sarah. The back door was ajar. He climbed in that way.

John couldn't crawl over the seat. The car was too small and he was too big. He placed his fingers on her neck, locating her pulse. It was good and strong. Warmth shot up his arm, another positive sign.

"Thank God," he muttered, letting out a sigh. How badly was she injured? He gently pulled her back, being careful with her neck. A bump was forming on her forehead, but there weren't any cuts on her face and no scent of a major blood loss. He brushed her hair away from her face. "Sarah? Can you hear me?"

She moaned and stirred. "Where am I?"

Afraid that she would hurt herself, he held her head still. "You're in your car. You were in an auto accident."

Sirens pierced the air, music to his ears.

She opened her eyes wide and looked around.

"Don't move, Sarah. Help is coming."

"Did I hurt him?" she asked.

"Hurt who? Did you hit someone?" The car was smashed up against the building as if she had deliberately hit it at a great speed. If someone had stood between her and the wall, they couldn't have survived, and John was fairly certain the scent of blood would be overwhelming.

"Brian," she said.

She wasn't making any sense. "Sarah, you didn't hit another car."

"No, the man in my car. Is he hurt?"

That's when Ray's scent hit him. What the hell?

Sarah closed her eyes and started to cry. "I don't feel good."

He wasn't feeling so well, either.

Lights swirled all around them and the sirens went silent. He wiped her tears away and kissed her temple. "Take it easy, Sarah. Help is here."

He hated leaving her, but the firemen had their job and he was only in their way. They secured her neck with a brace and covered her before they pried the door open. Once freed, she was placed on a gurney. He wanted to climb in the ambulance with her, but was told to follow.

John trudged over to her car and surveyed the damage. Placing his hand on the crumpled hood, he fell to his knees. She could have easily died. What the hell happened and how was Ray involved? If only he had taken care of the bastard when he had the chance, if only he had made sure Ray turned himself in, if only... Yeah, if only. His life was full of them. Someone tapped his shoulder. He jumped and fell on his butt.

"I'm sorry," Ashley said. "I didn't mean to scare you. Is she okay?"

He stood and brushed his backside. "I think so. I'm going to the hospital. If you want to close up the place..." He couldn't finish and turned away. If he were mortal, he'd probably be tearing up or crying. He certainly felt like crying. He'd never been so scared.

"Don't worry about anything. You do what you need to do."

She deserved a raise. A big one.

"Thanks, Ashley." He kept his back to her and waited until her footsteps indicated she'd headed toward the bar.

Sarah's purse lay in the passenger's footwell. He leaned in and grabbed the handle, causing her cellphone to fall out. Should he call Lori? He'd certainly want Lori to do the same for him. He picked it up and placed the call.

# Chapter 18

The doctor said Sarah was suffering from a mild concussion and if she wanted to go home—and no way was she spending the night at the hospital—someone would need to stay with her. But who? Lori would probably volunteer, and that made sense, but Sarah wanted John. She couldn't very well ask him, though. They'd barely gotten back together.

She sat on the edge of the bed, growing more frustrated by the second. Stupid sleeve wouldn't hold still and her arm was too sore to bend correctly. Bracing for impact wasn't the brightest move she'd ever made, right up there with intentionally crashing into a building. Doctor had said she was lucky not to have broken any bones. Instead, she'd overused every muscle in her body, especially her arms and legs. Ah, but what was a little soreness as long as she was free and still breathing?

John and Lori entered the cubicle during another unsuccessful attempt with her jacket and he came to her aid, holding it in place.

"Thank you," she said.

"Where's your coat?" Lori asked.

"It got...dirty." Sarah glanced at John and he gave her an apologetic smile. Even soaking the darn thing hadn't gotten the blood stains out and she had ended up tossing it in the trash.

Lori handed Sarah her scarf and purse. "As soon as they come back with your paperwork, I'll take you home"

"I can take her home." John took the scarf and carefully draped it around Sarah's neck. His loving touches nearly did her in.

Lori narrowed her eyes at John. "She needs someone to spend the night. I can do that. I've done it before."

"I can stay the night," he said. "Besides, you have to work tomorrow, I don't."

*Oh, yay!* Decision made. "Lori, I love you to death, but I think I'll feel safer with John around."

Which wasn't a total lie. Brian was still out there, probably waiting for her to be alone again. She forced back a shudder.

Her statement brought a smile to John's face and a frown to Lori's. Sarah grimaced at the hurt look on Lori's face, but her mothering was the last thing Sarah wanted.

"You better not take advantage of her."

"Lori!" Sarah chided.

He placed a hand on her shoulder. "That's okay, Sarah. She cares about you." He said to Lori, "I'm not Steven. And I'll be a perfect gentleman."

A perfect gentleman? She might be sore, but she was far from dead. Oh why did she have to get hurt?

"I'm sorry, I didn't mean to imply you were." Lori turned her back to John and spoke softly. "You call me if you need anything, okay?"

Sarah promised. Lori gave her a kiss on the cheek. When she left, Sarah was itching to follow. The hospital brought back too many memories. She just wanted to go. Anywhere else would be better.

"How many more hours must I wait for that nurse?"

John chuckled. "She's only been gone for five minutes."

When the nurse finally returned with the paperwork, Sarah would have run for the exit if not for her poor legs. John became her crutch and led her to a bench in the foyer. She waited while he brought his car around. A gust of frigid air blasted its way inside the hospital. Dang, the temperature had dropped considerably. Her jacket would not do for long-term, but she wasn't in any condition to shop for a new coat. Plus, she was officially without transportation. "Totaled" was the word she'd heard.

No coat. No gloves. Holding the stupid ice pack wasn't helping her retain heat, either, but the nurse insisted she take it for her forehead. Of course, her face was still bruised, so what was another bump?

The Bumblebee pulled up to the curb. John came rushing around the vehicle and dashed inside, probably afraid she'd come outside on her own. While she couldn't wait to leave, she wasn't in any hurry to rush out into the freezing air. He blocked the wind while escorting her and lifted her inside, keeping her exertion down to a minimum. Somehow she didn't think Lori would have gone to so much trouble.

Sarah tossed the ice pack in the cup holder, thankful to get rid of the cold thing. The seat belt cut into her ribs, which were tender from the accident, so she held it out, relieving the pressure.

John slid behind the wheel and nodded toward the ice pack. "Aren't you supposed to put that on your forehead?"

"Yes, but it's cold. I'm cold," she grumbled.

"As soon as the car warms up, you'll get some heat." He then took off his denim jacket and gave it to Sarah. "Here, put this on. It should help."

This wasn't his normal coat. Why wasn't he wearing his heavier... "Oh crap."

"What is it?"

"Your stuff is in my trunk."

"Don't worry about it. Now put on my jacket."

"Aren't you cold? Don't you need it?"

"No. I only wear it for show."

She liked the show he gave her right now. Even with the crappy way she felt, he left her breathless. What was she thinking? It's not like she could jump him. Dang it. And she really wanted to jump him.

As he drove off she attempted to put the jacket on the correct way, but it hurt to move and the seat belt kept getting in the way. Turning the jacket around, she slipped her arms through the sleeves and wore it backward.

John chuckled. "Do you need any help with that? I can pull over."

"Nope, I'm good." She snuggled inside and took in his scent. "Is there anything bad about being a vampire? So far it seems like the way to go. You don't get cold, you're stronger, hear better, see better, read people's minds, and don't age. What's not to like?"

"Well, you don't eat food anymore, and there is the whole 'stay out of the sun' thing."

"Yeah. I guess there is that." It sure seemed like a small price to pay, though.

Then there was his super healing. Boy, she wouldn't mind that right about now. Did he scar? She stared at his side.

He brushed his hand against his shirt. "Is there something on me?"

She blinked and shifted her gaze to his face. "No. Can I see?"

Though she hadn't elaborated, he nodded. At the next light, he lifted the shirt. The skin looked smooth and pale, as if she'd never stabbed him. She tentatively touched it and he gasped.

"Does it hurt? Or am I cold?" she asked, rubbing her hands together.

"It doesn't hurt and you're far from cold. I just forgot what your touch does to me."

The light changed and he drove on. Sarah pulled his shirt back down. The view was too irresistible.

John took her hand. Her heart started the old flip-flop again, telling her she'd been away too long. Knowing he was a vampire didn't change the way her body felt about him. It had only been two days and it seemed like an eternity. During those two days, she'd felt incomplete, like part of her was missing. And that part was sitting beside her. She'd never let him go again.

As if he could read her mind, John said, "God, I missed you. I'm so glad you're okay." He gave her hand a gentle squeeze.

"I missed you too."

Sarah laid her head back and closed her eyes. It wasn't like she hadn't gotten enough sleep during the day, but that accident had drained her dry and she must have dozed. In no time, he was parking the car.

He told her to wait until he came around to get her. Even though the last thing she wanted was a blast of cold air, she hated being waited on. "I'm not helpless," she muttered to herself.

He opened her door. "I know you're not helpless."

Damn super hearing.

He helped her untangle the seatbelt from the jacket and put it on the correct way. As she stepped out of the vehicle, she stumbled on her unsteady legs and nonchalantly reached out for John, hoping he wouldn't notice. Maybe it was a good thing she'd waited. He saw and gave her a smug look.

The muscles in her legs refused to work properly and she shuffled like an old lady, but John never said a word. When she reached the stairs, he seemed tempted to pick her up, but only offered his arm instead. She wasn't sure whether to be glad or upset. She didn't want him to think she couldn't walk, but she hurt. Eventually they made it to her apartment and he helped her settle on the loveseat.

"Where are your blankets?" he asked.

"There's one in my bedroom, on the chair." John left to get it. "You don't have to baby me, you know!" Now, why had she yelled?

He returned with the blanket and shook it open. "Will you drop it? I'm going to baby you, so just get used to it." He laid the blanket on her and tucked her in. "How's that? Do you need me to turn up the heat?"

His wrapping resembled a cocoon and her arms were trapped inside. She wiggled a bit and freed them. "I'm fine, the heat's fine. Thank you. Now, will you sit down?"

He was worse than Lori, but where Lori would have gotten on her nerves, he didn't. It was sweet how much he cared. When was the last time anyone, besides Lori, had babied her during an illness? Steven never had. In fact, he'd blamed her for disrupting his routine. Of course he'd blamed everything that went wrong in his life on her, probably still did.

And her mother? Hell, she probably hadn't babied Sarah even when she'd been a baby.

John picked up the ice pack and held it out. "Unless you want a bump the size of a baseball on your forehead, put this on."

"Okay," she said in defeat. Vampires must possess a super good memory, too. She put the pack up to her head and used the blanket as a glove, pretty much covering half her face. Not the half that could see him, though, no way would she block that view.

John shook his head and chuckled as he knelt on the floor beside her. "Here, let me. The cold won't bother me." He lowered the blanket and took the pack, gently placing it against her forehead. "You really scared me tonight, Sarah. I thought I lost you. What were you thinking?"

She had told the police everything that happened, including Brian's description and the part where she had deliberately driven into the building. John had paled more than usual after she admitted that. He might have yelled if they hadn't been in the hospital. Heck, he might still yell.

"I was thinking I could knock him out since he wasn't wearing a seat belt. Just my luck, I get knocked out and he goes free."

"Free." A look of remorse flashed across his face. "I should have never let him go."

"You said you didn't see anyone."

"Not at the wreck. Back at the garage."

"So, Brian *did* attack me at the garage."

"Why do you keep calling him Brian?"

"Because that's the name he gave me." After she explained, John informed her that Brian was Ray's middle name. After an unsuccessful attempt at getting her to meet discreetly, Ray had settled on abducting her. "What happened to not having to worry about this Ray or Brian or whoever? Were you lying?"

"No. I've been looking for the bastard ever since you told me about the news article."

"The news article? But that was about…" The air became thin and she began to hyperventilate. The serial killer had attacked her. Which meant, if not for John, she'd be dead? "Oh God. Oh God."

John put the pack down and held her face in his hands. "Calm down, Sarah. You're okay. I won't let anything happen to you."

She batted his hands away. "I'm not okay. You just told me I'm that killer's next target! How could you keep something like that from me?"

"Because I didn't want you to worry."

"That's not your job. You should have told me when I told you about that article."

He sat back on his legs. "And how exactly would I have explained myself? You didn't know about me then. I swear, as soon as I realized he hadn't turned himself in, I searched everywhere. If I thought there was any chance you were in danger, I would have protected you better."

And he would have, of that she had no doubt. "So what happened? How did he find me?"

John took her hand and ran his thumb across her knuckles. "I honestly don't know. It could have been chance. You were in the same area as before. Maybe he's been staking the place out. You don't know how badly I feel. I should have done better by you. I'm so sorry."

"It's not your fault. You thought you had taken care of it." Her anger dissipated while fear reclaimed her. Would she ever feel safe again? Sure, John helped, but he couldn't be with her twenty-four-seven. She concentrated on him stroking her hand, anything to keep from screaming. "We should tell the police we know who the serial killer is."

He looked at her as if she'd gone mad. "You can't tell the police that Ray is the serial killer."

"Why not? I want him caught!" Frustration caused her eyes to water. She wouldn't feel safe until Ray was behind bars.

"He will be caught. You've given them his description. Please trust me. If you even mention the words serial killer, they're going to ask a lot of questions. Questions we can't answer. Do you understand?"

How could she think reasonably when there was a killer on the loose? A killer after her? But John probably had resources the police didn't have. "I suppose so. Just don't expect me to be calm about this."

He smiled before kissing her forehead. "I'll do my best to take your mind off of it."

The forehead? Really? She might be sore, but her lips worked fine. She opened her mouth to protest and her stomach growled.

"When was the last time you ate?"

He did seem fixated on her dining habits. At least she knew why he didn't eat, special liquid diet, indeed. But when had she eaten last? "Lunch yesterday?"

"Yesterday?" He shook his head. "Sarah…you need to take better care of yourself. What can I fix you?"

Good thing he didn't ask what she ate for lunch. Ice cream and cookies weren't exactly nutritious. She sat up. "Food doesn't appeal to me right now, but I guess I can find something light."

John held her down. "No, you stay here. The doctor said you should rest."

It was just as well. That little movement had hurt.

# Chapter 19

John's idea of spending a day with Sarah without the prospect of sex might end up being a day of torture. After he fed her soup, she decided to take a shower, against his better judgment. She could barely stand. But as soon as she entered the bathroom and turned on the water, his thoughts turned carnal. Just knowing she was in there naked, wet, and soapy got him harder than hard. He needed to get his shit together or he'd blow this great opportunity to show her he was still a decent person, regardless of being a vampire.

Sarah emerged from the bathroom wearing a robe that only reached her knees. She had always worn slacks or jeans, never dresses or skirts and it had teased him to no end. Now her legs were bare, which wasn't helping his erection one bit. Damn, she was sexy. But if he kept staring, his boner would never leave, so he blinked and forced his gaze on her face.

"Would you help me dry my hair?" She pulled the towel free, uncovering a wet, frazzled mess.

"Sure." John followed her to the mirror, where she picked up the comb and started working out the knots. With each movement, she winced in pain.

"Come on. Let's get you somewhere more comfortable." Taking her hand he got a shock of heat. He couldn't wait to feel that warmth all along his body when he made love to her. His penis jerked in what little room he had in his pants. Damn it. He really was an idiot.

He led her back to the chair. Easier access and she'd be off her feet. When she settled in, her robe opened momentarily giving him a glimpse of heaven. Holy shit, she was naked under that thing. He could easily bury his face inside her and go to town.

Damn it. Shit. Crap. Not gonna happen. He quickly moved behind her, knelt on the carpet and nearly moaned at the pressure on his groin. Served him right for thinking.

He inhaled to clear his head, but got a whiff of her shampoo instead. It was some floral blend, enhancing her natural scent and making him harder than ever. Okay, so maybe he should stop breathing. He concentrated on working the knots free and ran his fingers through her hair.

When it came time to blow-dry it, the cord was too short for the nearest outlet, so he picked up the chair, with Sarah still in it.

"Whoa, John. What are you doing?" she asked, grabbing onto the arm rests.

He put her down. "Sorry. Wasn't thinking. There aren't any plugs near you."

She glanced over her shoulder toward the wall. "Oh. Then warn me, okay?"

Warn her? Well, damn. "Will do." She didn't stand, so he did as she suggested. "Hold on."

She stared at him with those beautiful green eyes as wide as they could get and gripped the arm rests while he lifted the chair and moved it near an outlet. He never wavered because she wasn't heavy.

"Impressive."

He flashed his eyebrows and smiled. She really was accepting his whole vampire thing. How did he get so lucky?

* * * *

Sarah leaned back in the chair while John ran his fingers through her hair and blow-dried it. His touch was pure torture. All she wanted to do was turn around and kiss the guy. And maybe fondle him a little. Or a lot. He was clearly interested—the bulge in his pants told her enough—but he probably thought she was too sore. Wasn't that the truth?

She could barely move around, let alone make love. And why was she naked under her robe? John was doing his best to be a gentleman and she was acting like a hussy. What kind of heartless bitch had she become? A horny one, apparently. After flashing him, she'd seen the error of her ways and tucked the robe between her legs.

The blow dryer cut off, ending her sensuous interlude. She wouldn't mind him doing this all the time, but only if he wanted.

He knelt in front of her. A slow smile spread across his face as he toyed with her hair. "I wouldn't mind doing that again. That's if you enjoyed it."

If she were feeling one-hundred percent, she'd more than enjoy it. "I did."

He brushed his fingers against her cheek and lingered there while he gazed at her with those shimmering blue eyes. His eyes were filled with such love and tenderness. And what had she done when she discovered his secret? Thrown his love back in his face. How did she deserve his love after that?

Tears ran down her cheeks.

His eyes widened. "What's the matter? Are you in pain?"

Sure, she hurt everywhere, but the only organ that mattered was her heart and it ached for him. "I'm sorry, John."

He furrowed his forehead as he wiped the tears away. "What are you sorry about?"

"For the way I treated you when I found out. I told myself if I ever discovered who came to my rescue, I'd hug them first then ask questions. I haven't even thanked you for saving my life that night. And now you're being so nice. I don't deserve you." The tears flowed a little more freely.

"Ah, Sarah. Don't cry. You were scared and confused. I'm just so happy you can accept me the way I am. That means more to me than anything."

He deserved that hug. She wrapped her arms around his neck, and rested her head on his shoulder. "Thank you for saving me. Thank you for being in my life. I hope you never leave."

Ever so gentle, his arms came around her. "I don't plan on it."

His voice sounded husky. She was probably tempting him again, but she liked being in his arms. Almost as much as kissing him. But probably not as much as making love, if they ever got around to actually doing that. She rubbed her cheek against his neck, which brought a gasp from him. "What do you feel when I touch you?"

He leaned into her touch. "I get a rush of warmth."

"But aren't you always warm? Isn't that why you don't need a coat?"

He pulled away and looked at her. "I don't need a coat because I adjust to the temperature. Except for touching you—and sunlight—I don't notice any difference."

"Wow, to never be cold or hot. I can't even imagine."

"Yeah, but I can never enjoy the sun on my face or the heat from a fireplace. You're the closest thing to that pleasure. Actually, you surpass it." He caressed her cheek as if in thought, then blinked. "You ready for bed now?"

Bed was the last thing she wanted. That, and being alone. Ray had already tried to abduct her twice, what was to stop him from trying a third time? Did he know where she lived now?

"He can't get you here." He held her face and stared at her intently.

"I know, but..." God, she sounded whiny. How could he stand it? She wasn't sure she could.

"Why don't we watch TV and when you fall asleep, I'll carry you to bed. And then after each time I wake you, I'll stay until you go back to sleep."

She liked that plan, but... "You have to wake me?"

"Doctor's orders. Remember?"

Oh yeah, doctor. But sleeping in John's arms? Now that was something she could wrap her mind around.

# Chapter 20

John sat on the loveseat, waiting for Sarah to get dressed. Darkness had finally descended, bringing a sadness along with it. Who knew spending a quiet day with her would end up being the best day of his life? He wanted to spend every second with her, but she did have a life, and a job. Heck, so did he, but he would remedy that later. Before he left for Wings, he insisted on taking her out for dinner. Those two tiny meals she'd eaten couldn't have filled her up. He'd told her she wasn't torturing him by eating in front of him, which had been all the encouragement she'd needed to agree on the date.

She emerged from her room, walking with a little more ease. "I think I'll be able to make it to work tomorrow. Guess I better call Lori for a ride."

He rose from the loveseat. "You don't need to call her. You can use the Xterra until the insurance settles things."

"What? I can't do that. How will you get around?"

"I don't need a car, but people question you when you're different and I try very hard to appear normal."

She eyed him suspiciously. "You don't need a car? Really?"

"Where am I going to go during the day? You can use mine. I'll be fine." He opened the closet and pulled out a blue coat.

"What's that? That's not mine."

"It is now. I told you I would replace it, so I bought you a new one."

She rushed to him and wrapped him in a hug. "I can't believe you did all this. Not just the car and the coat, but the way you've taken care of me all day. And after the horrible way I treated you. You're the best thing to ever happen to me. What would I ever do without you?"

He stiffened at her question. Did she really feel that way about him? He'd be lost without her. No one filled his heart like she did. When she died, she'd take his soul with her, whether or not she loved him back.

She placed a hand on his cheek. "What is it? What are you thinking?"

He buried his face in her hair, taking in her scent. "That I'm lucky to have you in my life. I love you so much, Sarah."

She squeezed him harder. "I love you, too."

In his wildest dreams he couldn't imagine the joy inside his heart at hearing those words. Heck, he never thought he'd ever hear those words. He cupped her face and gently kissed her. He'd been avoiding this kind of contact all day, afraid he might overreact. But she loved him. He could kiss her for that. "Oh Sarah, you don't know how happy you've made me."

Her laughter sounded wonderful. Now it truly was the best day of his life.

* * * *

Sarah sat in the Bumblebee and ran her fingers along one sleeve of her new coat. The padding was thicker than her old one and the color almost matched his eyes. She loved it. "When did you get it? You've been with me since last night."

John pulled into a parking spot and killed the engine. "I went out between wakeups."

"You left me?" *Argh!* What was with her whininess? It wasn't like he had to report to her.

"You were sleeping fine and I did have to feed."

Jealously flared out of nowhere. Who did he feed on? A man or a woman? And why did it matter? How silly was it she felt threatened by a meal? No sillier than wishing she were said meal. "Did you ever think of maybe feeding from…me?"

His eyes widened. "Uh, no."

"Why not?" Wasn't she good enough?

He closed his eyes and pinched the bridge of his nose. "I don't feed from people I know."

139

Well, that sort of made sense. She probably wouldn't want to eat hamburger if she had named the cow, except he said he didn't kill to eat, so wouldn't that be like drinking the cow's milk? So what was the big deal? And did he feed from men or women? Oh crap. Who was she to boss him around anyway? She certainly didn't want to anger him. "I'm sorry. I had no right to question you."

"Don't worry about it, okay? But if it makes you feel better, you're forgiven."

The hostess seated them in the back of the quiet restaurant. Almost like they had the whole place to themselves.

She picked up the menu and John did the same. Why would he do that? The waitress arrived with two waters.

"I'll have the chicken pot pie with rolls and a Diet Coke." Sarah put the menu down and smiled at him. This should be interesting.

He lowered the menu. "I'll have the same."

He'd have the what? Sarah waited until the waitress left before she bent over the table and whispered, "What are you doing?"

Mirroring her movements, John grinned and whispered back, "I'm having dinner with you."

She rolled her eyes. "No, silly. Why did you order?"

"Wouldn't it look strange if I went into a restaurant and didn't order anything?"

"But won't it look strange when you don't eat it?" She certainly hoped he didn't expect her to eat his dinner, too. She might be hungry, but she wasn't that hungry.

He sat back and folded his arms across his chest. "Oh, I'll eat it. Don't worry."

She frowned. What did he mean by that? All this time he could eat and he'd led her to believe otherwise? Why would he do that?

John laughed.

"What's so funny? I thought you couldn't eat."

"I never said I couldn't eat, just that I don't. I'll take care of it so don't worry. Just enjoy your dinner, okay?"

The questions in her head bombarded her. What did he mean he'd take care of it? If he could eat, why the story about his liquid diet? She'd love to ask him, but the place was almost too quiet. Anyone could overhear them. She would ask him later.

Their meals arrived, and after one whiff, Sarah's stomach grumbled, revealing how famished she really was. She broke up the crust and the pot pie steamed around her face. It was too hot at the moment, but the rolls were okay. She took one and buttered it. Three bites later, she bit her lip. "Damn!"

John, in the midst of breaking up his own crust, looked up and scanned the room. "What's the matter?"

"Oh, I went and bit my lip. I hate it when I do that. Now I'll probably bite it at least three more times." She fished out an ice cube and wrapped her napkin around it before placing it on her lip.

He slid from his side of the booth and scooted beside Sarah. "Let me help." He took the napkin and placed it on the table.

"Help how?"

Holding her chin, he leaned over and ran his tongue across her bottom lip. The soft sensation set her desire on fire and when he let out a little moan and pulled away, she wasn't about to let him go. She grabbed the back of his neck and planted her lips on his. This was what she'd been craving all day. This was what he'd held back. She ran her fingers through his hair and explored his mouth. God, he tasted good. Her body tightened with a need so strong she slid her hand to his waist. She was inches away from his crotch.

"God, Sarah, you have to stop," he said into her mouth.

Oh crap. John had been right to hold back. Kissing him was asking for trouble. Embarrassed at how she'd reacted in a public place, she apologized and released him so he could sit back on his side of the booth.

"What was that all about?" Damn, her mouth still tingled.

"How's your lip?"

She ran her tongue around and found no evidence of ever having bitten her lip. So he'd been healing her, not kissing her. Figured. "It feels great. Wow, you can be pretty handy. Of course, next time you could warn me so I don't attack you in public."

John laughed and said, "Will do. Now eat your dinner and try not to bite your lip again."

Curious, she had to ask, "Did I taste good?"

He let out a long breath and stared at her. "Eat."

She pouted when he wouldn't answer. Didn't seem fair. Of course, if she had tasted bad, he probably would have grimaced or something.

He skewered a carrot and slowly ate it, as if he wasn't sure what to expect. His eyebrows shot up and he smiled. "I forgot how much I liked carrots."

"It tastes good?"

"Yeah, it tastes great."

John took to his food as if he'd been starving and Sarah enjoyed her first meal in ages. It was nice eating with him and she couldn't understand why he'd never bothered before. If he was so concerned about her eating habits, all he ever had to do was join her.

He slowed halfway through his meal while she plowed on to the end. Once finished, she took and ate John's rolls too, since he wasn't going to eat them.

After she polished off the last roll, he leaned back and crossed his arms. "I knew taking you out to dinner was a good thing. I bet if we stayed in you'd only eat a sandwich or something small like that."

Sarah couldn't deny it. It'd been several days since her last decent meal. Cooking for one was no fun and going out alone unthinkable. Basically, she'd been living on soup and sandwiches. But did he have to be so smug about it?

After John paid the cashier, he took her hand and led her outside. A gust of wind slapped her face. He stopped. She pulled her hood up as his grip on her hand tightened. He stared out into the parking lot. She could have sworn he growled.

"What is it?" She looked out into the darkness and found the source of John's anger. Steven. Being cooped up all day, she'd never gotten a chance to get that restraining order. Why did he always seem to show up at the strangest places? Could she and John ever have a date that didn't end in disaster? "What should we do?"

John shrugged. "I can make him leave, but if he has an agenda, he'll just show up again. Or we can ignore him and hope he gets the message. Your call."

She squeezed his hand. She'd love nothing better than to see Steven leave, but ignoring him would work, too. John wouldn't let anything happen to her, she was sure of it. But before she could announce her decision, Steven approached them.

"Hi, Sarah. How're you doing?"

So much for ignoring the bastard. She leaned into John, whether to hide or seek comfort, she wasn't entirely sure. Probably a bit of both. Was Steven seriously starting a casual conversation?

"I'm fine, and you?" If she could pull the question back, she would. Damn stupid reflex.

"I'm doing well." Steven's gaze shifted to John then back at her. "Aren't you going to introduce us?"

Had hell frozen over? But before she could say anything, John offered his hand to Steven. "I'm John."

Steven glanced at John's hand and reluctantly took it. Sarah cringed. What information would he get out of Steven? Her accident? The baby? Crap.

"Aren't you that bartender at Wings?" Steven asked.

Please let him go, she prayed. But of course, John didn't. Steven didn't even try to get free.

"Owner, actually," John said. "Are you following us? We seem to run into you a lot."

Steven laughed nervously and John continued to hold his hand. "Why would I be following you? I just happened to come here for dinner and spotted you. No harm done."

What kind of garbage was Steven spewing? He didn't even live around here. All the times she had suggested the restaurant, he'd rolled his eyes as if she'd suggested they eat dirt.

John pulled Steven in close, their faces inches apart. "I suggest the next time you spot us, you keep on walking. Sarah doesn't want you in her life anymore, and I can't say I blame her, not after you killed her baby."

Oh God! No! Dizziness attacked her for a moment. What else did John find out?

"I don't know what you're talking about," Steven said, shooting an accusing look at her. "She fell down the stairs."

John abruptly released Steven's hand and then scanned the parking lot as if he heard something. She followed suit, although she had no idea what to look for. There wasn't anyone else in the lot. Not even a wandering pet. But then, his eyesight was probably a hundred times better than hers.

John glared at Steven. "Who sent you here?"

"I'm not following you and no one sent me here. You're nuts, you know that? You sure know how to pick 'em, Sarah. I'm outta here."

After Steven entered the restaurant, she confronted John. "What was that about?"

He led her to the Bumblebee and held the passenger door open. Well, maybe the parking lot wasn't the best place to talk. Sarah climbed into the SUV and pulled the seat belt across her lap, wincing at the tension across her chest. So much for thinking she was healing. When the driver's door didn't open, she looked up. John was nowhere in sight. Where had he gone? Shit. Did he go back to talk to Steven? Or maybe do something worse? She quickly unbuckled her belt and got out.

She headed back toward the restaurant when soft coughing noises caused her to stop. Down on the ground, toward the front of the Bumblebee, John was kneeling on the pavement, clutching his stomach. She rushed to his side. "John, what's the matter?"

"I'm okay. Please get in the car." He moaned and then doubled over.

"You're hurting. What can I do?"

He started to gag. "Please get inside, don't make me ask again."

Slowly, she stood. His retching became more intense and she took two steps back, the sound triggering the same reflex in her. Maybe leaving was a good idea. If she even got a whiff, there was no telling what she might do. She climbed inside the Bumblebee and put her head in her hands, ready to stick her fingers in her ears in case the sounds penetrated the interior. With the driver's window in her peripheral vision, she stayed in that position until John stood. She let out a relieved breath and straightened. God, what a wimp. She should have been there for him.

He opened the door and slid behind the wheel. Sarah pulled a small bottle of water from her purse, and held it out. When he only stared at it, she said, "To rinse your mouth?"

"Is there anything you don't carry around in that purse of yours?" he said as he leaned over to look into her bag.

"Yeah, the kitchen sink."

He chuckled before getting out of the car. If he was laughing, he must be feeling better. Why wasn't she?

When he returned, he put the empty bottle in the cup holder between the seats. "Thanks. Guess I misjudged how long I could hold it in. I'm sorry you had to witness that. Certainly wasn't my intent." He smiled weakly and her heart went out to him.

"Are you okay?" She placed her hand on his arm. He didn't seem ill, but it felt rude not to ask.

He smiled and patted her hand. "I'm fine. Embarrassed, but fine."

Embarrassed? That was it? She'd be feeling like shit. "So that's what happens when you eat?"

He nodded. "My stomach doesn't produce acid anymore, so it can't digest food. It's not as bad as it seems. Really."

Looked pretty bad to her. "So you can still enjoy the taste of food, but if you eat it…" She couldn't finish the sentence.

"Exactly," he said, smiling. "Bummer, huh?"

So much for enjoying meals with John. He could joke about it, but she wasn't sure she could. How could she ever eat in front of him again? To tempt him every day when he couldn't enjoy it was just plain cruel. Her mother had taught her that much.

"What were you doing with Steven?"

He draped his arms over the steering wheel and looked out the windshield. "I didn't believe him and I wanted the truth." He shook his head back and forth minutely.

"And what? Is he? Is he following me?"

John took her hand and gently squeezed it. He gazed at their union. "I don't know. I couldn't access his thoughts."

"Sure you did. How else did you know about…?" The question died on her mouth.

He shifted his gaze to her and furrowed his eyebrows. "The baby?" Sarah nodded. "Lori told me."

Lori? How could she? Sarah opened her mouth to protest, but John put his fingers to her lips.

"Now don't go getting mad at Lori. She meant well. I am sorry for your loss."

Lori always meant well. Didn't mean it was right. Her eyes sprung a leak and John wiped the tears away.

"Ah, Sarah. What did he do to you?"

His look of concern was too much. She stared out the side window. "He broke my heart," she murmured as the memories came flooding back.

*Sarah ran up the stairs, eager to tell Steven the news, and stopped at the large mirror at the top. Gazing at her reflection, she turned sideways and lightly touched her belly. How long would it take before she showed? She couldn't wait to wear maternity clothes. Movement in the mirror caught her attention, and she lowered her arm as Steven emerged from their bedroom. Grinning, she turned and faced him.*

*"And what brings a smile to my beautiful wife today?"*

*"I have wonderful news." She bounced up and down, unable to contain her joy.*

*He gave her a light hug before stepping back. "Wonderful news, huh? Well, go on and tell me before you explode."*

*"You know how I haven't been feeling well lately?" He nodded for her to continue. "I'm pregnant."*

*His smile turned into a scowl. No. The news was supposed to make him happy. She trembled knowing what would come next and automatically stepped back.*

*"This wouldn't have happened if you took the pill."*

*And it wouldn't have happened if he always used a condom, but some nights weren't worth the bother. "You said you wanted a family."*

*"Some day, not now!" He paced the hallway. "You'll just have to get rid of it."*

*His words stabbed deep. Tears blurred her vision. Her marriage was over. Nothing would fix it.*

*But get rid of her baby? Never. She stood, holding her head high. "You can't make me."*

*"How dare you disobey me!" He brought his hands up and shoved her.*

*The stairs loomed into view and she grabbed onto the first thing within reach—the mirror. Her momentum ripped it from the wall and together they tumbled down the steps to the foyer.*

So much glass. So much blood. Her dream had been ripped from her because she had dared to defy him. If only she had kept her mouth shut.

Would she be in mourning forever or would it take more time? One thing was certain: she could never tell John. He would kill Steven for sure.

John held her hand. "Lori thinks he's responsible, but said that you wouldn't press charges. Why not? He certainly seems deserving."

Except she'd been just as responsible. "Doesn't matter. I wanted him out of my life. He promised me the divorce if I dropped it. That's what I wanted."

"He doesn't deserve to live."

The anger in his voice startled her. His eyes were glowing with hatred.

"But you won't hurt him, will you? You're not a violent man. If you were, Ray wouldn't still be alive, would he?"

He hung his head. "No, he wouldn't. But that was before. Don't you realize I'd do anything to protect you?"

146

"I know." Sarah placed his palm against her cheek. "But John, Steven's out of my life, and I'm better off. Better off because I found you. If I can forget him, can't you?"

He looked away as if in thought. Could he forget or was the vampire inside of him wanting revenge? "Promise me you'll tell me whenever you see him. No secrets."

Relieved, she squeezed his hand. "No secrets. I promise."

John nodded and started the engine. They drove in relative silence until he turned toward her apartment.

"You missed the turn to Wings."

"Why would I go there?"

"So I could drop you off."

John sighed heavily, a sign she recognized as frustration. "I'm taking you home. I'm not going to force you to drive tonight."

She certainly didn't want him mad, not over something stupid, so she kept quiet and remained that way until John pulled into her parking lot. He helped her out and escorted her to her door. When he handed over the keys, he was quiet, but his face gave nothing away. If he was angry, he hid it well.

John fished his cellphone out of his pocket and glanced at it. "I have some business to take care of that shouldn't take long. If it's not too late, do you mind if I come back after I'm done?"

"You're not mad at me?"

He returned the phone and cupped her face, igniting her desires. His glimmering eyes pierced her soul. "Sarah... I could never be mad at you. You make my life worth living. I want to be with you."

How'd she get so lucky to find someone like him? Someone who didn't lose their temper on a whim, who was happy in her company and not concerned with appearances? She smiled and placed one hand over his. "I'll be waiting."

He rubbed his thumb across her cheek. "I'll be as quick as I can." After kissing the top of her head, he spun her around and nudged her toward the door. "Now get inside and lock the door."

"Yes sir!" She saluted and laughed. As she shut the door, she smiled. John was hers and she couldn't ask for a better man.

# Chapter 21

After checking in with Lori and assuring her friend she'd be at work the next day, Sarah grabbed an afghan and her book and curled up on the loveseat. The place was lonely without John. She missed his scent, his presence. In less than a month, he'd managed to become a huge part of her life and she hoped he'd be in her life a good long time. But would he want to stick around when she looked older than him or did he want to turn her into a vampire, too? Would that be akin to proposing?

If he asked to turn her, would she say yes? Probably. Maybe. He'd never mentioned what was involved or what the success rate was, only that it was a curse. The curse would be to watch loved ones grow old while remaining young, so if she was like him, then it wouldn't be a curse anymore, right? No one meant more to her than John. Sure, she hadn't known him all that long, and she had some time on her side, but the idea made her smile. Being a vampire with John would be better than perfect.

She opened her book. There were only about fifty pages left and she was at the part where she really hadn't wanted to put it down. She should have it finished before John returned. It would certainly make the time go by faster. Faster was good. She pulled the afghan up and dug in.

Just as she got to the part where the hero's life was in danger, someone knocked on the door. She recoiled and dropped the book. Good Lord. Was she jumpy enough? John had only been gone fifteen minutes and Lori would have called first, so who the heck could it be? Straightening and stretching her legs, Sarah slowly stood. As the day wore on, the pain had subsided. True, she couldn't run worth a damn, but walking without pain would do for now.

She shuffled to the door and looked through the peephole. The hallway was empty. Probably some kids playing a prank. She padded back toward the chair when there was another knock. She looked a second time and her heart lodged in her throat.

It was Steven.

* * * *

John opened his office door. Perry was sitting behind his desk, reclining in his chair. He might have been irritated if he wasn't so relieved.

"I wasn't sure you'd come so quickly. Thanks," John said.

"You said it was urgent."

"And you tend to forget to charge your phone." Movement from behind caught John's attention and he turned around. How desperate had he sounded for Perry to bring the Head of the Committee?

"Hello, John."

"Hello, Barnet." John closed the door. He didn't extend his hand in welcome, a common occurrence between vampires and a gesture that had taken him years to remember. No one liked having their thoughts read inadvertently.

Barnet, a rare vampire who'd been turned in his forties and actually sported some gray in his dark hair, wasn't a particularly tall man, nor was he overbearing, but he'd earned every vampire's respect because they knew he truly cared. Many considered him a father figure, John one of them. Barnet had stepped in and taught him all about being a vampire. There wasn't a man he respected more.

"I was disappointed you didn't stay after your last meeting, but it is nice to see you back in society. I trust the bar is doing well?"

At the time, John had still been living as a hermit. He hadn't stayed because being with other vampires was almost as bad as being with mortals. Now he felt bad that he hadn't. "It is."

"Okay, Johnny, what kind of trouble did you get yourself into now?" Perry asked.

Good old Perry, no beating around the bush for him. "I didn't think I had done anything to get myself in trouble, but there is a problem and I need help."

Barnet came around and sat in the chair in front of the desk. "What kind of help?"

John couldn't sit. He wasn't sure how much trouble he had caused and as he thought about Sarah and everything, his nerves bunched up. He needed to move or else he might blow a circuit, so he paced the restrictions of the room. "I interfered but now he's back. I don't know what I did wrong. And then there's Steven."

"Relax, John," Barnet said. "You're not on trial here. Slow down and start from the beginning."

Relaxing wasn't possible, not until Sarah's safety was ensured. John continued pacing while spilling all the details of the events that had occurred since saving Sarah from the serial killer. The only thing he omitted was her unique resistance to mind manipulation. Perry had never mentioned it so John suspected the man had never tried. He wasn't ready to share everything, if he ever would be.

"You're making me dizzy, Johnny. Cut it out," Perry said. "Who's Steven?"

John stopped and leaned against the door. He folded his arms across his chest, hoping that would keep him from exploding. "Sarah's ex. We ran into him tonight and I tried to read him, but all I got was static. From what I know, the only way that could happen—"

"Is if another vampire has control," Barnet finished. "This doesn't sound very promising. It almost sounds like you have an enemy, John."

"Me? I just assumed..."

"That someone was after Sarah?" Barnet said. "If they were, wouldn't they just take her?"

"I guess." Except most likely no vampire could control Sarah, but John couldn't share that theory without telling them about her.

"I think someone's toying with you. Did you make any enemies I don't know about?"

"No. Not that I know of." He'd never stayed at any of the meetings long enough to even warrant an enemy, but if another vampire discovered Sarah and was drawn to her, would they resort to these games? Games like tampering with his steps? And he had to go and install the camera so the stairs weren't in view. Could he be any stupider? "Damn it."

"You thought of someone?" Barnet asked.

"No. But if someone is controlling Steven, they're doing a really good job of it. I didn't sense anyone at the restaurant and I would have investigated further, but I couldn't leave Sarah alone unprotected."

"We'll check it out," Barnet said. "Give me the addresses of everyone involved and I'll make some calls. We'll get to the bottom of it." He stood and Perry followed suit, acting much too quiet.

John jotted down the information and handed the paper over. He shoved his hands in his pockets. "You don't know how much I appreciate this. Trying to do it on my own has been impossible."

"You always have us. We're family." Barnet smiled. "Do you think you might turn her?"

John felt the blood leave his face. "I hadn't even…"

"Too soon, huh? That's okay. I look forward to meeting her…someday, then."

Someday? If John had his way, it would be no day.

* * * *

Sarah's heart pounded fiercely. What the hell did Steven want? Why couldn't he just leave her alone? Better to remain quiet, that way he'd think she'd gone to bed and would go away.

He knocked again. She reached for the light switch, but what if he saw it go out? How light-tight was the front door? Instead, she prayed for him to leave.

The doorknob jiggled. *Oh God!* Her heart stopped for a moment. But the door was locked. It was always locked. Even before all the weirdness happened in her life, she'd locked that door. She relaxed and breathed easier. He couldn't get in.

"Sarah?" He knocked again. She put her head in her hands and closed her eyes. *Dear God, please make him go away.*

The sound of a key sliding into the doorknob jerked her upright. What the… She had locked the door, but the bolt… *Shit!* It wasn't engaged. Stupid, stupid, stupid. She ran to the door, but with stiff planks for legs, she stumbled over her feet. Before she could reach the bolt, the door was opening.

How dare he? This was her home, not his. Something in her erupted in rage and she stood her ground.

He staggered back when he saw her. "You're here."

151

"What do you want? And how did you get a key?"

"Hey, I'm very resourceful." He shut the door behind him. "And what I want, is you."

His words, uttered in a low voice, were like ice cubes down her back. What the hell was that supposed to mean? Her anger morphed into fear and she shivered.

In her periphery, she judged the distance to her bedroom. If she caught him off guard, she could lock herself inside and wait for John. That door didn't have a key hole. But could she make it in her condition? The little running she'd done had taken its toll on her poor legs. Oh crap. She had no choice.

Without warning, she dashed for the bedroom. She'd reached the doorway when her leg cramped up and she stumbled. He tackled her and she landed on her stomach, knocking the breath out of her and bringing tears to her eyes.

"Scream, and I'll kill you," he said.

He'd do it, too. Oh God! This couldn't be happening. Where was John?

# Chapter 22

John raced back to Sarah's apartment with a lighter load. Mike had graciously accepted being the full-time bartender, and without John begging, either. Now with his nights free, John could spend them protecting Sarah, either by keeping watch over her place at night or out searching for Ray. He'd do anything to keep her safe.

He only hoped he didn't have to keep her safe from him. After he had healed her lip, it had taken a tremendous amount of willpower to stop. Not because of how she tasted—and damn, she tasted better than life itself—but because when he kissed her, well, thinking became difficult.

He entered the parking lot and slowed to a jog. It may have been late, but people were still up and he didn't need anyone seeing him whip by. He took the steps, two at a time, and raised his fist to knock on her door, but it was ajar. She had locked it when he left; he had heard it click. Frowning, he entered the apartment.

"Sarah?" Sounds of movement, followed by sobbing, came from the bedroom, compelling him in that direction. "Sarah, what's the matter?"

The sight that greeted him punched him in the gut. With her arms above her head and her wrists attached to a set of cuffs threaded through the headboard, she was bound and gagged as someone's sex toy. Naked from the waist down, she had twisted her body keeping her back toward the door and the sheets curled around her legs as if she had attempted to cover herself and failed.

He fell to his knees beside the bed. The gag in her mouth was wet and loose and he removed it easily enough, but she kept her head away and wouldn't look at him.

"Oh God, Sarah! What happened?" The scent of sex was strong and so was another. He clenched his teeth. If he ever ran into Steven again, the man wouldn't live through the encounter.

She didn't move or answer. John placed his hands on the cuffs. How could he free her without hurting her in the process?

"Nightstand," she murmured.

"What?" A key lay on the bedside table and he picked it up. This didn't make any sense. He inserted the key and the instant one cuff came open, she yanked free from the headboard, grabbed the sheet, and covered herself up. She brought up her knees and hugged them while the cuffs dangled from her wrist. He reached out to remove them, but she shied away, so he backed off.

"Sarah, sweetie, it's okay. He won't touch you again. Tell me what happened."

Her response was stone-cold silence.

"Sarah, say something. Please," he begged.

She rested her head on her knees and looked toward the window. "Please go," she whispered.

He couldn't leave her, not like this. He never wanted to leave her again. But she needed help. He could call 9-1-1, but would that get her to open up? Probably not. But Lori could. "I'm just going into the other room for a minute, but I'll be right back."

Slowly he rose and backed away. She never moved a muscle. He shut the door on his way out.

His phone didn't have Lori's number, but Sarah's did. He really should add her number and prayed he'd never have to use it.

"Hey, Sarah. What'd you forget?"

It was déjà vu all over again. For once he'd like to call her with good news. "It's not Sarah."

"Please let this be a pleasure call." Lori might have been going for funny, but the tension in her voice came through.

"I'm sorry, but you need to come over to Sarah's. While I was at Wings, she was... I think she's been raped. She won't talk to me."

"Shit. I'm on my way. Make sure she doesn't clean up. No shower, no washcloth, nothing. Do you hear me?"

He knew the routine. "I hear you. Just hurry."

After he hung up, he rushed back to the bedroom. She'd curled into a fetal position, facing the window. He walked around the bed and knelt in front of her. She shut her eyes when he approached.

Trying to be gentle, he talked softly. "Sarah, I called Lori. She's on her way."

As soon as the words left his mouth, tears flowed from her eyes. He wanted to hold her, to comfort her, but wasn't sure she wanted him. A murderous rage filled him. If he found out a vampire was responsible, he would seek his revenge, the Committee be damned. But right now Sarah was more important, so he pushed the homicidal thoughts away. She was his first priority and always would be.

"If you want to talk, I'm here."

For fifteen minutes, they sat in silence. This wasn't fair. He'd just gotten her back and now he might lose her. Some women never recovered from rape.

Lori let herself in and stopped at the bedroom door. She waved for John to follow. Before he had a chance to shut the door, she bombarded him.

"What the hell happened? I thought you were staying with her."

He dragged her into the living room and ignored her rant. As calmly as he could, he relayed how he'd found Sarah, but saying the words brought the memory as if he were reliving it. He placed the key in Lori's hand and said with a cracked voice, "She won't let me near her to remove them."

Lori rubbed his upper arm and nodded. "I'm sorry for the outburst. It's not your fault. I'll find out what happened."

He could have listened to their conversation—and he was quite tempted—but Sarah deserved her privacy. Instead, he zeroed in to the television next door. After what seemed like an eternity, Lori emerged from the bedroom. She plopped down in the chair.

"That bastard." She looked him in the eyes, hers holding fury. "Steven had a key and let himself in. I convinced her to go to the hospital and report it, so she's getting dressed. They'll contact the police there."

John gripped the loveseat. He never thought he'd ever have the courage to kill someone, the Hippocratic Oath was still a part of who he was, but with Sarah's life in danger, killing would be easy.

Lori leaned forward, placed her hands on her knees, and glared at him. "Are you going to be there for her? Because if you can't, you better leave now."

The woman was seriously nuts if she thought he was leaving Sarah now. "I'm not going anywhere. Sarah's the most important person in my life. I love her."

She leaned back and nodded. "Good. She'll need all the support she can get."

Sarah called for Lori. Her voice barely reached the room. It hurt his heart to hear her so weak.

Lori stood. "Why don't you go get your car and drive it up to the entrance? I'll get Sarah and we'll meet you."

He hated leaving her, but she'd probably be more comfortable without him around so he left and did as Lori asked. After he had pulled in near the stairs, he cranked up the heat. According to the gauge in the SUV, the outside temperature was twenty-three degrees. Much too cold for Sarah. He would make her as comfortable as possible.

The back door opened and Lori helped Sarah inside. She kept her head down and not once during the drive did she raise it. That couldn't be a good sign.

John dropped them off at the emergency room and found a parking spot. When he arrived in the waiting room, Sarah was sitting and leaning against her friend. Should he sit beside her or would she be more comfortable if he didn't? She still hadn't looked his way. He sat across from her.

The nurse called Sarah. John and Lori were told to wait.

Wait? Why not stake him and lay him out for the sun? She had to be all right. His life would be nothing without her. He would be nothing without her. His arms and legs twitched with nervous tension and he nearly pulled his hair out. Feeling like he'd blow a gasket if he sat still any longer, he stood and paced within the waiting room.

Three police officers, two men and a woman, walked down the hall Sarah had taken and John suspected they were there for her. She'd better tell them the truth this time. He needed Steven behind bars to keep from killing the bastard. Twenty minutes later, the two male officers came out to the waiting area and approached him.

"Are you John Pennington?" one of them asked.

He acknowledged he was. They wanted his side of the story. Relief coursed through him. He was proud of her for pressing charges. It couldn't have been easy and he wished he could have been with her. After he told the officers what he knew, they asked if he'd let them into the apartment. Why him? Why not Lori? What if Sarah needed him? But when Lori told him she thought it might be a while before anyone could visit Sarah, he gave up. Besides, the odds that Sarah would want him right now seemed pretty slim. At least the trip would keep him busy and he could straighten up the place.

Upon arrival at Sarah's apartment, he showed them her room. He could still see her there, bound to the bed, and his heart ached. If it was this bad for him, he could only imagine what she would experience. The police inspected the bedspread and found semen, taking a sample. They took plenty of pictures and bagged the handcuffs. John asked what would happen next and got the best news yet.

There was an arrest warrant out for Steven.

\* \* \* \*

Sarah closed her eyes as she lay on the narrow hospital bed. Steven had done much worse in the past, but she'd never had any witnesses before. While she was glad to be free, she wished someone else had found her, anyone else besides John. What he must think of her.

No one could visit until after her examination and questioning. Not that it mattered. She didn't want anyone with her anyway. She felt violated in more ways than one: first Steven, then the police, then the doctors.

Once the police and doctors were through, Lori came inside her little screened-off cubicle, but not John. That couldn't be good. Sure, she had shied away from him and told him to go, but only because she was embarrassed. It had nothing to do with not wanting him. Was she dirty in his eyes? Did she repulse him? She must have, because he couldn't even sit beside her in the waiting room. Damn. It wasn't fair. She'd just told him she loved him, and she still did. But did he still feel the same or had Steven ruined it all? Her chest tightened and her nose tingled. The tears would come if she let them.

Lori explained about John's trip and then proceeded to try and soothe her, but Sarah didn't want soothing. She wanted John.

A while later, Lori jerked in her seat. She fished her cellphone out of her pocket and looked at the display. "I'll be right back," she said and then left the room.

Sarah was alone again and almost welcomed the tears.

A few minutes later, Lori came back around the partition. "The nurse says you'll be able to leave soon. You doing okay?"

Sarah nodded. "I just want to go home."

"I know, kiddo. Listen. John's back. He's out there waiting. Can I send him in?"

The moment of truth had arrived and Sarah wasn't sure she could face it. It would break her heart if he didn't want her anymore. Better to get it over with, though. "Okay."

Lori left her and seconds later, John appeared around the partition. Sarah sat up. He looked as miserable as she felt. With tears in her eyes, she held her arms out, hoping. Not a moment later, he was holding her, comforting her.

She cried. She was home.

# Chapter 23

John stood when Sarah and Lori entered Wings. He had come down earlier and saved a table in the back. Good thing he had. The place was getting crowded.

He gave Sarah a light kiss on the lips, which is all he'd allowed himself to do for the past week. It was damn hard—he wanted her so badly—but she'd been through a lot. How could he make advances when the last time for her was so…traumatic? He had suggested a trip to his house for the weekend to get her away from the memory of that night. The way she'd jumped at the idea gave him hope. A new place meant a fresh start.

He held the chair for Sarah, but she continued standing while Lori sat in the neighboring seat.

Sarah placed her hand on his arm. "Can I talk to you in private?"

Lori laughed. "Is that code for making out?"

"No, it's code for I want to talk to him in private." Sarah swatted Lori on the arm.

He wouldn't mind the making out part, but Sarah seemed serious, not playful. He handed Lori a menu. "Dinner's on me." He swept his arm toward the back exit. "After you."

Sarah led the way to his office and closed the door after he entered. Her face was all scrunched up with worry and she wrung her hands. Okay, definitely not wanting to make out.

"What's the matter?"

She shifted her weight from one foot to the other, then back again. Her mouth opened and closed like a fish in action.

He placed his hands on her shoulders, keeping her still. "Sarah, just spit it out."

"You aren't going to fake eat tonight are you?"

"Fake eat?" The question completely caught him off guard and he burst out laughing. Seeing the pained look on her face didn't help any, it made it all the more precious.

She frowned and placed her hands on her hips. "So glad I can entertain you."

He stifled the last laugh. "Sorry, Sarah. I never heard anyone call it that before."

"Well, I didn't know what else to call it. You're not going to, are you?"

Of all the things to worry about. "No, I don't plan on eating. If she asks, I'll say I ate earlier. Okay?"

She let out a long breath and placed her hand over her heart. A hint of a smile showed on her face and she nodded. "Good. I was so worried... I don't want you to ever feel you have to...you know."

The things she let bother her were so petty compared to the things she didn't. Steven had raped her and she wanted life to go on as usual. If it upset her, she hid it well. But getting sick in front of her? A disaster.

"Come on," he said. "We better get back before Lori comes looking for you."

Lori smiled when they returned to the table. "It doesn't look like you made out."

Sarah ignored her so he did the same. "What can I get you ladies from the bar?"

* * * *

The last thing Sarah wanted was alcohol. She would be wide awake and alert when she got John into bed that night. All week he'd treated her like a fragile figurine and frankly, she was tired of it. Guess if they were to ever have sex, she'd have to initiate it. And by gosh, they would have sex. She would not let her ex win.

She ordered a Diet Coke and Lori ordered a Jack and Coke. John left to fill their orders.

When he returned with their drinks, they placed their dinner order. By the time they were done eating, the sun had set.

"Is there anything else I can get you?" John asked.

Sarah shook her head. Would Lori take the hint?

"Yeah, I'd like another Jack and Coke." Lori leaned back in her chair and stretched her legs.

Sarah inwardly sighed. She couldn't very well kick her friend out, and she couldn't abandon her, either. "I changed my mind," she told John. "I'll take another Diet Coke."

"Coming right up." He saluted and headed for the bar.

"He sure is sweet on you," Lori said. "I don't think he's taken his eyes off you all night."

Sarah turned in her chair and smiled back at John. Yeah, he was sweet, maybe too sweet. She hoped to see some wild by Sunday.

"I better go make room for that drink. I'll be right back," Lori said.

Sarah tore her gaze away from John to acknowledge Lori's statement and gaped when her friend passed Perry on the way to the restroom. He pulled a one-eighty at Lori's retreating figure and Sarah shook her head. Of all the people to show up. He slunk into the seat across from her and settled himself in. She silently groaned.

Perry grinned wide, flashing his white teeth. "Good evening, Sarah," he said in a voice dipped in honey. "How do I always get so lucky to find you alone?"

At their last meeting, she'd had no idea he was a vampire, yet he scared her. And now that she knew? Heck, he still scared her. She just didn't trust him or the way her body reacted to his touch. His bright green eyes sparkled with mischief.

"You said you would behave," she said.

"Yes, but that was before you knew what I am. Does that knowledge change anything?"

"I didn't tell John about your visit because you said you would behave," she said through clenched teeth. "Do you want me to change my mind?"

He held his hands up in surrender. "Don't worry, Sarah. I didn't come to harass you, I came to see Johnny."

Did that mean he had news about Ray? She'd opened her mouth to ask when Lori returned.

"Who's your friend?" Lori grabbed her seat and once she got a good look at Perry, she turned her wide-eyed face Sarah's way and mouthed, "Oh. My. God."

Perry was a good-looking man, Sarah couldn't deny that, but his package was deceiving. As much as it pained her to introduce him, she ceded. "This is John's friend, Perry Davenport. Perry, this is my friend, Lori Forester."

Perry took Lori's hand and kissed it, similar to the move he'd made on Sarah when they'd first met. Lori ate it up.

"So, you're Perry, huh? Sarah mentioned you, but failed to tell me how good looking you are."

"And she didn't tell me what a beautiful friend she has, either. I guess that makes us even." He flashed a smile at Lori and she giggled. Uh oh. Not a good sign. Sarah didn't want them hooking up. What might Perry do?

John came back with their drinks and placed them on the table before sitting beside Sarah. "Hey, Perry."

She nonchalantly placed a hand on his arm and squeezed. He glanced down at her hand before looking up. She pointed to Perry and Lori with her eyes, but maybe her fear came out instead. Or maybe John sensed it. Whatever, she hadn't planned on him getting mad. When he turned toward Perry, his look could have wilted flowers.

"Are you behaving yourself?"

Perry clutched his chest as if in pain. "Now Johnny, I'm being good, really."

"Who said you had to be good?" Lori asked.

Perry gazed at Lori and grinned. "Oooo, I like her, Johnny." His eyes almost smoldered.

Oh crap. Sarah had seen that look several times from John. Bad enough Lori was interested. Did it have to go both ways?

Lori scooted her chair closer to Perry. "Do you live around here or are you just visiting?"

He weaved his arm around hers and took her hand with both of his. Lori grinned and desire flashed in her eyes. They were so intimate, Sarah felt like a voyeur.

"I'm only visiting, but that doesn't mean we can't have fun tonight, does it? They plan on leaving soon anyway, don't you, Johnny?"

Sarah stared at Lori. How could this be happening? Sure, Lori was a big girl, but Perry was a vampire. And vampires liked to...do what? Feed? Have sex? Have sex while feeding? Crap. Just because

John never tried any of that on her, didn't mean Perry wouldn't on Lori.

John stood and tapped her on the shoulder. "Sarah, can you help me for a minute?"

How could she leave the two of them alone? They might not be here when she got back.

"Can you get me another on your way back?" Lori asked as she held up her drink. "It suddenly got very hot in here."

Okay, so Lori had no plans on leaving quite so soon. Slowly, Sarah rose, still feeling apprehensive. John grabbed her elbow and helped her up, and, after relaying Lori's order to Heather, led her to his office.

Once they were out of earshot, she asked, "Do you think it's a good idea to leave Lori alone with Perry?"

He shut the door and faced her. Cupping her face tenderly, he wiped everything from her mind. The whole week she had craved his touch, but he'd been so distant that she doubted he'd ever touch her again.

"Sarah, relax. Lori is fine. You know how Perry can be. It's not the first time he's ever been out with a mortal. Besides, it seems Lori is enjoying herself."

His loving strokes put her in a trance, but his words woke her up, and they weren't comforting. "How do I know he's not controlling her or something? How do I know he hasn't tried to control me?"

He grasped her shoulders and placed his forehead against hers. "First off, he doesn't do that. Despite what you think of the man, he has his pride. Something will happen only if she wants it. Okay? Secondly, if he had tried with you, he wouldn't have succeeded and he hasn't said anything."

"You haven't told him?"

He shook his head.

"How come?"

He shrugged. "It never came up."

It never came up or he didn't want Perry to know? Was John still afraid for her safety?

"Listen, Lori will be fine. If she's not interested in him on her own, he'll walk away. Trust me."

Which meant Perry wouldn't walk away because Lori was clearly interested. Crap.

Sarah wrapped her arms around John and nestled her head in his shoulder. If only they were at his house already. "When can we leave?" Nah, she wasn't anxious.

A chuckle rumbled through his chest as his arms came around her. Contentment. Security. She could stay like this forever.

"Soon as I talk to Perry."

She reveled in his embrace, but the sooner she released him, the sooner they could get on the road. Plus, she really wanted to know what Perry had found out. When they returned to their table, she found Lori had scooted up against Perry. If she moved any closer, she'd be in his lap.

John placed his hands on the table and leaned into Perry's ear. "We're ready to leave."

Patting Lori's hand, Perry said, "Don't go anywhere. I'll be right back." He flashed another smile Lori's way. She practically swooned. Perry stood and glanced at Sarah before following John.

Lori's eyes got that star-struck, glazed-over look. She was either under Perry's control or had completely lost it.

"Are you okay? Do you need some air?"

Lori blinked, coming out of her trance. "Wow! What a guy. And is he hot!"

There was no stopping her now. Once Lori latched onto someone, that was it. But seeing Perry again made Sarah wonder. "What do you think of his eyes? Do you think they sparkle?"

"Sparkle?"

"Yeah, you know. Glimmer, like glitter?"

Lori raised an eyebrow. "No. They sure are a pretty green, but otherwise they look normal to me. Why do you ask?"

"How about John's eyes?"

Lori cocked her head. "John has beautiful blue eyes, but you already know that. Where are you going with this?"

"I thought I saw them sparkle. Must have been the light playing tricks on me." So Lori didn't notice. The eyes of every vampire Sarah had ever met sparkled. Why was that?

"Whatever. And by the way, Perry offered to walk me to my car later. Hell, maybe I'll get lucky tonight."

"Lori!"

"What? If he's willing, I'm willing. It's not every day you run into someone like that."

More accurate than she'd ever know. Sarah shook her head. "Just be careful, okay? I really don't know him that well. I'm concerned for you."

Lori's face softened and she smiled. "Hey, don't worry about me, I'll be fine. It's not like it's the first time for me or anything like that. You two run along and have a fun time, and hopefully I will, too," she said, giggling. Lori was absolutely glowing.

John returned carrying his bag and Perry resumed his position next to Lori. Sarah could only shake her head. Telling the couple goodbye seemed like a waste of time. Had they even heard her? They never looked up.

Once the doors to the Bumblebee closed to listening ears, Sarah started with her questions. "Did Perry find Ray?"

John frowned and shook his head. "I'm afraid not. Ray hasn't been at his house all week, or any of his other known locations. It's like he's vanished. I'm guessing your accident scared him off."

She'd never scared anyone off. Why now? "Are they quitting?"

"No, of course not."

"But if they don't have anything else to go on…"

"There are other theories."

"What kind of theories?"

He looked away. "They aren't important. Just know no one has stopped, okay?"

How could they be unimportant? It was her life they were talking about. She turned his head her way and disregarded the pleasurable zap. "I'm not frail, John. I know you think you need to protect me, and don't think I haven't appreciated the fact you've been around the past week, but you can't do it all. I have to fend for myself during the daylight hours. You can't be there all the time."

His pained expression weighed heavy on her shoulders, but how else would she get to the truth? The man wouldn't tell her anything if he could help it.

He took her hand into both of his. "You're right. I can't be there all the time. I wish I could, you don't know how much I wish I could. I don't want anything bad to happen to you. You're too important to me."

"Then tell me, so I can protect myself. If I'm left in the dark like I was before, I won't be prepared for anything."

He hung his head low as if he'd lost a fight. Maybe she'd finally gotten through.

"Okay, I'll tell you what I think, but you have to know it's only speculation. I don't have any proof, yet."

"Okay," she nodded. "What do you suspect, then?"

"I tried to determine why Ray came back to attack you. It didn't make any sense. I've never had any problem with suggestions before. It shouldn't have happened this time either. But after we ran into Steven Monday night, I became a bit suspicious."

She told herself to let John tell his story without interrupting, but when he mentioned Steven's name, she couldn't help herself. "What? You said you couldn't read his mind. Did you lie? Would it have prevented—" She couldn't finish the question.

John widened his eyes and shook his head. "God, no, Sarah. I didn't get anything from him. I swear. I wish I did, then I might have been able to prevent it."

Of course, he was right and she was just overreacting. He would have done anything to prevent Steven's assault.

"When I tried reading his mind, all I got was static. Someone had control."

"When you say someone, you mean another vampire, don't you?"

Being the polite guy that he was, he merely smirked and nodded when he could have given her a look that said *Duh*. Why wouldn't he mean another vampire? What human could do that?

"Anyway, with Ray coming after you, it makes me wonder if someone is controlling him, too. Perry and Barnet are looking into it."

"How many vampires live in the area?"

"In Dayton? Just me. Perry visits occasionally. If anyone else passed through, they haven't contacted me."

While Sarah didn't care for Perry, he wouldn't be helping if he were the culprit, would he?

"I wish I knew who would come after me that way," John said.

"What do you mean come after you? Aren't I the one being attacked?"

"Yes, but think about it. Whoever is doing this knows how important you are to me. Ray would be in jail, not suddenly back into your life. And while Steven has his issues, would he really sacrifice his freedom in such a manner?"

"But I wasn't in your life when you sent Ray to the police."

"Yeah, that's the only flaw in my reasoning. Told you it was a theory."

Was fate righting a wrong because Ray hadn't killed her on that night? Well, fate could take a shit bath. She wouldn't give up without a fight, even if it meant acting like some crazy, paranoid person.

Sarah looked out into the garage. Here she was on the brink of a nice, relaxing weekend, only to start it stressed out to the max. Would she spend the rest of her life looking behind her? Because vampires didn't age—they could go at it forever. They could hurt John forever. It seemed as if the oxygen in the SUV thinned to nothing.

He pulled her close. "Sarah, it'll be okay. I won't let anything happen to you. This is why I didn't want to say anything."

His presence soothed her as nothing else could and she relaxed. One way to stop all the madness would be if he turned her, but he never mentioned that possibility. She'd give him more time, but if he didn't bring it up, she certainly would. "No, I'm glad you told me. I needed to know. Maybe I'll see something during the day that you can't." She pulled away and sat up straight. "Enough of this. Let's go start our weekend."

He grinned and his eyes sparkled a little brighter. "Anything for my sweetie."

Sweetie? She'd never been anyone's sweetie before. She kind of liked it.

# Chapter 24

The trip to Urbana was shorter than Sarah expected. Forty miles should have taken nearly an hour, since the route comprised mostly of minor thoroughfares. Instead, John arrived in under thirty minutes. Talk about a lead foot. And keen eyesight. And maybe that controlling bit. Geez, no wonder vampires had never been discovered.

He turned into a driveway and she squinted through the window. She'd assumed he lived in a normal neighborhood, but driveways this long didn't exist in normal neighborhoods. How big was his place? It certainly was secluded enough. Trees lined both sides of the driveway for what seemed like forever, but lights up ahead told her they were almost there. Anticipation nearly caused her to jump up and down in her seat. When he drove into a clearing, her jaw dropped.

What kind of trick had he played? How was this place just a house with a yard and a garage? She had pictured the kind she grew up in—a one-story ranch—not a castle, and how could that not be a castle what with a two-story turret out front?

"John, you've been holding out on me," she said as she unbuckled the seatbelt. "This place is huge. It's beautiful. How could you not live here all the time?"

He shrugged as he undid his belt. "I got lonely out here by myself."

Well, the place was isolated, probably a perfect vampire hideaway, but without any family... Maybe someday she could be his family. She wouldn't mind living here.

She'd hopped out of the Bumblebee and headed toward the home when she spotted the covered porch. She stopped and clutched her chest. How many times had she dreamed of having such a place to sit outside and read? She ran, anticipating all the wonderful things she would discover, but halfway there she remembered their luggage, and her manners. She pulled a one-eighty and plowed into John.

"Oh!" she exclaimed. He grabbed her shoulders and held her upright. "Sorry," she said. "I came back to help with the luggage."

"It'll wait," he said, grinning. He turned her toward the house. "Come on. You're anxious to see it, so let's go see it."

Sarah stepped up to the porch. "It has a swing?" Those afternoon reading sessions were looking like a strong possibility. Except John wouldn't be able to join her. Her jubilation deflated a bit. "Maybe when it's warmer we can sit out here at night?"

He hugged her from behind. "I'd like that. And you could always come out and enjoy the sun, too." He placed a kiss atop her head and then opened the front door. She walked inside, but after he shut the door, she became blind. She put her hands out to keep from hitting anything.

"Sorry," he said. "I keep forgetting."

A light came on and the brightness caused her to shield her eyes for a moment. She stood and stared at the curving staircase. The mahogany handrail gleamed. "Bet you slid down the banister when you were a boy, huh?"

"Not if I wanted to keep my hide."

Hmm, she didn't believe he hadn't attempted it at least once.

"Over to the right is the dining room," he said as he pointed. Curtains covered the curved windows of the empty room, but not a speck of dust could be seen. "As you can probably guess, it doesn't get much use."

She found him grinning at her. "I'm sure there are lots of rooms you don't use. The kitchen? The bedrooms?"

He nodded. "Yep, don't really have a need for them anymore."

No wonder he didn't live here, too big and empty for one person.

"What's over here?" she asked, indicating the room to the left. She gravitated to the huge stone fireplace and pictured a roaring fire and maybe a bearskin rug lying in front. Did they even make those anymore? She'd find something soft and furry.

"The living room."

One lone couch occupied the wall across from the fireplace and thick drapes covered the windows. She pulled back a panel and discovered plywood. "Are all the windows like this?"

"They are down here. I have foil covering the upstairs windows. I hope all this darkness doesn't depress you."

"I don't think that's possible." As long as she was with him, she didn't think anything could. "What else you got?"

He led her toward the back. On the right, she passed the largest kitchen she'd ever seen. What a waste. The little breakfast nook would have looked cute with a round country table and chairs filling the spot; instead it stood barren. The room on the left contained another turret.

Definitely a castle.

"I can see where you spend your time," she said. The family room contained a huge selection of electronics. The TV, which she swore was larger the one he owned in his apartment, rested inside the turret. In the cabinet underneath, he'd stored every conceivable game console, and maybe a DVD player for good measure.

"Yeah, well, what can I say?"

"Do you use the upstairs at all?" Did he even have any beds?

"The shower is upstairs, but don't worry, a bedroom is clean and ready for you. Come on." He took her hand and pulled her along up the stairs.

At the top, he stopped in front of the door across the hall, to the right of the landing. He placed his hand on the knob. "This was my parents' room. I thought you might enjoy using this one."

He swung the door open and she stepped inside. A large four-poster bed greeted her first and when she bounced on the mattress, she spotted the fireplace situated between the closet and bathroom. *Hello, God.* She was in heaven. "Oh, John! It's lovely."

More curtains covered the turreted windows in the far corner. Even without the view or light, the area would make a great sitting room. She entered the bathroom. Damn thing was larger than the kitchen in her apartment. And the tub? Big enough for two people.

He came up from behind and wrapped his arms around her. "I remodeled this room a few years ago. You don't think I overdid it, do you?"

She leaned against his chest and reveled in his closeness. Something she'd been missing since…forever. Now it was just the two of them, alone, and she was healthy. Her poor, excited heart was probably giving everything away and if he didn't know what she had planned next, he was an idiot.

Her idiot, though.

She turned in his arms and gazed into his glimmering blue eyes. A strand of hair partially covered one eye and as she brushed it away she continued running her hand to the back of his head. His silky hair slipped through her fingers and she nearly fisted it. Instead, she pulled him toward her. He didn't resist.

A sensuous charge raced through her the moment their lips touched. She grasped his shoulder, afraid she might swoon, but he compensated just fine. With one hand, he grabbed her butt and pulled her close, pressing up against her and driving her crazy with need, while he held the back of her head with his other hand. He sought entrance with his tongue and she obliged. God, he tasted good.

Time to get him naked.

\* \* \* \*

John had been afraid Sarah would reject him. Instead, he held a wildcat in his arms.

Her blouse had disappeared somewhere and she tugged on his shirt. He pulled away enough so he could remove it. With his shirt sailing through the air, she slid her fingers over his chest and played with his nipples. He nearly popped out of his jeans.

This was happening now. Was she ready? Was he? She kissed him again, wiping the questions away. All he'd wanted was her, under him, since the first night he saw her. He broke the kiss and before she could say anything, scooped her up and carried her to the bed. After kicking off his shoes, he climbed in and lay beside her. He traced the contours of her face and stared into her beautiful green eyes before he leaned in to taste her sweet mouth again. He couldn't get enough. When she unbuttoned his jeans and brushed against his burgeoning erection, his cock jerked and he hissed in a breath. Sweet Jesus. He held her hands and stopped her. If she touched him… Damn, he wanted this to last.

"Me first, please," John said. Sarah nodded and let him continue.

Slowly, he ran his hand down her taut stomach, discovering the huge bruise across her chest and tiny, older scars scattered over her belly. Gently touching the bruise he asked, "Does it hurt?"

She shook her head and said, "No, not anymore."

"What are these from?" One larger, jagged scar started from under her slacks and ended at her belly button.

She brought her hands over her stomach. "I fell and took a mirror with me."

Fell? No, pushed. Damn, she could have easily died along with her baby. His heart ached all over again for her loss. He bent down and, after pushing her hands away, slowly kissed the bruise and each scar, her warmth spreading throughout his body. She arched up to meet him. When he finished, he looked up, smiling. "Remind me to kiss that seat belt, too."

She laughed, but when he removed her bra and fondled her breasts, her laughter died with a gasp. He sucked on one perfect nipple, flicking it with his tongue. Moaning, she ran her fingers through his hair, leaving trails of heat. God, he wanted her now. He quickly removed her slacks and panties and then paused as another scent intoxicated him: her arousal. His fangs emerged.

Damn it. He shucked his own pants while he willed his teeth to retract. Maybe one day he could bite her, but not their first time and certainly not without her permission.

Once his fangs retreated, he climbed on the bed and admired her. How had he gotten so damn lucky? She was beautiful. And all his. He ran his hands up her calves, so soft, so warm. When he reached the apex of her thighs and stared at her sex, she tensed. He bent down for a taste but his fangs returned. Damn it all to hell! Maybe next time he could take his time with her. That's if he could ever control the stupid things.

He kissed his way up and hovered over one lovely breast. Unwilling to risk another fang appearance, he settled for licking one nub while he massaged the other between his finger and thumb. As he lay over her, the luxurious heat returned, especially when she ran her hands down his back. He moved up and nuzzled her neck. Her artery thumped as if in anticipation. Hell, so did his heart.

He positioned himself to enter and paused. What if he was too big? What if she was too small? Or worse yet, what if he lost control?

"What is it?" she asked.

"I don't want to hurt you."

She caressed his face. "You won't. I'm ready for you."

As if to prove it, she arched up. That little touch set off a spark and propelled him forward. He thrust inside her. Heat. Moisture. Tightness. She encased him in pleasure. He'd never felt anything so mind-blowing. So perfect.

She licked his nipple and grabbed his ass, getting him hotter. He drove into her as she opened wider for him.

She gripped him harder and tensed beneath him. Her breaths came in short puffs. He kissed her just as she came, her moans filling his mouth, her body trembling in release, milking him for all he was worth.

An explosion of erotic proportions ripped through him. He cried out as he spilled into her. His home. His everything.

Once he recovered, he lifted up and found her crying. His heart clenched as his worst fears were confirmed. "Sarah? Oh God, I hurt you."

He moved to slide off her, but she held him close. Wiping her eyes, she shook her head, but more tears flowed.

"What is it, then? Why are you crying?" He brushed her tears away.

"I never knew it could be like this, John. I never realized." She put her arms around his neck and held onto him. "I love you so much."

Relief flowed through him. Happy tears. He could handle happy tears. After wrapping his arms around her, he flipped over so he was on bottom. He nuzzled her neck. "I know what you mean. It's like you were meant for me. I love you, too, Sarah. Forever and with all my heart."

\* \* \* \*

Sarah rested her head on John's chest, enjoying the sound of his beating heart while she recovered from the best sex ever.

John was perfect. She'd thought he might feel cold, but he'd matched her temperature almost immediately. In fact, he kept her warm. How that was possible when he didn't generate any heat she didn't know, but she wouldn't complain.

She stared at his nipple. It teased her. Heck, he teased her. She could go for another round, but he probably needed recharging or something. Didn't all men? She ran her hand over his smooth chest and his nipple hardened at the touch. Ah, couldn't let the other one feel left out, so she flicked her tongue over the nub next to her mouth. A hardening under her thigh brought her head up.

Then again, he wasn't like all men. His beautiful blue eyes practically glowed at her.

Boldly, she ran her hand down his stomach and grasped his growing penis. He leaned his head back and closed his eyes. She'd known he was big, but goodness.

"Unless you're prepared for another round, I'd stop if I were you."

She smiled. "You don't need to recover?"

He opened his eyes and stared at her. "Apparently not."

Life couldn't get any better. Well, it could if he turned her, but she wouldn't bring that up. Not yet. She kissed him instead. "Well, then, get ready for round two."

"As you wish." He held her tight and sat up.

With ease, he lifted her by her hips and placed her over his erection, filling her. She nearly came right then and there.

Love, vampire style. *Oh yeah.*

# Chapter 25

Soft light filtered in from the bathroom. Sarah slept peacefully, her head on his shoulder, and he was afraid to move. Not that he needed to move—he didn't need to do anything—but he couldn't disturb her. She hadn't been sleeping well the past week.

Each night since her rape, John had left before she retired for the evening so she could bolt the door behind him. Sure, he could have waited until she slept and slipped through the window, but acting normal made him feel normal. Plus, he didn't want her to think he couldn't leave her alone. If he appeared confident nothing would happen, she felt confident.

So while she thought he had departed like any sane boyfriend would, he had actually camped beneath her bedroom window. At first, he'd wanted to make sure Steven or Ray or another vampire didn't come nosing around. Then she had cried out. Afraid he'd missed something, he climbed to her bedroom window only to discover she was having a nightmare. He'd been tempted to climb in and comfort her, but he'd only end up scaring her more, so he'd stayed outside and prayed they wouldn't last long. She'd never been loud enough to wake the neighbors, just loud enough to pierce his heart.

Now she was quiet and her angelic face seemed at peace. Her eyes rapidly moved beneath the lids and her lips slightly curled up at the corners. He smiled with her. She deserved a good dream for a change. Right now, he was living better than any dream he could imagine.

And it was all because of Sarah. She was certainly full of surprises. After what Steven had done, John wasn't sure if she'd ever want sex again. She did and then some. And while his recovery time seemed remarkable, even to him, she took full advantage of it. Wherever did she get the energy? But number five had been her limit and she had finally conked out.

She stirred and opened her eyes. Her forehead furrowed in that confused expression he loved, but when she looked up and saw him, she smiled.

"What time is it?" she asked, rubbing her eyes.

Glancing at his watch, he said, "Around five. Go back to sleep, you've only been out about four hours."

She frowned. "I don't want to. I'm not tired," she said yawning.

He raised his brows. "Oh, you're not, are you?"

"I don't feel tired." She sat up. "It's hard to tell what time it is with all the curtains. How do you ever know when the sun is out?"

Sitting up with her, he rubbed her back, enjoying the silky texture of her skin. "Well, you see, I have this watch..."

She stuck her tongue out. "Smart ass." Then she gave him a quick kiss. "Have I told you lately that I love you?"

That kiss was much too quick for his tastes. "Yes, but I'll never tire of hearing it."

Cupping her face, he planted his lips against her. Even after holding her for hours, heat bloomed. Their tongues tangoed, her arms went around him, and his erection returned. No way would she have enough energy for another round, so he reluctantly broke the kiss and lay back on the mattress, bringing her next to him.

"I wish I could stay here with you forever," she said. "Would you want that, too?"

He'd want that more than anything, but she couldn't be saying what he thought she was saying. "You know I would, but the commute can get kind of old, don't you think?"

"Sure, I guess," she said with a frown.

"What are you thinking?"

She placed her arms on his chest and propped herself up. Hair flying every which way, she gazed at him with a hopeful expression. She looked so adorable. "I was thinking I could be with you forever if you turned me."

"What?" he sputtered. If she had slapped him, he wouldn't have been as shocked. His heart nearly stopped. "Do you know what you're saying?"

"I know I love you more than anything. I know I don't ever want to lose you. Why not turn me?"

In a way, he felt flattered. He'd never thought she would want this life. Heck, he didn't want it. "Sarah, this isn't a decision to be made lightly. It would be life altering. There would be no going back."

"I know that, don't you think I know that? Don't you want me?"

He hugged her tight against him. "That's not it, Sweetie. Don't ever think that. My life would be incomplete without you."

She pushed away and sat up. "All the more reason to turn me, right? And if I'm like you, then Ray and Steven can't hurt me. I would be safe."

"Is that what this is about? You don't feel safe?"

She ran her finger across his chest in little curlicues. "You always make me safe, but I get the impression you don't feel the same. I love you, John. If I want it and it would solve our problems, why not do it?"

"What about having children? I can't get you pregnant, but there is in vitro fertilization. Or you may decide later you'd rather be with someone…human." And if that thought didn't slice and dice his heart. "But once you turn, you won't be able to conceive."

She turned away and drew her legs up. Had he just given her a reason to leave him? Most likely, he'd ripped her heart with memories of her lost child.

He pulled her back toward him and found her crying. The pain in her face broke his heart. "I'm sorry. I didn't mean to hurt you."

"There was a time when I wanted children more than anything," she said quietly, avoiding John's gaze while she swiped at her tears. "But Steven took that away from me."

"Yes, I know you lost the baby, and I am sorry for your loss, but that doesn't mean—"

She shook her head. "That's not what I mean." The tears started falling again. She laid her head on his shoulder and spoke softly, "I'm damaged. I can't… I can't have children."

He closed his eyes. Rage boiled inside him. That man had done nothing but hurt her from the day they met. "I knew I should have killed him."

Sarah took his head into her hands, forcing him to look at her. "No, John. You're not that man and Steven's not worth it. Haven't you told me that a hundred times? But don't you see? It doesn't matter anymore. I want to be with you now. I want to be with you forever."

Anger ate at his insides and he could think of nothing but the sheer pleasure he would feel squeezing the life out of Steven. Sarah was right, though. He might be able to get away with the crime, but not at the expense of losing her.

She swung one leg over his body, startling him. After pushing him back down onto the mattress, she laid her head on his chest and rubbed his arms and shoulders. The massage helped lift the rage out of his system. This wasn't right. He should be consoling her, not the other way around. When she planted little kisses on his chest, he hugged her tight. She'd known exactly what he needed. He never wanted to let her go, but could he turn her?

"I understand what you're saying."

She tensed in his arms. "I see a 'but' in your future."

He couldn't resist and grabbed her ass. "Yes, and it's a very nice butt."

She laughed and swatted his hand away. "Stop it. You know what I meant."

"Yes, I know what you meant. *But...* I need you to wait. I don't know if I could stand it if you came to hate me."

She struggled to sit up so he loosened his hold. "I don't think I could ever hate you, John."

"Stranger things have happened."

"Fine. How much time are you talking about?"

"How about a year? Could you wait a year? If, after you've learned everything, you still feel the same way, I'll get permission." And he hoped for her sake she would have changed her mind by then.

"Get? But I'm giving you my permission."

He smiled. "I know, but I need the Committee's permission, too."

"How come?"

"Because the Committee doesn't want just anyone to be a vampire and in order to keep control of the population, rules have been put in place. They investigate all turnings to make sure everyone agrees and also to make sure the turnee is...worthy. Most of the time it's just a formality, but if there's any doubt, the Committee will know and disapprove the turning."

And wouldn't there be plenty of doubt where Sarah was concerned? It wasn't like anyone could get into her head. True, they would probably jump at the chance to have her turn, but what would happen if after they still couldn't read her thoughts? A vampire who couldn't be read could be a dangerous vampire. But that was an issue he'd worry about later. If it even became an issue.

She chewed her bottom lip and looked down, furrowing her forehead in thought. "A year, huh?" She placed her hands on her hips. "You know, I could get killed in a year. Hell, I'd be dead now if you didn't interfere that first time. Why should I wait?"

He sat up to meet her and smoothed the hair away from her face. "Because I'm asking? I know what the risks are, but aren't you the one who wanted to take it slow in the first place? I'm not going anywhere, Sarah."

Breathing heavily through her nose, she clenched her jaw and thinned her lips. Had he screwed it all up?

Finally she relaxed, leaned forward, and hugged him. "Okay John, I'll wait a year."

Relief flooded him and muscles he hadn't realized were clenched were now relaxed. This was a fight he didn't want because he couldn't win it in the end. Hugging her tight against him, he smiled. "Thank you."

Bending his head down, he nuzzled her and inhaled her sweet scent. While he was content with holding her, she kissed and nibbled his neck, a sensitive spot for him.

"John?" she said between kisses.

"Yes?" Her kisses sent a trail of heat all the way to his loins.

"That last time we made love, did I see your fangs pop out?"

She was still kissing and nibbling his neck, and with each kiss and nibble his penis became stiffer. She must feel it since she was sitting right on top of it, but her question caught him off guard and his desire slackened a bit. If she'd only seen them the last time they made love, he must have done a pretty good job of hiding them. Still, he wished she hadn't noticed at all. "You might have, why?"

He moved his head to see her, but she held him close and continued her kissing and nibbling.

"Is it sexual? Biting, I mean. Does making love to me cause you to want to bite me?"

Was she curious or concerned? He couldn't tell with her anymore. In fact, he was finding it hard to talk—her mouth was driving him nuts. "I was told it's sexual. But I promise. I won't lose control."

"You don't know, then? You've never done it?"

She nibbled on his ear and he almost jumped off the bed. "You're my first."

She pushed back and gaped at him. "I'm your first?"

Thank goodness she'd stopped. He wasn't sure he'd be able to control himself much longer. Clear-headed once again, he nodded. "Since turning into a vampire, yes."

She seemed to consider his statement for a while then asked, "Were you told if I would I enjoy it?"

Okay, it was curiosity and not concern. "What is it Sarah, what are you asking?"

"Don't get me wrong, everything with you has been beyond my wildest dreams. But if biting me, taking my blood, makes it better, I want you to do it. Are you willing?" She chewed her bottom lip and raised her eyebrows in the cutest smile he'd ever seen.

For as long as she lived, he would probably never understand her. He'd love nothing more than to experience that particular mixture, not to mention sampling a larger portion of her wonderful blood, but he never thought she'd be the one to bring it up. Of course, he didn't think she'd bring up turning, either.

"I only have Perry's word on this, and we both know how he is, but he told me that biting while making love creates a bond like nothing else. That he never manipulated their minds, that they never knew he bit them, and that he left them all extremely satisfied." John chuckled. "His words, not mine. I don't know how much of it to believe, but yeah, if you're willing, I'm willing."

"Okay, then." She promptly jumped off him and headed for the bathroom.

He stared at her retreating body. What the hell had happened?

\* \* \* \*

Sarah opened the cabinet beside the tub and ran her hand over the fluffy white towels. Pretty, but not what she needed for The

Bite, an event she'd just now named because when she thought back on this night—and she was sure she would—she wanted a name for it.

The first time she had spotted John's fangs, she was curious what set them off. The second time, she knew. It gave her a thrill knowing she could make him lose control like that.

She opened the cabinet under the sink. Bingo. Smiling, she grabbed the bottle and closed the door.

If biting made sex better, why not do it in the tub? The thing was definitely large enough and she'd already pictured them making love in the water. Now she could add biting to the mix. Or, rather, The Bite. Oh yeah.

She turned on the faucet and poured in a small amount of bubble bath. The flowery scent drifted from the heat of the water. Perfect.

"What are you doing?" John asked from the bedroom.

He was being polite in not following her, she was sure of it. She silently laughed, remembering his expression when she'd left him sitting on the bed. He'd been ready to bite her then. Well, it wouldn't take that long to get him back in the mood.

Heck, was he ever out of the mood?

She strolled to the door and peered around the corner. John was still sitting where she'd left him and smiled when he saw her. "Are you coming back?" he asked.

Shaking her head, she said, "Nope, you're coming here. Remember that big tub?"

He leaped off the bed. "We're taking a bath?"

She eyed his erection. Nope, never out of the mood. Ah, to be a vampire. Somehow she would get him to move that year up several months.

Once the tub filled, Sarah eased herself into the warm, bubbly water. Leaning against one end, she waited as John entered, facing her. He really was unbelievable. She admired the muscles in his chest and arms and loved the solidness when she caressed them. A trail of hair traveled down his flat stomach to his manhood. John naked was a wonderful sight indeed.

But, right now she wanted more than a view. She leaned forward and kissed him on the mouth, slipping her tongue inside. He sucked on it and that did it for her. She became wet and it had nothing to do with the bathwater. He pushed her back against the tub and slowly caressed her breasts with his hands. When he played with her nipples, passion ignited and she moaned into his mouth.

Whoa. Who was turning who on? Damn, if she didn't get those fangs to show, she might come before he bit her and she didn't want that. Time to get to work. She kissed her way to his neck and nibbled on his ear. He gasped. Much better.

"Are you ready?" he asked breathless against her ear.

Afraid to ruin the mood with a raspy voice, she nodded. She held onto his shoulders in case the pain caused her to grab.

John nuzzled her neck and wrapped his arms around her, holding her still. Loving the way he embraced her and knowing he'd never really hurt her, she relaxed a little. He entered her with a thrust and bit down. She gasped, expecting pain but floating in unadulterated bliss. She arched up to meet him as every muscle clenched in need.

A wonderful sense of warmth spread throughout her. With each thrust, something amazingly tight wrapped around a body part she couldn't possibly own. But the best part of this experience was the delicious sweet-coppery flavor filling her mouth. She wanted more.

Was she feeling his pleasure, too? Damn, it felt oh so goood. She hovered over the edge of an orgasm and rode it as long as she could.

When the first shudder hit her, it came from both inside and out, squeezing and being squeezed, more intense than she'd ever experienced. She grabbed him tighter as both orgasms hit her. It was more than her poor mind could handle.

\* \* \* \*

John moaned. He should stop feeding, but he was so close to coming. Plus, he'd never tasted anything so sweet, so intense. He just wanted a little more.

Sarah shuddered as she came, her contractions the spark to ignite his own orgasm. Wave after wave of pleasure washed over him. Would it ever end? He hoped it wouldn't.

Her scream cleared his mind. Damn it. Was he still drawing her blood? He released her neck and licked the site, healing the holes. She lay limp in his arms.

"Sarah?"

No response. What had he done? How much had he taken? Oh God.

He tapped her face. "Sarah! Sarah! Wake up!"

Her eyes flickered opened and she trembled. Oh thank God. Seeing her awake brought him some relief.

"Are you okay?"

She grabbed onto his shoulders as her breathing came out in bursts. "Yes, I think so. Wow! Did you feel that? How great was that, huh?"

He wasn't feeling so great. He'd thought he'd killed her. "Are you sure? You were out for a while."

"How long?"

Much too long. "Long enough. Are you dizzy?"

She leaned back against the tub. "Well, yeah, a little, but I figured it was from the sex. Didn't you feel what I felt?"

The sex was phenomenal, but he wouldn't admit that. "I don't know what I felt. But when you screamed and passed out... Well, let's just say you scared the crap out of me."

She caressed his face and kissed him lightly on the lips. "I'm so sorry. But you don't have to worry. I'm fine. Deliriously, wonderfully, fine." She picked up the washcloth and held it out. "Here. Why don't you clean me up?"

She did seem rather euphoric. But also pale. He'd lost control, taken too much and she was paying the price. He could never do it again. He would never do it again. Not if it put her life in danger.

\* \* \* \*

The buzz from The Bite still thrummed through Sarah's body. Okay, *now* she'd had the best sex ever. Too bad she'd scared John. The poor man really looked frazzled.

He washed her as if she were a delicate piece of glass and stared at her face the whole time. Was he afraid she'd suddenly pass out or something? Yeah, she felt a little weak, but she'd felt worse after giving blood.

After he finished washing her, she took the cloth and worked on him. But her wrist felt as if someone had tied a fifty-pound weight around it. Holding up her arm became difficult.

"That's it. We're done here." John lifted her with ease and sat her on the edge. He pulled one of the fluffy towels from the cabinet, but when she reached for it, he pushed her hands aside and promptly dried her off.

"I'm okay."

He grunted in response.

She stood and he wrapped the towel around her. The room tilted to one side and she grabbed onto his arm for support. Okay, so maybe she was a little dizzy. That was all the invitation he needed. He picked her up and carried her to the bed.

He turned a deaf ear to her protests.

"Shit," he said. "The bags are still in the car." He found his jeans on the floor and pulled them on. "I'll be right back. Don't move."

He was such a worrywart. She grabbed his arm. "Can you bring me a brush and mirror before you go?"

He went back into the bathroom. She didn't really need to brush her hair, well, maybe she did, but she was curious about her neck. He'd sucked on it long enough.

When he returned with the items, she lifted the mirror and examined where he'd bitten—flawless. "Dang, John. You do good work."

"It's all part of what I am," he grunted.

The frown on his face worried her. "John? I'm okay. Really."

Her words didn't seem to comfort him. He leaned over and kissed her forehead. "Please stay in bed. After I get the suitcases, I'll bring you up something to eat."

This wasn't exactly how she'd thought the night—or morning—would end, but she would do anything to ease his mind. "I promise I won't go anywhere."

He relaxed and a thin smile appeared on his face. Then he was gone.

After brushing out her hair, she lay back on the mattress. Her eyelids kept closing, but she fought sleep. Maybe he had taken too much blood, but she certainly wasn't going to admit that. It might have helped if she'd eaten beforehand. Or had taken vitamins. Next time she would be more prepared. She smiled. Oh yeah, if she had any say, there would be a next time.

Getting him to agree would be the challenge.

# Chapter 26

"I said no, and I mean it."

"I'm sorry, John." Crap. Sarah stood in the breakfast nook pouting while John stormed into the family room. She'd patiently waited until Sunday morning before broaching the subject of biting. She hadn't expected his anger.

He hadn't touched her since The Bite, not exactly the way she wanted to remember the event. Granted, she'd slept for nearly ten hours after their bath and that was without a meal, which he hadn't woken her for. So waking up weak, groggy, and with a major headache only fortified his stance and made her job even harder.

She sat beside him on the couch, thankful he didn't get up and walk away. "I didn't mean to upset you."

He fiddled with a loose thread on the cushion. "I know you didn't. Do you want to watch a movie?"

Too bad he didn't ask *what* she wanted to do, not that he'd agree to it anyway. Somehow she'd get him in the mood. She just wouldn't bring up biting, not until later anyway.

"Maybe after breakfast." If she ate, he'd have to notice she was better.

For a vampire, he'd certainly stocked the kitchen well: frozen dinners, canned soup, even her favorite cereal. Eating in front of him was still the pits, but if it got him to relax, she'd do it. She grabbed a bowl and filled it.

John followed and, leaning against the counter, picked up the box and studied it. "I still don't know how you can eat this stuff."

Without a dining set in the house, she stood at the counter and ate. "It's filling and has all the vitamins I need. If you don't want me to eat it, why'd you get it?"

"I got it because you like it."

She hoped she hadn't ruined the best weekend ever by sleeping through most of it. As she chowed down, questions about his eating habits came to mind. She would eventually become a vampire so there were some things she should know.

"John, how often do you eat?"

Putting the box down, he answered, "If I didn't expend much energy or get injured, every other night." He smiled. "Of course, when we started dating, I overfed, thinking I would lose control if I didn't, but that never happened."

"Not even once?"

He shook his head. "Nope. I had my own misconceptions of what a vampire might do in a relationship. It's what kept me isolated for so long. Seems I was worried about nothing." He grabbed the counter and stared at her intently. "Just because my fangs extend doesn't mean I have this uncontrollable urge to bite."

Message received. Too bad, though. It would have been a way around his refusals.

"How much do you take?"

"Not much. Less than a pint. If I'm injured, I'll need more, so then I would find another donor. I won't put someone's life in danger because of my needs."

Is that what he thought? That he'd put her life in danger? Somehow she'd show him he was wrong. "So when you turn me, I won't be some raving monster, ready to devour anyone I see?"

He smiled. "No. *If* you are turned, that won't happen. I would be with you to help."

She'd said when. He'd said if. She needed him to say when, because it would be when. She would be a vampire. But, first things first. At least she'd made him smile. After a few more spoonfuls of cereal, she risked the next question. "Have you gone out since we got here, or did you get enough from me?"

He frowned at her question and looked away. So much for the smile. Maybe she should have her head examined.

"No, I haven't gone out since we got here and yes, I did get enough from you. Can we change the subject now?"

Crap. She was making him angry again. That was not conducive to lovemaking. "Sure. Do you really want to watch another movie or are you in the mood to play one of your video games?"

His face lit up as his frown curved into a smile. "You'd really play a video game?"

That was much better. Video games would get him to relax and have some fun. "Yeah, I'd play a game. They aren't hard, are they?"

* * * *

First John crushed her in video bowling, then he flew past her in video golf, all while the stereo blasted. Sarah might be a horrible gamer, but she loved her music and, after inquiring whether or not his ears could handle it, enjoyed it loud. John didn't care, he'd learned to adjust his hearing long ago. Whatever made her happy, made him happy. Well, most things, anyway.

He couldn't believe she still wanted him to bite her. But how could he explain how dangerous it was without scaring her away? Eventually, he'd get her to understand or she'd grow tired of asking.

Would they ever have fun again after that unfortunate incident? Because of him she'd nearly died. He wouldn't risk making love for fear of injuring her further. Staying away was damn hard, though. He missed her touch, her kisses. But her health was more important.

Although... She was looking a lot healthier now. Her color had improved from a ghastly pale to a nice pink, probably from eating regularly since waking. And she seemed energized, which she expended by dancing between her golf turns. Maybe after lunch he could test the waters, so to speak. He didn't want this weekend to end on a downer.

Sarah had just finished putting on the eighteenth green when the music changed to Clash's "Rock the Casbah." She spun toward him and tossed the controller his way. While gyrating her hips, she caressed the curves of her body.

He sat on the couch and stared. What should he do? Should he get up and join her or enjoy the view? Before he could decide, she unbuttoned the first three buttons of her blouse.

He obtained a full-blown hard-on and it only took two seconds. There was testing the waters and then there was testing the waters.

"What are you doing?"

187

"Hush. I'm dancing. You sit there and relax." She swiveled her hips to the music and unbuttoned another button.

Relax? Was she nuts? He'd been trying to do that ever since she'd passed out, and had nearly succeeded. But with her ass moving every which way and her hands caressing those luscious breasts of hers, he was anything but relaxed. He was turned on so high he could probably sing soprano.

The remaining buttons came undone and she slipped the blouse off her shoulders. Ah man, she wore the pink, lacey bra. When he'd first spotted that thing in her bag, he couldn't wait to see her in it. She looked better than he imagined.

Moving to the music, she shimmied the blouse behind her, as if she were drying off her back, shaking her breasts in the process. Damn. If she wanted sex, he'd be more than happy to oblige. He stood.

She pointed to the couch. "Down."

Her bossy voice made her hotter. He plopped back onto the couch, letting gravity do its job. Okay, so she had an agenda. She'd better get a move on because he wasn't sure he could wait much longer. Bossy or no bossy.

She twirled the blouse over her head and threw it at him. It landed at his feet, but he didn't reach for it. He couldn't stop staring. She gyrated to the music while she seductively slid her hands from her hips to her belly and unbuttoned her jeans.

She slid them down her legs, slow and sensual. Ah, geez. The panties matched the bra. He might have groaned. God, she was beautiful.

She tossed the jeans somewhere and danced over to him. Standing in her underwear and swaying her hips, she extended her hand. It took his frazzled mind a moment to catch on. Finally. He placed his hand in hers and rose.

That pleasant rush of warmth he'd missed the past day was mixed with an unexpected electric jolt. His heart raced.

She stilled with her eyes closed and mouth smiling. "Nice."

It was more than nice. Try intense. He moved in closer, but she came out of her mini-trance and pulled him to the middle of the room.

"Stay."

Like an obedient dog, he obeyed, if only to see what she had in mind. Because what he had in mind had nothing to do with dancing and a whole lot to do with them naked on the floor. Hell, right now they wouldn't even have to be naked, only the important parts.

She danced her way behind him, her fingers playing across his stomach and sides. The T-shirt came free from his jeans, but she couldn't remove it without his help. He obliged by slipping it over his head and tossing it aside. She lightly kissed his back, sending little heat waves with each touch, while her fingers burned a path over his nipples. Forget about her agenda. He spun around. She licked a nipple and grabbed his ass, grinding herself into him. A penis couldn't explode, but she was certainly testing that theory.

She offered her back and danced up and down against him, removing her bra and panties in the process. The bones in his legs decided to take a vacation. He grabbed her shoulders, partly for balance, but mostly to start in toward her breasts. She shrugged free, twirled around, and wagged her finger at him.

Actually wagged her finger! What the hell?

She gripped his waistband and tugged the button free. All right. Now she was getting somewhere. He closed his eyes and concentrated on breathing while she worked the jeans over his aching, extended member and off his legs. When she came back up, he'd take over, no more waiting.

But instead of coming up for more dancing or whatever, she wrapped her warm, moist mouth around his cock. He gasped as pleasure, heat, and a little buzz shot through his groin. She stroked him with her tongue as if she knew exactly what he enjoyed and if she wasn't careful, she would end up with a present. While her mouth was better than nice, it wasn't enough.

She stopped to catch her breath, and damn, he had to, also, but he took that opportunity and pulled her to her feet.

"Hey, I'm not done."

"The hell you're not." He lifted her by her hips. "Hold on."

She took his meaning right away and put her arms around his neck and her legs around his body. He found his target and thrust into her. Hot. Moist. Tight. Heaven. Oh yes, he was in heaven.

"Sweet Jesus!" she exclaimed as she grabbed onto his back and dug in. "I'm a sex junkie!"

He almost laughed at her remark because she voiced his words exactly, but once he entered her, her excitement seemed to mix in with his own, creating a mental overload. That wonderful fullness he'd felt when he bit her returned. Just like she knew where to suck earlier, he knew where to rub. She arched her head back and moaned.

But he wasn't biting her now. Was this some lasting affect or a permanent event? Whatever, he was taking advantage.

He kissed her, savoring the flavor he'd missed. What the hell was wrong with him, staying away like he had? She was fine. She was more than fine. She was his.

Each thrust brought him double waves of pleasure. Each thrust brought his release closer. Then she clenched and it was as if he felt it both ways. The sensation took him over the edge. They climaxed almost simultaneously.

She screamed and went limp.

"Sarah?" He held her up, but the intense orgasm drained him quicker than he anticipated. A cramp skittered across his belly. He stumbled and her dead weight pulled him forward. He fell to his knees.

Suddenly conscious, she grabbed his shoulders, but the effort was late. Instead of falling back on his haunches, he continued going forward. He extended one arm to brace their fall while holding her with the other. Once his free hand hit the floor, he slowly lowered her, ending up on his hands and knees. He desperately sought air. The last time he had felt this drained, she had stabbed him.

"Oh, shit!"

"What is it? Are you alright?" Sarah cupped his face. "You look paler than usual. Did I do something wrong?"

He wished he could alleviate her fears. But he needed blood and it was at least five hours until sunset. If he let on… Shit! She'd want to help. He couldn't let her do that.

"I'm okay. I just need to get my breath. I guess I'm not used to all this activity." And sex burned more energy than he'd imagined. Why hadn't Perry ever mentioned that? "What about you? You pass out again?"

She grinned. "Maybe. It was pretty intense, don't you think? But you weren't biting me, so you can't blame it on that."

No, he couldn't. And he shouldn't be in such dire straits if he had taken enough earlier. So maybe he had miscalculated and she'd passed out for other reasons. Like, a massive orgasm. Didn't mean he would feed from her again.

Sarah scrambled out from under him. "What can I do?"

John rolled onto his back as a cramp rippled across his stomach. He cringed. Ah, shit. Maybe if he lay still, he could keep the pain away and the worry off her face. "There's nothing you can do. Give me a few minutes." Like, maybe three hundred.

"You need blood, don't you? You lied when you said you got enough."

"I didn't lie, it was a valid assumption." He *so* did not want to get into that conversation. "Let me rest awhile. I'll be okay." Vagueness wasn't lying, was it? He would be okay, as soon as he fed.

She leaned in close, concern marring her beautiful features. Her scent hit him hard, though, and his fangs extended. What was that bit about not having an uncontrollable need to bite? Yeah, that worked for sex. For food, not so much. He couldn't very well tell her to back off without her being suspicious. Shit.

"John, I want to help. Take some blood from me." She waved her arm over his face.

He gently pushed her away. "I'm not going to feed off you, Sarah. I'll be okay. I can wait."

"You'd rather have a stranger than me?" Tears formed in her eyes.

Damn it. They were going to have this conversation whether he liked it or not. "I can control myself with a stranger. I don't know how much control I have with you. Okay?"

With concentration, he managed to retract his fangs. Slowly, he raised himself to a sitting position. Maybe that would ease her fears.

"Oh." She sat back looking defeated, but clearly thinking. While glancing about the room, she gnawed on her fingers. It was fascinating watching her while she figured out a solution.

Her face lit up. "I could order a pizza!" She sprang to her feet and started searching the room.

What the hell was she thinking? "I hate to tell you this, but I don't need a pizza," he said, trying to sound lighthearted.

Uncomfortable sitting there exposed, he grabbed his jeans. He was putting them on when she passed by, still naked as ever, still sexy as ever. "Sarah...please get dressed."

She looked down as if she'd forgotten she was walking around nude. "Oh, sorry." She bent over and picked up his T-shirt. She didn't look any less sexy wearing his shirt, but it was better than nothing.

Her searching was driving him nuts. "What are you looking for?"

"The phone and a phone book."

"You'd be looking forever, then. I don't have either. I have my cell, who do you need to call?"

"I need to call a pizza place, but I don't know what's nearby. Oh, the computer!" She ran over to it. "Do you think you can come over here? I don't know which address is closest, since I have no idea where we are."

With speed a turtle would easily beat, he managed an upright position and headed toward the computer. The jaunt exhausted him and he placed his hands on his knees. "Why are we ordering a pizza?"

"So you can feed on the delivery person."

"What?"

"So you can feed on the delivery person." She enunciated each word as if he were an imbecile. Hell, maybe he was. His mind certainly wasn't working correctly.

"If I order a pizza to be delivered, then I'll have the delivery person come inside while I get their money. While he...or she, is here, you do your thing." She looked up at him with hope in her eyes. "That would work, wouldn't it?"

Again, he was amazed with the way her mind worked. He kissed the top of her head. "Yeah that would work."

And to think he was ready to sit in agony for five hours.

\* \* \* \*

One large ham and pineapple pizza, her favorite. Sarah would have preferred a small, or even a medium, but there was a minimum delivery amount. She clicked on the order button. They'd better send a guy. If they sent a pretty girl... Well, she wouldn't think about it.

John sure could be grumpy when he was hungry. And while it stung he wouldn't consider feeding from her, she understood why. Didn't mean she liked it any, or that she believed it. He believed it, and that's all that mattered right now.

As much as it pained her to see him suffer, in a way it made him more human. Or maybe all men were grumpy when they didn't feel well, whether they be vampire or not. And he was clearly uncomfortable with her walking around in his tee, so before he got more upset with her, she went upstairs and fetched her robe as well as a shirt for him. Not that she wanted to cover that luscious chest of his, but maybe it would make him feel better. When she returned to the family room, John was shaking his head.

"What now?" She handed him the shirt.

"I thought you were going to get dressed," he grumbled.

Yep, still cranky. Maybe it wasn't the tee after all. "I don't want to get dressed yet. I'm hoping to take a shower later. What's wrong with my robe?" He'd seen her in it before and never said anything.

"Nothing." After putting the shirt on, he leaned back against the cushions and closed his eyes.

Since he was moving rather sluggishly, the plan was to wait in the living room. She walked up and nudged his knee. When he opened his eyes, she grabbed his elbow.

He shook her off. "I don't need any help. I can do it myself."

Except his idea of doing it himself meant he couldn't.

Standing there with hands on her hips, she declared, "John Pennington, stop acting macho and let me help you!"

He raised his eyebrows. A small grimace formed on his face. "Sorry. You're right." He reached out. "Would you help me up, please?"

Sarah put his arm around her shoulder and they slowly made it to the living room. It was nice feeling needed for a change.

Not fifteen minutes later, the doorbell rang and she jumped up nervously. He nodded to let the person in. Of course, let him in. What the heck was she thinking? She opened the door. The cold air whipped inside and the light nearly blinded her. Too long since she'd seen the sun and strangely she hadn't missed it. Clutching the robe together, she waited a moment for her eyes to adjust. A young man stood on the porch. She let out a relieved breath. Thank God.

The pizza boy pulled a flat box out of a padded case and handed it to her. The aroma of Italian seasonings teased her nose and caused her stomach to rumble. She hadn't thought she was hungry, but damn, that thing smelled delicious.

"Can you come in while I get my purse?" She closed the door when he came inside.

"Don't you like the light?"

"Not really." She placed the pizza on the stairs and picked up her purse. Before she could ask how much she owed, his eyes glazed over and he stepped toward John in a jerky fashion. Talk about cool. Would she be able to do that when she became a vampire?

"Sarah, do you mind?" John asked her, but kept his eyes on the boy.

She stared at John. What? He wanted her to leave? "Can't I watch?"

"I'd rather you didn't. Just take the pizza and go."

"But you always watch me eat. Why can't I watch you?"

Pizza Boy stopped walking. "You owe me fifteen dollars."

John's eyes widened in surprise. The kid's eyes glazed over once again. "I can't argue with you and control him at the same time. Not in my weakened state. Please go."

"But John, how am I going to understand if you—"

"Now!"

His voice reverberated throughout the whole house and she took a step back. A lump formed in her throat and her nose tickled. He'd never yelled at her like that before, not even when she might have deserved it. She didn't deserve this. Tears formed as she threw her purse down, spilling the contents. "Don't forget to pay him," she spat, stomping up the stairs. "He deserves a big tip, too."

She ran inside her room, slammed the door, and hurled herself on the bed. Oh God. What had she done? She'd yelled at John. Yelled at him! Why couldn't she just keep her mouth shut?

# Chapter 27

*"The only thing you'll remember is coming in, getting paid, and leaving."*
John sent a mental image fortifying his command.

The delivery boy stuffed the money in his pocket—twenty bucks seemed generous enough, any more might look suspicious—and let himself out while John hid in the living room. As soon as the door shut, he went to the foot of the stairs and looked up.

He rubbed his jaw. How badly had he screwed things up? Losing control of the boy had been the final straw and he'd snapped. He hadn't meant to yell, it just came out. The scared and hurt look on her face stabbed him deeply and if he hadn't been in dire needs, he would have stopped her from storming away. It appeared he had some groveling ahead of him.

After putting her purse right and placing the pizza on the counter, he took the stairs two at a time and stopped at the door. He reached for the knob, but prudence told him to knock.

No answer. Well, he'd warned her. He opened the door.

Her scent was everywhere, but no sign of Sarah. He checked the bathroom. Nope. Closet empty, too. Where could she have gone? The drapes in the corner moved. "Sarah?"

She didn't answer, but she didn't have to. She hitched her breath. As he approached the window, her scent became stronger. "I know you're behind the curtains. Come out please."

"Not yet," she said with a tremble in her voice.

"Please. I need to see you."

He held the thick material in his hand, ready to expose her.

195

"Stop!" she said and pulled the drapes together. "Some of the foil is loose."

He released the fabric as if it burned and dashed into the bathroom. His heart pounded to be free. Damn, he'd come close. To what, he didn't know. He didn't want to know.

"Are you away from the window?" she asked.

"Yes." He shut the door. No light had seeped through the curtains—he would have noticed that right away. But how easy would it have been for her to expose him to the sun? If she were truly angry... No, no. She wasn't like that.

"It's safe now," she said.

He slowly opened the door and peeked through the crack. Not that he didn't trust her, but she might have left a gap in the drapes unintentionally. She stood beside the windows facing the wall, head bent forward. The only light came from the bedside lamp. The curtains held.

"I'm sorry I yelled," she said. "I didn't mean it. It won't happen again."

Ah, shit. He should have known what his yelling would accomplish. She was probably waiting for the fists to fly. God damned Steven. "Sweetie, look at me."

She didn't move. He took a chair and pulled it beside her. The scent of her fear wafted toward him as he took a seat. It killed him that he still threatened her, not because he was a vampire, but because he was a man. He hooked his index finger around her pinky. She jerked back, but he held on and tugged. "Come here."

Slowly, she let him pull her into his lap, but she wouldn't look at him. Her discomfort nearly broke his heart.

"You have nothing to apologize for," he said. "You had every reason to be mad at me. I wasn't prepared for your curiosity and I took it out on you, and that's no excuse. I'm sorry, Sarah. I had no right to yell at you the way I did."

Slowly she turned her head toward him, her eyes glistening with tears. "You're not mad at me?"

"If I were, what do you think would happen?"

She stared down at her hands.

"I would never hit you," he said as he lifted her chin. "Never."

She fell against him and put her arms around his neck. Tears trickled onto his shoulder, wetting his shirt, but he didn't think they were from sadness. Besides smelling her fear or anger, he'd never been able to read her emotions, but for some strange reason he could feel her relief. She transferred it when they touched. He closed his eyes and sighed as he hugged her.

She buried her head in the crook of his neck. "Will I ever be able to watch?"

And now they were back to the issue at hand. Feeding had never been sexual. He bit, he ate, and that was that. But since the unfortunate event? Yeah, just thinking about biting her stirred his groin. What would happen if she watched him feed? Would he get off on that? He shuddered at the thought.

He wouldn't lie to her, but telling the whole truth wasn't an option, either. Not until he learned more. "You're going to have to give me time to get used to the idea."

She lifted her head and sniffled. The tears caused her eyes to become a brilliant green and made her nose red. She was adorable. "You don't like doing it, do you?"

She was also observant. Now he was the one to look away.

"You don't like being a vampire?"

"It wasn't the choice I would have made."

She played with the hair behind his ear. "I know, but if you weren't a vampire, I'd have never met you."

He held her face and heat blazed a trail to his heart. "Ah, Sweetie. I can't imagine life without you, either."

He kissed her softly, but when she ran her fingers through his hair, his penis sprang to life and his fangs emerged. Damn. He broke their kiss and looked away.

She held his head. "Let me see them."

Oh great, just what he needed.

Gently prying his upper lip, she exposed his teeth then ran her thumbs over the points.

He pulled away before he could prick her. Sure, he'd eaten and he probably wouldn't attack her, but why test that theory? "Be careful."

"They're not so bad, John. You make them seem so much bigger than they are."

They sure as hell felt huge. Her ministrations and his fear were enough of a distraction—his erection deflated and his fangs retracted.

Her eyes widened. "That is so cool. I can't wait until I have a pair. Then I could bite you."

Bite? He swallowed and his pulse quickened.

She raised her eyebrows and cocked her head. "Why do I think you'd like that?"

Before he could answer, she straddled him, lowered her head, and placed her moist mouth on his neck. A blaze of heat spread from the contact. She bit down. Good God. He jerked upward as his fangs emerged and his erection returned with a vengeance. Did she know all his sensitive zones?

His jeans were the only thing between him and heaven. She hadn't broken the skin, but she continued gripping his neck while she freed his cock. He must be crazy letting her do this. Hadn't he nearly passed out the last time? She certainly had.

She touched him and he almost exploded. He arched his back and grabbed her hips. She opened her mouth long enough to say, "I want you in me."

Denying her anything was impossible.

\* \* \* \*

The sun had set, putting an end to their little vacation away from reality. If only she could stay in John's bed. If only they knew who had it out for him. If only she was a vampire. Because if she were a vampire, she was pretty sure she wouldn't have to worry about number one and number two.

Sarah tidied up the family room while John went upstairs to fetch their bags. He still looked paler than usual, no thanks to her. She had finally gotten him fed and what did she do? She nearly attacked the man. Not her proudest moment, but damn, he brought it out in her.

She *was* a sex junkie, provided the sex was with John.

When he returned, she stood and reached for her coat and scarf. "Ready?"

"No, not yet. Would you sit down, please?"

She did as he asked. "Everything okay?"

He nodded and sat beside her. "Everything's fine. I have something I want to give you." He took her hand, palm up, and placed a gold chain in it. "My father gave this to my mother and I would like you to have it."

A charm looped through the chain. Three teardrop shapes interlocking, each in a different shade of gold: rose, white, and yellow. She held it up and let it dangle. "Oh, John. It's beautiful."

"It's a trinity knot. The white stands for devotion, the rose for true love, and the yellow for passion. It's how my father felt about my mother, and it's how I feel about you." He took it and placed it around her neck.

She fingered the charm. "Are you sure? I mean, it was your mother's."

"And she intended for it to be worn by the woman I chose."

Somehow, it comforted her, knowing John would always be with her. "Thank you. I'm never taking it off."

"I love you." His whispered breath caressed her ear and sent pleasurable shivers through her body.

She hugged him tightly. Ah, he felt so good in her arms, smelled good, too. The mix of soap and man got her juices flowing. She leaned back and gave him a light kiss. "What am I going to do?"

He looked at her curiously. "What do you mean?"

"I'm hopelessly in love with you and I want you all the time. I wasn't kidding earlier when I said I was a sex junkie. That's what I feel like when I'm with you."

He chuckled. "You're not alone. I feel the same way."

"Do you think it will last? This strange connection when we touch?" Although, that last time wasn't quite as intense as the first. She had still shared his experience, but it had been fuzzy, not sharp. And she hadn't passed out. Maybe she was getting used to it, or she was better prepared.

"Considering I have no idea why it happened, I can't say. I suppose I can ask Perry the next time I see him."

"Perry?" Just the mention of his name put cold water on her libido. "Isn't there anyone else you're friends with?"

John kissed the top of her head and chuckled. "Come on, let's get you home." He helped her up as he stood.

She didn't want to go home, not unless he was there, too. What if Steven came back? Or Ray? And if a vampire was controlling those two, how could she fight them? Somehow, she'd get John to spend the night.

# Chapter 28

Pink and orange clouds hovered over the eastern horizon as if on fire, and John would be one ball of it if he didn't get his ass in gear. He rushed cautiously down the streets, sticking beside the buildings, his dark clothes a useless camouflage as dawn approached and lit up the area. So he not only had to avoid the sun, he had to avoid any onlookers. Guess that was what he got for being greedy.

When Sarah had asked him to spend the night, he'd had no problem obliging. It beat camping outside, which he would have done otherwise. He had planned to leave well before sunrise, but six turned to seven and then her alarm went off. He had to stay and say good morning, right? One kiss led to another and then another until she practically pushed him out the door. At least one of them had some sense.

Traffic became heavier, forcing him into a normal gait. By the time he arrived at Wings, his heart was racing and not from exertion. He quickly unlocked the door and entered the stairwell. The door shut with a slam as he leaned against it in relief. Damn, he'd cut that close.

He trudged up the stairs as emptiness settled over him. Day would be damn lonely without her. Playing games would pass the time, but he preferred playing with her. This past weekend had shown him what he could have. He still wouldn't rush her, though. She needed to understand what she was getting in to. If after the year, she still wished to be a vampire with him, then his life would be complete.

When he reached the landing, he froze. Someone had left his apartment door ajar. What the hell? He sniffed the air and relaxed. Damn man had nearly given him a heart attack. He opened the door to Perry lounging on the couch, playing a video game.

"Hey, Johnny!" Perry said, sitting up. "About time you got home. Couldn't stay away from the little lady, huh?"

"What are you doing here? Have you learned something new?" Because, truly, the man wouldn't think of calling with news that important.

"Not yet. Came to talk, but you weren't here, so I let myself in through the bedroom window."

So if Perry came in through the window... "Why was the door open?"

"I left it open for you."

Sometimes it wasn't worth the bother trying to understand Perry.

John shut the door and tossed his coat and keys on the counter. Perry didn't usually stay during the day—claimed John would kill him with boredom—now he was stuck. Maybe the day wouldn't be so bad after all. "What did you want to talk about?"

"Just curious about how your weekend went, that's if you're willing to kiss and tell as they say. But man, how come you never told me about Lori? Friday night turned out better than I expected. I could easily see her again. Maybe we could double-date."

"I doubt that would ever happen. You do realize Sarah doesn't like you, right? And hitting on her friend isn't helping matters any."

Perry frowned. "She doesn't like me? Really? I thought she was playing a game. Huh."

John sat in the chair and stared at his friend. How blind was the guy? He didn't want to add to his friend's woes, but still needed answers. So he pulled a Perry and changed the subject. "So you and Lori, huh? Did you bond?"

"Bond?" Perry laughed. "Yeah, right. She was great in the sack and quite tasty." Perry wagged his eyebrows. "Nothing special, though. Well, except she does have these moves—"

"Enough." John held his palm out. "I thought you said when you feed during sex it creates a bond."

Perry laughed. "Yeah, about that. I was kind of talking out of my ass, hoping to interest you in sex again. That's why I said it. I mean it's fun, but bonded? No, that's a fairy tale."

John gaped at Perry. He suspected many things Perry told him were fabrications, but he'd honestly hoped that one was true. What the hell had happened with Sarah?

"Johnny? Anyone home?" Perry waved his hand in front of John's face, bringing him out of his trance. "Hey, I'm sorry. I guess it didn't go well with Sarah, then?"

John scrubbed his face. Maybe he was using the wrong word. "So when you bite during sex, you don't feel her pleasure as well as your own?"

Perry's eyes widened. "Uhhh, no. Are you saying… Did you… You mean feel, like you were her?"

John nodded.

"Damn."

"What does it mean?" And why was he asking Perry? His chances of getting a straight answer out of him were slim and none. He probably should be talking to Barnet.

"I have no idea. I've been with hundreds of women, but never experienced that. You might want to ask Barnet when he stops by tonight."

"What? Why is he coming? You told me you didn't find anything."

"I didn't. Don't know about Barnet. I happened to run into him last night."

"Why didn't he call me?"

"He might have if I didn't tell him I was coming over. Said he wants to talk to Sarah, get her side of the story." A guilty smirk crossed Perry's face. "Oh yeah, I guess you should make sure she's here, huh?"

John resisted the urge to smack Perry, as if it would have done any good. The man remembered what the man wanted to remember.

Did Barnet just want to talk or was he planning on reading Sarah's memories? What would he do when he was unsuccessful?

\* \* \* \*

Sarah practically floated into work, high from the weekend, high from love. And while that was all good, emptiness was settling around her. Whatever John's bite had done to them was fading, and fast.

He really was a drug and she was going through withdrawals.

She shouldn't complain. Being with John was better than life itself, but that connection made it more so and she wanted it back as sharp as it had been after The Bite.

She hung up her coat, stashed her purse in the desk drawer, and headed toward the break room for some much-needed coffee.

"Seems we both got lucky this weekend, huh?"

Sarah jumped at Lori's voice and spun around. Had the whole company heard? Fortunately, they were the only ones in the room. "Is it that obvious?"

"Sure it is. I haven't seen you this happy since...hmm...never. John really agrees with you, huh?"

"I love him."

"Yeah, I got that." Lori sat at a table. "You never told me about Perry, though. Man, that guy is hot. He sure knows how to give a girl a good time, too. I swear, he has these moves—"

"Enough." Sarah held her palm out. "Do I really need to hear this?"

"TMI? Still, I've never had anyone suck on my neck like that and not give me a hickey."

"He gave you a hickey?" Sarah sat and took a sip of the hot drink, wishing she could have spiked it with something strong. Like whiskey or brandy, anything to dull the uneasiness in her chest.

"No. Aren't you listening? But the way he went at me, I was pretty sure I'd have one, but there's not a mark there. Whatever he did, sure felt good. No one's ever been able to make me come three times in one night!"

Sarah choked on her coffee, spewing a mess all over the table. Perry had fed on Lori. That bastard!

"Sorry." Lori grabbed a paper towel and some disinfectant and cleaned off the table. "I gave him my number, but he hasn't called. If you see him, can you find out if he's interested in another time? I wouldn't mind being his friend when he visits. You know, the kind with benefits."

"Benefits?" Sarah took another sip.

"Yeah. His fuck-buddy."

The coffee never made it down her throat.

\* \* \* \*

John looked at his watch. "Sarah will be here soon. Would you disappear for a while?"

Playing video games with Perry wasn't nearly as fun as playing them with Sarah, but it passed the time and beat being alone.

"Why? You plan on doing the nasty?" Perry nudged him in the ribs and cackled.

"Just go down to my office. You can play on the computer there."

"Yeah, like I won't be able to hear you."

"She doesn't know that."

No sooner had he said the words than the downstairs door slammed. Finally. Euphoria mixed with a burning need filled him and he rushed into the hallway. Sarah climbed the stairs, wearing a pretty pink blouse and black slacks under her blue coat. When she reached the top, he picked her up and twirled her around, so thankful to have her in his arms. She squealed delightfully and gave him a hello kiss he would never forget. She tasted so sweet and her warmth radiated all the way to his growing erection.

Perry cleared his throat. She stopped abruptly and John silently cursed.

"Hello, Sarah. You're looking fetching today." Perry was still sitting on the couch, but craned his head to look out into the hall.

John moaned and slowly let Sarah stand on her own. "Look who was waiting for me when I got home this morning. But he's going downstairs. Aren't you, Perry?"

He ushered her into the apartment and helped remove her coat. Perry stood and took her hand. "Johnny tells me you don't like me. Why is that?"

John rubbed his face. Crap. What the hell was Perry doing?

She stammered, "He... He shouldn't have said that."

Perry stared down at their hands. "So it's not true?"

John fought the urge to pull his so-called friend away—the vampire most likely enjoyed the rush of warmth Sarah emitted—but he needed to remain civil. "Perry, leave her alone."

Perry grabbed her by the shoulders and kissed her. Shock nailed John to the floor. She pushed Perry away and slapped his face.

"What the hell?" John got his feet working and rushed to stand between the two of them. He wanted to punch something. Perry's face looked like a good target.

She touched her mouth. "You bit me! What? Lori wasn't enough? Now you felt the need to sample me?"

Perry sat back on the couch, his face scrunched in bewilderment.

She pulled her hand away. Blood covered her fingers and the scent triggered John's fangs.

He clenched his fists as a mixture of anger and betrayal burned through his veins. "Perry, are you insane?"

"That does it," she muttered, then looked up at John with guilt in her eyes. "I didn't want to have to tell you this, but Perry hit on me when he visited me in Lima."

She couldn't have shocked him more if she had punched him in the gut. "What? Why didn't you tell me this before?"

She glanced briefly at Perry, who was currently staring at the carpet. "Because he said he would behave. So if that's behaving, I don't want to know what it's like when he's bad."

"I think I'll go downstairs like you wanted. We'll talk later." Perry zipped around the other side of the coffee table and shot out the door.

John fumed. If Sarah hadn't grabbed his arm, he wasn't sure what he would have done. Murder seemed like a good idea, and what vampire would blame him? Perry had basically attacked his woman.

"I'm sorry, John," she said.

His anger abated out of concern for her. "You have nothing to be sorry for." With a forceful will, he retracted his fangs as he gently lowered her jaw. "Where did he hurt you?"

She pointed, and while he was tempted to lean in and lick it all better, his emotions were mixed up and one taste of her blood might be the thing to put him over the edge. Losing control was not an option. Instead, he licked his finger and rubbed the wound. The bleeding stopped.

"John, if you want to talk to Perry, I can come back tonight."

He wiped his finger on his thigh, afraid even to get a sample. "No. You just got here."

He grabbed her hand. The couch was littered with game controllers and Perry's indentation. Hell no, not there. He dragged her to the bedroom. After flipping on the light, he shut the door as she sat on the edge of the bed.

She'd never been in his bedroom before and she glanced around in curiosity. The double bed—a recent addition—and dresser took up most of the space, but then he only used the room to store his clothes.

She stared at the floor. "Can he hear us down there?"

"I don't care." And he didn't. He sat on the bed beside her. "What did he do in Lima?"

She closed her eyes and took a moment. That moment nearly killed him. "He didn't hurt me. He just wanted to know if his touch did anything to me."

"And? Did it? Does it?"

"Does it matter?" The scent of fear emanated from her.

John grabbed her hand, getting a rush of her warmth and a faint zip up his arm. "It won't change how I feel about you if that's your concern. But I need to know, okay?"

She stared at him with tears in her eyes. "I told him I didn't feel anything."

"Did you lie to him?"

One tear slipped down her cheek. "I don't like Perry. I love you."

Dear God, she'd lied. He pulled her into his arms. "I know you do. I love you, too. But this sure as hell complicates things."

"You blame me for—"

"No." He held her back. "I don't blame you for anything. You understand? It's not your fault Perry's acting like an ass," he said, loud enough so the man would hear. "But Barnet's coming over tonight and he wants to talk to you."

"Me? What for?"

"I don't know. I assume it has to do with Ray or Steven. He's probably hoping to access your memories." He rubbed his face. "Guess I have no choice but to tell him about you now."

"What are you afraid of? You think I'm going to choose one of them over you?"

That thought had crossed his mind.

She pushed him onto the mattress and straddled his hips. "Let me tell you something, John Pennington. Yes, I felt a spark when Perry touched me. And yes, it scared me. Then I realized, it's just a spark. When I touch you, it's a hundred—no a thousand—times better. Perry's a spark. You're a God-damned electric plant. You hear me? There's no comparison."

"Yeah, but who knows how you'll react to other vampires?"

"John, I was attracted to you long before I even touched you. Perry repelled me at first sight. I'm yours, you idiot."

He laughed. Yes, he was an idiot. "Come here."

He pulled her down and kissed her—her mouth soft and complying—ran his tongue over her healed wound, and tasted a trace of her blood. His fangs emerged.

She broke the kiss and stared at his mouth. "You like my blood, right?"

Oh, God. Not again. He willed his fangs to retract and sat up, keeping her straddled over his lap. Too bad she wasn't wearing a dress or skirt—the access he could have—then maybe he could postpone this conversation for another time. He stared at the buttons on her blouse. Maybe there were other ways to distract her. "My aversion has nothing to do with how you taste, okay?"

He flicked open the top three buttons, eliciting a gasp from her and exposing the black bra with the little red bow. God, he loved her sexy underwear and hardened at the sight.

"What are you afraid of then?" she asked.

The clasp was in front for a change. He reached to unhook it, but she slapped his hand away.

"Answer me, John."

He could overtake her easily, but at what cost? Her anger? Her rejection? But in essence, wasn't he rejecting her? Her blood? "Why is it so important that I bite you?"

She leaned her forehead against his. "Because ever since you did it, I've done nothing but crave for you to do it again. Not want. Crave. You created a connection between us and I felt whole for the first time in my life. But it's fading, and I don't like that feeling. It's like you're leaving me. I know it's silly, you're right here and what we have is great. But your bite triggered some wonderful need and instead of needing a certain vitamin or chemical, I need you to take my blood. Not Perry. Not Barnet. You. I need to know I'm yours. Do you get it?"

Oh he got it all right. He'd been feeling the same way all day. But what she was asking, or needing… "What if I lose control?"

"I don't think you will. I know you don't consider me food and don't want to consider me as food, but would it help if you thought of me as dessert?"

A nervous chuckle escaped. Dessert. That might work. "You're killing me, you know that?"

"And you kill me a little with every no. Please, John. Bite me. Show me I'm yours." She tilted her head and moved her hair, exposing her neck. When he made no move toward her, she pulled his head down and whispered, "Dessert."

He inhaled her scent, triggering his fangs. He grabbed her shoulders. "We leave the clothes on, you hear?"

Because any other distraction could prove fatal.

"Sure, John."

Her heartbeat reverberated in his ears. The scent of her arousal hardened him to the point of pain. Then again, she was sitting right on top of him.

The artery in her neck beckoned him. He bit. The sweet delicate taste swirled across his tongue and down his throat. He did this for her, not for him. If he kept repeating that mantra, maybe he would be able to stop.

She gripped his shoulders and moaned in pleasure, as the emotion transferred to him. Their connection strengthened, sharpened. He could almost pinpoint when it reached the max, as if it were some kind of fuel gauge.

Her orgasm shocked and overtook him—he hadn't even been touching her anywhere erotic—and he nearly came in his pants. The imaginary gauge read full. He stopped sucking. But now he was horny as hell. Now he needed her. He licked the bite marks away and kissed her on the mouth, claiming her. She ran her fingers through his hair and sucked on his tongue. Kissing wasn't enough. He stood with her in his arms and laid her on the bed. Without much fanfare, he slid her slacks off and groaned at those sexy black panties. No time to admire. His shoes and jeans quickly joined the pile on the floor.

He entered her and came after only two thrusts. She cried out his name and then promptly fainted. Okay, so maybe it was the sex that knocked her out. Nearly took him away, too. He collapsed beside her, his lungs searching for oxygen.

"Sarah?" He patted her cheek. At least she didn't look pale. Not like last time.

Eyes blinking, she faced him. "You okay?"

"Not really. I don't like seeing you knocked out like that."

"But it wasn't the blood. You know that, right?"

He touched her cheek and smiled. In a way, he hated her being right, but was relieved all the same. "Yeah, I know."

A smile spread across her face as she reached out for him. "I'll make sure to eat first next time. Then maybe I can stay awake, huh?"

He pulled her into his arms. Next time. He couldn't believe he was actually considering it. "Vitamins, too. You start taking supplements. Especially B12. And iron."

"I love you, John. I feel so much better already."

Strangely, so did he. That emptiness he'd felt earlier had disappeared and their connection was back, stronger than ever. But why the hell did it come at the cost of biting her?

# Chapter 29

John tossed the last controller back into the cabinet. Watching Sarah leave for work had been easier than it had been leaving her that morning. Contentment? Maybe. Maybe she was his drug. Or vitamin. Whatever, he'd gotten a healthy dose and the uneasiness had disappeared.

Until his door opened and Perry entered.

John straightened as the anger returned with a vengeance. "If you're smart, you'll stay downstairs. Or better yet. You stay here. I'll go downstairs. Just be gone at sunset."

He went to the door, but Perry blocked his way.

"Johnny, we need to talk."

"Talk about what? How you attacked my woman? Or how you came on to her in Lima? What else have you done? You're supposed to be my friend."

"I am your friend, man. Listen, it's not what you think."

"What am I thinking, Perry? Hmm? Tell me what I'm thinking. Because right now I'm thinking about throwing you out into the sun!"

Perry held up his hands, palms out. "I didn't do this to hurt you, I swear. But when I discovered I couldn't read or control her, I wondered what mess you got into. Plus, I was curious, okay?"

That news sat in his stomach like that chicken pot pie had. "Did you tell anyone else? Did you tell Barnet?"

"Hell no. I didn't expect to react to her so…intensely, so I certainly wasn't involving another vampire. It was bad enough I had to deal with you."

That admission lit a fire in John. In a flash, he wrapped his hands around Perry's throat and squeezed. "Are you behind everything that's happened to her? Her car? The abduction? Her rape? Because if you are, so help me…"

*"Don't be an asshole,"* Perry communicated telepathically, since John made it unlikely for him to speak aloud. He stared at John, not even making a move to get free. *"Whoever is doing this doesn't have her best interests at heart. I could never hurt her, okay? Never."*

John pushed Perry away. "You sound like you love her."

Perry rubbed his neck. "Love? I doubt it. You know love and me don't go together. But desire? Oh yeah, especially after—"

Perry stopped with widened eyes, looking guilty on so many levels.

"Especially after what?" John grabbed his stomach as something inside twisted. "What did you do to her in Lima?" Perry lowered his head and kept quiet. "Answer me, damn it."

Perry spoke to the floor. "She told you. I talked to her then left."

Lies, all lies. John grabbed Perry's arm, establishing skin contact. Perry struggled at first, then relaxed in surrender.

*Sarah lay sleeping on the hotel bed, the covers twisted around her legs. He approached her and took her hand, enjoying the warmth as it shot up his arm. When she stirred, he stilled until he determined he hadn't woken her. He sniffed her wrist, inhaled the scent of jasmine and his fangs emerged. Slowly, gently, he bit down on the fleshy part of her hand, savored her blood, and became instantly aroused.*

No! He didn't. John shoved Perry away in disgust, his heart aching from the betrayal. "You're not welcome here anymore."

"Johnny, listen."

"No! Friends don't do what you did." John opened the door and started pushing Perry out, but the man moved like a stubborn octopus. "Get the fuck out of here."

Perry grabbed the door frame and shot out toward John. Next thing John knew, Perry had twisted him around, pinned his arms behind his back, and had him kissing the floor. He struggled to get free, but with Perry's knee digging into his back, he couldn't get any leverage.

"Get off me!"

"When I'm finished. Listen, I'm sorry. What I did was…inexcusable. I know that. But she's not the same now, Johnny. You don't have to worry any longer."

John stopped struggling. "What are you talking about?"

"The draw. It's diminished."

"The what?"

Perry climbed off John and shut the door. "The draw. That intoxicating scent that pulled me toward her. Isn't that how she affects you?"

Slowly, John stood. Her scent. It was different for Perry than for him. His worst fears materialized. "Ah shit. How many more vampires do I have to worry about?"

"No, that's just it. Her scent, while nice, no longer gave me this insane desire to…well, you know. And then when I held her hand, that warm feeling just…fizzled. Kind of depressing if you ask me. I needed to know if she tasted any different."

"You had no right to kiss her!"

"I couldn't just come out and bite her, now could I? But she's different, Johnny. She's practically…normal."

Normal? That word did not describe the exquisite flavor he had sampled not thirty minutes ago. Nor the hard-on it gave him. "Explain."

"There was still a little zing, but like her touch, not very noticeable. Did nothing for my libido, that's for sure. So whatever you two did, it changed her."

While he was pleased Sarah no longer affected Perry, it still didn't change the fact his former friend had gone after his girl and basically assaulted her. No, Perry wasn't getting away with that. Killing might not be an option, but something else was. In a flash, John shot his fist out and connected with Perry's face with a resounding crunch. The man went flying over the counter and crashed into the cupboards. The refrigerator teetered before settling upright.

Perry jumped up and rubbed his jaw. "Feel better now?"

"A little." Very little.

* * * *

At five-thirty, Sarah walked into Wings, still feeling radiant from that nooner. In fact, the whole afternoon had gone by in a blur, thanks to John.

She had thought she'd have to do more convincing before he finally relented and fed from her, but maybe he'd felt a little needy after learning about Perry's betrayal. Whatever changed his mind, thank goodness he had. The uneasiness in her chest had disappeared. Contentment took its place.

She wouldn't mind The Bite being a recurring event, with or without their clothes on. Minus the visit from Perry, of course. Would it be the same when she became a vampire? She could only hope.

John greeted her at the door and pulled her into his arms. Delight, grief, and a touch of titillation overwhelmed her when his lips brushed against hers in a brief, chaste kiss. She still wasn't used to feeling his emotions.

Customers filled the restaurant, but no sign of Perry.

"He's upstairs," he said, as if he knew who she was looking for. But then, who else?

"Are you two still friends?"

"No."

And that was the reason behind the sadness. "Oh, John. I'm sorry." As much as she disliked Perry, he was John's friend.

"I told you, you have nothing to be sorry for." He indicated to an area behind her. "Go take that booth. I'll join you in a minute."

Guess they were waiting for Barnet down here. Not that she blamed him. She didn't exactly want to see Perry, either. Maybe once the sun set, they could leave the noisy dining room and find something to pass the time. Something to lift his spirits. She could think of many somethings, especially now that he owned a bed. Wonder when he'd bought that?

John placed a menu on the table and slid in beside her.

"What time do you expect Barnet?"

"I don't know. If it gets too late, and you want to go home, don't worry about it. But while we wait, you can have dinner. Did you even eat lunch today?"

By the time she'd left John's, she hadn't had time to get anything nourishing except what she could find in the vending machine at work. But he probably wouldn't think cheese puffs and popcorn were all that healthy or filling. Still, how could she eat in front of him when he was in such a distressing mood? "No, but—"

"No buts, you're eating," he said and continued by whispering in her ear, "I can't have you fainting on me tonight, now can I?"

All her internal rants quieted and her heart rate picked up when he licked the outer edge of her ear and squeezed her thigh. Oh yeah, fainting would be bad. So bad. She'd like to experience the whole shebang for once.

She ordered the chicken fingers only because she could treat it as snack food. When her meal arrived, she tore it into tiny pieces and ate it like popcorn. Snacking was easier, especially when she put the plate between them. She pretended he didn't take any by choice, not because he couldn't eat.

During her nibbling, Perry slid onto the bench across from them. Oh God, now what? Her appetite spoiled, she pushed the plate away.

John put his arm around Sarah in a protective manner. "What do you want?"

"I came down to tell you I'm leaving," Perry said. "And to apologize."

His eyes sparkled in misery, sending her into a guilt trip when she had no reason to feel guilty. Still...something had changed between them. When he'd held her hand back at John's, she would have gotten a larger whap from static electricity. And her heart had reacted, but not so much from the attraction, but from fear of the unknown. His kiss and subsequent bite had only made her furious. So what did it mean? Was she finally immune to him?

Perry clasped his hands on the table. "I'm sorry, Sarah. For everything. Kissing you. Biting you. Lima. My behavior was inappropriate and it won't happen again." Massaging his jaw, he turned his attention to John. "I hope you can forgive me. Your friendship means everything and I was stupid not to realize that sooner." With that, he left.

She didn't know what to make of it, but Perry's apology seemed sincere. John sat quietly, staring at the table, either in deep thought or zoned out. Was he even breathing? She couldn't tell.

"You okay?" she asked.

"I'm fine." He pushed the plate back toward her, without making eye contact. "Now eat."

He didn't sound so fine, he sounded depressed. She'd love nothing more than to make him feel better—a little fellatio would benefit them both—but when she suggested they wait upstairs, John nixed it. He didn't want to put Barnet out since he wasn't familiar with the place.

Instead, John brought over two game consoles to pass the time. After feeling like a total idiot on the last two trivia questions—like it was common knowledge which counties bordered Mali, wherever the heck that was—Sarah was ready to call it a night when John excused himself and headed for the front door. An older gentleman had entered. Was he

Barnet? Did vampires even have gray in their hair? They talked a bit, but never shook hands. John brought him over.

"Sarah, this is Barnet Groves. Barnet, Sarah."

His age threw her first. Probably the myth playing with her, but she'd assumed all vampires were turned young. This man appeared a good ten to fifteen years older than John. No wonder John thought of him as a father figure. He looked the part. His button-down shirt and dress slacks made him appear distinguished, like an important businessman minus the suit. But his eyes were a big giveaway. While they weren't as blue as John's, they sparkled like every other vampire she'd encountered. Fascinating.

"It's a pleasure to finally meet you," Barnet said.

"Same here." She offered her hand, but John took it instead.

"Why don't we go upstairs where it's more private?" He kept her hand and led the way to the stairs, where he indicated Barnet go up first. All during the jostling inside his apartment, he seemed to make a great effort to stay between her and Barnet.

John offered the chair to Barnet then sat beside her on the couch. Not once had he let go of her hand.

"You know, John, I was hoping I could talk to Sarah in private for a minute."

John shook his head and stared at the carpet. "I'm sorry, sir, but there's something you should know before I can do that."

Barnet leaned forward. "What's the matter?"

"You can't read her mind."

"Is that what this is about?" Barnet leaned back and smiled graciously at Sarah before returning his attention to John. "You know I won't hurt her, but it's common practice when a mortal has knowledge about our race. I promise not to get too personal."

"Not what I mean. I mean you can't. Physically. Can't."

Barnet raised his eyebrows and stared at Sarah. He seemed to inhale slowly, as if trying to capture her scent, unlike the sniffing way Perry had always done it. Was he trying to control her, too? After a moment, he looked away in thought. "Has she offered you her blood?"

John furrowed his brow. "Yes, and I've fed from her. Why does that matter?"

"How long ago."

"About seven hours. Again, why—"

Barnet snapped his head up. "Has Perry met her? Before you took—"

"Yes," John growled. "And he's lucky he's still alive."

For biting her? Or for something else? Anger flashed from John to her through their clasped hands. She needed to calm him, but how? "I'm afraid they've had a falling out because of me."

"Not because of you. Because of Perry." John turned toward Barnet. "He assaulted her and I sent him away. Am I going to have to send you away, too?"

"Assaulted?" Barnet's eyes widened and he seemed to examine her from his chair. "How?"

"He bit her."

"He nipped me on the mouth," she said.

"He kissed you and bit you and he, well... He's lucky I didn't kill him." John's anger hit her so hard, she might have attacked Perry if he stood in the room. She breathed deep and pushed serene thoughts John's way. Like the way he touched her after making love and the way he took care of her after her accident.

Barnet raised his hands in a placating manner, but sadness filled his eyes. "It's okay, John. I understand."

John's breathing slowed. "How is that possible when I don't even understand it?"

"Then let me try to explain. Do you know Katarina Koenig? She's one of Victoria's friends."

"Maybe. I think so. Why?"

"Right after Christmas she introduced me to a young man. She was just as protective of him as you are of Sarah and no one could read or control him."

"I'm not an abnormality?" she asked.

Barnet smiled. "Oh, don't get me wrong. You're an abnormality. In all my years as a vampire, I've never seen your kind. I always thought it was a story, a myth. The Perfect Mate."

"I've never heard of that story," John said.

"If you had stayed at Headquarters for longer than the meetings and got to know your fellow vampires, you might have. I'm surprised Perry didn't say anything, though." Barnet glanced at Sarah and grimaced. "Or maybe I'm not. That man never thinks before acting."

"My kind? You make me sound like an alien."

"Not alien. Just different. But since John has fed from you recently, I'm not sensing anything unusual. And I'm sure if John allowed it, your touch wouldn't feel all that different, either. After a day, though, maybe I would. Justin created quite a stir."

John squeezed her hand and fear flowed into her at the mention of Barnet touching her. So that's why he'd kept her from Barnet. The idiot was still afraid she'd pick some other vampire over him? She gave him a reassuring squeeze back. "Who's Justin?"

"Katarina's...mate, for lack of a better word. When she arrived in Atlanta, it had been several days since she fed from him and his signal, draw, or whatever had returned. I didn't feel anything, and neither did any of the other males who were there, but Victoria and Hilde, two of our Committee members, did. They only wanted to be near the young man, but Katarina went into attack mode. That's when we, the Committee, decided to sequester Justin until we could figure out how to handle him."

"You put him in jail?"

Barnet laughed. "Not really. More like a hotel room. It kept him safe, but by then Victoria and Hilde couldn't stay away from the room. Katarina refused to leave him alone, didn't trust anyone near him, which forced her to feed from him again, not that he minded. He practically begged her to. Once she did, Victoria and Hilde lost interest."

John relaxed considerably at this information. "What did Hilde's husband think?"

"Not good thoughts, I'm sure, which was another reason for the lock up. Hilde was only curious, I believe that. I think she finally convinced Rolf, too. But Victoria is unattached and hasn't been with anyone since her husband's passing. I'm afraid Justin's allure hit her hard. It didn't help that the effects of Katarina's feeding were only temporary. A few days later, Victoria felt the allure again. Luckily, Hilde had already left with Rolf."

"What happened with Justin?" she asked.

"Katarina originally brought him to get permission to turn him. In light of the circumstances, and the fact no one could coerce him into it, we granted it."

"Did that stop the draw?" John asked.

Forget the draw. Would it stop their connection to one another? But Barnet might not even know that part. Of course, if it meant being with John forever, she could give it up. She'd miss it, though.

"I'm sorry. So, so sorry." Barnet lowered his head. "The process didn't take. He can't be turned."

"What?" She bolted off the couch. "Are you saying I can't be a vampire?" Did this mean her time with John was only temporary? Would he leave her when she got too old? Pain radiated from her chest and the room darkened as if some black hole swallowed it up.

# Chapter 30

John couldn't have heard Barnet correctly. To find someone like Sarah and then not be able to keep her? It was some kind of sick joke. Or maybe it was the curse of being a vampire.

"John."

Barnet's worried tone caused John to look up. Barnet stood and moved toward Sarah, who was wavering in her stance.

"Sarah." John grabbed her around the waist before she fell.

Tears streamed down her face and she gripped his arm. "Tell me it's not true."

He helped her back onto the couch and held her close while she cried. If he could, he'd be crying right along with her. Barnet might as well have ripped his heart from his chest.

"I'm sorry. I can only imagine how hard this information is to take, but I thought it was better to be blunt. If it's any consolation, Katarina and Justin are just as upset. The Committee is currently searching for similar cases in other countries, although, I think if there were any, we would have heard about them. There has to be something we're missing because if the story is true, and it's beginning to seem that way, I find it hard to believe a Perfect Mate cannot become immortal."

John held her and stroked her hair, calming himself as much as soothing her. "So what now? Do I feed from her every day to keep the vampires away? I'd end up killing her."

"Katarina believed the same thing, but so far Justin isn't showing any ill effects. I'd guess you wouldn't have to go to that extreme since there aren't any other vampires around here."

"Are you forgetting the vampire controlling Steven and possibly Ray?"

"That I did. But from what you told me, it has to be a female because I believe a male would have taken Sarah by now."

"And you've had no luck?"

Barnet shook his head. "No. I wish I had better news." He rose. "I'll leave you two alone. But one more thing. I'm trying to keep a lid on this Perfect Mate business. Until we have more information, I don't need every unattached vampire going out half-cocked looking for the impossible. We're liable to have ourselves one big mess then."

"You don't have to worry about me," John said.

"I suppose you're right. Guess I should be having this conversation with Perry." Barnet groaned and shook his head. "I'll see myself out."

After Barnet left, Sarah broke down again.

"Hey." He held her face and wiped the tears away. "I'm not giving up hope and you shouldn't either. That's just one case, it might be different with you. Besides, you agreed to wait a year anyway. A lot can happen."

Her voice hitched. "But what if I'm not different. What if there isn't anything. I'll get old and you won't."

"You don't worry about that. I'm not going anywhere. You're stuck with me. You hear?"

He kissed her deeply, tasting her tears. She possessed him body and soul and no amount of time would ever change that. If it came down to it, he'd prove it, but hoped he'd never have to. For now he would make her forget and show her how much she meant to him.

* * * *

Something brushed across Sarah's lips. Opening her eyes meant waking up and since she didn't want to do that, she swiped at her mouth, but nothing was there. Must have been a dream. Then it happened again. She opened her eyes to a darkened room. John smiled as he gave her another light kiss on the lips.

"Mmm, good morning," she murmured.

She was determined to make it one, too, especially since John had spent all last night doing whatever he could to help her forget Barnet's words. Live in the now and enjoy it. Why fret over stuff she couldn't control?

Kissing a trail from her mouth to her neck, he said, "Good morning to you, too, sleepyhead. It's almost six-thirty. I hope you don't mind me waking you a little early."

Hell, with a wake-up call like that, he could wake her early every morning. Who needed sleep? Oh wait, she did.

He pulled the sheet away and exposed her naked body. The coolness of the room gave her a slight chill and a few goose bumps. He kissed his way to her breast and lightly licked her nipple, opening the floodgates to her sex and heating her up. She gasped. How had he managed to turn her on so quickly? After kissing his way down her stomach, he lingered at her belly button before he slowly worked his way back up to her other breast and suckled that one. She arched into him, wanting more.

"What are you doing?" Well, she knew what he was doing, just not why and she was almost not caring either way, it felt so good.

He spread her legs and positioned himself between them—"I'm having breakfast"—then kissed his way back down her belly.

Having breakfast? Since when did he—oh hell. She pulled away and tried to close her thighs, but he held her tight.

"Relax, will you? God, you smell wonderful." He ran his tongue over her folds. "Taste good, too."

Not hard to believe since his experiences transferred to her, but relax? He was kidding, right? His ministrations were sending her over the edge of that huge cliff called orgasm. Didn't hurt that he knew exactly where to lick and suck. Why wouldn't he if he could experience what she felt? He flicked her clit with his tongue while fingering her insides, rubbing the perfect spot. The man was too good. She tensed every muscle, her nerve endings on fire. Before her world exploded, she grabbed her pillow and put it over her face.

The climax ripped through her and she screamed with ecstasy. Even John moaned.

He removed the pillow from her face and said, panting, "Damn. It's like waking from a wet dream." He grabbed some tissues from her nightstand and cleaned himself. "I might have problems taking your blood, but I certainly love the side effects."

"Tell me about it," she said and laughed. "How am I supposed to get ready for work now when I don't even want to get out of bed?"

John tossed the tissues in the trash before snuggling in beside her. After brushing the hair from her face, he leaned over and gave her a proper good morning kiss, making her tingle all the way to her toes. How could her body be craving him again? Was it never satisfied?

Moving his lips to her neck, he said, "I'm sure you'll manage. At least you don't have to run back home."

She was sure he was only joking, but it didn't stop the guilt from forming. "You know, you could drive home and I could take the bus to work."

John lifted his head and frowned. "Sarah...I was only teasing. I told you, I don't need the car. Quit feeling guilty." He glanced at the clock, sat up and scooted toward the edge of the bed, but stopped and gave her another kiss. "God, you taste good, but I do need to get going."

She rose up on her elbows and ogled him while he slipped on his jeans. Too bad he wasn't undressing, though. Then again, she'd get to see that after work, which reminded her... "By the way, I'll be late tonight."

He picked up a shoe. "You got a meeting?"

"With a client at six-thirty, at the coffee shop around the corner."

He spun around, frowning. "It's not at your work? Don't you usually meet your clients there?"

Now he was giving her the willies. "It's not uncommon for me to meet at an owner's establishment and it was the only time she could meet. Should I be worried?"

His face softened. "I'm sorry. I'm being overprotective. Again. But if you don't mind, I'd like to be at that coffee shop waiting for you."

"Okay, but I really have no idea how long I'll be."

"Doesn't matter. Okay? It'll make me feel better."

"Well...as long as it makes *you* feel better."

"Was that sass? Were you sassing me?" He bent down and tickled her in the ribs.

Laughter burst out of her and she couldn't stop. The guy was relentless. "I give. Please. Just stop."

But his tickles turned more sensuous and the next thing she knew, his jeans were off and he was in her. Ah yes, the perfect way to start a day.

# Chapter 31

After packing her briefcase and dressing for the weather, Sarah headed toward the elevators. Thank goodness the shop was around the corner. She could avoid the garage altogether. That place always seemed creepier after work than it did in the morning. Someday she'd be able to walk through it without her heart hammering away. A day after Ray and Steven were captured, most likely.

She stepped outside and the frigid air attacked her with a vengeance. Good old February. One day the weather would be warm, teasing of things to come. The next day, cold and hard, saying, "Fooled you!" At least it wasn't snowing. Hugging the briefcase, she used it as a shield to block the wind. Light shone through the coffee shop window. Thank goodness. If forced to wait outside, she'd freeze for sure.

Before Sarah could reach for the knob, a middle-aged woman with long, auburn hair opened the door and offered her hand. "Ms. Daugherty, I presume?"

Sarah took her hat off and shoved it in her pocket before shaking the outstretched hand. "Yes, I am. Are you Ms. Delany?"

"Yes, good to meet you."

The handshake seemed unusually long. Her grip was strong and either she liked holding hands or she was a vampire trying to get information. Crap. But wait, if she were a vampire…

Neither a sparkle nor glimmer shone in her eyes. Just plain old brown. Sarah relaxed. John's paranoia was starting to rub off, not that it would take much.

"Come in and have a seat. Kind of nippy out there, isn't it?" Ms. Delany closed the door and rubbed her arms.

"I'll be glad when spring arrives." Sarah placed her purse and bag on the floor and hung her scarf and coat on the back of the chair before settling in.

A tray of muffins and a coffee carafe, along with some plates and cups, sat on the counter. Were they the only two in the shop? If anyone worked in the back, they were quiet.

"Oh I do love the spring." Ms. Delany carried the tray to their table. "Sorry for not meeting at your office, but I didn't think it was an appropriate place to approach you regarding a job."

This was about a job? "I'm sorry, but I don't do the hiring—"

"Oh, not for me. I want to hire you."

The woman couldn't be serious. If this was an interview, it was the strangest one she'd ever had. She hadn't even sent out any resumes. She looked around the shop. "A job? Here?"

Ms. Delany laughed as she sat, but it sounded strained and fake. "Oh no, not *here*. My friend owns this place and is letting me use it and with it being close to your office, I thought it would be more convenient for you. I run my own business. I heard great things about you during your job up in Lima and it intrigued me." After passing the plates out, she placed a muffin on each and then poured coffee in the cups.

Goosebumps formed on Sarah's arms and she fingered her necklace. Maybe she should leave. Ms. Delany kept staring as if she wanted to kiss and after that handshake, well, it was downright creepy. Sarah had never been hit on by a woman before, but there was always a first time. "While I'm flattered, I'm not really looking for another job. I enjoy working at Miller and Thomason."

"Ah, but you can stay and hear me out, can't you? Here, have a muffin. They really are quite delicious." Ms. Delany took a bite and smiled.

Sarah wrung her hands together . Why not stay? John would arrive shortly and she could use him as an excuse to leave and show she was into men, not women. Besides, maybe the job would be fun. Or pay more. She picked up a muffin and bit into it. The flavor of blueberries filled her mouth. Damn, they were good. But then, blueberry muffins were her favorite. She added creamer to her coffee and took a sip. "Okay, I'm listening."

Ms. Delany explained her business, while making sure Sarah's cup stayed full. And with the frigid weather, Sarah gulped the coffee down. Hey, maybe that's what she needed to stay awake after a sexy session with John: caffeine. She'd certainly put it to the test tonight.

"What do you say? Think you could stand to work for me? I'd pay to relocate you."

"Relocate?" Sarah blinked several times. Damn eyelids were getting heavy. She'd only slept maybe a total of four hours the night before and it was catching up with her. Okay, so maybe the caffeine wouldn't work tonight. She fought to appear attentive, while the table begged her to rest her head.

"Oh. I'm sorry. Didn't I mention? The job is in Detroit."

Sure, John would probably follow her anywhere, but Detroit? It had to be way colder than Dayton. If she were to move anywhere, it would be south, where summer lived year-round, especially since it appeared she wouldn't be a vampire.

Her chest tightened. Crap. Why'd she have to think of that again? It was what kept her awake most of the night as it was. Her heart grew heavy and her nose tingled. No! She would not cry. Must think positive thoughts. If John had hope, so could she.

Ms. Delany placed her hand over Sarah's. "Ms. Daugherty?"

Sarah took a deep breath and put the vampire business out of her mind. What were they talking about? Her head was getting fuzzy. Oh yes, the job. "I'm really flattered, but I'm afraid I'll have to decline. I'm not looking to relocate at this time. Thank you for the muffin. It was delicious." She bent over for her things and the room spun sideways. Whoa, what was that? She grabbed onto the table for fear of falling over. If she didn't know any better, she'd think she was drunk.

"Oh dear, are you okay?" Ms. Delany asked.

Pinpricks of fear tingled over Sarah's skin. Not drunk. Drugged. What the hell was in that coffee and who was this woman? She had to leave before she passed out, but her mind was already foggy. Slowly, she rose and reached for her coat. "I'm fine. I just need some air."

Ms. Delany dashed to Sarah's side—a little too quickly—and grabbed Sarah's elbow. Her grip rivaled that of John's. "You don't look at all well. Why don't I help you to the ladies room? Maybe some water would help."

Oh shit. Was Ms. Delany the vampire behind everything? If so, why not put that vampire strength to use? Then again, maybe she wanted Sarah unconscious first, so she couldn't make a scene. Or call for John.

John! God, please let him be outside.

\* \* \* \*

A woman, huddled inside her coat as the wind whipped her hair around, walked past John and stared at him as if he'd come from another planet. Had he forgotten to zip? He looked down at himself. Oops. In his hurry to leave, he'd put on his jean jacket. Not exactly proper outwear on what appeared to be a blustery evening. No way was he going back to change. He'd already gotten a late start as it was. Of all the days for Mike to have car trouble.

If the temperature had dropped considerably, maybe he should have brought the Xterra. Guess he'd have to keep Sarah warm in other ways. Or warm her up after their walk. He didn't have a bathtub, but the shower could hold two, provided those two didn't mind being close and intimate. He smiled. Oh yeah, they would have some fun in the shower tonight.

He had just turned the corner toward the coffee shop when the back of his neck tingled and his stomach twisted. Now what? He'd already fed.

His name reverberated through the air and was abruptly cut off. *Sarah!*

He bolted for the door and plowed inside. Sarah was entangled amidst a table and chair, using them as an anchor while a woman grabbed her around the waist.

"What are you doing?" he barked.

The woman dropped Sarah. In a flash, she'd disappeared out the back.

Damn it. She must be the vampire responsible. If only he'd nabbed before yelling, he might have captured her or at least seen her face. No way was he chasing her though. Sarah came first.

She hugged one chair while her legs were wrapped around another. When she saw John, she scrambled to her feet, but her motor skills were sluggish and she fell back into the pile of chairs. What was wrong with her? He rushed to her aid, freeing her from the offending pieces. She stayed on the floor and looked up at him with squinty eyes.

"Sarah, are you okay? Did she hurt you?"

He lifted her, but her legs were wobbly and she couldn't stand. Instead, he lowered her to the floor and placed her in his lap.

Her head moved erratically before her glazed-over gaze locked onto his. She blinked several times then placed an unsteady hand against his cheek. "John? You came."

She'd been drugged and was fighting the effects, but he didn't think she would last much longer.

"Yes, sweetie, it's me. Do you remember what happened?"

Her words were slurred and he strained to make out what she was saying. "Vampire. Tried to fight. God, you're beautiful. Did I ever tell you that?"

"It's okay, you're safe now." He hugged her tight. Damn, he'd almost lost her again. If he had been a few minutes later... No, he couldn't think like that. He was here and she was safe. And she would be safer once he took her home. He stood with her in his arms.

"We going somewhere?" she asked.

"In a minute." He flipped a chair upright and lowered her onto it, then grabbed a table and scooted it up to her. "Can you sit here without falling?"

"Sure, John." She grabbed onto the table and placed her head on the surface with a rather loud thud. John cringed.

Once he determined she wouldn't topple over, he locked the front door then headed in the direction the vampire had taken.

Wind whipped in through the open door of the kitchen. Only dumpsters stood in the alley, not that he expected she'd be waiting for him. He shut the door and headed back toward Sarah. She hadn't moved, but she was humming "Rock the Casbah." Of all the songs... He shook his head. What the hell had she ingested?

Muffins littered the floor and a carafe had rolled up against the counter. He sniffed and tasted each. While the muffins seemed fine, he discovered a chemical substance in the coffee. Should he take her to the hospital? No, if the vampire had wanted her dead, she'd be dead. He would take her home and let her sleep it off. But before he could do that, he needed to clean up the mess. Sarah's fingerprints were sure to be everywhere.

It didn't take long for John to straighten up. He bundled up Sarah and carried her home, not able to relax until he arrived at his stairwell. He opened the apartment and lowered her to the couch.

She wasn't down but a second when she covered her mouth and gagged.

Shit. He picked her up and rushed to the bathroom. He had just gotten her situated over the toilet when she heaved. Holding her head so she wouldn't bang it against the seat, he waited for her to finish, then wet a washcloth and wiped her mouth. As he placed the cloth in the sink, she became limp in his arms. She had finally passed out.

What had he done to cause this vampire to hurt him like this? And why did she have to involve Sarah at all? Sarah didn't deserve any of this. She only had the misfortune to love a vampire. If it weren't for him, she wouldn't be in this mess.

He carried her to the bedroom and gently placed her on the bed. After getting her outerwear off, he removed her shoes, uncovering her socks. Penguins. His chest tightened and everything inside him ached to cry. She'd been out cold the last time he'd seen those socks. Maybe he should suggest she get rid of them. They certainly didn't bring her luck. He covered her with a blanket and lay beside her. An unfamiliar scent lingered on her clothes. The scent had to belong to the vampire responsible, but who the hell was she?

John pulled out his cellphone and punched in Barnet's number. He didn't even give the man a chance to say hello. "I saw the vampire. She's attacked Sarah again. Can you come?"

"Perry's probably closer. I'll call—"

"No! I don't want him here."

"Okay, John. I'll be there as soon as I can."

He lay back down beside her. Her breathing seemed normal and when he took her pulse he found it to be a tad fast, but strong. How was he ever going to do right by her?

He lost track of time, but her chest had risen one thousand one hundred and thirty-four times before Barnet appeared in the doorway. John hadn't even heard him enter the apartment.

"How is she?"

John stood. "She's been drugged. I'm hoping it only knocked her out, since her heart rate and breathing are normal. But if I can't rouse her in a few hours, I'm taking her to the hospital."

"Can we talk in the other room? I feel like we're disturbing her."

"Do me a favor first? The woman's scent is on Sarah's clothes."

Barnet took two steps, then stopped. "When did you feed from her last?"

"Not since your visit. But I can trust you, right?"

Barnet placed his hand on John's shoulder. "Yes, you can trust me. Just don't be mad if I enjoy this, okay?"

John nodded. He pulled the covers down, stood back, and crossed his arms.

Barnet took Sarah's hand, leaned over and sniffed. "She's rather exotic, isn't she?"

The urge to pull Barnet away came fast and strong. John clasped his hands behind his back. "She's affecting you?"

"Not much. A little bit of warmth and a touch of wild meadows. She smells like home. Is that what she smells like to you?"

"Home, yes, but it's strawberries for me." John gritted his teeth. "Jasmine for Perry."

"Interesting." He sniffed her sleeve and then jerked upward. "Impossible."

"Who is it?"

"You didn't recognize her?"

"I only saw her back. Why? Should I know her?"

\* \* \* \*

Sarah was fighting a losing battle and she couldn't even see her attackers. But they were everywhere, she could feel them. Flailing her arms, she hit them several times before they restrained her.

"Sarah, stop!"

His voice was familiar, but why? Someone pinned her arms and she squirmed. "Let me go," she cried.

"Sarah, open your eyes."

Were they closed? Was that her problem? She opened them and found a man straddling her. The light source behind him kept him in shadows. He was the reason she couldn't move. She screamed when he clamped a hand over her mouth.

"Sarah, it's me, John. It's okay. You're safe."

John? She blinked her eyesight into focus and took in his scent. It was him. She stopped squirming and tears sprang from her eyes.

He removed his hand, crawled off her, and then lifted her into his arms. "It's okay Sarah. You're going to be okay."

She hugged him tight, his wonderful scent calming her. He was real and he was holding her. She cried until the memory of her nightmare faded.

"Where are we?" she asked.

"At my apartment. I didn't think you were ever going to be lucid. Do you remember anything?"

Unable to find a tissue, she grabbed the sheet and wiped her face. When she sniffled, John excused himself and came back with a roll of toilet paper. "Will this do?"

She nodded and used some to blow her nose. "Thanks." Breathing easier, she fought to remember the events, but it was as if a fog had settled over everything. "I remember going to the coffee shop and meeting Ms. Delany. Then it gets fuzzy. But I think she's a vampire."

John looked away and was quiet for a moment before speaking. "And you'd be correct."

She scooted back against the wall. "So you caught her?"

He paused longer this time. "No, but we know who she is." He met her gaze. "Used to go by the name of Danielle Delaveaux."

"Danielle? Your Danielle? I thought she was executed."

He chuckled, but there was no joy behind it. "Surprised us, too."

"Are you sure it's her?"

"Barnet is. He smelled her on your clothes. I never got a chance to imprint her scent after my turning, she was taken away before I could do that. Maybe if I had..."

She grabbed his arm. "Don't go blaming yourself for something you had no control over. So what happened? How is she alive?"

"We don't know. Barnet's checking into that."

"What do you think her plans are, since she didn't...you know, kill me?"

He closed his eyes and tilted his head back. "Something sick and twisted, I'm sure. I'm just thankful I was there when you screamed. If I had been a few minutes later..."

She hugged him. "Don't. I'm fine. You got me."

He didn't return the hug and the disappointment stung.

She pulled away. "What's the matter?"

"This is all my fault. You don't know how sorry I am to have dragged you into all of this. Maybe you'd be better off without me in your life."

"Don't say that. How could you know? She's doing this, not you. Would you have me blame myself for what Steven did to me?"

John flinched. Good. She'd made her point.

"But Sarah—"

She covered his mouth. "No. This isn't your fault. None of this is your fault. Don't you realize how happy you've made me? Even with all the craziness we're going through? Don't take that away from me. Please don't do that." Tears she thought had dried sprang to life once more.

"Ah, Sarah," he said and then hugged her tight.

She clung to him. She never wanted to let him go. "I love you, John."

"I love you, too."

It took some effort, but she was able to compose herself enough and pull away. With the room so dark, she had no idea if it were day or night. "What time is it? How long was I out?"

He looked at his watch. "Seven-fifteen."

"In the morning? Crap. I'm going to be late for work." She scooted to the edge of the bed, but John grabbed her arm.

"What do you mean work? You're not going anywhere."

"John, stop it. I'm fine." She wrenched her arm free, but when she put weight on her feet, her legs gave out. She would have fallen if John hadn't caught her.

He picked her up and placed her back on the bed. "You can't even stand," he said as he sat beside her. "You're not going back until this is over."

Was he trying to pick a fight? Didn't he realize what he was saying? "Don't go there. I won't have you telling me what I can or cannot do. I've lived that life before and I won't live it again."

He placed his head in his hands. "Oh God, Sarah. I don't mean to sound controlling. Please understand. I can't protect you if you go out there."

She pulled his hands away. He was going to look at her when she spoke. "So you want to imprison me?"

He placed his hands on her shoulders. "That's not what I want to do. When this mess is over with, things will be different."

"Yes, but how long will that take? I can't live my life around uncertainty. Danielle may strike tomorrow or wait a month. We don't know, do we? I can't have other people controlling what I do. That isn't any way to live. I could get hit by a bus tomorrow and this Ray and Danielle mess won't matter a bit."

"Don't talk like that."

"Well, it's true."

"Damn it. I wish I could turn you now. I'd do it."

"You mean it? You wouldn't make me wait?"

"I'd do anything to keep you safe." He dropped his arms and lowered his head. "But even if Barnet is wrong and it worked, I still can't turn you without permission, so what am I supposed to do?"

Stupid permission, but she certainly didn't want to cause John any problems. Then again, Barnet could be correct and she couldn't be turned. "Trust me?"

"I do trust you."

"Then please don't cage me up like an animal. I can't live that way."

He jumped up and paced the small room. "I know, I know! I'm sorry. I know I don't have any right." After a few moments, he stopped. "Can you do me a favor?"

"What kind of favor?"

He took her face into his hands. "I'm not asking you to give up your job or your friends, but do you think you could not go into work today? You're really in no shape and I'd feel so much better having you close. Can you do that for me? Would you do that for me? Please?"

While Sarah could quickly recover from the physical abuse Danielle inflicted, the mental abuse John was suffering might not be so easy to repair. The agony on his face could easily be erased with one little word. He wasn't asking for much. "Yes, John. I can do that."

# Chapter 32

"Do you have any plans for Valentine's Day?" Lori asked Sarah.

They were sitting in the break room, eating their lunch. John seemed to think Sarah would be safer if she stayed at work all day and she had no problem with that. The less she traveled the better. Why make it easier for Danielle to capture her?

"Valentine's Day? Is that coming up?" Sarah asked before taking a bite of her sandwich.

"Yeah, silly, it's tomorrow."

Sarah had never really cared for the holiday. It was just another day to make lonely people feel lonelier. Not that she would feel lonely this year, but then she didn't need a holiday for John to prove his love. He showed her every day. She didn't even have to ask him to feed from her last night and his initiation made it all the sweeter, since it appeared he'd done it out of enjoyment instead of some insane need to protect her. "If John has made any plans, he hasn't shared them with me."

Lori opened a small bag of chips. "What's been going on with you two? You've been quiet about him and that's not like you."

What should Sarah say? That spending a night with John led to another and then another? And then after dinner each night, he had made love to her until she'd been too exhausted to move and each morning more of her stuff had magically appeared.

The fiend. Ah, but he was her fiend.

She smiled. "I think I moved in with him."

Lori went ballistic, which was better than Sarah had anticipated. "You think? When did that happen? When were you going to tell me? Are you crazy?"

Sarah took another bite of her sandwich. Lori would eventually calm down.

"Have you learned nothing from your relationship with Steven?"

That last question stung. "I thought you liked John. He's nothing like Steven."

"I know that, and I do like him, but Sarah, you haven't even known him a month. Don't you think you're rushing things a bit?"

Maybe, but there was no way she could tell her friend the truth. Being vague was the only way to go. "I love him, Lori, and he loves me."

"So, what, did he propose?"

"No, he didn't propose." Did vampires even get married? Would a legal document even work with him? She'd get old, but he wouldn't. Oh God, she didn't even want to think about that. Still, what would pass for the exchanging of vows? The exchanging of blood? Hmm. Maybe that was how she could become a vampire. Wasn't that how it worked in the myth?

"Then why did you move in with him?"

Because he was a sneaky little bastard. When would he learn he only had to ask? "Because I love him, why else? Don't spoil this for me, okay? I've had the best couple of days so far."

Lori shook her head slowly. "I don't know. I hate seeing you make the same mistakes again."

Sarah was getting weary defending herself where John was concerned. "I'm not making a mistake. Besides, I haven't made any commitment with him. I'm not even giving up my apartment."

Lori's eyes lit up. "You're not?"

"Not yet. He'd rather I wait a year."

"Okay, then," Lori said, and opened up her lunch bag.

"That's it? That's all I had to say, that I wasn't giving up my apartment? Boy, I wish I had led with that bit of information." Sarah laughed in spite of herself.

The day progressed as normal days did: meet with client, file, repeat. A few minutes after four o'clock, her cellphone rang displaying Lori's name. Sarah laughed as she answered the call. "You too lazy to walk over to my office?"

"I'm down in the garage. I just got back from a client's and didn't watch where I was walking and I cut my leg. It's bleeding all over. Can you bring me the first aid kit?"

"What? Do you need to go to the hospital?"

"I don't think so. Bring the first aid kit and you can decide for yourself. But hurry, okay? I parked next to your Bumblebee."

Sarah disconnected the call and ran to the break room. After opening several cabinets, she found the kit. She rushed back to her office and grabbed her coat and purse, just in case she needed to drive. How the hell had Lori hurt herself so badly? Sarah was usually the klutz.

On her way out the door, she waved at Linda, who was busy chatting on the phone. Sarah arrived at the garage, rushed toward the Bumblebee, and abruptly stopped. Lori's car was parked beside it, but her friend was nowhere to be found. As a matter of fact, she'd never told Lori her nickname for John's SUV, which could only mean…

It was a trap and she'd walked right into it. Shit.

A hand covered her mouth and something pricked her neck. She jumped and squealed at the touch. Oh God. Not again! As the garage grew dimmer, the first aid kit slipped through her fingers.

\* \* \* \*

John scrolled through the many different Valentine flower arrangements. Buying flowers in the computer age was less personal, but, for someone who couldn't venture out into the sun when most stores were open, sure made the process easy.

He'd never thought he'd buy flowers again. The last time had been for his mother's funeral. He also never thought he'd be comfortable feeding from Sarah, yet once he became used to the sensations, he was able to take control and actually enjoy it. Having her taking vitamins and iron and eating more nutritiously helped, too. She hadn't passed out the last time they made love, either.

He'd made his selection of pink—of course—and white roses when his neck tingled and stomach twisted. The last time that had happened, Sarah had been nearly abducted.

He rubbed his neck. It was only four-thirty, so the chances Danielle had captured Sarah were pretty slim, especially since Sarah was at work. But, what if… He grabbed his cellphone. She could yell at him all she wanted, but he needed to hear her voice or he'd go stir crazy.

237

He placed the call and promptly went to her voice mail. Damn. Had she let that thing die again? Maybe he should get her a charger for her office. He called her work number and the receptionist answered the phone.

"Hi, Linda. Would you get Sarah for me please?"

"I'm sorry, she stepped out. Would you like her voice mail?"

Sarah wasn't there? Where would she be going, and without her phone? His stomach twisted tighter. "How about Lori?"

"No, she's out with a—Oh wait. She just walked in. Hold on."

"This is Lori, how may I help you?"

"It's John. Do you know where Sarah is?"

"If she's not in her office, then I guess I don't. What's up?"

He massaged the tingling in his neck. Something was wrong. "Can you check and see if she's left for the day? Her phone isn't working and I'm a little worried."

"Is there a reason you have to know where she is every minute? Because that's not a healthy sign. Neither is having her move in with you when you've only known each other a month."

Shit. He didn't need this right now. "She's only staying with me until Steven has been caught. I'm not trying to control her. I just want to keep her safe and I don't trust Steven. Would you check, please?"

"Oh. I hadn't thought about it like that. Give me a minute. I'll call you back."

He stood and paced the room. He needed to calm down. Get the facts first. Jumping to conclusions wouldn't solve anything.

Someone knocked at his door and he jumped. Yeah, his nerves were shot or he would have heard—he sniffed the air—Heather climbing the stairs. He opened the door.

"Hey, Boss. Someone left this at the bar and said it was urgent you get it." She handed over an envelope. "Also, the contractor called. They'll be out Monday to work on the back steps. What made you go with cement?"

He flipped the envelope over and something inside shifted. It only stated his name. No address. No return address, either. Who would be sending him an urgent note? His stomach twisted. Oh shit.

"Hey, you okay?" Heather asked.

"I'm fine. Thanks." John closed the door behind Heather. He ripped open the envelope and Sarah's necklace fell to the floor. Oh

God! Sarah! With shaky hands, he picked it up. A piece of paper stuck out of the envelope. He read it twice before it registered.

*She's in Urbana. You know the address.*

He collapsed on the couch. Danielle had abducted Sarah. Who else? But how did she do it? The sun hadn't set.

His phone rang. Lori. He pushed the answer button.

"Hey, John. I looked all over. Her computer is still on and your car is in the garage, but her purse and coat are gone."

He needed to ease her worries because he was worrying enough for both of them. "It's okay, Lori. She just got here. She's not feeling well and came home. Thanks for looking, though. I appreciate it."

"Oh, okay. Have her call me when she's feeling better."

"I will. Thanks again."

He disconnected the call and stared at the note. Danielle wouldn't expect him to do anything until the sun set, which meant he could get the upper hand if he arrived beforehand. But how? How was he going to get to his car? How was he going to drive it? And how was he going to do all that and keep from turning into a crispy critter?

Shit, shit, shit.

# Chapter 33

John stood at the back exit of Wings, roll of foil in hand, tape in pocket. Shade shrouded the alley making it safer, but not completely safe.

The one thing he'd been told over and over—avoid the sun at all costs—was the one thing he had to face. Barnet had tried talking him out of this madness, to wait for him, but John wouldn't hear of it. Bad enough to wait the ninety minutes until sunset, but then to wait another two hours for Barnet's help? Wasn't happening. Nothing would stop him from saving Sarah from that bitch who had turned him. And the only way he would have the upper hand on Danielle was if he showed up sooner than she expected.

Wearing more clothes than normal—jacket, scarf, gloves—John had covered as much skin as possible. He'd even snatched Pete's Looney Tunes ball cap, wishing it were a sombrero or one of Sarah's knit caps. His ears and face were still exposed.

He took a deep breath to calm his wildly beating heart and then opened the door, praying he would survive the trip. Even in the shade, the brilliant blue sky blinded his eyes. If only he'd found some sunglasses. Not much he could do about that now. He lowered the bill of the cap and stepped outside.

So far so good. He stopped at the first beam of light, waited for the traffic to clear and then zipped across. Getting the brunt of the sun, his right ear and cheek burned for a moment, but John continued on his way. He'd heal, but at a cost. Each time he ventured out into the sun, the toll added up. By the time he arrived at the garage, he staggered as if he'd drunk one too many beers. A lone passerby would certainly aid his cause, but he wouldn't sit around and wait.

He stumbled to his Xterra and opened the door. Sarah's scent hit him hard. Despair weaseled in to take hold, but he refused to let it control him. He would save her from Danielle and nothing was going to stop him. He pulled the tape out of his pocket. The glass was already tinted, but how much of the harmful rays would it block and which rays were harmful? Better to be safe and cover the suckers. He left openings for the side mirrors and kept half the windshield clear. His destination lay northeast, away from the setting sun. He should be good. If not, he'd find out how well the glass was treated.

With the last window covered, he'd tossed the tape onto the passenger seat when a lone person ventured inside the garage. John hesitated for only a moment—Sarah would need him at his best— and he fed as quickly as possible.

While in the city, he avoided any street forcing him into the sun, but once he hit the freeway, he was in the clear. He arrived in Urbana in record time.

To prevent giving away his arrival—one of the disadvantages to owning a bright yellow vehicle—he parked several houses down in a copse of trees. The sun wouldn't set for another fifty minutes, but the tree line and hills would create darkness sooner. At least, he hoped so. He climbed out of the vehicle and headed for his neighbor's yard, avoiding the sun as best as he could.

A small forest of pine trees divided the homes and John crouched between two, safely in the shade and hidden from anyone's view. With her mouth gagged, Sarah was hugging a tree— her wrists and ankles bound—in the middle of his yard, sitting in what little sunlight remained. Danielle was most likely hiding in the house or in the barn, somewhere protected. Was she alert, watching for his arrival, or lackadaisical, confident he wouldn't arrive until well after sunset? He hoped for his and Sarah's sake it was the latter, because there wouldn't be a better time to strike.

* * * *

Sarah leaned her head against the tree. She hadn't seen anyone since she awoke, but could only assume Danielle was behind it all. Why else be tied up like bait?

She tugged on the restraints again, but like the last time the cable ties only cut into her skin. Nothing she did seemed to loosen them.

Poor John. Most likely Danielle had informed him of her capture, probably enjoyed torturing him like that. He must be going crazy with fear. He wouldn't be able to leave Wings until the sun set, which meant Sarah would be sitting out in the cold for at least thirty minutes after. What would happen during that time? Would she see Danielle then? Oh crap.

John appeared out of nowhere and he wasn't a burning fireball. Oh thank heavens. She yelled at him to hurry—because if he could be out in the shade, so could Danielle—but the gag muffled her words.

"Wow, you got here sooner than I expected," Danielle said. "I'm impressed."

"Shit," John muttered. Remorse filled his eyes.

He stared at Danielle as she emerged from the barn. She looked almost normal, wearing a flowered blouse and dress slacks. But there was a huge difference between this woman and the woman Sarah had met at the coffee shop. The auburn hair was now a long and wavy blonde and the plain brown eyes were gone, replaced with a sparkly ice blue, so pale they were almost white.

"I was hoping Barnet was wrong," John said.

"Didn't you know? He's never wrong."

He stood. "Fine, you got me. Let Sarah go."

"Now, why would I do that? If I only wanted you, I could have had you. But you hurt me, John, and now it's my turn."

Steven appeared behind John and held out a gun. Sarah screamed a warning that came out all garbled, but John took heed and spun around.

A muffled pop sounded and John stumbled back. What was that? What was happening?

Another pop. Again, John jerked. Clutching his stomach, he turned around. Blood spread out from the wounds. Oh God, it was Steven. Sarah screamed at him, "Stop shooting! Stop shooting!" But her words were useless. She couldn't even understand herself.

John staggered toward her, his face in shock. "I'm so sorry."

A louder shot went off. She jumped. Blood sprayed from his mouth and hit her face and coat. John fell to his knees. She cried, screaming out his name. On his way to the ground, he grabbed her shoulder and his hand brushed her neck. Oh, the pain. The horrible pain.

# Chapter 34

Sarah opened her eyes to the last traces of the debilitating pain she'd felt at John's touch. How long had she been out? Shade covered the area completely. Maybe five, ten minutes? Hopefully that was the end of her knockout events. They were giving her a headache.

The gag was long gone and she could breathe freely, but her throat constricted when she remembered John collapsing. So much blood. So much pain. Regardless of what he had told her, how could he survive all that?

However, she was still alive and bound to the tree, so he must have survived. Why keep her if he'd died?

Sounds of ripping and laughter filled the air. What the hell was going on? She scooted around the tree to see what the commotion was about and nearly burst out crying.

Oh God. What was Steven doing?

Using a knife, he cut the clothes off John and tossed them aside. John lay still as death, with a stake protruding from his chest. He was covered in blood.

"John!" *Oh please don't let him be dead.* She strained to get free, but the cable ties weren't any looser and they cut into her tender skin again. Damn it, she'd gnaw her wrists free if she could.

John blinked.

Thank God, he was alive, but he wouldn't remain that way when the sun came up. Steven was making sure of that. Or make that Danielle—wherever the hell she'd disappeared. No doubt she

244

was controlling him. He'd never even flinched when Sarah had yelled John's name.

If only she were a vampire, she'd be able to snap these restraints free. She stared at her sleeve, covered in blood. John's blood. Was that the answer? Would it turn her? Hell, what did she have to lose? Nothing, that's what. She sucked off all she could reach. It tasted sweet, not the coppery flavor she'd experienced whenever John bit her. After ingesting what she could, she waited. Please let it have worked.

A small cramp formed in her stomach and lasted a few seconds. That was it? She'd gotten the impression turning hurt a lot. Whatever, as long as it worked. She took a deep breath and yanked on the ties.

Pain shot up her arms and she cried out, but the plastic never budged. Oh God. She rested her forehead against the tree. How was she going to get them out of this alive?

\* \* \* \*

John stared up at the darkening sky. Two shots in the front, one in the back and they all hurt like the dickens. But the worst pain came from his chest and it had nothing to do with the stake. He'd failed Sarah.

Steven cut the jeans and shirt free, not caring about nicking his skin. As if he wouldn't notice another stab wound or four. Several tugs later, John lay naked to the universe. Come morning, if he wasn't freed, he'd be one crispy critter and Sarah would be…what? No matter what Danielle had in store for her, it couldn't be good.

Steven left him and headed for the barn.

John wiggled his fingers and toes and hope flared. A stake to the heart should have rendered him immobile from the neck down, so if he could move, then the stake hadn't completely pierced his heart. If Danielle got wind of that, she might readjust it. Better to play it cool and hope for a chance at freedom.

Sarah called him for the second time. He'd been afraid to look at her earlier, but sucked it up and turned his head. Oh, what she must be going through. Danielle had been remotely curious as to why Sarah screamed out the way she had before passing out. If only he could take back that touch.

"Ah, I see the little freak has come back to join the living," Danielle said as she emerged from the barn. "And how are you, John? Are you comfortable?" Laughing, she sat on the ground beside him and gazed at his body, especially the lower half. "What a shame."

"What are you going to do to him?" Sarah asked.

"What does it look like? I'm going to execute him."

"But why? He's never hurt anyone."

"Danielle doesn't care about anyone but herself," he said as he struggled for breath.

"Now John, is that any way to treat me? If it weren't for me, you'd be an old man by now, if not dead, wouldn't you? I gave you the greatest gift anyone could give and all I asked in return was for you to love me. Instead, you sentence me to death and fall in love with that freak. That whore." She stood and ambled over to Sarah. "That's why I'm doing this, dear Sarah. Revenge."

"But he wasn't involved in your sentencing," Sarah said. "You have to know that."

"He was the reason behind it all. That's what I know."

"So how did you escape?" John made sure he sounded weak, although his raspy voice was real enough. His lung was most likely punctured. But the more he could get her talking the better his chances of getting him and Sarah out of here. He just needed time. Time for Barnet to arrive. Time to heal. Time for the stake to completely dislodge from his heart. Unfortunately, he didn't think he could get Danielle to give him an hour. Or three.

Danielle strolled back to John. "Luck, pure luck. My guard took pity on me and freed me. We stole the cremated remains of a human and put them in my place. In return, I gave him sexual pleasures. However, I got bored with him and he became belligerent. The risk of him blabbing everything became too high, so I made sure he met with a fatal accident."

"But now your secret's out."

"No thanks to you. You just couldn't keep it in your pants, could you? As long as you were miserable, I was happy. And I made sure you were miserable, if not downright frustrated. Did you have fun with those steps?"

"That was you?"

"I really thought when she stabbed you, that would be the end of it, especially when you were forced to tell her the truth, but no. You had to go and make up." Danielle puckered her lips in an evil sneer and made kissy noises. "You two make me sick. I want to be happy. So if I have to come out to be happy again, well, then…"

She shrugged. "I got away once, I can do it again. It's not like the Committee has all these resources to find me, you know."

"But they know you're alive now. You don't think they'll catch you?"

She tipped her head back and laughed. "They'll try, I'm sure. But you see, I don't have any problem manipulating humans like they do, and human lackeys come in very handy during the daylight hours, especially when they're...pliable. When the human wants to do what you suggest, it makes it less problematic. And downright fun." She walked over to Sarah. "I have to say, Sarah, Steven is quite the lover. Although he's not nearly as endowed as our dear John, he did show me a trick or two. I'm amazed you ever left him. But then, he never beat me. Of course I never gave him reason to."

Sarah winced. "Is that how you always knew where we were? You made Steven follow me?"

"That was part of it," Danielle answered. "The bug I put in your apartment helped. Steven only made it more interesting. I sure did enjoy your expression when he kissed you at the hockey game. I only wish I could have seen what he did to you in your apartment. Did I hear you moan in pleasure?"

"Stop it," John said.

"Or what, John? Hmm? You going to come to her defense?" Danielle paced between John and Sarah. "You know, I didn't make you for her. I made you for me."

"And what I wanted never came into play?"

"If you had given me a chance, you would have come around. But nooo. What was it about me you didn't like, huh? You seemed to enjoy everything I gave you up until the bite."

"The truth would have been good."

"Fine. Then I'll give you the truth. You broke my heart, John. First when you rejected my love and again when you started loving *her*." She pointed at Sarah. "Now I want you to feel the pain you've caused me. To suffer as I've suffered all these years. And what better way to make you suffer than for you to know Sarah will be with Ray until her final breath and that there's nothing you can do about it."

"What?" Sarah yelled.

Ray emerged from the barn.

"No!" Oh, God. Not Ray. John's chest tightened. "You're the reason he never turned himself in?"

"Dear John, I intercepted in all your do-goodings. He's just the first you noticed." Danielle wagged her finger back and forth. "Don't you know you're not supposed to interfere?"

"And what the hell is this? Please don't do it. Even you can't be that cruel."

"Then you don't know me very well. But to show you I'm not completely heartless, I'll let you say goodbye. That's more than you ever gave me." Danielle headed for the barn. "Sarah dear, I plan on freeing you. Do be good and not run away or fight, because if you do, you'll be leaving with Ray immediately and won't be able to say goodbye to John. Do you understand?"

Sarah nodded, "Yes, I understand."

Danielle zipped inside the barn and returned with small pruning shears. She snapped the ties that bound Sarah, who immediately started rubbing her wrists.

Danielle kicked Sarah in the hip. "Go on. I don't have all night. But you even touch that stake and you're out of here."

Sarah nodded and crawled over to him, shaking her legs in the process. She knelt beside him, her face lined with worry and spotted with his blood. Damn. How much had he gotten on her?

If only he could reassure her. Tell her not give up hope. Ask her to feed him. But not with Danielle hovering about. Why propel her to speed things up?

"Oh, John." Sarah reached out to touch him.

"Don't. I can't hold back the pain for you."

Ignoring him, she cupped his cheek and winced, but when she closed her eyes, the pain dissipated. He took a long, painless breath.

Danielle squatted beside them. "You must be a witch, dear Sarah. However did you do that?"

*"Sweetie, don't tell her. Don't tell her."* John closed his eyes. What he wouldn't give to talk to Sarah freely.

"I...I don't know. *John? Did I hear you in my head?*"

He opened his eyes. What the hell? *"I don't know. Did you?"*

Danielle frowned for a moment before her face lit up. "You know, there is this story about the Perfect Mate. Could it be possible? Oh, this is too delicious. Too perfect. Have you fed from her? I bet you did. Maybe I should sample her before I give her over to Ray."

"No!" John yelled. "Don't you touch her, Danielle."

"Well, now you've made up my mind."

Danielle grabbed Sarah by the waist, disconnecting their link and the relief she brought him. The pain hit him anew and he gasped. Sarah struggled, but threats of Ray made her stop.

Standing behind Sarah and holding her still, Danielle pulled Sarah's hair back and yanked her neck to the side. The look of horror on Sarah's face ate at John. In one swift movement, the vampire sank her teeth into Sarah's neck. But before Sarah had a chance to cry out, Danielle pulled away and spit out the blood.

"Oh yuck!" She threw Sarah to the ground and spit a few times before wiping her mouth. "That is the most disgusting thing I've ever tasted."

Blood oozed from Danielle's mark, leaving two little trails down Sarah's neck. It might have been disgusting to Danielle, but her sweet scent caused his fangs to extend.

"That wasn't any fun," Danielle said. "I'm ready to end this now. Sarah, say your goodbyes. You have five minutes."

Sarah crawled over to him and held his face. "I love you."

She couldn't erase his pain. Her fear was too strong. "Promise me you won't give up."

"I'll try. But John—"

"No try. No buts. Just promise. *You're a smart woman. If anyone can escape Ray, it'll be you.*"

"Okay." She brought her lips to his and kissed him softly. "*What about you? Will my blood help? Can you bite my lips, tongue, anything?*"

He still couldn't get over communicating this way with her and tried to lighten the otherwise dour mood. "*I thought you'd never ask.*"

She smiled against his mouth, and for a moment he thought he'd succeeded, but then a tear dripped onto his cheek. "*Oh, John. I'm so scared.*"

"*I know you are. I am too. Just know I'll do everything I can to find you, okay? Now press your tongue against my fangs.*"

She did as he instructed and he bit down. Her sweet essence trickled in his mouth and sent a shocking jolt through his system. Damn. When had she gotten so potent? Energy rushed through him: healing him, giving him strength. The power that charged through him from the small amount he sucked made him wonder what it would be like if he struck a vein. He'd probably heal in minutes instead of hours.

"Good Lord." Danielle yanked Sarah up by her collar. "I'd tell you to get a room except I don't want you two together. Now say night-night." She stuck a needle in Sarah's neck.

"I love you," were the last words Sarah spoke before passing out. Danielle flung Sarah to the ground. She landed beside him, her hand limp on his chest.

"Sarah? *Sarah!*" Silence greeted him. "No!" He couldn't lose her, not like this.

"How touching—not. Okay, Ray. You can have her, now."

If John was to save Sarah, this was his only chance. Her blood was working wonders through his system. Once Danielle left, he'd be able to remove the damn stake on his own and go after the killer. Danielle's death would come later. Of course, it all hinged on Danielle; if she kept control, he was sunk.

As Ray approached Sarah, John said, "You lay a hand on her and you're dead, do you hear me?"

Ray bent close and laughed in John's face. "I don't think you're in any position to threaten me."

John couldn't have planned it any better than if he'd commanded it. He spit in Ray's face and—praying it worked—sent a verbal command. *"Grab my throat and tell me to go to Hell."*

Ray followed the orders, but with that zombie look. Wouldn't take long before Danielle noticed.

*"Where are you taking her?"* An address flashed across his vision. Yes, he'd been there. *"You will not harm Sarah. You will release—"*

Danielle slapped his face, cutting off his connection. "You don't think I've noticed how you've been moving? And how you controlled Ray? Seems I missed a vital organ."

She held another stake. As she brought her arm down, he shot his up and grabbed her by the wrist. Her eyes widened in shock. He sat up and reached for the weapon, but a punch to the jaw—courtesy of Ray—distracted him, giving Danielle the advantage. She wrenched free and plunged the stake into his chest. Excruciating pain exploded as his heart split in two. He cried out and collapsed to the ground, no longer able to move his arms or legs. Damn her!

She spoke to Ray. "You will do to Sarah whatever brings you pleasure. Now take her and leave."

Ray slung Sarah over his shoulder like a sack of grain and walked out of sight.

John used everything inside him to get Ray to stop, but either Danielle was controlling him or that stake had done its job. The rage inside overtook the pain and John roared. "This isn't over Danielle. Barnet is on his way."

Danielle knelt beside his head. "I hate to break it to you, but it is over. I really don't care if you're saved or not because you'll never find her in time, if at all. Sarah will be dead in a most unpleasant way and I'll have my revenge. Now forgive me, but I must gag you. Don't want the neighbors hearing you scream when you're frying in the sun. You understand, don't you?"

Holding his head still, she shoved a ball into his mouth and secured it in place with a leather strap, clamping his jaw in place. He couldn't bite the ball free and loosening the straps would be impossible without the use of his hands.

"Bye-bye, John." She waited as Steven emerged from the barn and together they walked away.

This wasn't over. Barnet would arrive in time and John would find Sarah. She was strong, she would survive. Hope was all he had left. He looked to the sky and prayed.

251

# Chapter 35

Sarah awoke with one monster of a headache. She was getting downright pissed at being knocked out all the time. Certainly couldn't be good for her brain. Of course, her brain was the least of her worries. Ray lurked around here somewhere.

The basement stunk of mildew and other unpleasant odors she'd rather not identify and the cold floor penetrated through the thin mattress. Her coat and shoes were missing, but she still wore her clothes. She thanked the Lord for that small favor.

No sign of Ray, though. She moved to sit up, but two foot-long straps attached to the wall and secured around her wrists kept her arms above her head. Damn it. She reached for one of the knots, but couldn't get her hands to meet. At least her feet were free. Using the straps for leverage, she hoisted up into a sitting position. The knot holding her left wrist loosened and her heart skipped a beat with hope. If she could only get her mouth on the stupid thing, she could grab the knot with her teeth, but no such luck there, either. Instead, she worked at making her hand as small as possible so she could slip it free. With Ray out of sight, now would be the best chance to escape.

The door to the basement squeaked. Sarah froze.

As Ray descended into the hellhole—wearing only jeans—each step of the wooden staircase squealed in protest. He took a bite of an apple and the juices ran down his chest. Was he just showing off his muscular body—he apparently hit the weights on a daily basis—or getting a start on things? She didn't want to think of what things he might have in mind.

He looked her way when he arrived at the bottom, stopped, and raised his eyebrows. "Did you enjoy your nap?"

She refused to answer. Maybe if she didn't play his games, he'd lose interest.

Taking another bite from his apple, he strolled toward her and sat on the mattress. He extended his free hand. She looked away, but he held her chin and forced her to face him. Her hammering heart nearly punched a hole through her ribs.

"Do I disgust you?" he asked.

Looking at him, she'd say no. His body wasn't disfigured in any way and his smile probably charmed many a girl. Unfortunately for many women, this package was deceiving.

"Do you want a bite?" He offered the apple.

Did he really expect her to take the bait, or was it part of his game? Either way, she wasn't falling for it.

"Not hungry, huh?" He released her and laughed as he stood. "Are you going to be this quiet all night? Maybe if I found something to talk about." He spun around and searched, as if unfamiliar with the room, but he probably knew exactly where everything was kept.

"Ah!" He approached the workbench on the far wall. The room was darker on that end, but she could still make out his movements. He put his apple down and picked something else up. When he turned around, he held something large and shiny. A knife! She gasped.

"Hey, a reaction, that's great. Are you scared?"

Maybe her silence was the wrong approach. Forcing a smile, she said, "Of course not. I'm just not fond of knives."

"You're not? Don't you use them in the kitchen? How could you even cook without one?" He returned, knelt beside the mattress, and brought the blade to her face. "Or did you have an unfortunate accident with one?"

Her reflection flashed off the shiny metal and her throat constricted. "Please don't."

He smiled. "Don't what?"

She didn't want to look at the knife, but when he moved it down to her chest, her gaze was glued to the weapon. Was he going to cut her? He brought the tip down to the top button of her blouse and popped it off with ease.

"Oops, looks like you lost a button." With his free hand, he caressed her face.

Okay, so he was trying to make her afraid. She looked him in the eyes, determined not to show her fear, but the knife made it damn hard.

"You're pretty, you know that?" He ran his index finger down her throat, across her collarbone until he reached the next button. "But something's missing."

He brought the knife-wielding hand up and ripped her blouse open. Clink, clink, clink. Buttons ricocheted off the wall and floor. The blade scraped across her cheek and she jerked back, hitting the wall. Shit.

He took a deep breath and nodded. "That's better," he said. "You look scared now."

Well, duh. Her tremors could probably set off a Richter scale and the neighbors could probably hear the pounding of her heart. But John had told her not to give up, so she wouldn't. His life depended on it, too. So how the hell could she get free without being cut to shreds?

Ray stared at her chest. "You have a lot of scars. What happened to you?"

When she didn't answer in the amount of time he allotted, he stuck his hand inside her bra and squeezed her breast. Pain shot through her, bringing tears to her eyes, and she shrieked. She longed to zone out, to go to that special place she'd gone whenever Steven had abused her, but if she went there, she might not come back.

He let up on the pressure. "Answer me or I do it again."

"Pushed." She gasped for breath. "Down the stairs. Broke mirror."

"Pushed? And you survived. Wow." He pinched her nipple and leaned in close to her face, the scent of apple strong on his breath. "I sure hope you survive the night. I could use the challenge."

She gritted her teeth against the pain he inflicted. She'd suffered enough at Steven's hands, but he'd never used a knife and he'd always apologized afterward. Somehow she didn't think Ray cared that much.

"Why don't we take a look and see what you have to offer." He took the tip of the knife and sliced her bra apart, nicking her skin in the process. She inhaled through the sting.

The restraints and the wall kept her from moving away, but her feet were free. Before he could touch her again, she brought up her knee and knocked him over. The knife clamored as it hit the floor. If only she could have clocked him in the head. Unconscious would have been so much better.

"Now why'd you go and do that?" He leaned over and retrieved the knife.

While he looked away, she worked at freeing her hand.

Ray held the weapon and gazed at it as if he were mesmerized. He brushed his fingers lovingly over the shiny blade, either cleaning or comforting it. When he turned his attention back toward her, she expected a scowl, not a half-smile. Slowly, he rose, holding the knife by his side. She prepared for a lunge, but he strolled to the foot of the mattress instead and knelt.

"You know, Bethany enjoyed being tied up when I fucked her," he said. "Said it gave her a better orgasm. Me, I liked it when she was really scared. Not that acting crap she was into. Unfortunately, by the time I got real fear from her, I'd gone too far."

The paper had mentioned Bethany, his first victim. Sarah needed to distract him, but how? Normally fear shut her up, but since he was intent on getting her to talk, she obliged, hoping time would be her friend. "What did Bethany do to you?"

At the mention of Bethany's name, he gazed into Sarah's eyes and cocked his head. "She didn't do anything to me. She loved me. I loved her."

"But you killed her."

"I didn't mean to. But when she became truly terrified, I wanted more. Her fear was a fuel I hadn't expected. I'm hungry for it."

"So, if I'm not scared, you'll leave me alone?" Talk about grasping at straws.

He tipped his head back and laughed. "Oh, you'll feel fear. Question is, will you survive? Bethany couldn't. Neither could the others. I really am curious."

Ray placed the knife down on the mattress and crawled toward her. Oh shit. She brought her legs up and used the straps as leverage to stand. Before she could gain her balance, he grabbed her feet and pulled, yanking her arms against the restraints. *No!*

Pain exploded in her right wrist, but her left hand slipped through the restraint. *Holy shit!* She held on with her fingers. No better time to take him out. The blade was within reach. She only needed to get one good kick in.

*Disable him. Get free.*

Of course fighting was exactly what he wanted, but what choice did she have? She couldn't very well lie still while he tied her up.

She twisted and kicked as he pulled her down on the mattress. His strength won out and he immobilized her by kneeling on her legs. Pain kept her movements to a minimum. Broken legs would not help.

"I like your cat socks. You wore those penguin ones back at the garage. You got a collection or something?" He stared as if he expected an answer.

If she remained quiet, he might actually break her leg. "I do."

Ray laughed. "Man, I'd like to see that."

"Then let's go. You can have them if you want."

"Nice try." He smirked as he unfastened her pants. Grabbing the waistband, he dismounted and pulled them off her.

Free from his grasp, she sat back up. He reached for her again and she kicked out at him, frantic. Terror took over and her kicks became wild, weak, and ineffective. He even laughed as if she were playing some kind of game and maybe it was a game to him, but it was all too real to her. After her futile attempts to knock him silly, he finally grabbed her right ankle and slipped a rope over her foot. Pulling the noose tight, he secured the other end to the floor. All the twisting and turning couldn't prevent him from doing the same with her left.

Great. Not only was she tied up, she'd aroused him in the process.

"That's better." He stood with his hands on his hips, looking pleased with himself.

She was spread out and vulnerable to whatever he had in mind. All her hopes hinged on one free hand. Would it be enough? She held both straps so he wouldn't notice the difference.

He straddled her, making it hard not to see—or feel—his growing arousal. Closing her eyes and zoning out was inviting, but not knowing would only be worse—she could lose her opportunity for escape—so she kept her attention on him. He picked up the knife and slowly ran the tip across her breasts, searing her skin, leaving a trail of blood. She screamed.

If she could strangle him with one hand, she'd do it now. How much more could she stand before her chance arrived?

*Be brave. Be patient. John is counting on you.* She repeated the mantra in her head.

Ray ground his erection into her belly. "Tell me now you're not scared. Once fear gets into you, it will eat at you. You can't just turn it off."

Sarah knew all about fear. But the fear she had lived with was nothing like this. He brought the knife up. Blood dripped from its tip. Would he cut her face next?

He patted her cheek and moved downward. She held her breath as he brought the knife to her panties. When he cut them away, she let out a breath.

Crap. She hadn't meant to relax. Relaxing was bad.

"So the thought of me fucking you doesn't scare you as much as...what?" He hovered over her and brought the knife up to her face. "This?" Tears trickled from her eyes. "Huh. Maybe I can get you to change your mind."

He placed the knife on the floor once again and cupped her face with both hands. The gentleness of his touch confused her until he slammed his mouth down on hers. Instinctively she clamped her jaw shut and jerked her head.

He pulled away and ran his fingers over her mouth. "Off limits, huh? Bet I can change that, too."

Ray nuzzled her neck and then licked his way to her breast. He lingered there for a moment. No nuzzling, no licking, just his breath tickling her skin. The bite caught her off guard. Searing pain shocked her system. Sarah screamed, but his mouth covered hers in a hungry kiss. He situated his body over hers.

His tongue invaded her mouth. *Gross! Bite down, bite down!* But wait. This was the distraction she needed. Her opportunity for escape. Slowly, she slipped her hand free. The knife lay beside her somewhere. Could she find it in time? To keep him distracted, she whined. "Oh God, please stop."

"Say it again. Say it again." He grabbed her breast and squeezed.

"Stop." Ignoring the pain, she felt along the side the mattress. Cold metal met her fingers. Freedom. Carefully, she traced the blade to the handle.

*You can do this, you can do this.*

"God, I want you." He sat up and focused on unbuttoning his jeans.

Now! She took the knife and thrust it into his side. Sudden warmth covered her hand.

His eyes widened in surprise. "What the fuck?"

She held on and waited. Shouldn't he fall over? Instead, he grabbed for the knife, but fear and determination helped keep her grip. She stabbed deeper and twisted the handle.

"You bitch!" He screamed and backed away. When the knife slid out, the wound gushed. Grabbing his side, he fell across her leg. Blood spilled across his belly and dripped onto her legs.

Bile burned its way up her throat, but she fought it. Time to beat feet. She cut the other strap and rolled Ray off so she could reach her leg restraints.

Once free, the rush of adrenaline, fear, or maybe shock shook her entire body. She stood on unsteady legs. The blood covering her hand caused her stomach to roll. She dropped the knife and yanked off her blouse, using it to scrub her hand clean. After tossing the ruined bra to the floor, she grabbed her pants with shaky hands and put them on. She was so cold. She needed something for her nakedness. For warmth.

On the work bench. Her coat.

She stepped over Ray and the room swayed. Crap. Her nausea returned. She bent over and slowed her breathing, gathered her bearings. Once the room stilled, she stumbled to the bench and retrieved her coat.

John had said she could do it, and she had doubted him. Never again. She was free, empowered. Now she could save him. But how? She had no idea where she was or how far away Ray had taken her. The neighbors. *Duh.* They could call the cops. Somehow she'd get to John. After zipping up her coat, she rushed to the stairs.

Ray tackled her legs. She screamed and landed hard on the floor. What the hell? Why wasn't he dead? Turning on her back, she kicked, hoping to dislodge him. He brought his hand up, holding the knife. As his arm came down, she twisted. The blade missed her thigh and hit the floor where it flew from his hand. He roared.

She kicked his head until he stopped moving. And then she kicked him again.

Her heart hammered away. Was he dead now? Had she killed him? She picked up the knife and stood. A puddle of blood grew underneath him. An encouraging sign, but she backed up the staircase for a few steps, just to be sure. No more surprises for her. No sirree.

He hadn't moved. Good. Sarah turned around, took a step up, and then stopped, as did her heart.

"Damn it! Do I have to do everything myself?" Danielle stood at the top with her hands on her hips.

\* \* \* \*

John stared at the sky. How much time had passed? Five minutes? An hour? Clouds had formed, covering up the stars and making it hard to judge. Was Sarah still alive? God, he didn't want to think the worst, but it was hard since he had nothing else to do but think. Action was impossible.

How could he have let that bitch get away?

"Johnny? Are you alone?"

Perry's voice—spoken low—came from the neighbor's yard. Not the person John had expected, but anyone would be better than no one. John nodded.

"Is it a trap?" Now Perry's voice came from above. A tree, maybe? Or the roof? John couldn't blame him for being cautious, seeing how he was caught in a stake and bake.

John shook his head.

Perry appeared in a flash. "Damn, Johnny. She had to stake you twice?" He reached toward the gag, and then stopped. "Maybe I should remove the stakes first. I don't need you yelling out. Or biting me."

As much as John wanted the thing out of his mouth, he couldn't argue with Perry's logic. Hell, he couldn't argue at all.

Perry grabbed hold of the wood. "This will smart a bit."

*Stop talking and just—*

Perry yanked them free. John screamed through the gag. Why did they hurt worse coming out? But when he moved his fingers and toes, the pain became inconsequential.

Perry removed the gag. "Danielle's a little kinky, huh?"

John spit out the ball. "Help me up. I need to get Sarah before it's too late."

"You're not going anywhere until you feed." Perry glanced at John's nakedness. "Or get dressed. Sit tight."

John had no energy to argue or move. He certainly wouldn't be any help to Sarah in this condition.

A few agonizing minutes later, Perry returned with a man slung over his shoulder.

"Is he my neighbor?" John asked.

"Hey, I can't help it if you live in the boonies. Beggars can't be choosers." Perry laid the man next to John. "Feed. The sooner you do it, the sooner we can get Sarah."

John prayed that however he found her, she was alive.

# Chapter 36

"Are you sure you know where you're going?" Perry asked for the third time.

"Yes, yes, yes," John said. "It was his Piqua address. Besides, I haven't gotten anything else to go by. She has to be there, Perry. She just has to." Why did it seem his SUV drove slower than usual? Didn't this thing go faster than one-forty?

He'd visited the Piqua house once, when he'd first gone looking for Ray. When the address had appeared in his vision, it made sense—it was the closest. Still, the twenty-five-plus miles were farther than he liked.

"Listen, Johnny, I know you don't want me around. So after we capture this bastard, I'll leave you alone."

John didn't want to deal with Perry right now, but couldn't leave him hanging, either. Perry might be a pain in the ass, but he'd come through and helped when needed. "I can't forget what you did, but I can forgive you. Now that I know how to control her allure…"

The words died on his mouth as an image of Sarah lying dead came to mind. No! She can't be dead. He'd feel it, wouldn't he?

Perry placed a hand on John's shoulder. "We'll find her, Johnny. Have faith." He plucked at a piece of foil they'd missed when tearing the stuff off the windows. "I can't believe you actually went out into the sun. What was it like?"

Good ole' Perry, changing the subject. Right now, John was happy to think of anything other than the unthinkable. "Hot. And bright."

"According to Abe, it's bright only because you're not used to it. He has those UV windows at his house and said that after the first week, he didn't need the sunglasses anymore."

Abe was one of the Committee members and Perry seemed to know them all rather intimately. Whether because he was always in trouble or because he liked to be in the know, John wasn't sure. Most likely a little of both.

"How long has he had them?"

"About a year. The Committee is looking to install them on all their vehicles now just in case they ever have to venture out into the sun."

A year? Damn. Barnet was right. John had been foolish not sticking around at the meetings. He might have discovered this sooner. To bring sunshine back into his house intrigued him. Wouldn't Sarah love that, too? Of course, if she didn't survive... No! He must stop thinking like that.

The street appeared up ahead. Finally. He slowed, but still took the turn on two tires, which squealed on the pavement. Perry was wise to keep his mouth shut.

John had pulled to the side of the curb across from Ray's house and reached for the door handle when Perry grabbed his arm.

"Slow down. If we barge in, Ray might... Well, do you really want to surprise him?"

No, he didn't. But he was so damn close to her, it made it hard for him to think straight. He just wanted her back in his arms.

"Fine," John said. "First one who sees him takes control."

The old neighborhood was quiet. John and Perry walked up to the house as if they belonged, but instead of knocking, John quietly turned the knob. The door was unlocked.

Perry grabbed his hand and said telepathically, *'I'll go around and check the windows. If I see him, I'll stop him.'*

John nodded. Slow and steady. No sudden movements. He wasn't about to startle the killer. But when he stepped inside the house, he was hit with the stench of death.

All bets were off.

* * * *

Sarah backed down the staircase and into the basement as the vampire headed her way. Shit. Now what? Ray she could kill. Danielle was more like…invincible.

"Sarah!"

John was here? He was alive? Free? Danielle covered her mouth and pushed her against the wall before she could call out.

"I swear you two will be the death of me," Danielle said.

Sarah still held the knife in her hand. Stabbing a vampire wouldn't kill them, but it had incapacitated John. Maybe a poke in the stomach would be enough to escape, or at least warn John. Sarah shot her hand out, hoping to catch Danielle off guard, but Danielle was quicker and grabbed Sarah's wrist.

"Nice try." Danielle jabbed the knife into Sarah's belly and sliced. "Sorry it has to end this way, dear. You had rather impressed me with your escape techniques, but I can't have you live." She dropped the knife and backed away with a smile.

Sarah slid down the wall holding her stomach. What the hell? The knife wound burned something fierce—though not as bad as she might have assumed it would—and drained her of energy, but she still had her wits. And her lungs. "John! Danielle's down here."

Danielle's eyes widened. Was she wondering why Sarah hadn't died? Well, Sarah was wondering the same thing. Sure, it had taken Ray several minutes to die, but he didn't have a twelve-inch gash in his gut, either. John appeared at the top of the stairs and Danielle headed for a window.

"Don't let her get away," Sarah said. No way was that bitch escaping again and if John saw her wound, he might let Danielle go.

A small window exploded, glass flying inside as Perry flew through the opening feet first. Danielle backtracked toward the stairs. John blocked her way.

Danielle spun around and pointed toward Sarah. "You're not going to save your bitch? She's dying as you stand there."

"I'm okay, John." And damn, if she didn't sound okay. But feeling? Well, she was a bit winded and her stomach hurt, and maybe she felt a little woozy, like she could sleep. Was that shock? The outside of her coat showed no signs of her bleeding, the zipper had kept the knife from slicing the coat along with her, but it was plenty wet inside.

Perry grabbed Danielle by the arms and pinned them behind her back. "I got her."

John turned toward Sarah and stopped. His nose flared as he stared at her. Crap. Maybe he couldn't see her blood, but he smelled it. Anger flashed in his eyes. He ripped the leg off the workbench. Splinters flew and Ray's apple tumbled to the floor. John rushed Danielle, impaling her with the wood. Blood sprayed. Danielle screamed. Perry dropped her and she lay in an unmoving heap.

"I still win," Danielle said. "When she dies."

"Shut up or I'll chop your head off," John said.

Sarah hadn't witnessed John's staking, but the violent act caused her to gag. And man, if that didn't hurt her stomach more.

"It's okay. It's over." John's appearance and words soothed her. She only hoped they were true. He reached for her zipper. "How bad?"

"I don't know, but..." She put her hand over his, keeping him from unzipping, and glanced at Perry. "I don't have a blouse on."

Perry turned his back. "I'll just call Barnet and let him know what's going on."

John unzipped the coat. "Oh my God."

Blood had soaked her pants and covered her belly. How the hell was she still alive? Or even conscious? Something didn't look right, though. Where was Ray's bite mark? Where was the cut Ray had made?

"I think I'm okay," she said.

"The hell you are." Gently, he ran his hands over her stomach, and then licked the wound. His tongue created a link to his conflicted emotions. While he enjoyed the taste, he hated himself for doing so and feared for her life. Getting a powerful rush from her blood only compounded his issues.

He'd had a similar reaction when he fed with that stake in him. Something had changed between them. Something good.

He closed her coat. "I don't understand. There's more blood here than from the little cut I found. Are you hurt somewhere else?"

Sarah shook her head. Little cut? Danielle had sliced her open. And how had Ray's cut healed so quickly and not even left a scar? Could it be? "John, could taking your blood heal me? I also had this cut—"

"What are you talking about? I never gave you my blood."

"No, but I took it." She pointed to the smudges on her coat where she had sucked it off. "And since then we were able to talk though our touch." She took his hand. *"Like now, right?"*

"Right..." He furrowed his forehead as if he was trying to make sense of it all. She was trying to do the same.

"I'm healing fast. Does that mean I'm a vampire now?"

He shook his head. "You're not a vampire. Your blood is too strong."

"But I'm...different."

"That you are, Sweetie." He kissed her long and deep. "That you are."

# Chapter 37

"Happy Valentine's Day." John stared at his sleeping beauty as she lay upon the bed in his Urbana house, and laid another kiss on those luscious lips of hers.

Sarah stretched her arms out over her head. "Valentine's Day is February fourteenth, not March fourteenth."

"Says the calendar, not what's in my heart. Besides, we didn't get to celebrate it properly."

It had been a busy month. After Danielle's staking, her hold over Steven had severed and the police found and arrested one confused man. Sarah didn't have to worry about her ex any longer.

Ray's picture had ended up on TV when his body was found in the remnants of an accidental house fire. Sarah had done her part and contacted the police, informing them that he had been the one who had tried to abduct her. The police had announced that Ray was the serial killer they'd been searching for, giving the families of the murdered women closure.

John had been tempted to leave Danielle in the basement with Ray when they torched the house, but Barnet wouldn't hear of it. He wanted the Committee to deal with her, to make sure her death was witnessed by a panel. Last John heard, she'd been beheaded and burned. Every one of the Committee members, plus Perry and a few other vampires, watched the event. John would have attended, but Sarah would have wanted to go, too, and he refused to have her in the vicinity of the one person who'd nearly taken her away.

"You ready for breakfast?" Sarah brushed her hair back.

He kissed her neck. Who knew a bond could be so freeing?

When she had taken his blood, her cravings went away and her allure to other vampires disappeared. And then there was her miraculous healing. Sure, she'd slept for a good long while after being stabbed, but she was alive. He shuddered thinking what would have happened if she hadn't had the foresight to take action.

They had relayed the information to Barnet. That was the part Barnet failed to mention in that Perfect Mate story, a story the Committee was beginning to think wasn't just a story: So in love they share and forever be together. It wasn't enough they shared love, they needed to share blood, too. Had the author meant to be vague? Barnet would most likely find the answer to that. But if John had only heard the story before, he might have figured it out sooner. Or better yet, Sarah would have.

Her act of desperation to become a vampire had sealed their bond and changed her forever. Not that they could read each other's mind—they were closed to one another that way—but even after a month without another drop of his blood in her system, they could still communicate telepathically.

In Atlanta, Justin eagerly took Katarina's blood, thus ending months of unrest. The Committee was still debating on whether or not to announce the discovery of Perfect Mates. Barnet was sure it would cause an upheaval, with every vampire bent on finding their own. Maybe that would occur, maybe it wouldn't. But John was fairly certain it took more than just a blood exchange to be bonded.

While Sarah and Justin were not vampires, it appeared they were immortal. Whether they aged, only time would tell, but John suspected they wouldn't. And while they still ate regular food and could go out into the sun, they healed quickly and never seemed to be drained from feeding, not that John needed much from Sarah-- one draw could sustain him for days. And wasn't that what the Perfect Mate was all about? The story, or documentary, wouldn't make sense otherwise. Regardless, she was stuck with him. Not because of their bond or her blood, but because he couldn't see loving anyone like he loved her.

He took in her wonderful scent and licked her neck. Making love to her now was tempting, but he had other plans. "Not yet. I have a present for you."

"A present?" She sat up holding her out her hand. "Ooh, ooh, hand it over."

"I'm sorry, it's not that kind of present."

She frowned. "What kind of present is it, then?"

"A good one, I hope." Grinning, he climbed off the bed and offered his hand. When she took it, he led her out to the hallway and down to his old room.

"What are we doing here?"

"You'll see." He opened the door and ushered her inside the darkened room. Circular in shape, his childhood bedroom was the upper part of the turret over the dining room. He walked over to the curtains on the east side and slowly pulled the cord to open them, welcoming the morning sunshine.

"John, what are you doing? The sun's out." She tugged on his arm to get him out of what she thought were harmful rays. "John, what kind of present is this? Are you trying to kill yourself?"

"Surprise!" he said, laughing.

She stared at him. "Surprise? What do you mean, surprise?"

"I got those UV windows Perry told me about. Isn't it amazing? They work. I don't feel anything." He squinted out over the lit up yard and continued, "It's been over fifty years since I could enjoy the daylight. I forgot how beautiful it could be."

She stood beside him and took his hand. Fear trickled over through their touch.

He turned toward her to appease her worries and instead nearly lost it. He caressed her face. "I didn't think it was possible, but you're more beautiful in the sunlight." He kissed her lightly on the lips.

"This is my present?"

"Well, yeah. I don't want you to have to spend the rest of your life in the dark." He picked up a little box from the sill and got down on one knee. "Sarah, I know it's backward since we're bonded, but I promise to love you and cherish you forever. Will you marry me?"

He opened the box. The marquis-cut diamond ring sparkled in the sunlight.

She gasped and put her hand up to her mouth. Her eyes glistened with unshed tears. "Vampires can get married?"

"Well, yeah. What do you say?"

The smile slowly spread across her face. "Yes, John. Yes, I'll marry you," she said, nodding her head silly.

He slipped the ring on her finger, then lifted her and twirled her around. "Thank you, Sarah Daugherty. I'll do right by you, I promise."

And he had forever to show her, too.

# ACKNOWLEDGMENTS

My deepest thanks go out to my very first readers: Stephanie, Mary, and Jan. It couldn't have been easy reading such a rough story, but your encouragement was all the motivation I needed to pursue this new career of mine (and seek some much-needed training!). And this book also wouldn't have stood a chance if not for the critiques I received from the following writer friends: Kathleen McRae, Kristine Krantz, Kimberly Lesczcuk, and Jennette Marie Powell. Thank you, thank you, thank you!! To my editor, Paige Christian: Thank you for helping this story be the best it can be (even through my griping). Lastly, no book is complete without readers and if you read this book—THANK YOU! I hope you got as much joy from reading as I did from writing it.

# ABOUT THE AUTHOR

Stacy McKitrick always had stories in her head; she just never knew what to do with them. Then one day she decided to give writing a try and discovered the passion she'd been looking for all her life. Her stories contain paranormal characters, but her practical nature needs to make their existence plausible, as well as give them that happy ending (because it's all about the love). Living in her own happy ending, she resides in Ohio with her husband, Jim and their two grown children.

You can find her at www.stacymckitrick.com

Thank you for purchasing this book

Sign up for my newsletter to receive new release announcements, sneak peeks of future books, and bonus content. I sometimes even give away stuff.

http://eepurl.com/-Auwz

Now read on further for the first chapter of
BLIND TEMPTATION
(Book 3 in the Bitten by Love Series)

# BLIND TEMPTATION
## Chapter 1

When life became rough, nothing worked better at soothing her spirit than the silky texture of her handkerchief. Now if she could only get her life upgraded to rough.

Victoria sat with her head down, the smooth material failing miserably to calm her. She couldn't have heard the Head of the Committee correctly. Never in all her years had she been called into his office for disciplinary action.

"Do you understand me?" he asked.

"You had a meeting without me?" she asked. "What have I done wrong?"

Barnet came from behind his desk looking more fatherly than her own father had. The smattering of grey in his hair only enhanced that image. He sat in the chair beside her. "Victoria, we're concerned. Staying holed up is not healthy and it's not been fair to the other members."

"I am not holed up. I go out." Just because she lived at Headquarters, which was her right, didn't mean she stayed in her room. The Underground Atlanta shopping mall was but a doorway away.

"The Underground is not going out. Seeing the stars, walking in Centennial Park, driving to an assignment, now that's going out."

She didn't even know where that park was located. Had it even existed before 1967? And what was so great about seeing the stars? They couldn't have changed. But what he was asking her to do...
"You don't play fair, Barnet."

"Don't go there, Victoria. We've been more than fair. Forty-plus years of exile is long enough. Actually, it's been too long. If you wish to remain on the Committee, you will attend class tonight."

"Why can't you just give me the manual? I'll read it. I promise."

Barnet smiled. "That would kind of defeat the purpose. We want you out of Headquarters, mingling with the population. You can't get that with reading."

"And a driving class is supposed to accomplish this? I don't even own a car."

"Are you afraid to drive? Is that it?"

Not so much driving, only what driving stood for, but she wouldn't admit that. "Can't very well be afraid of something I've never done before."

He rose. "Then there is nothing to discuss."

"But Barnet..."

"What?"

"Is this at least an adult class?"

He let out an exaggerated sigh. "I won't lie to you. It's possible the class will be filled with teenagers. Most adults already know how to drive. As Henrik should have taught you."

She moaned. It was worse than she'd thought. "You can't do this to me! They're going to treat me like...like one of them."

"Only if you act like one."

Oh, what did Barnet know? He hadn't been turned at seventeen. No, his turning had happened after his forty-second birthday.

"The school thinks you're twenty-two. You act like twenty-two, they'll treat you accordingly."

How about if she acted three hundred and eighty-one? How might they treat her then?

\* \* \* \*

The front door slammed and Ben all but jumped off the couch. That's what he got for reading 'Salem's Lot. Vampires. He shuddered. Thank God they didn't exist.

273

The scent of lilacs preceded Susannah's entrance. "Ben! I'm so glad you're here."

"Where else would I be?" he muttered. Sometimes he really wondered about her mind. Had turning forty done that to her? Is that what he had to look forward to next year? Papers to his right rustled and the scent intensified. Ben marked his spot in the book and turned toward his sister. "What's wrong?"

"My instructor for tonight's class quit on me. Last minute. I can't afford to cancel this class. I need you to teach it."

Ben laughed. Sometimes Susannah had a rich sense of humor. She sure knew how to play it, acting all serious. "That's a good one."

"I'm not kidding."

*Shit.* "Why can't you do it?"

"Because I'm already teaching another class."

"Then put them together."

"I can't. It's the driving portion. Do you want to take that one over instead?"

"Very funny."

She placed her hand on his knee. "I'm sorry, but I need the money. *We* need the money. You have to help me, here."

"No one's going to believe I can teach them the rules of driving."

"You've taught it before. You know the class."

His pulse raced. Yeah, but that wasn't the point and she knew it. "Can't you just cancel tonight's class? I'm sure you'll find someone."

"Not last minute. And not at the rate I can afford to pay. Please, Ben. I haven't asked for much, have I? I let you live here."

He rose. "So you're saying if I don't do it, you'll kick me out? Nice, Suze."

She grabbed his arm. "No, of course not. But if I cancel this class, we may both be out. I'll be short on rent. Your tutoring income can't cover it."

He sat back on the couch. "You said it was enough."

"Normally, it is. But…"

The emergency room. *Shit.* He covered his face. "I told you I shouldn't have gone."

"Like I was going to stitch you up. Sure. Next time maybe I will." She was getting angry. Her voice raised an octave, usually a good indication.

He puffed out a breath. "Suze, I want to help, but if I'm the teacher on record—"

"You won't be. I will."

"That's fraud."

"No one's going to know. After I'm finished with my driving class, I'll take over yours. Please, Ben."

Who in their right mind would believe he could teach driver's education? Maybe agreeing would make her see what a terrible mistake it was. "Fine. I'll do it."

"Thank you, thank you, thank you." She hugged him tight and nearly knocked him over. "Now hurry up and get changed. Class starts in an hour."

Crap. What the hell had he gotten himself into?